flying
witch

Chihiro Ishizuka

9

Contents

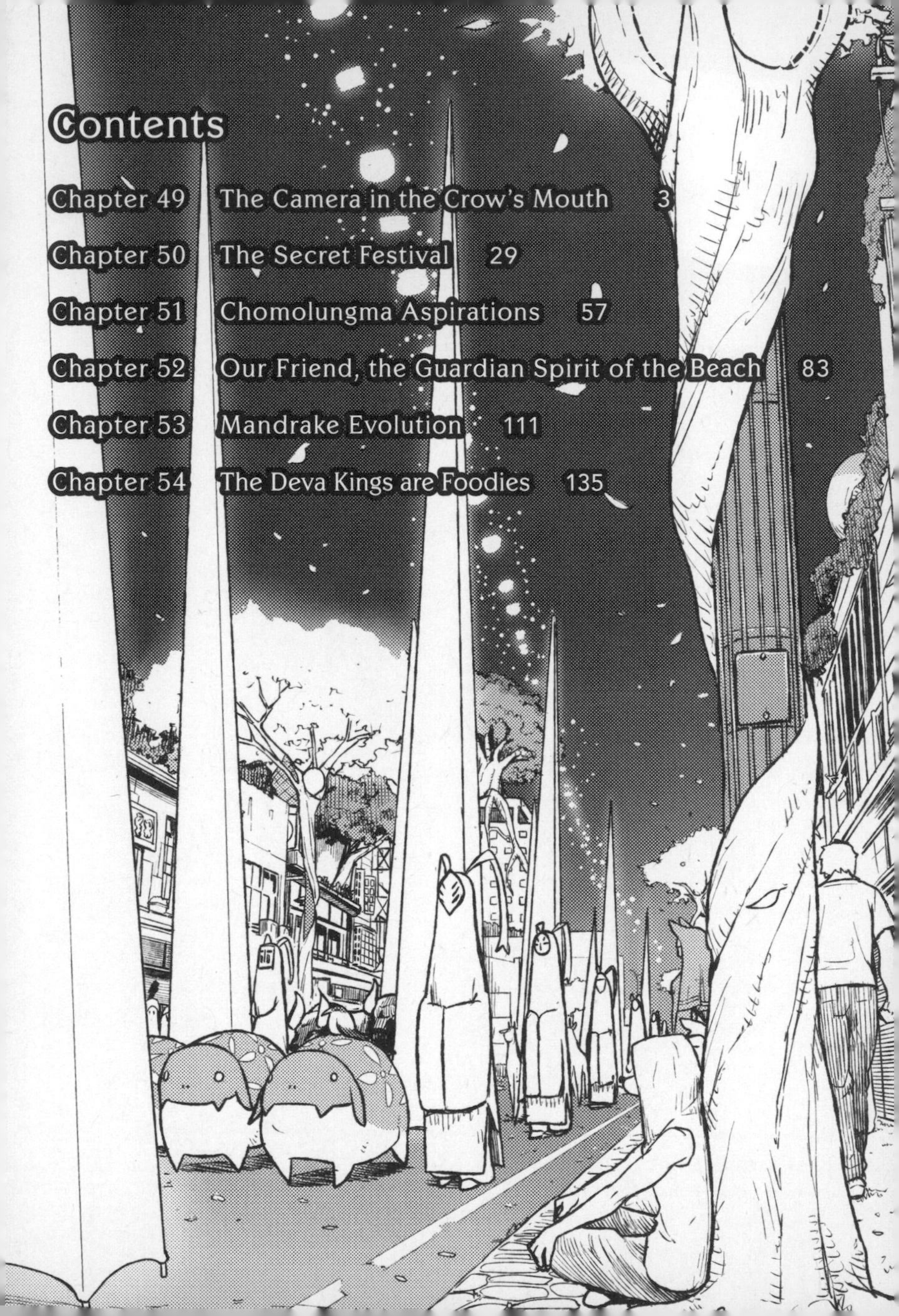

Chapter 49
The Camera in the Crow's Mouth

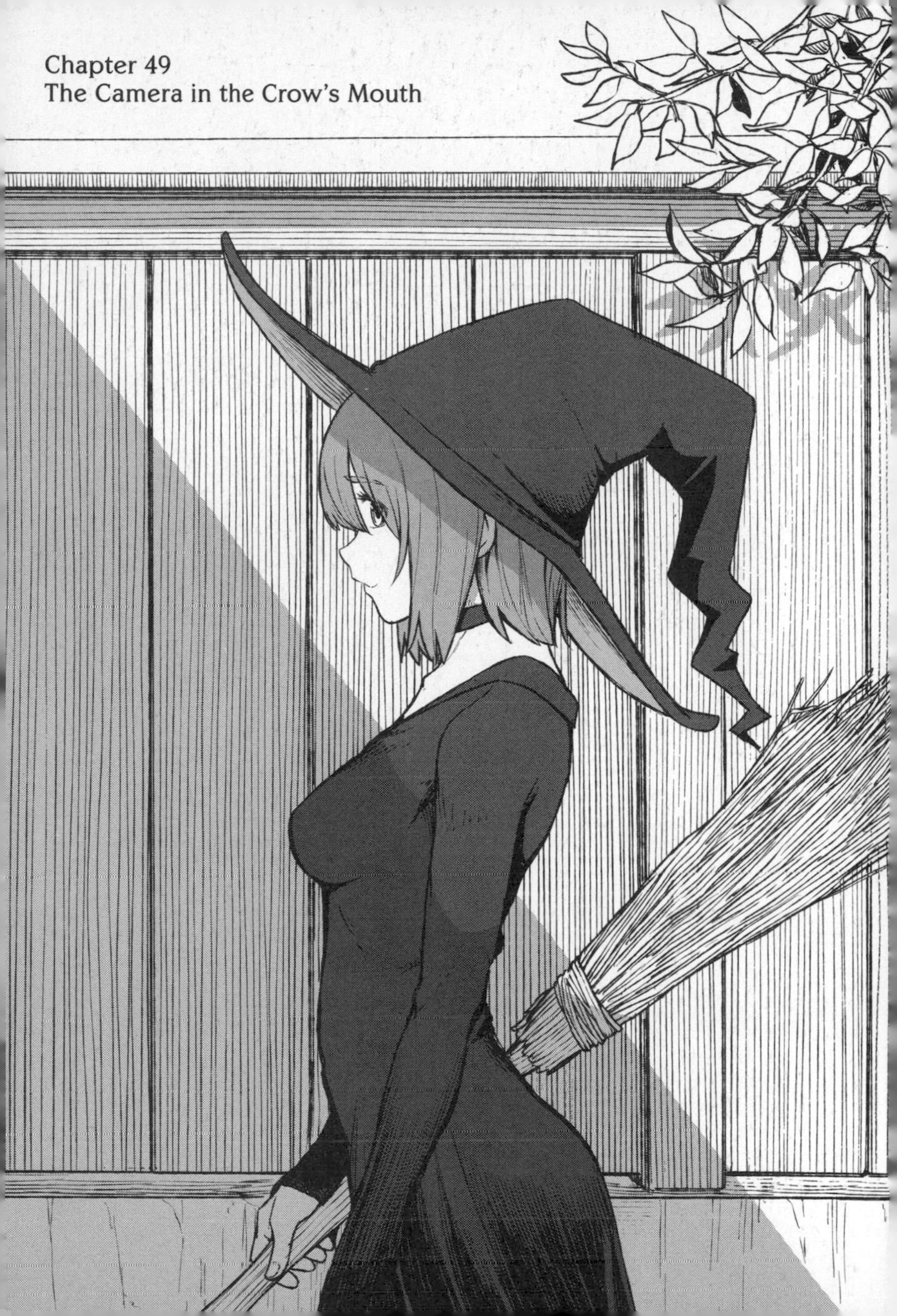

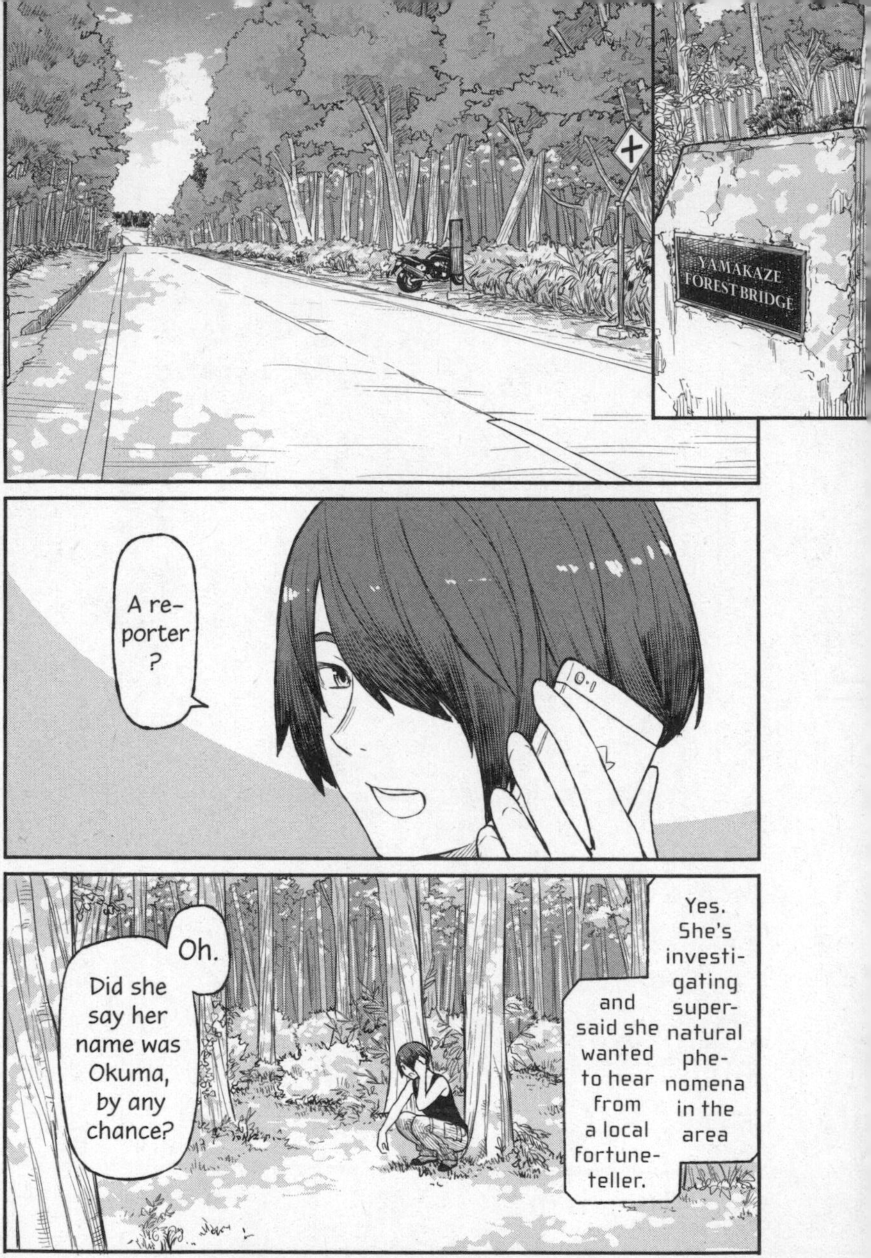
YAMAKAZE FOREST BRIDGE
A re-porter?
Yes. She's investi-gating super-natural phe-nomena in the area
and said she wanted to hear from a local fortune-teller.
Oh.
Did she say her name was Okuma, by any chance?

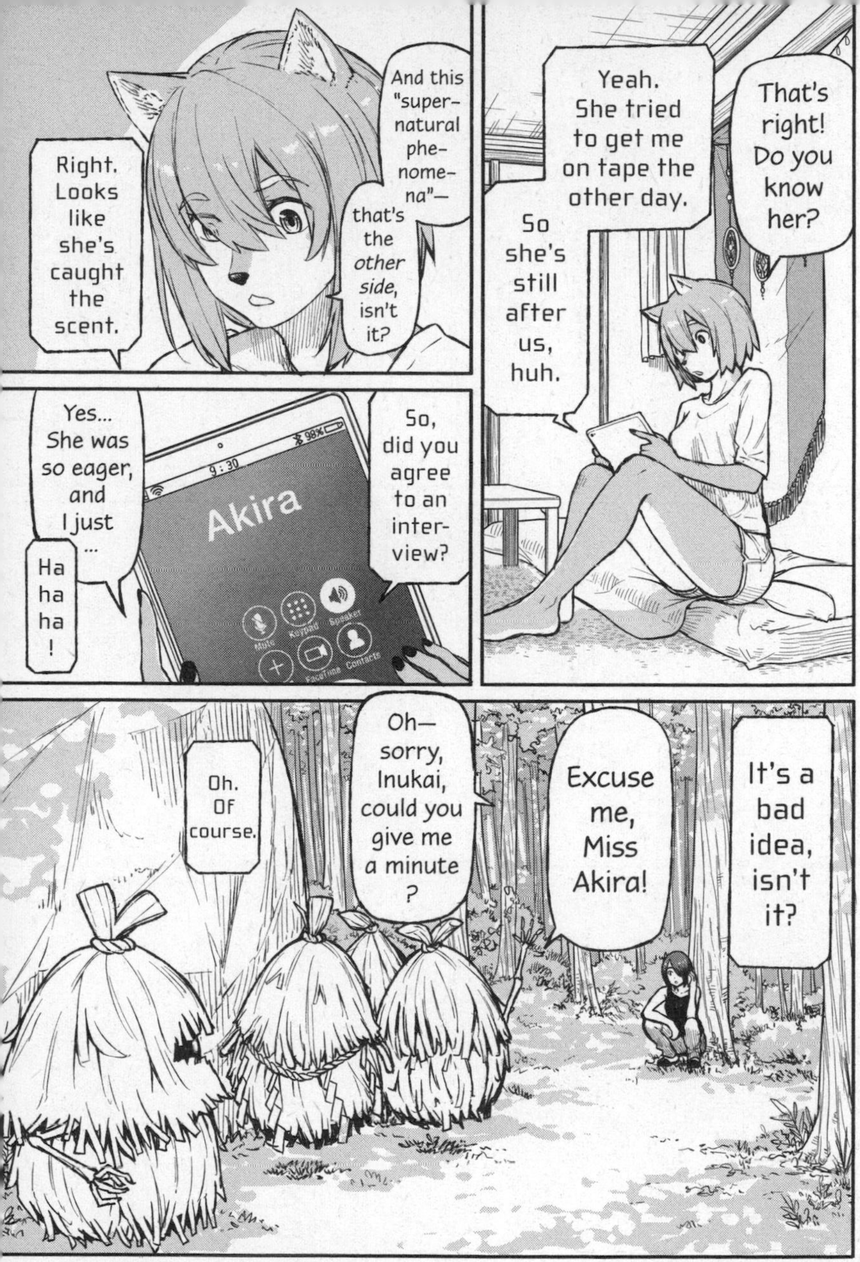
That's right! Do you know her?
Yeah. She tried to get me on tape the other day.
So she's still after us, huh.
And this "supernatural phenomena"—that's the *other side*, isn't it?
Right. Looks like she's caught the scent.
So, did you agree to an interview?
Yes... She was so eager, and I just ...
Akira
Ha ha ha!
It's a bad idea, isn't it?
Excuse me, Miss Akira!
Oh— sorry, Inukai, could you give me a minute?
Oh. Of course.

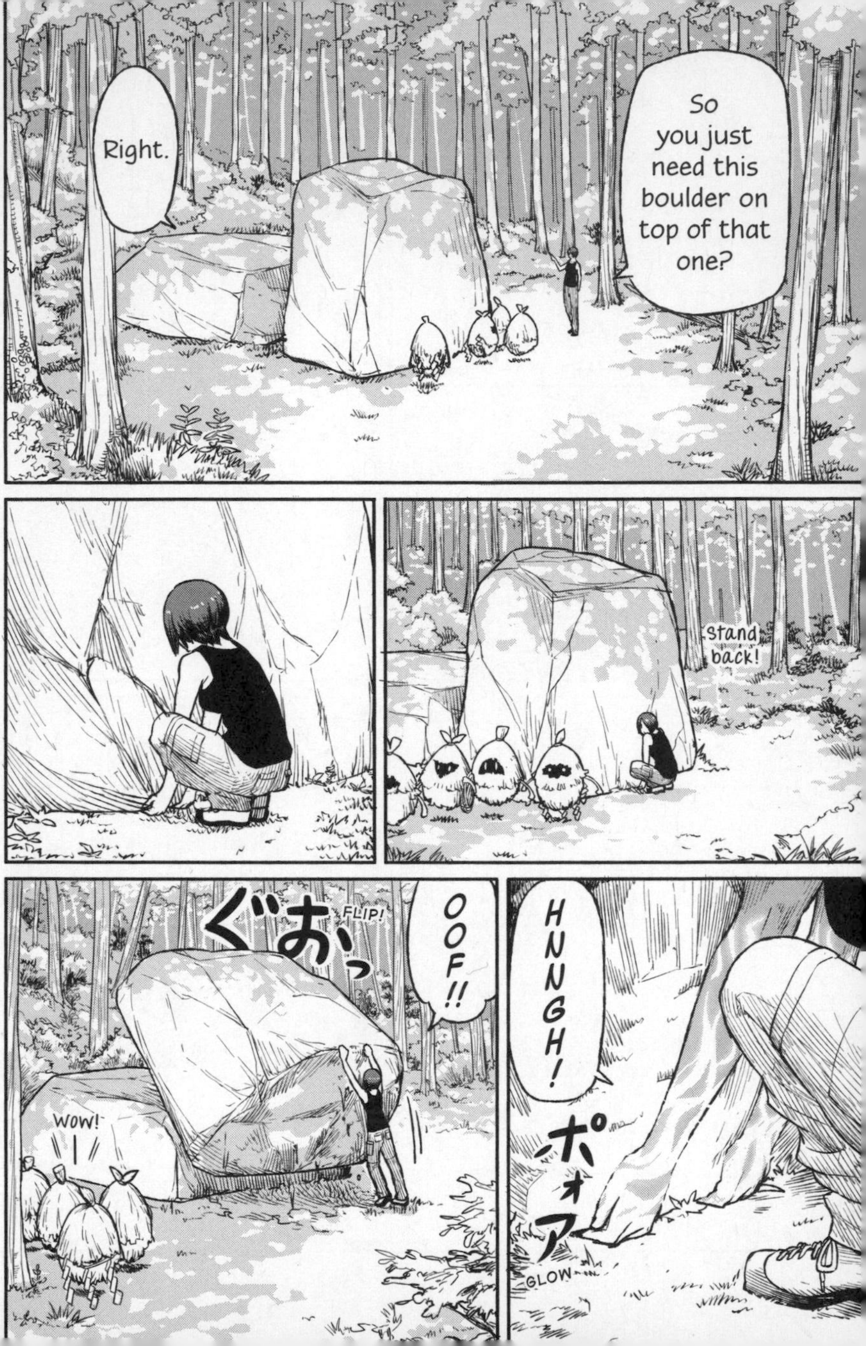
So you just need this boulder on top of that one?
Right.
Stand back!
HNNGH!
ポォア
GLOW
OOF!!
ぐおっ
FLIP!
WOW!

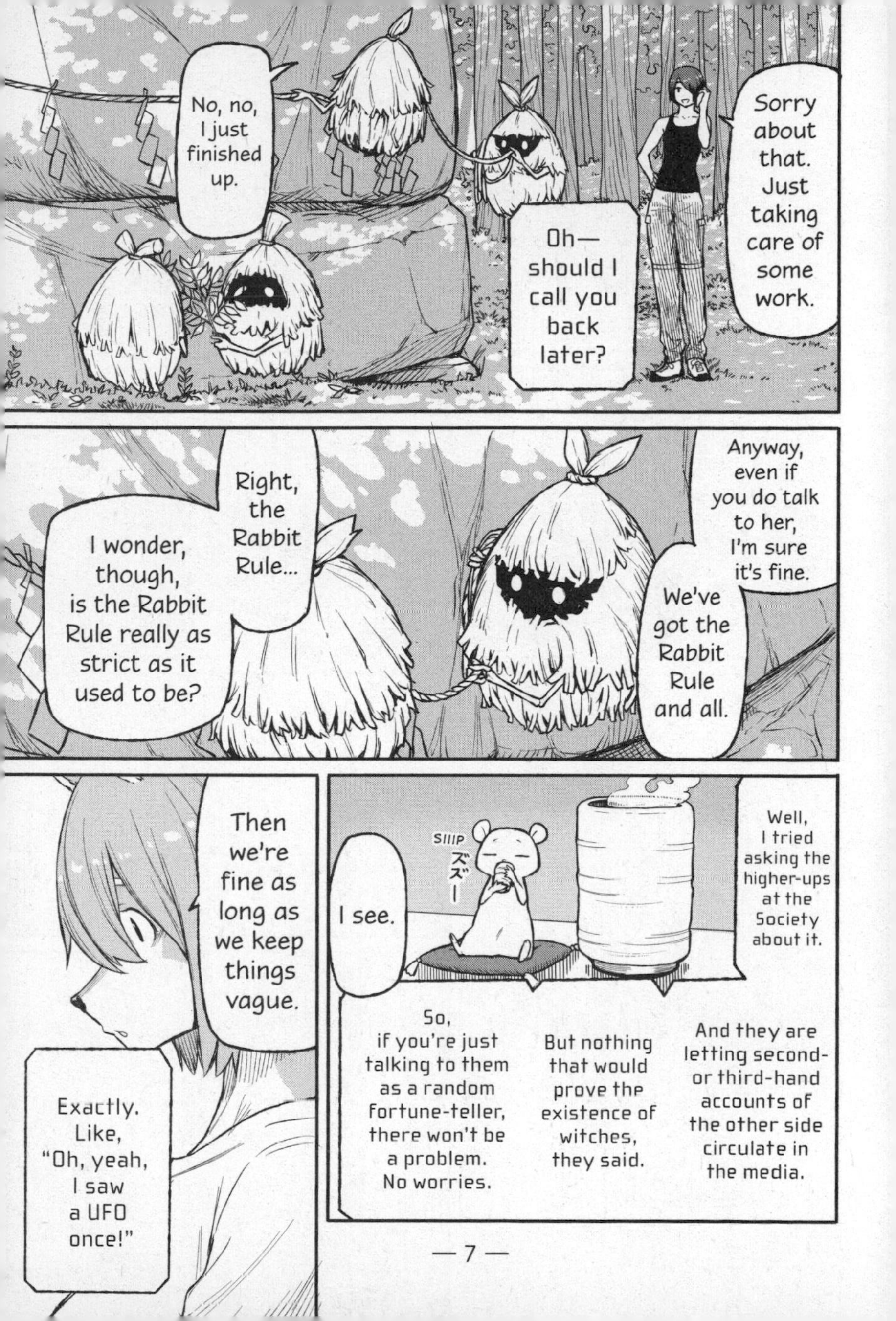
Sorry about that. Just taking care of some work.
Oh— should I call you back later?
No, no, I just finished up.
Anyway, even if you do talk to her, I'm sure it's fine.
We've got the Rabbit Rule and all.
Right, the Rabbit Rule...
I wonder, though, is the Rabbit Rule really as strict as it used to be?
Well, I tried asking the higher-ups at the Society about it.
SIIP
ズズー
I see.
And they are letting second- or third-hand accounts of the other side circulate in the media.
But nothing that would prove the existence of witches, they said.
So, if you're just talking to them as a random fortune-teller, there won't be a problem. No worries.
Then we're fine as long as we keep things vague.
Exactly. Like, "Oh, yeah, I saw a UFO once!"

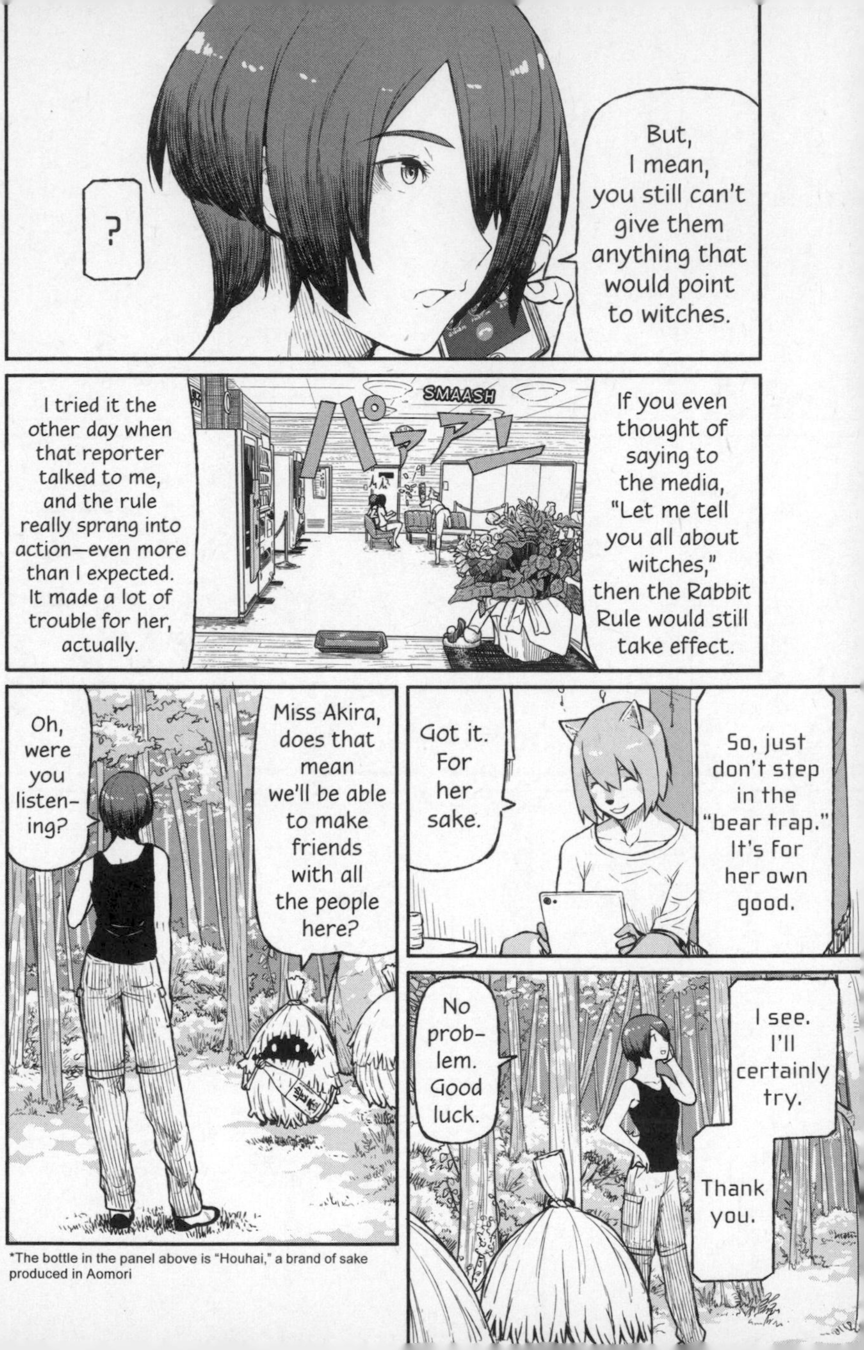
But, I mean, you still can't give them anything that would point to witches.
?
If you even thought of saying to the media, "Let me tell you all about witches," then the Rabbit Rule would still take effect.
SMAASH
I tried it the other day when that reporter talked to me, and the rule really sprang into action—even more than I expected. It made a lot of trouble for her, actually.
So, just don't step in the "bear trap." It's for her own good.
Got it. For her sake.
I see. I'll certainly try.
Thank you.
No problem. Good luck.
Miss Akira, does that mean we'll be able to make friends with all the people here?
Oh, were you listening?

*The bottle in the panel above is "Houhai," a brand of sake produced in Aomori

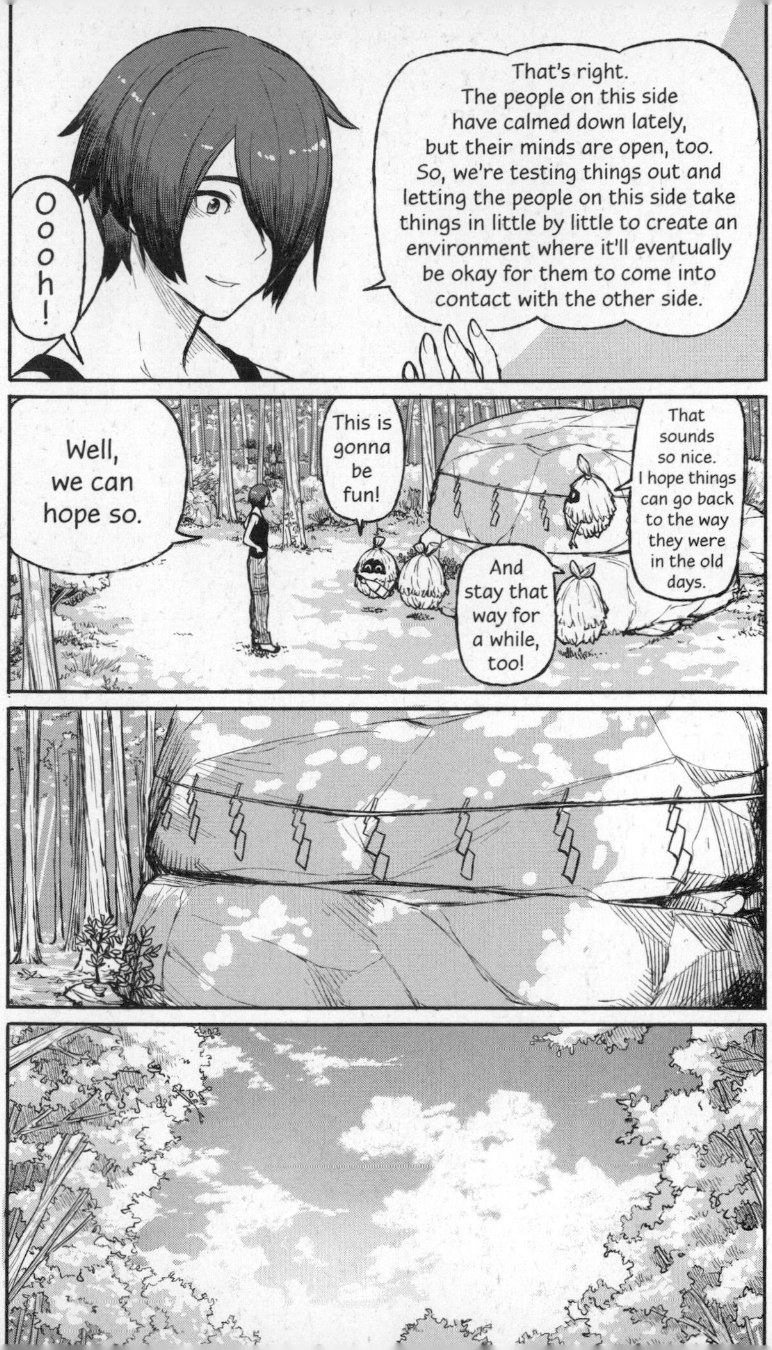
That's right. The people on this side have calmed down lately, but their minds are open, too. So, we're testing things out and letting the people on this side take things in little by little to create an environment where it'll eventually be okay for them to come into contact with the other side.
Oooh!
That sounds so nice. I hope things can go back to the way they were in the old days.
And stay that way for a while, too!
This is gonna be fun!
Well, we can hope so.

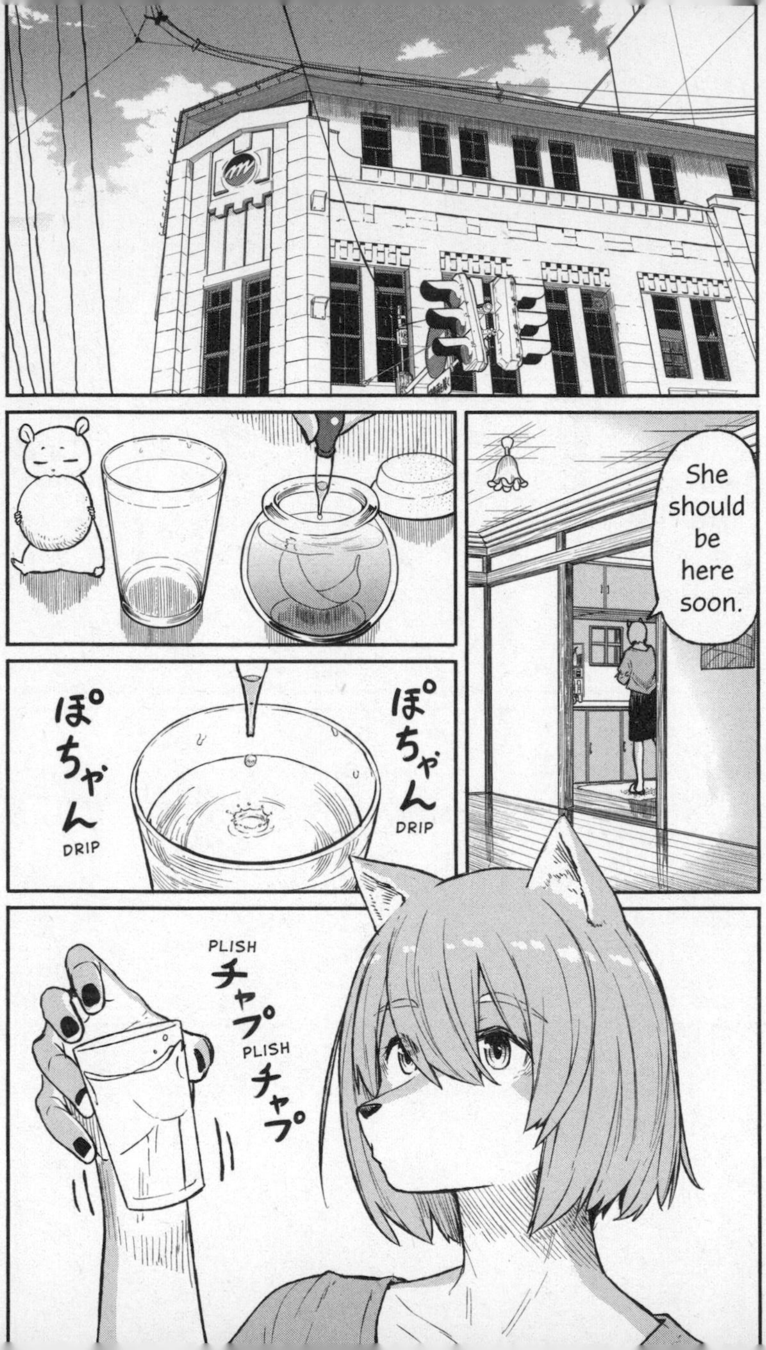
She should be here soon.
ぽちゃん
DRIP
ぽちゃん
DRIP
PLISH
チャプ
PLISH
チャプ

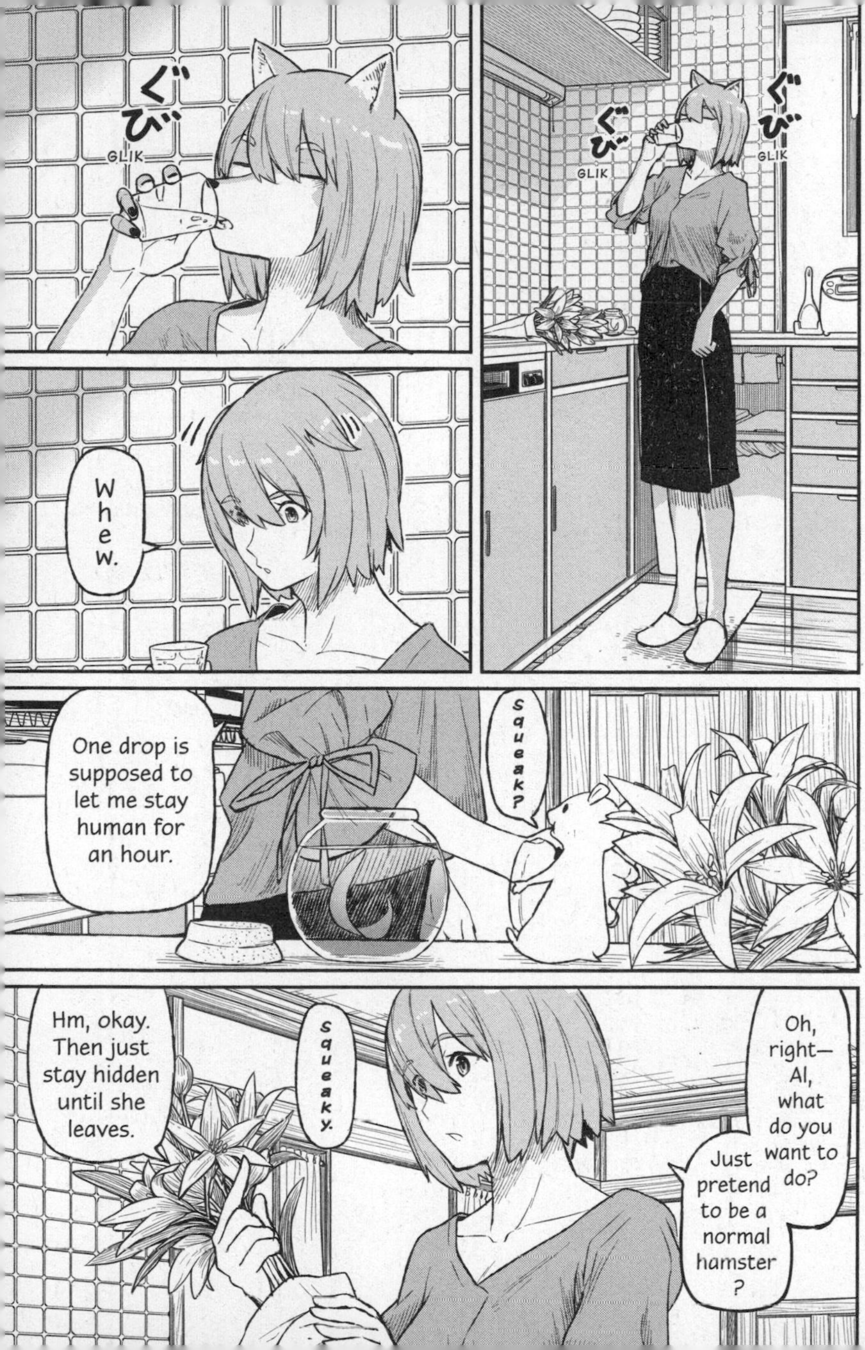
ぐび
GLIK
ぐび
GLIK
ぐび
GLIK
Whew.
Squeak?
One drop is supposed to let me stay human for an hour.
Oh, right— Al, what do you want to do?
Just pretend to be a normal hamster?
Squeaky.
Hm, okay. Then just stay hidden until she leaves.

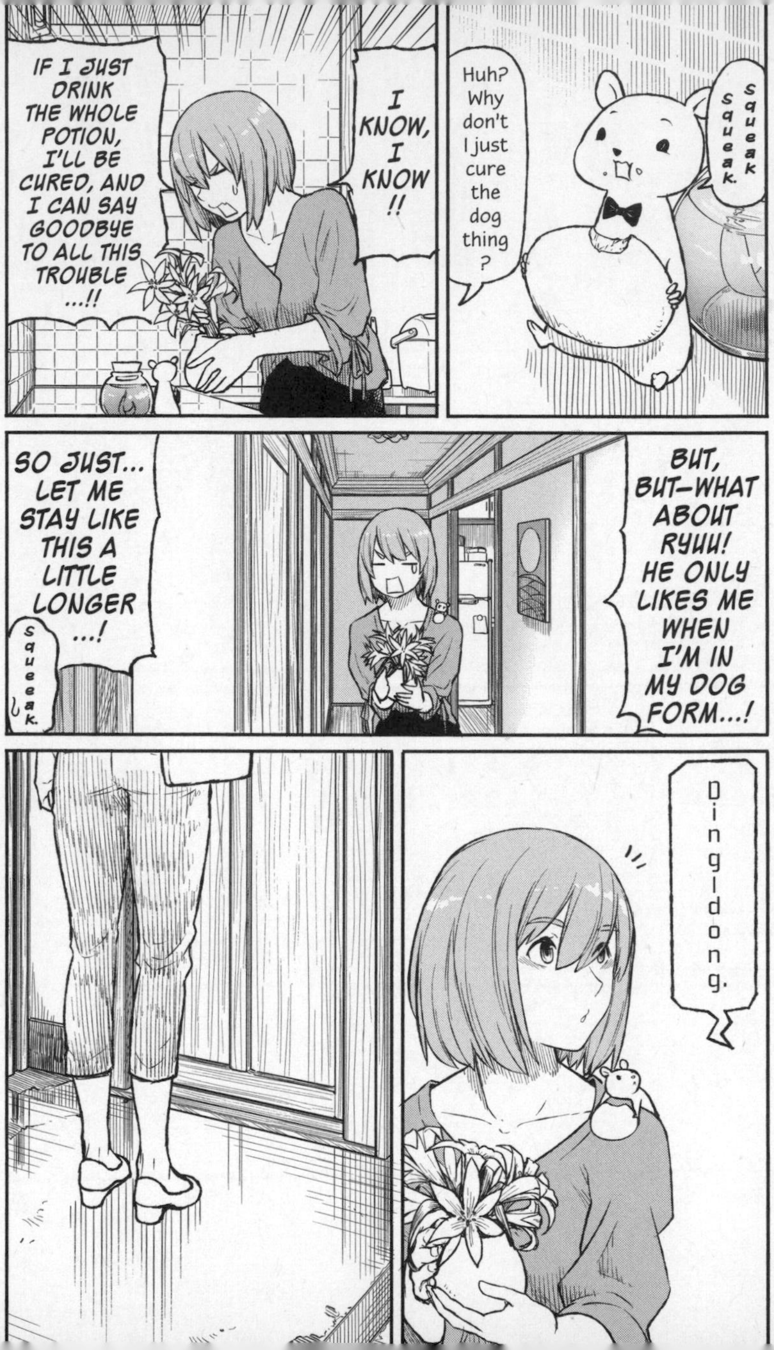
Squeak squeak.
Huh? Why don't I just cure the dog thing?
I KNOW, I KNOW!!
IF I JUST DRINK THE WHOLE POTION, I'LL BE CURED, AND I CAN SAY GOODBYE TO ALL THIS TROUBLE ...!!
BUT, BUT—WHAT ABOUT RYUU! HE ONLY LIKES ME WHEN I'M IN MY DOG FORM...!
SO JUST... LET ME STAY LIKE THIS A LITTLE LONGER ...!
Squeeeak.
Dingdong.

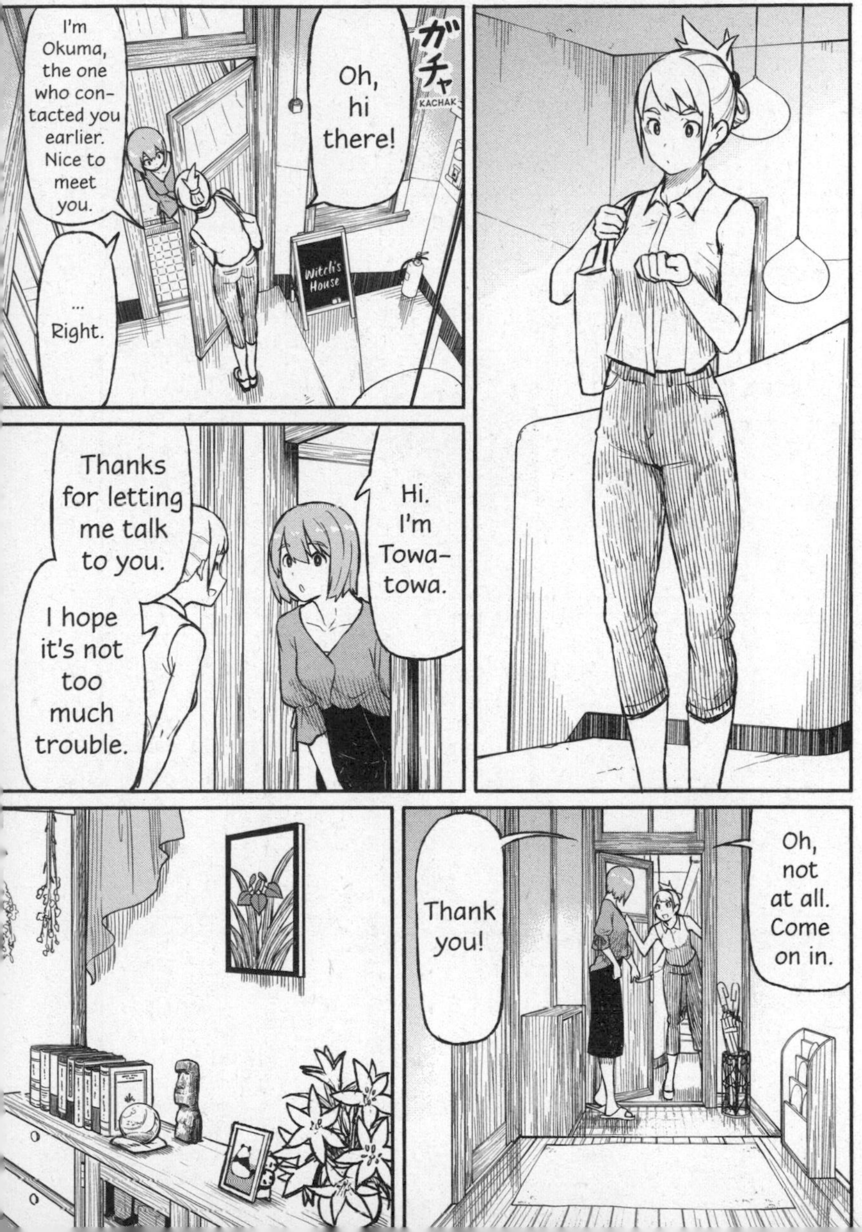
ガチャ
KACHAK
Oh, hi there!
I'm Okuma, the one who contacted you earlier. Nice to meet you.
... Right.
Witch's House
Hi. I'm Towatowa.
Thanks for letting me talk to you.
I hope it's not too much trouble.
Oh, not at all. Come on in.
Thank you!

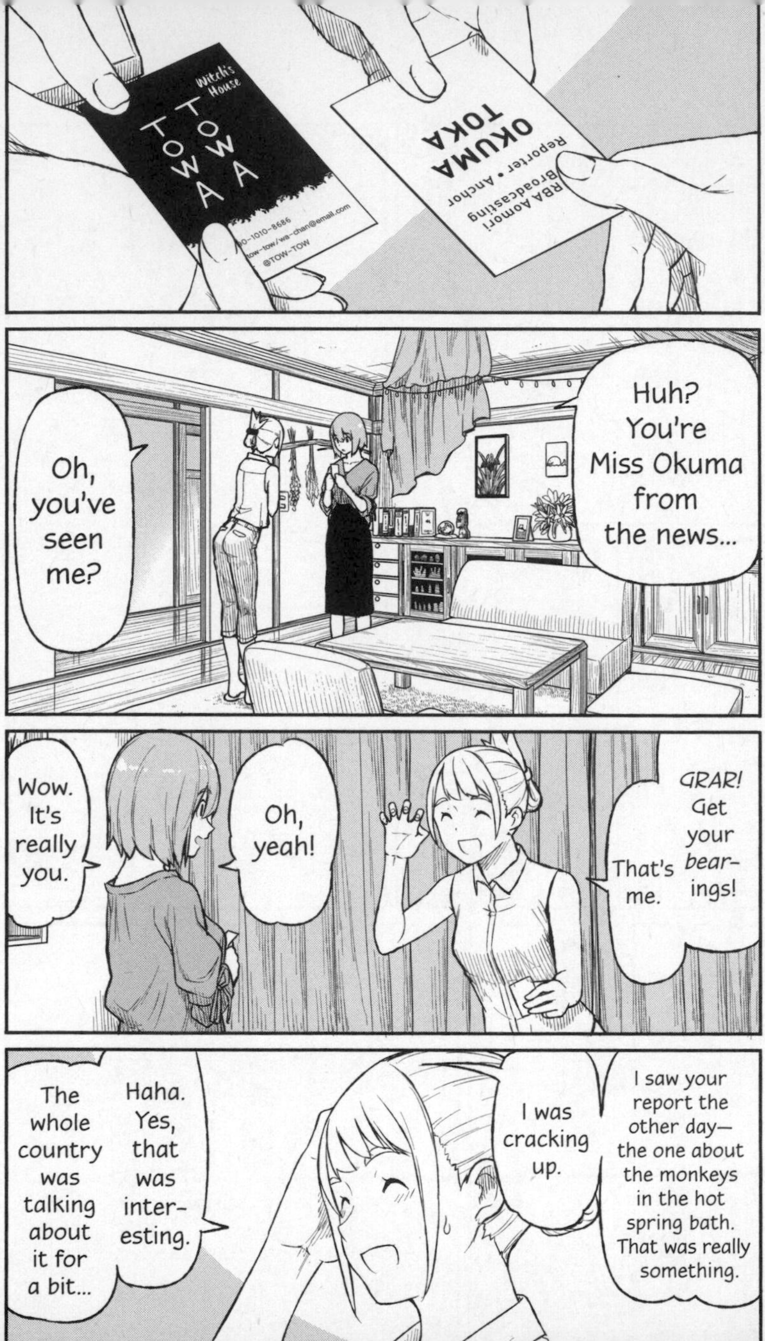
OKUMA TOKA
Reporter • Anchor
RBA Aomori Broadcasting
Witch's House
TOWA TOWA
@TOW-TOW
Huh? You're Miss Okuma from the news...
Oh, you've seen me?
GRAR! Get your bear-ings!
That's me.
Oh, yeah!
Wow. It's really you.
I saw your report the other day—the one about the monkeys in the hot spring bath. That was really something.
I was cracking up.
Haha. Yes, that was interesting.
The whole country was talking about it for a bit...

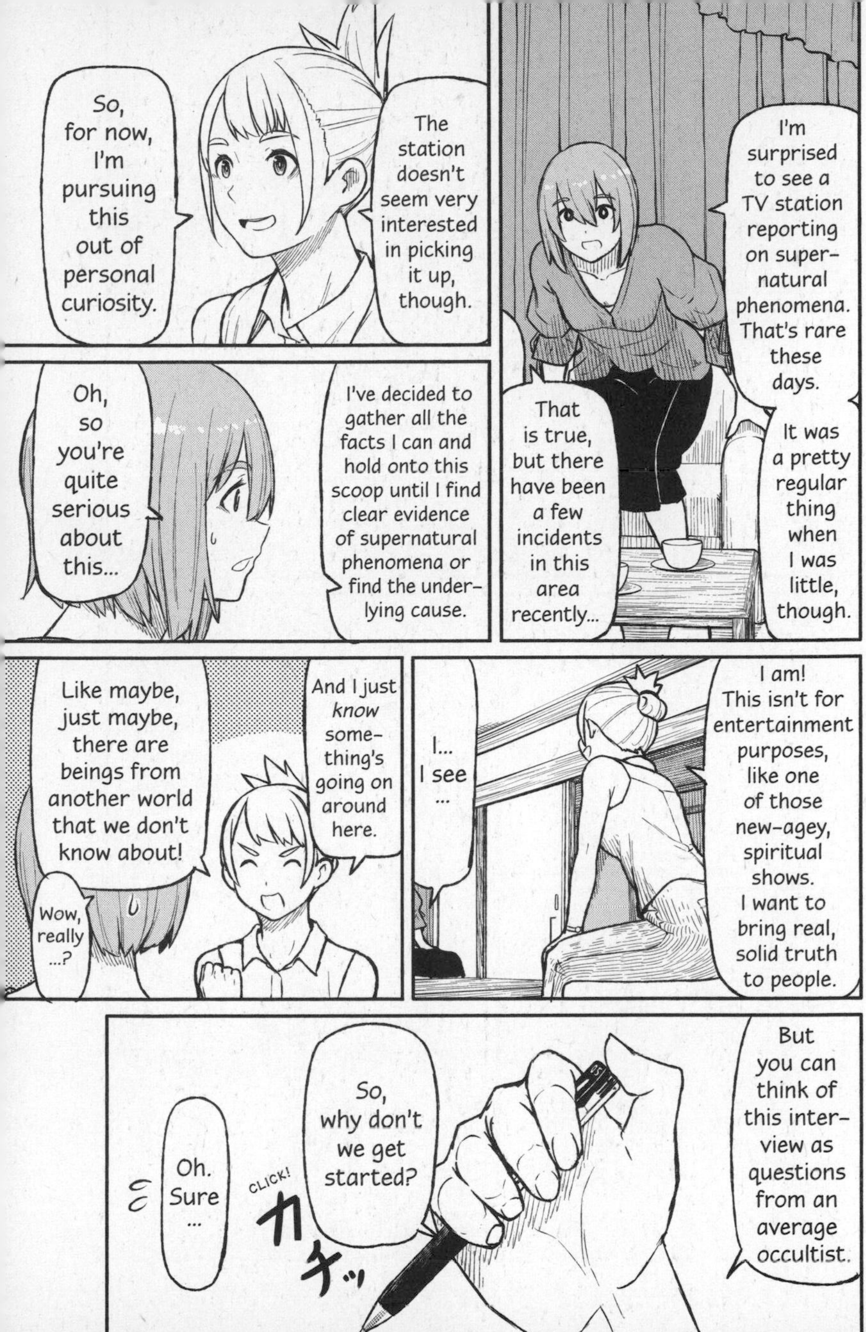
I'm surprised to see a TV station reporting on supernatural phenomena. That's rare these days.
It was a pretty regular thing when I was little, though.
That is true, but there have been a few incidents in this area recently...
The station doesn't seem very interested in picking it up, though.
So, for now, I'm pursuing this out of personal curiosity.
I've decided to gather all the facts I can and hold onto this scoop until I find clear evidence of supernatural phenomena or find the underlying cause.
Oh, so you're quite serious about this...
I am! This isn't for entertainment purposes, like one of those new-agey, spiritual shows. I want to bring real, solid truth to people.
I... I see...
And I just *know* something's going on around here.
Like maybe, just maybe, there are beings from another world that we don't know about!
Wow, really...?
But you can think of this interview as questions from an average occultist.
So, why don't we get started?
CLICK!
カチッ
Oh. Sure...

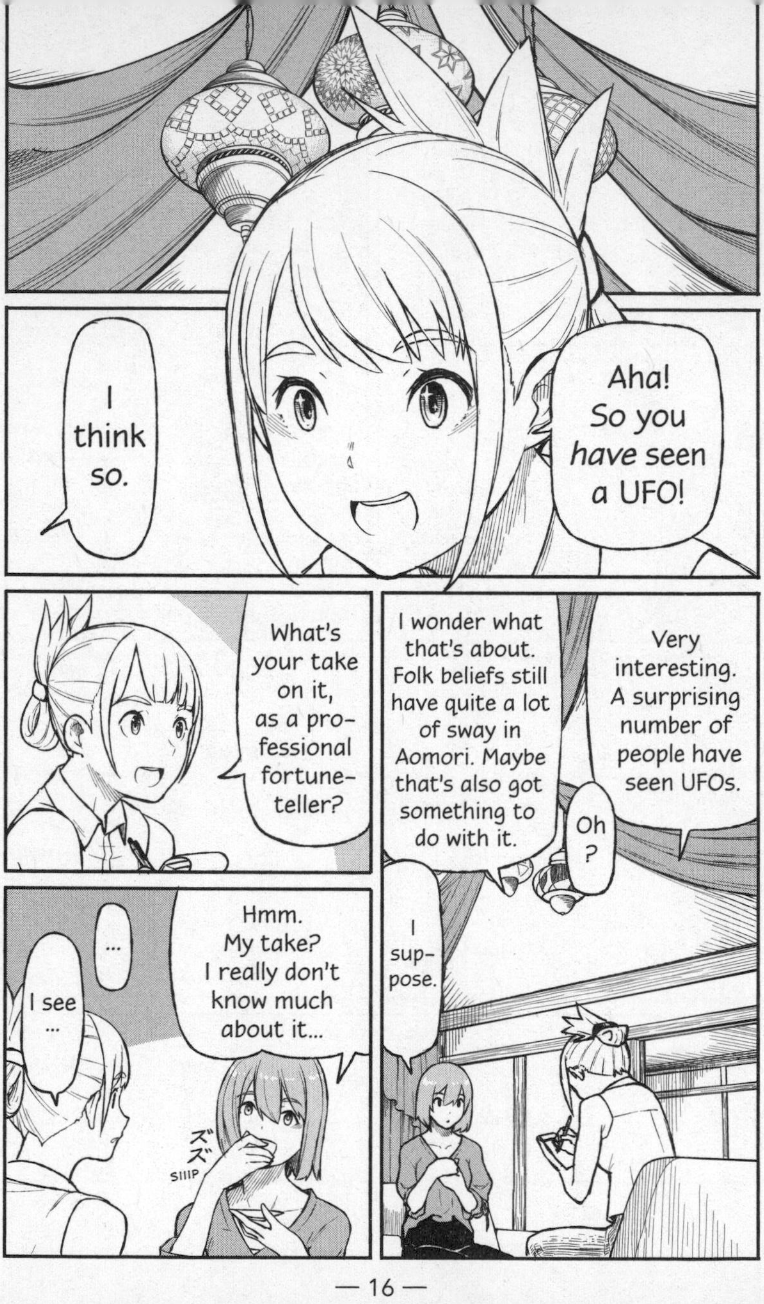
Aha! So you *have* seen a UFO!
I think so.
Very interesting. A surprising number of people have seen UFOs.
Oh?
I wonder what that's about. Folk beliefs still have quite a lot of sway in Aomori. Maybe that's also got something to do with it.
What's your take on it, as a professional fortune-teller?
I suppose.
Hmm. My take? I really don't know much about it...
...
I see ...
ズズ
SIIIP

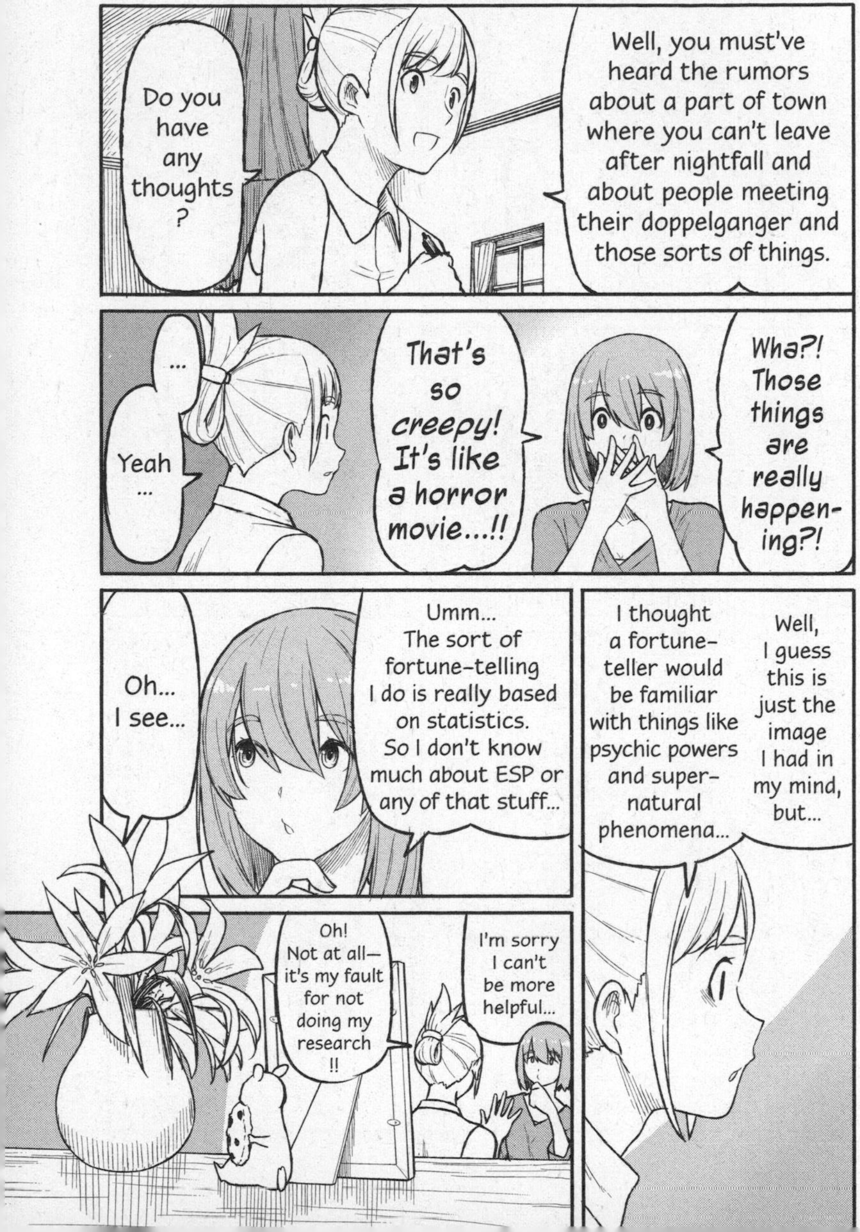
Well, you must've heard the rumors about a part of town where you can't leave after nightfall and about people meeting their doppelganger and those sorts of things.
Do you have any thoughts?
Wha?! Those things are really happening?!
That's so *creepy*! It's like a horror movie...!!
...
Yeah...
Well, I guess this is just the image I had in my mind, but...
I thought a fortune-teller would be familiar with things like psychic powers and supernatural phenomena...
Umm... The sort of fortune-telling I do is really based on statistics. So I don't know much about ESP or any of that stuff...
Oh... I see...
I'm sorry I can't be more helpful...
Oh! Not at all—it's my fault for not doing my research!!

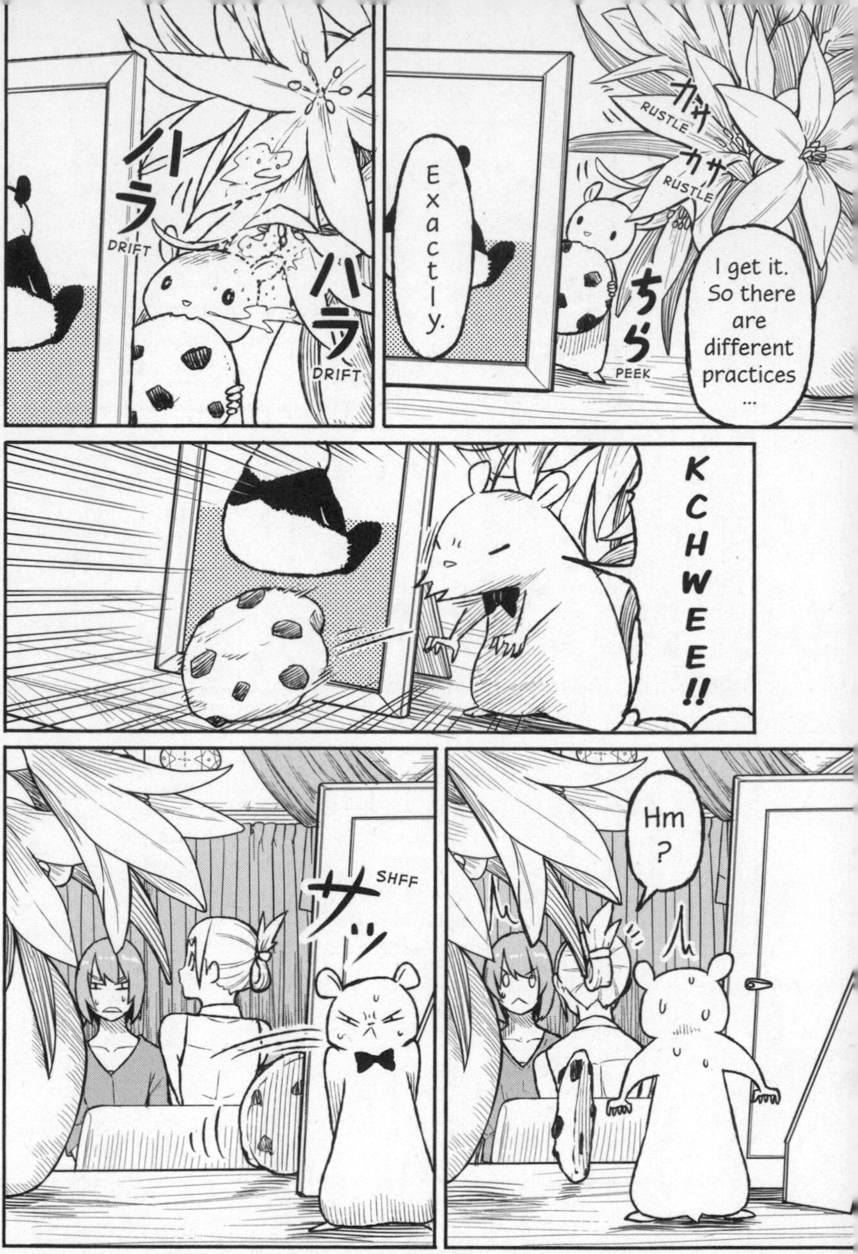
カサ
RUSTLE
カサ
RUSTLE
ちら
PEEK
I get it. So there are different practices ...
Exactly.
ハラ
DRIFT
ハラ
DRIFT
KCHWEE!!
Hm?
ん
サッ
SHFF

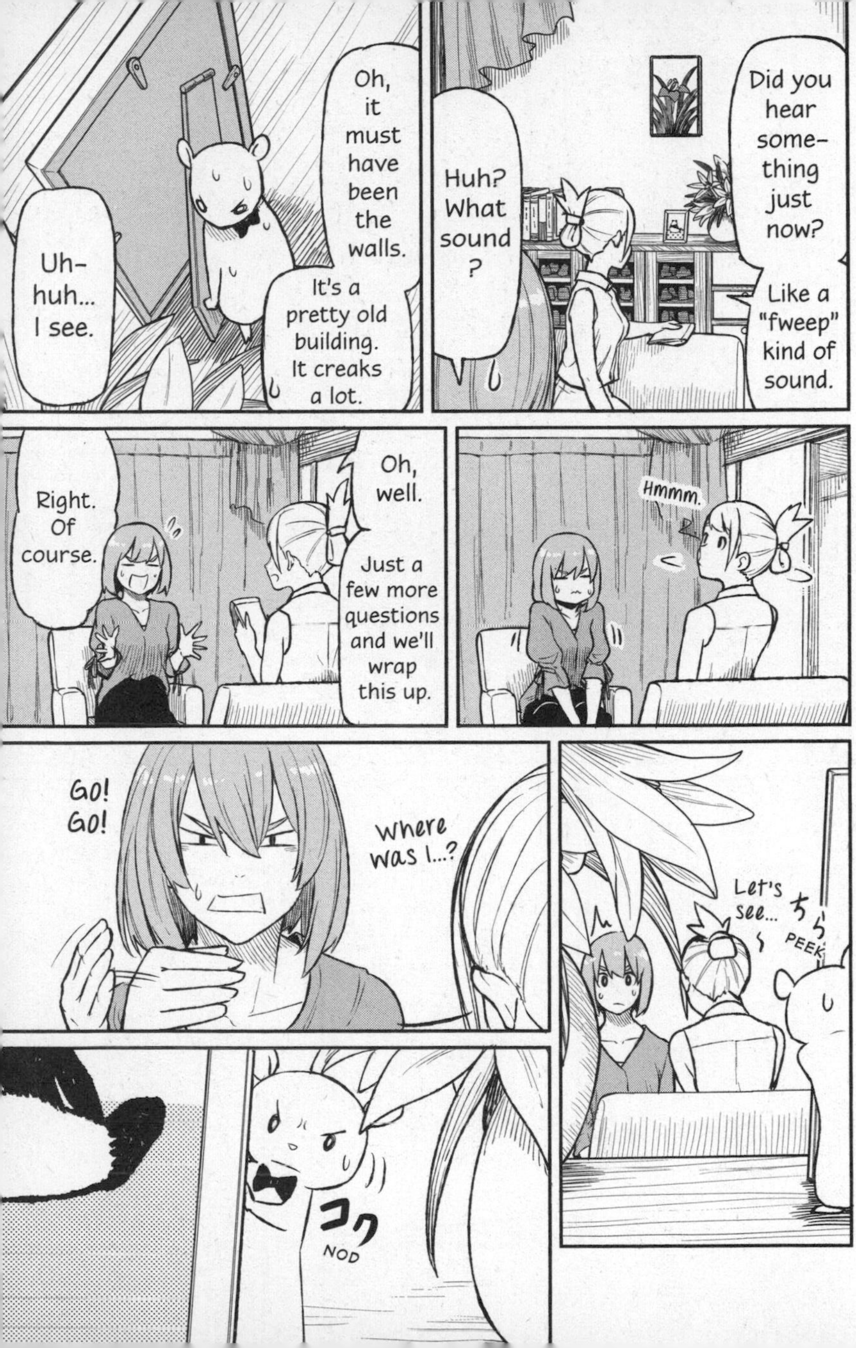
Did you hear something just now?
Like a "fweep" kind of sound.
Huh? What sound?
Oh, it must have been the walls.
It's a pretty old building. It creaks a lot.
Uh-huh... I see.
Hmmm.
Oh, well.
Just a few more questions and we'll wrap this up.
Right. Of course.
Let's see...
ちら PEEK
Where was I...?
Go! Go!
コク NOD

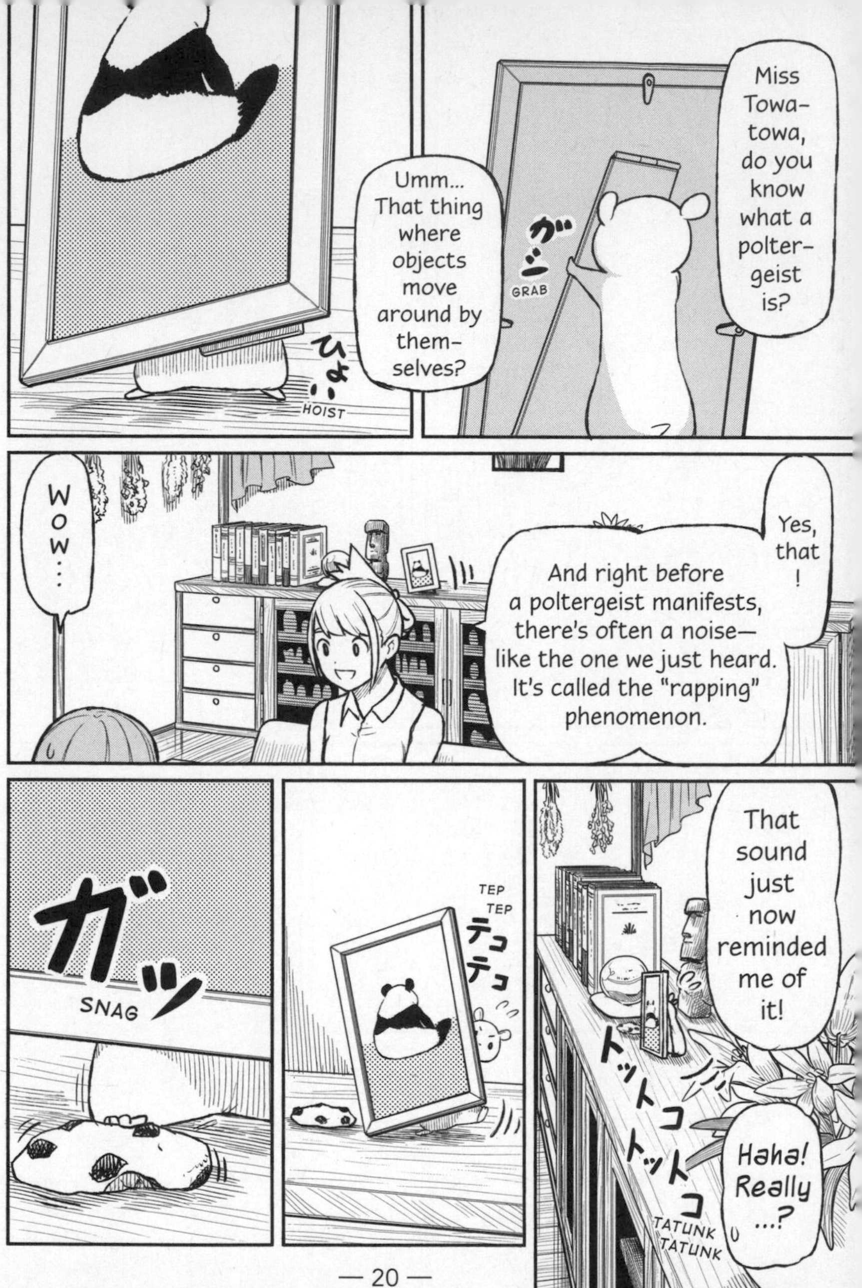

Miss Towa-towa, do you know what a polter-geist is?
ガッ
GRAB
Umm... That thing where objects move around by them-selves?
ひょい
HOIST
Yes, that!
And right before a poltergeist manifests, there's often a noise—like the one we just heard. It's called the "rapping" phenomenon.
Wow...
That sound just now reminded me of it!
トットコトットコ
TATUNK TATUNK
Haha! Really ...?
テコテコ
TEP TEP
ガッ
SNAG

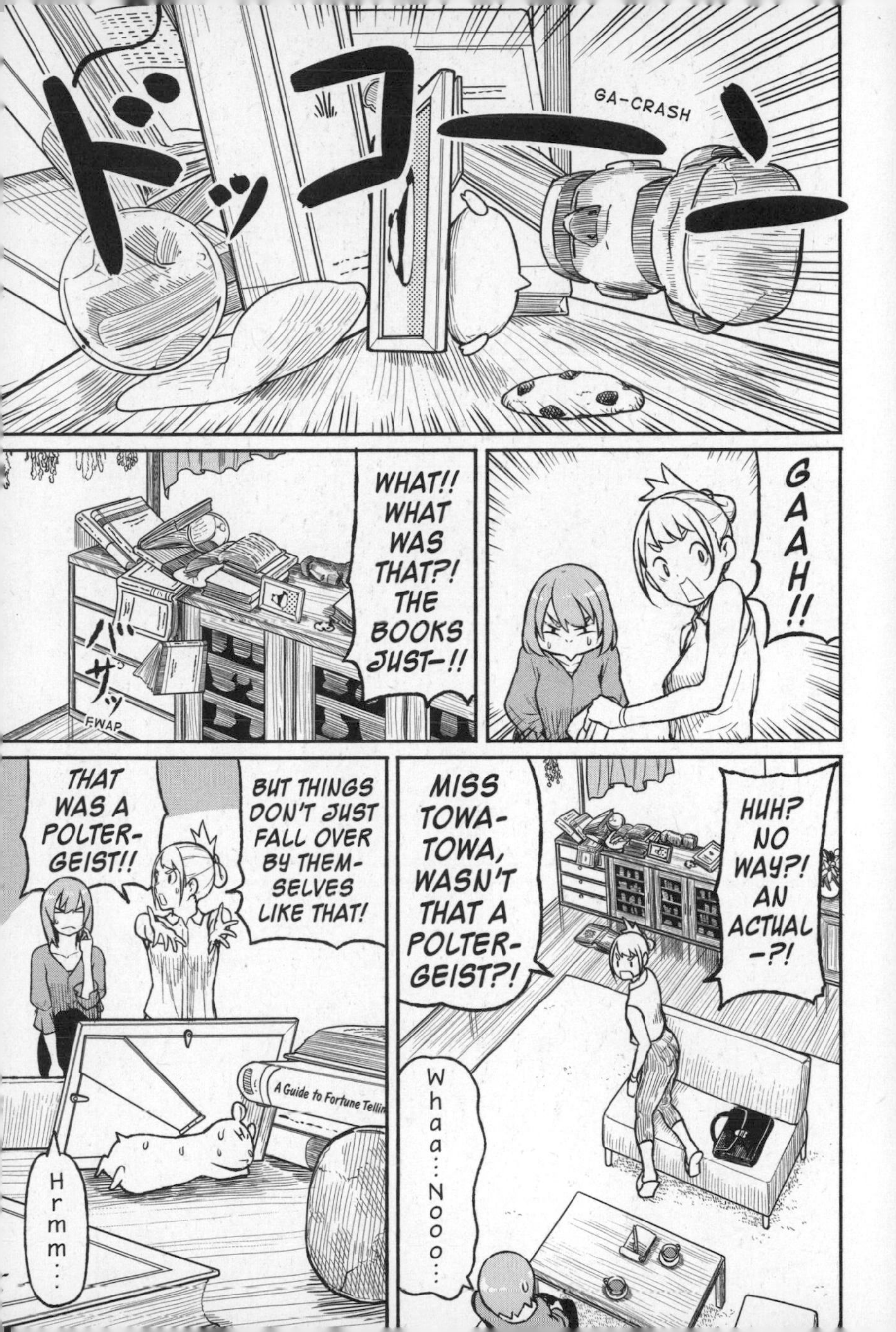
ドゴーン
GA-CRASH
GAAAH!!
WHAT!! WHAT WAS THAT?! THE BOOKS JUST-!!
バサッ
FWAP
HUH? NO WAY?! AN ACTUAL-?!
MISS TOWA-TOWA, WASN'T THAT A POLTER-GEIST?!
Whaa...Nooo...
BUT THINGS DON'T JUST FALL OVER BY THEM-SELVES LIKE THAT!
THAT WAS A POLTER-GEIST!!
A Guide to Fortune Tellin
Hrmm...

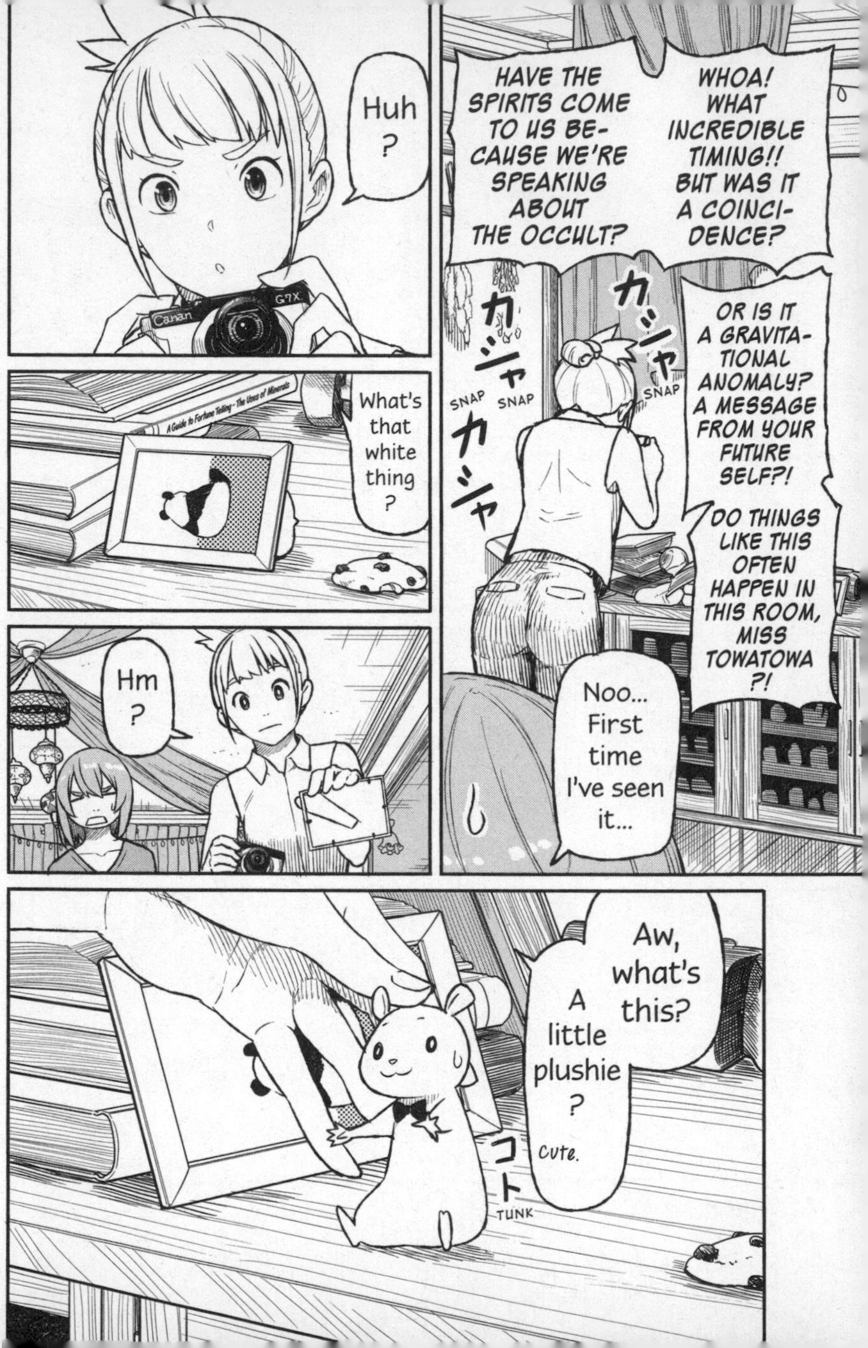
WHOA! WHAT INCREDIBLE TIMING!! BUT WAS IT A COINCIDENCE?
HAVE THE SPIRITS COME TO US BECAUSE WE'RE SPEAKING ABOUT THE OCCULT?
カシャ SNAP
カシャ SNAP
カシャ SNAP
OR IS IT A GRAVITATIONAL ANOMALY? A MESSAGE FROM YOUR FUTURE SELF?!
DO THINGS LIKE THIS OFTEN HAPPEN IN THIS ROOM, MISS TOWATOWA?!
Noo... First time I've seen it...
Huh?
Canan G7X
What's that white thing?
A Guide to Fortune Telling - The Uses of Minerals
Hm?
Aw, what's this?
A little plushie?
Cute.
コト TUNK

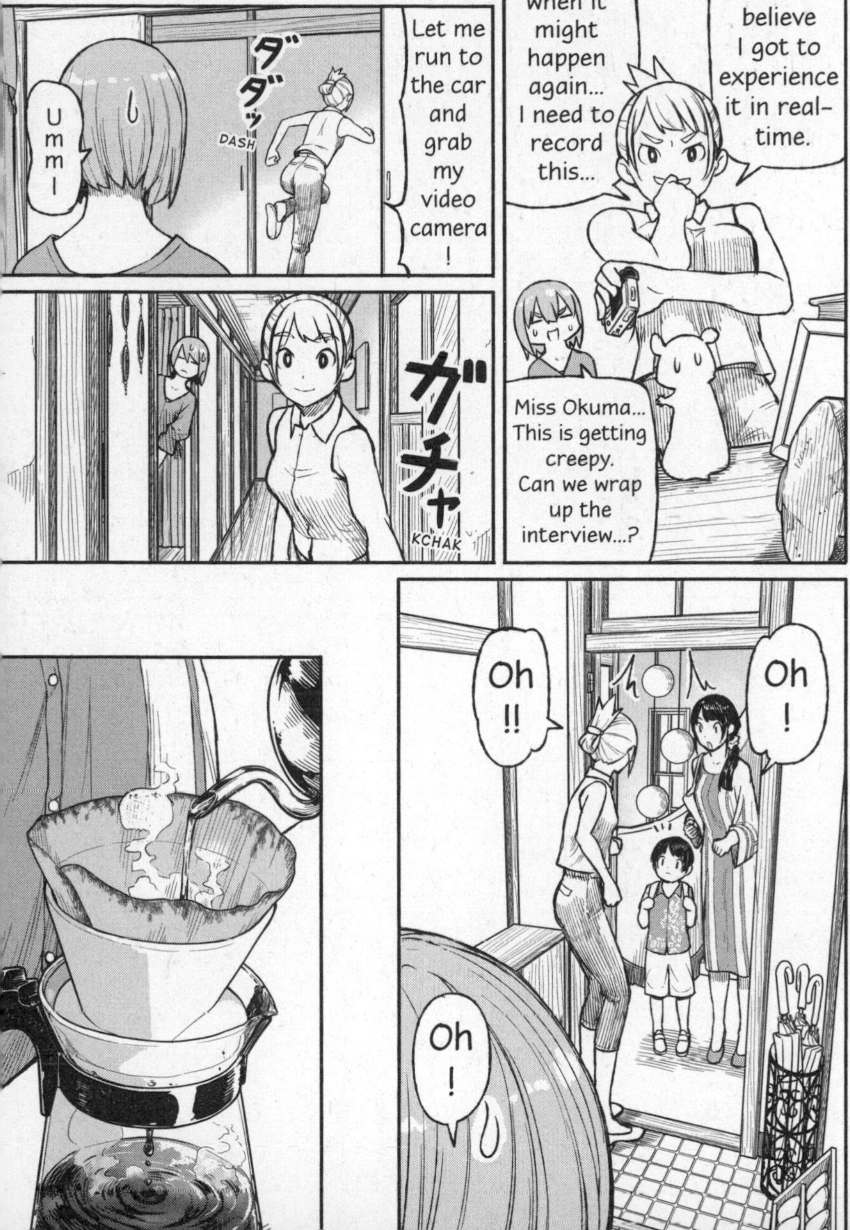
Ooh, I can't believe I got to experience it in real-time.
No telling when it might happen again... I need to record this...
Miss Okuma... This is getting creepy. Can we wrap up the interview...?
Let me run to the car and grab my video camera!
ダダッ
DASH
Umm!
ガチャ
KCHAK
Oh!
Oh!!
Oh!

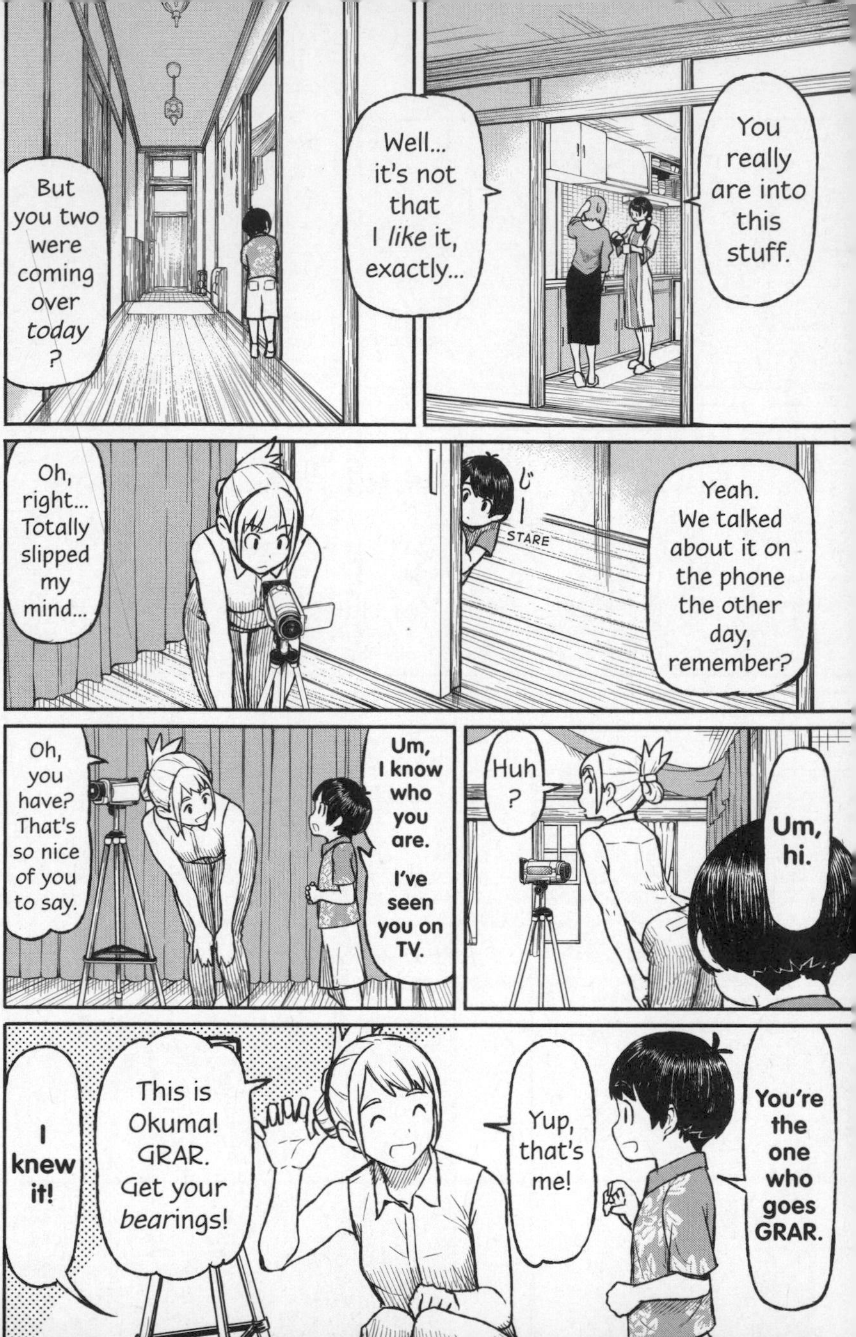

You really are into this stuff.
Well... it's not that I *like* it, exactly...
But you two were coming over *today*?
Yeah. We talked about it on the phone the other day, remember?
じー
STARE
Oh, right... Totally slipped my mind...
Um, hi.
Huh?
Um, I know who you are. I've seen you on TV.
Oh, you have? That's so nice of you to say.
You're the one who goes GRAR.
Yup, that's me!
This is Okuma! GRAR. Get your *bearings*!
I knew it!

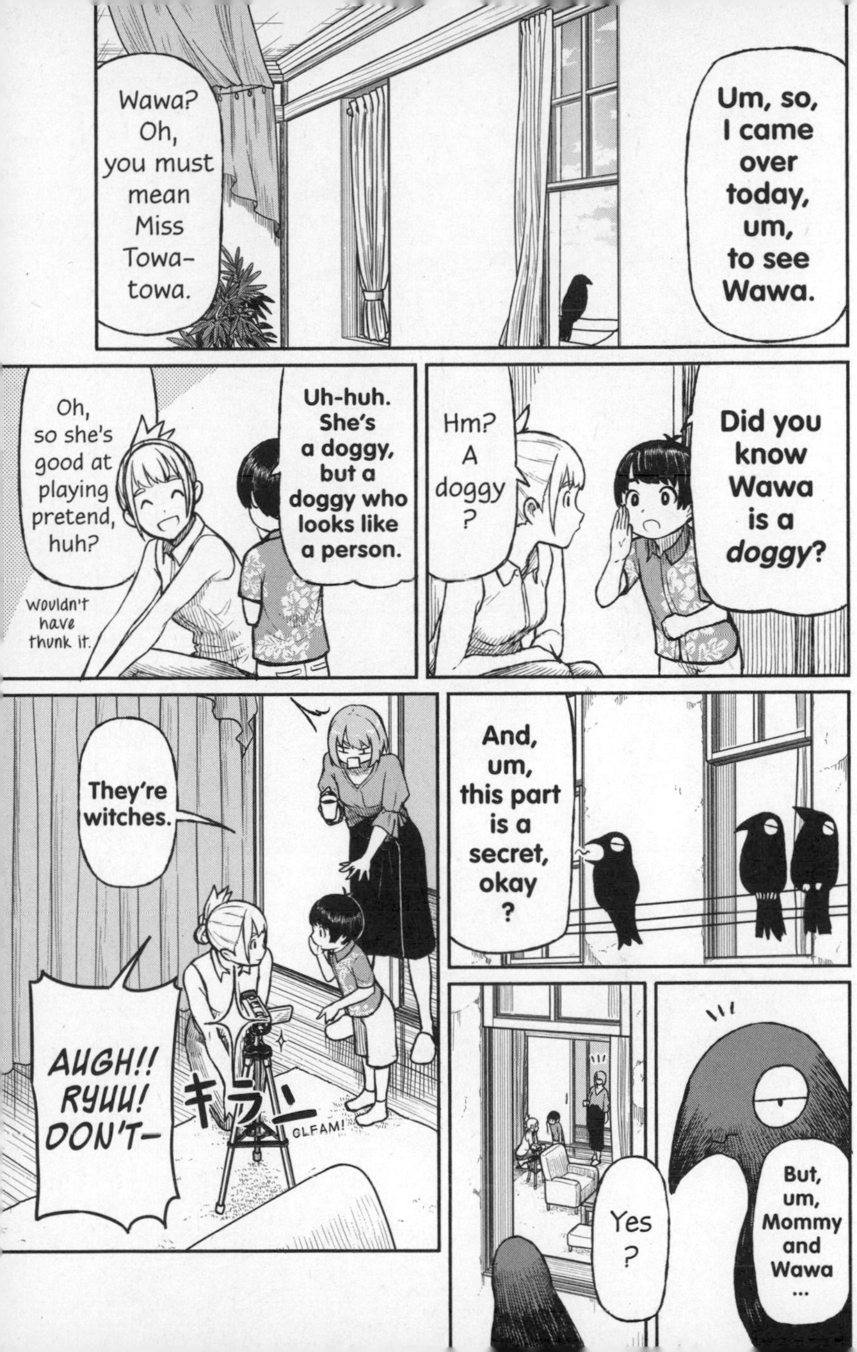
Um, so, I came over today, um, to see Wawa.
Wawa? Oh, you must mean Miss Towa-towa.
Did you know Wawa is a *doggy*?
Hm? A doggy?
Uh-huh. She's a doggy, but a doggy who looks like a person.
Oh, so she's good at playing pretend, huh?
Wouldn't have thunk it.
And, um, this part is a secret, okay?
But, um, Mommy and Wawa ...
Yes?
They're witches.
AUGH!! RYUU! DON'T–
キラーン
GLEAM!

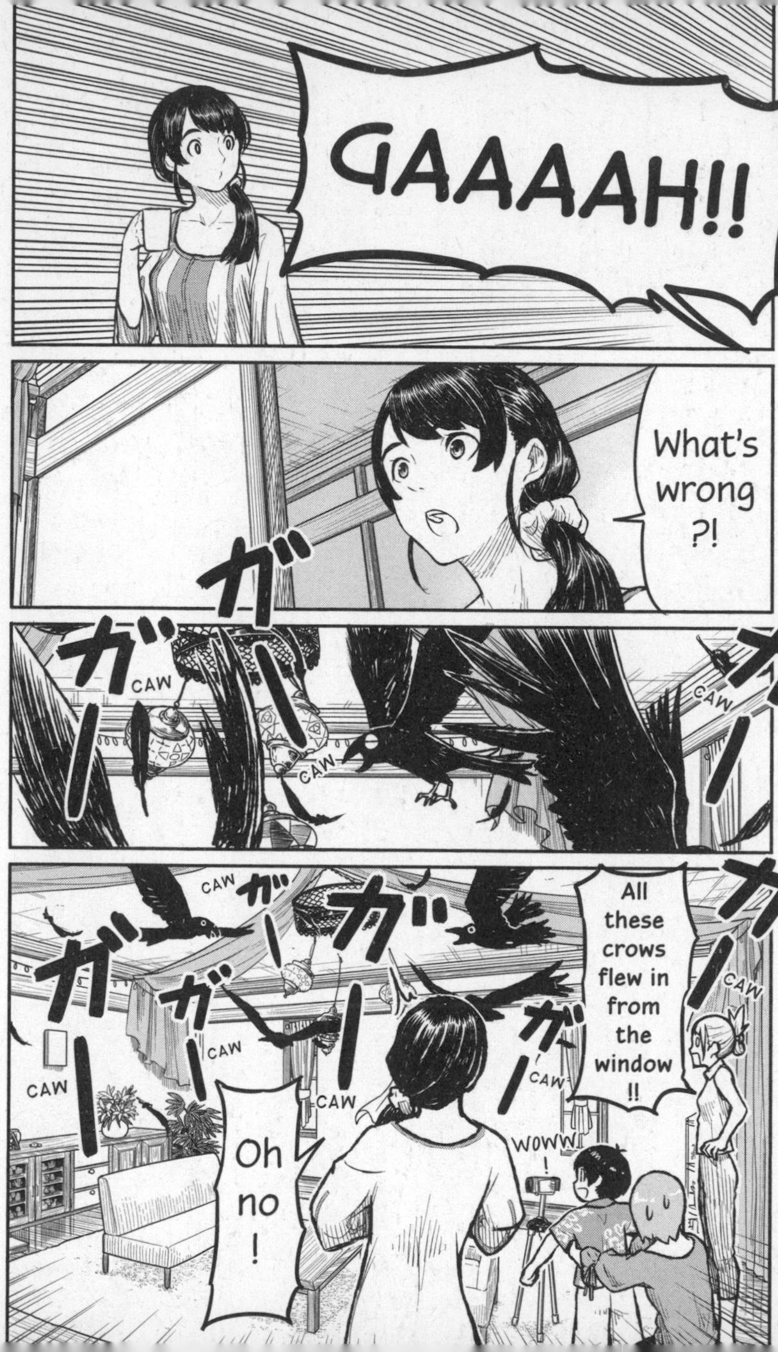
GAAAAH!!
What's wrong ?!
ガー
CAW
CAW
ガー
CAW
ガー
ガー
CAW
All these crows flew in from the window !!
WOWW !
ガー
CAW
ガー
CAW
Oh no !
ガー
CAW
ガー
CAW
ガー
CAW

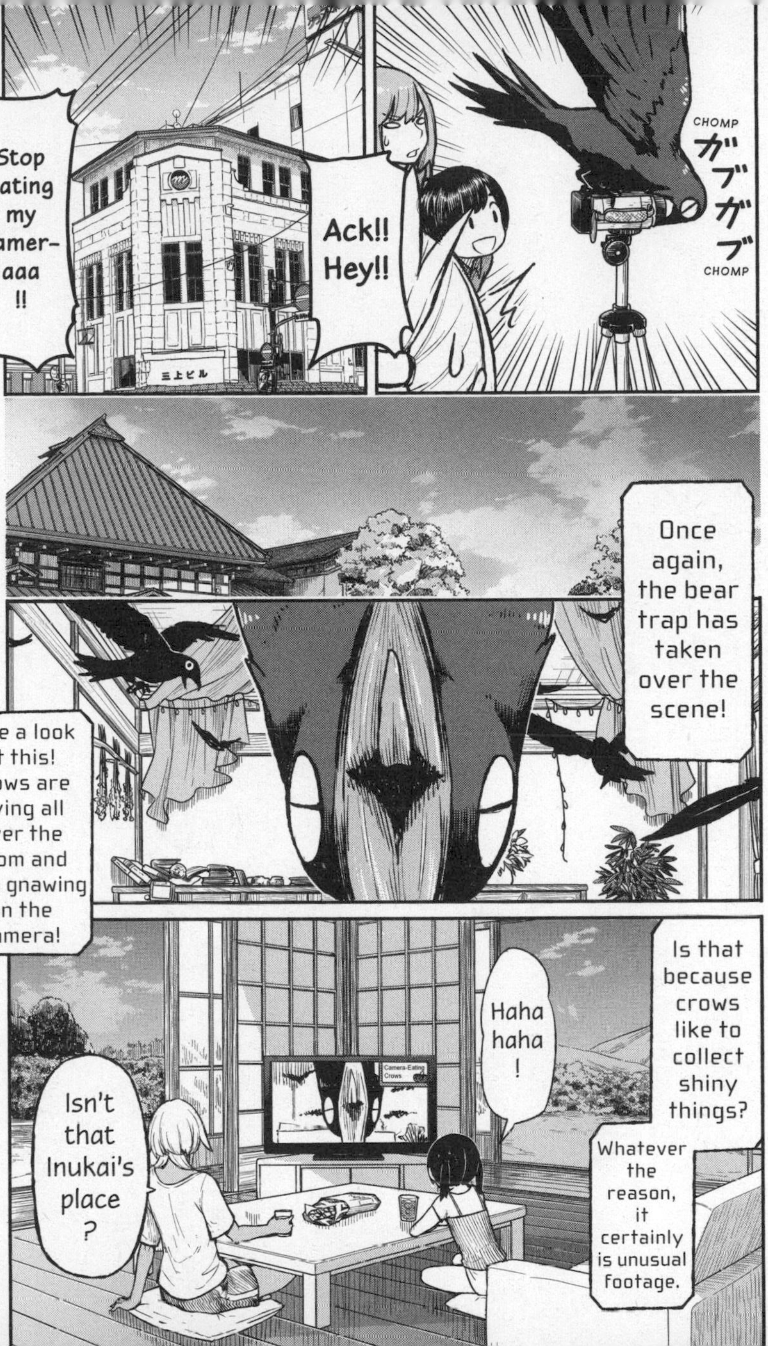
CHOMP
ガブガブ
CHOMP
Ack!! Hey!!
Stop eating my camer-aaa!!
三上ビル
Once again, the bear trap has taken over the scene!
Take a look at this! Crows are flying all over the room and even gnawing on the camera!
Is that because crows like to collect shiny things?
Haha haha!
Camera-Eating Crows
Whatever the reason, it certainly is unusual footage.
Isn't that Inukai's place?

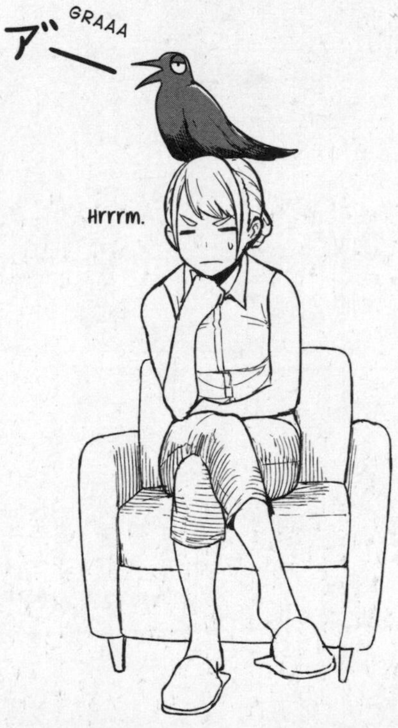
アー
GRAAA
Hrrrm.

Chapter 50
The Secret Festival

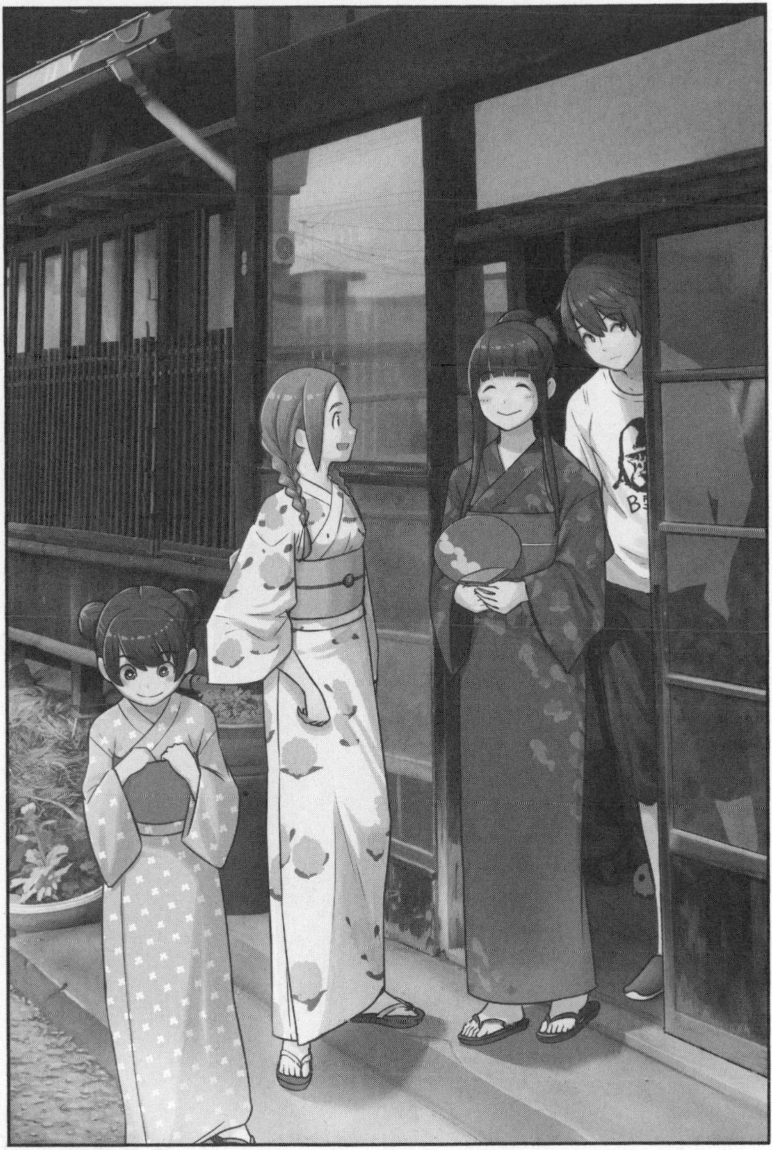

Flying
Witch

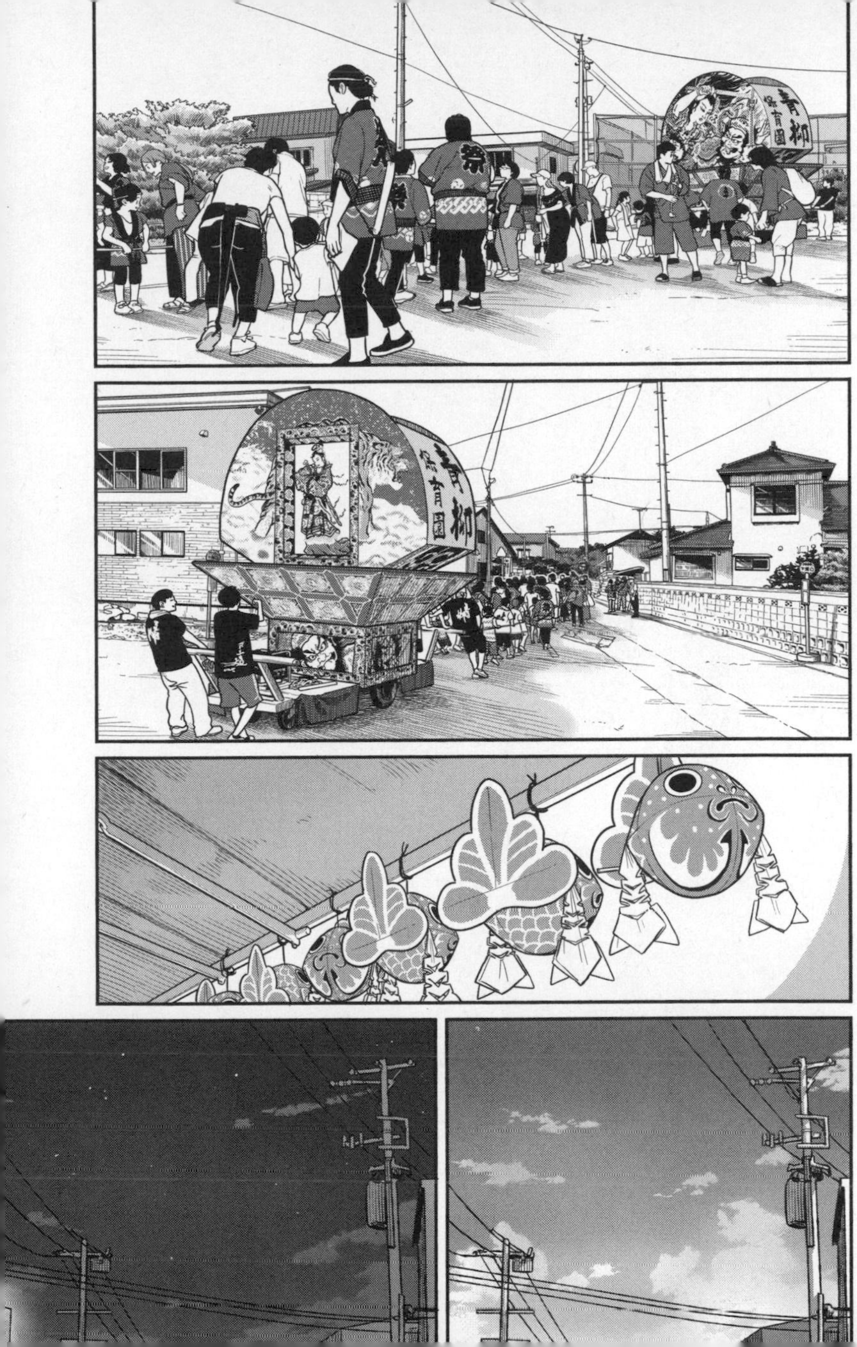
青柳
保育園
祭

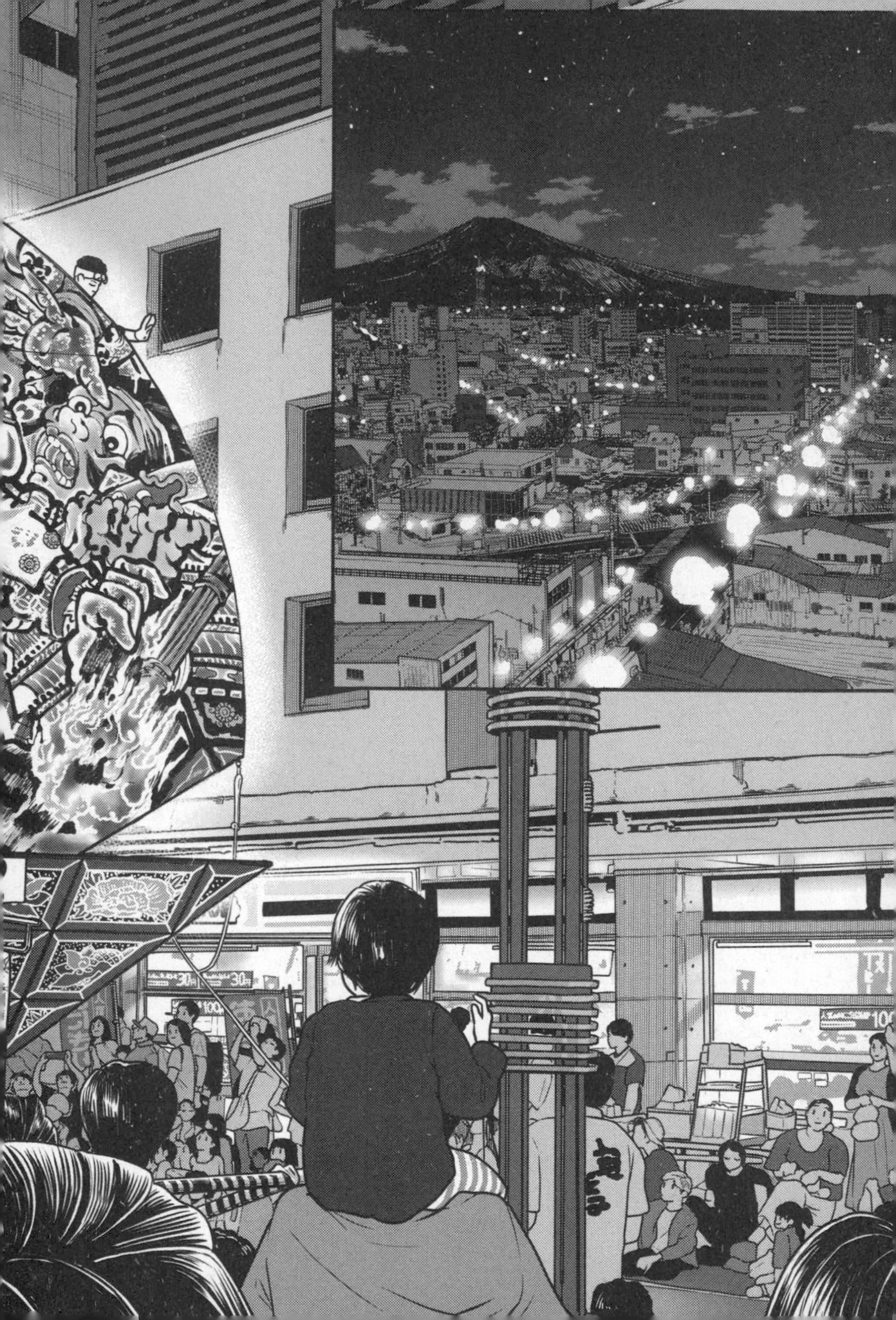

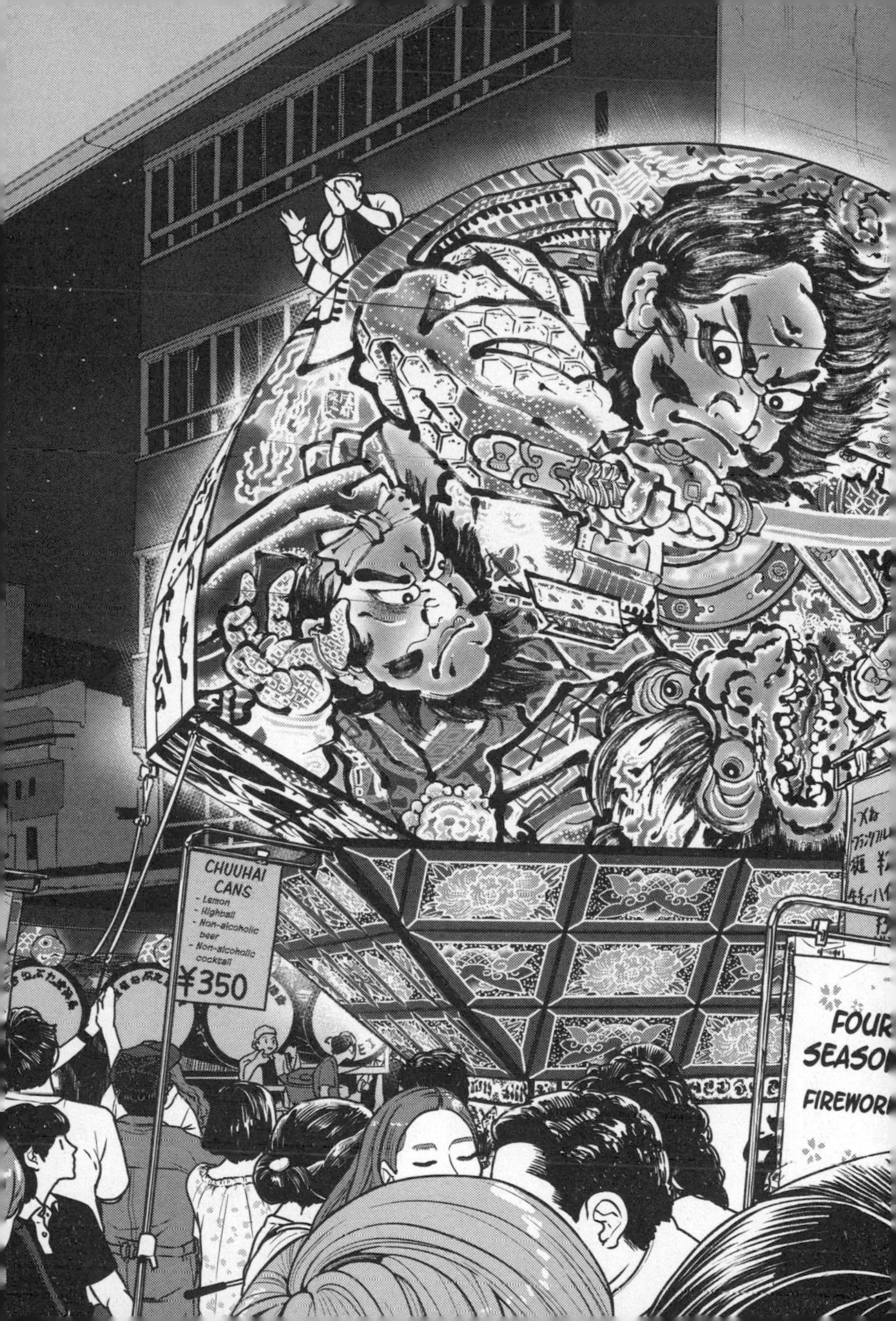
CHUUHAI CANS
- Lemon
- Highball
- Non-alcoholic beer
- Non-alcoholic cocktail
¥350
FOUR SEASO
FIREWOR

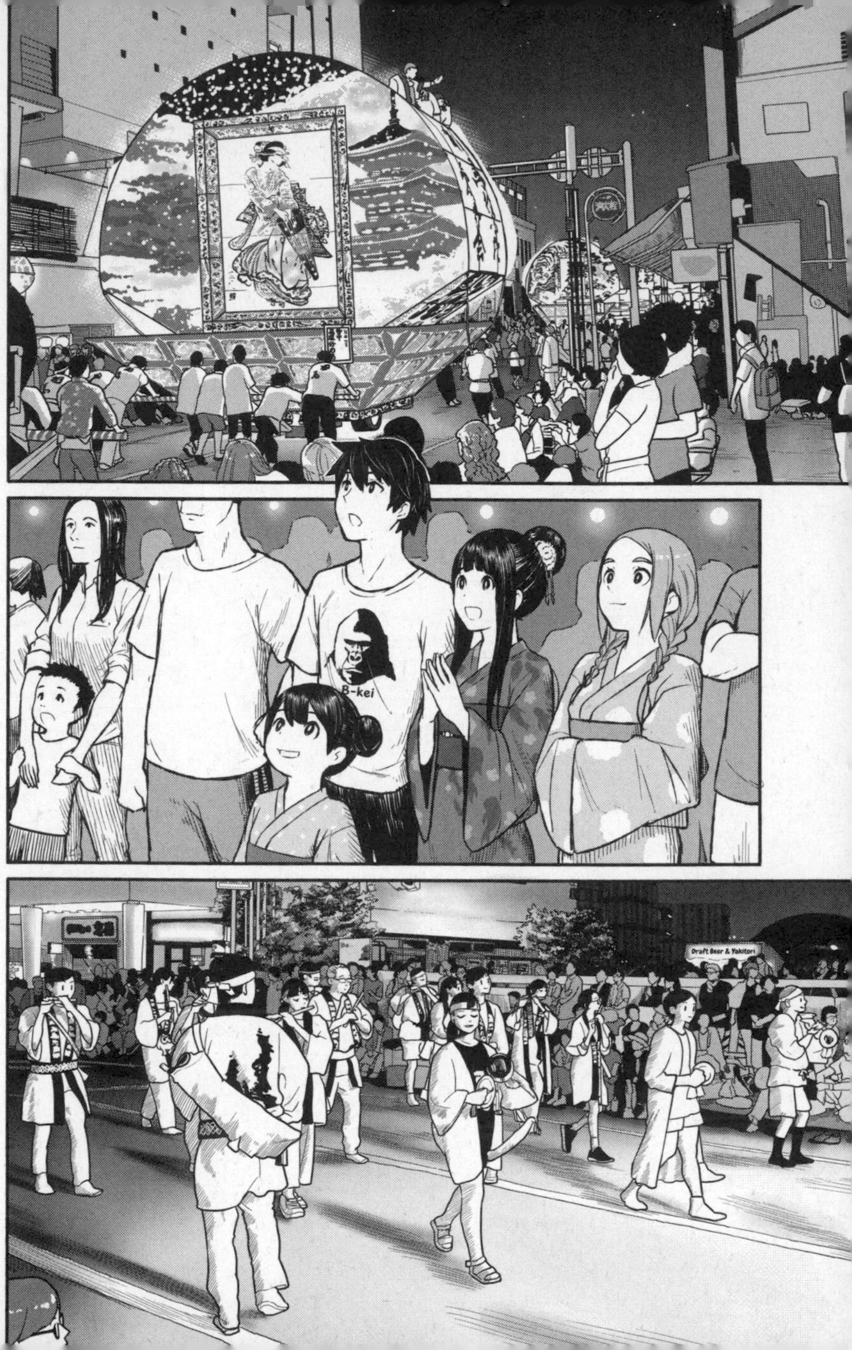
B-kei
Draft Beer & Yakitori

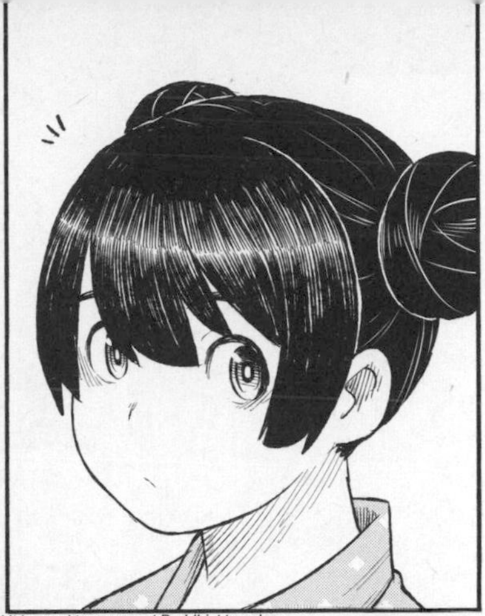

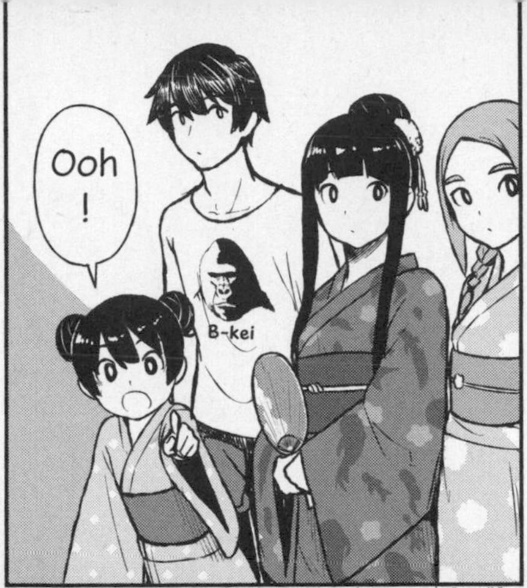
Ooh
!
B-kei

Note: The symbol in the middle of the float's signage is known as a "manji," and it is used to represent Buddhist temples.

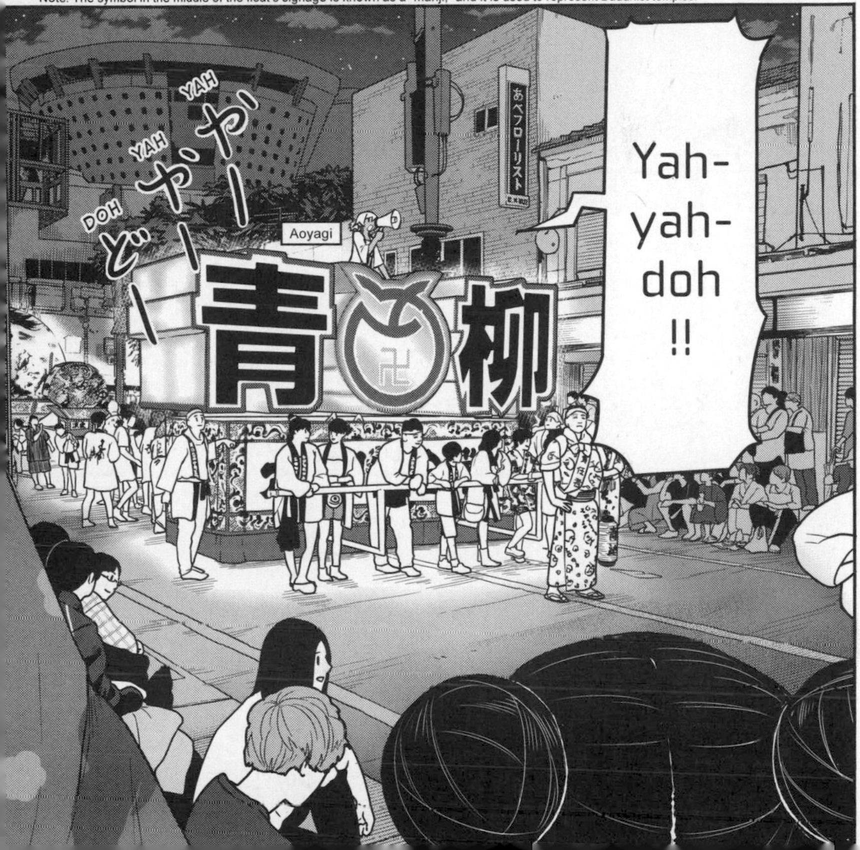
Yah-
yah-
doh
!!
あべフローリスト
YAH
やー
YAH
やー
DOH
どー
Aoyagi
青柳

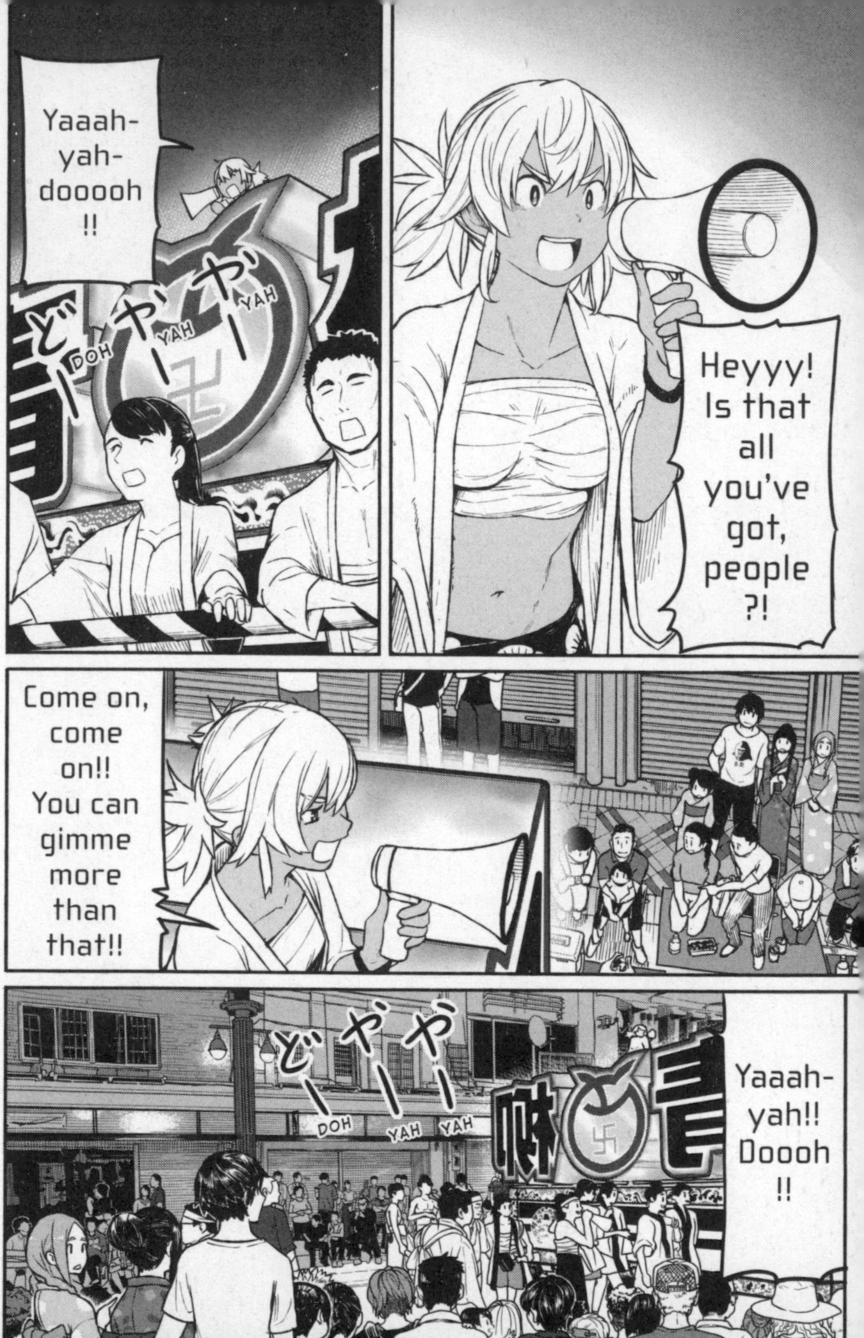
Heyyy! Is that all you've got, people ?!
Yaaah-yah-dooooh !!
DOH YAH YAH
Come on, come on!! You can gimme more than that!!
Yaaah-yah!! Doooh !!
DOH YAH YAH

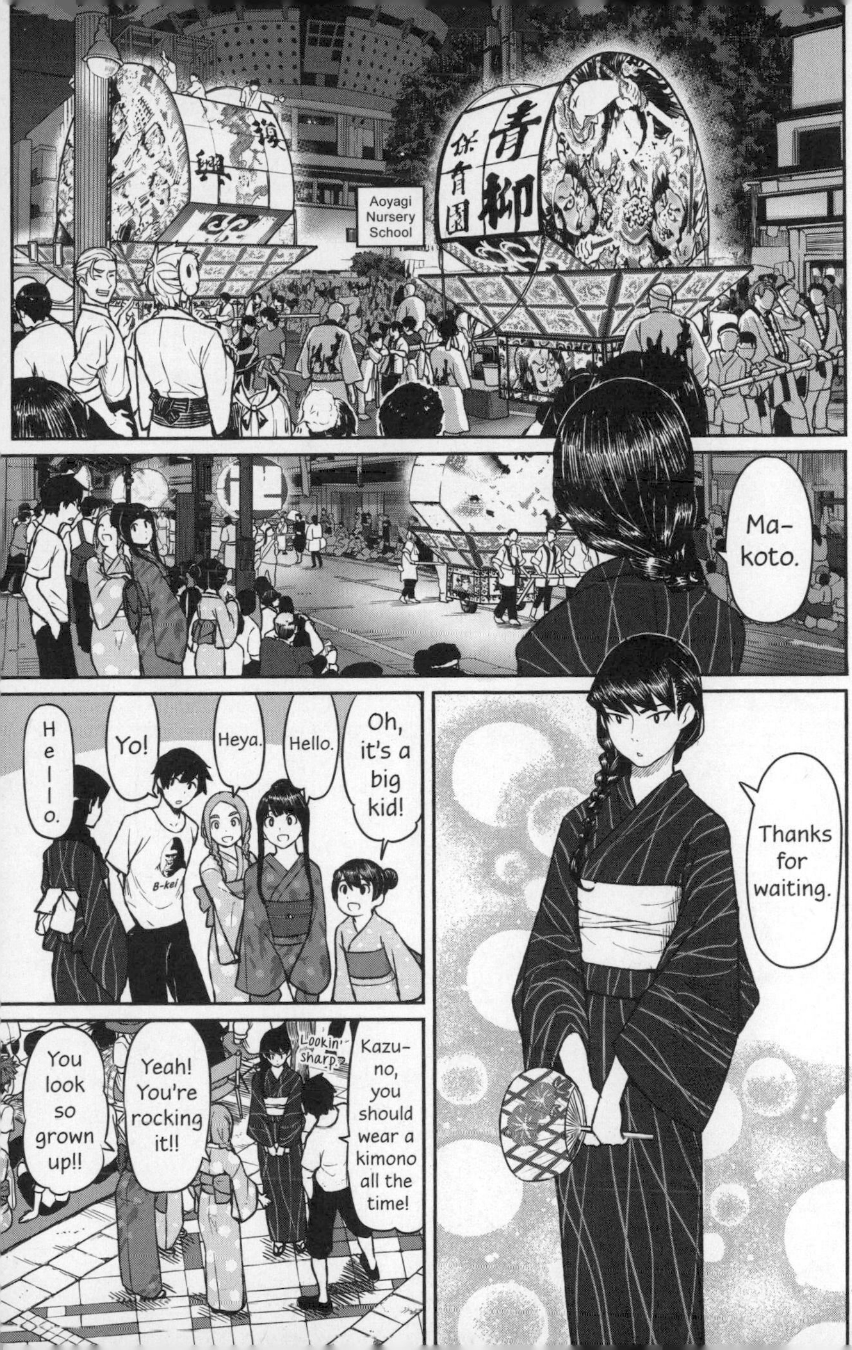
Aoyagi Nursery School
Ma-koto.
Thanks for waiting.
Oh, it's a big kid!
Hello.
Heya.
Yo!
Hello.
Kazu-no, you should wear a kimono all the time!
Lookin' sharp.
Yeah! You're rocking it!!
You look so grown up!!

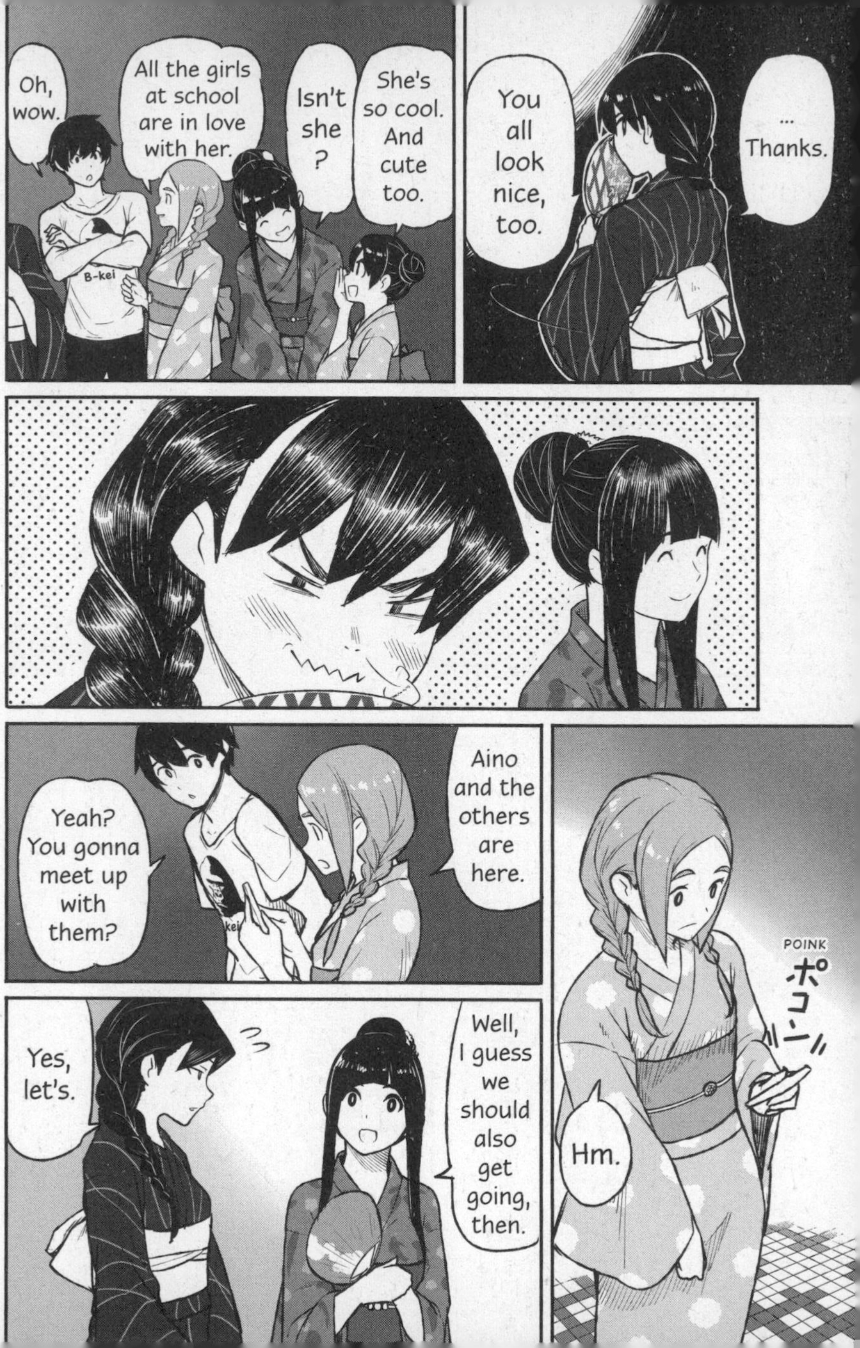

... Thanks.
You all look nice, too.
She's so cool. And cute too.
Isn't she?
All the girls at school are in love with her.
Oh, wow.
B-kei
POINK
ポコン
Hm.
Aino and the others are here.
Yeah? You gonna meet up with them?
Well, I guess we should also get going, then.
Yes, let's.

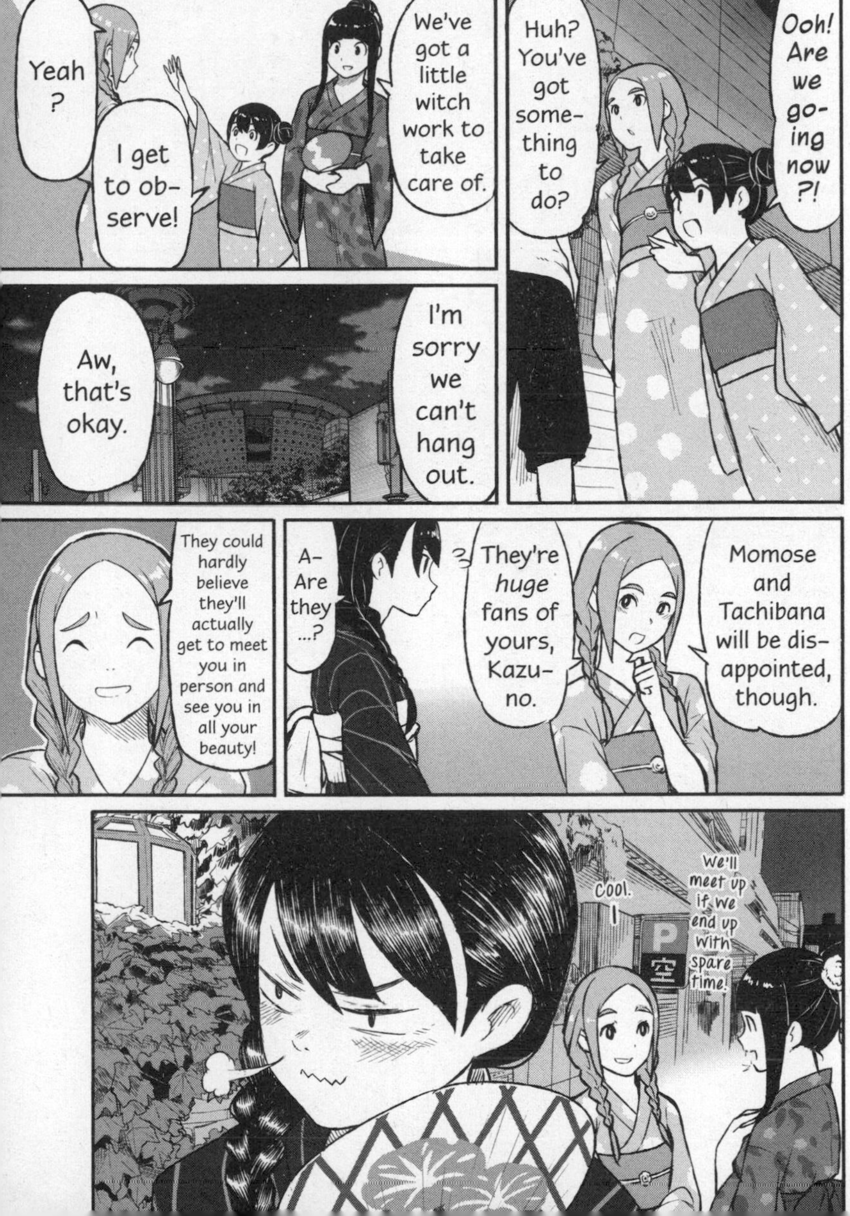
Ooh! Are we going now?!
Huh? You've got something to do?
We've got a little witch work to take care of.
Yeah?
I get to observe!
I'm sorry we can't hang out.
Aw, that's okay.
Momose and Tachibana will be disappointed, though.
They're *huge* fans of yours, Kazuno.
A- Are they ...?
They could hardly believe they'll actually get to meet you in person and see you in all your beauty!
We'll meet up if we end up with spare time!
Cool. I

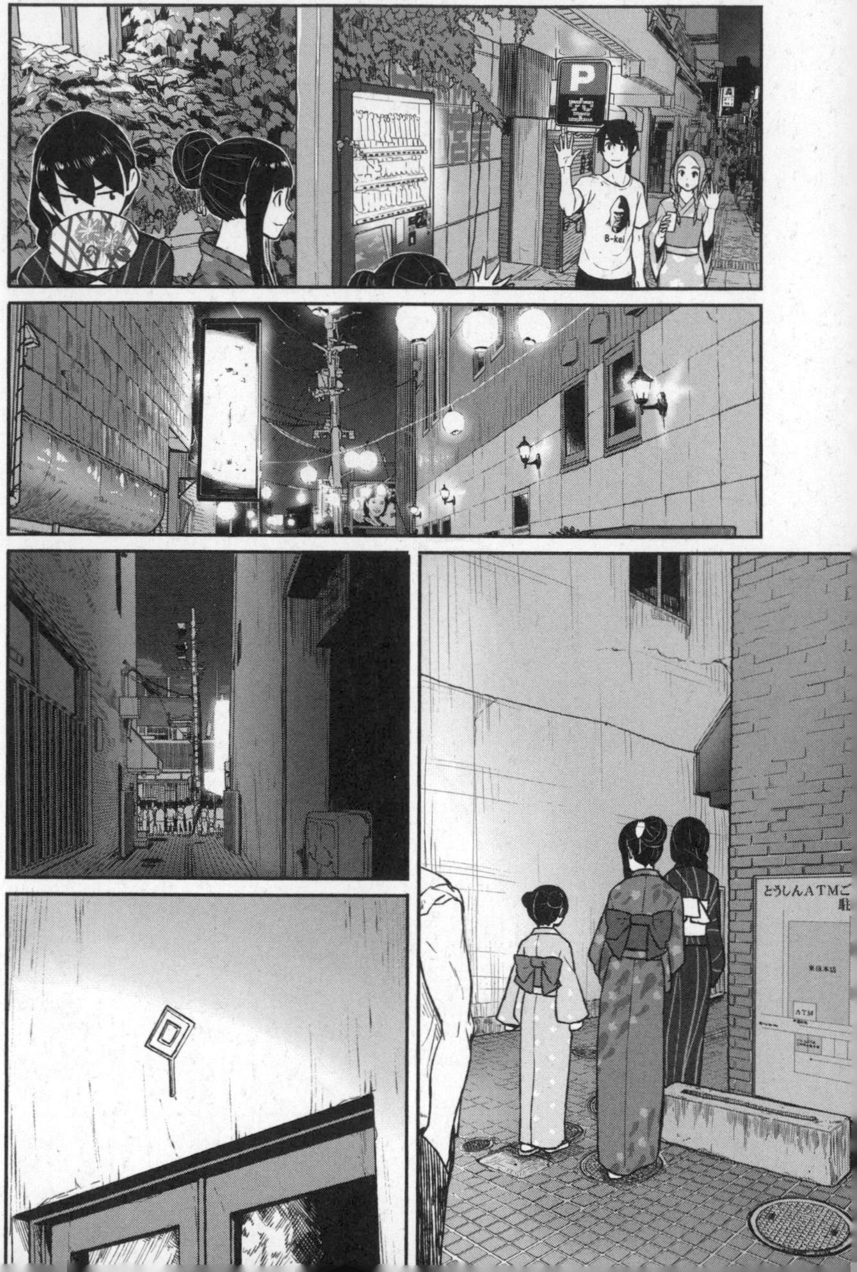
P
B-kei
とうしんＡＴＭご
駐
ATM

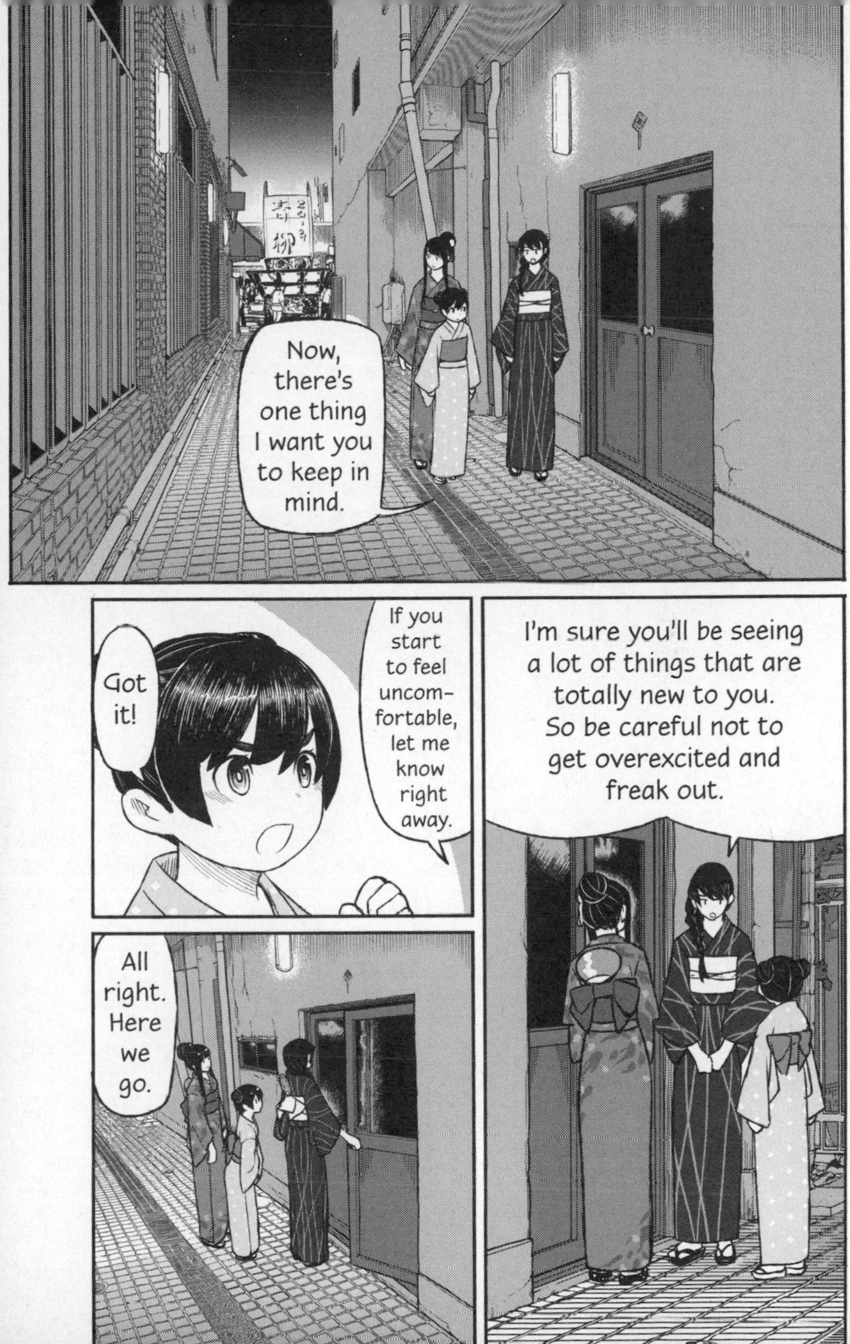
Now, there's one thing I want you to keep in mind.
I'm sure you'll be seeing a lot of things that are totally new to you. So be careful not to get overexcited and freak out.
If you start to feel uncom-fortable, let me know right away.
Got it!
All right. Here we go.

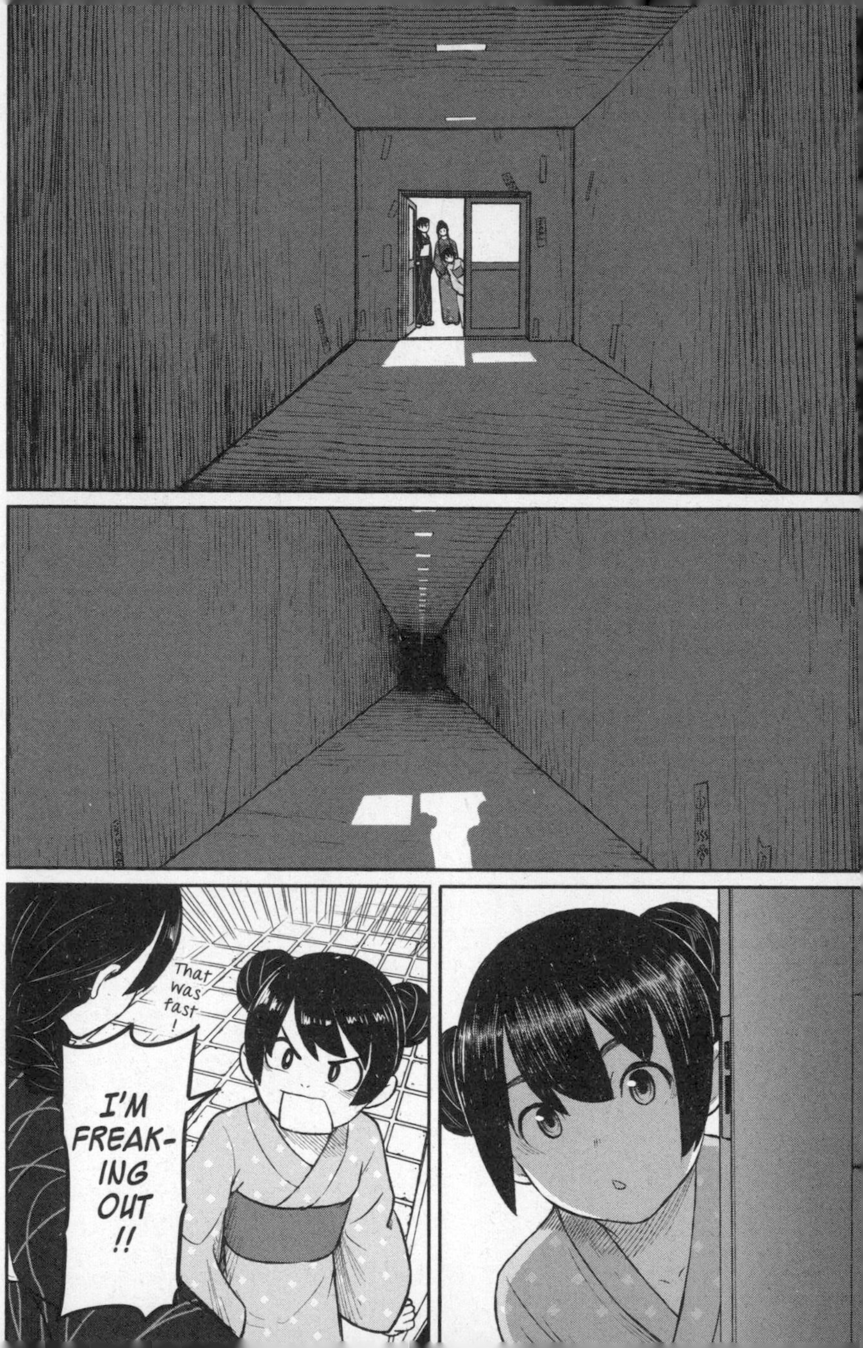
That was fast!
I'M FREAKING OUT!!

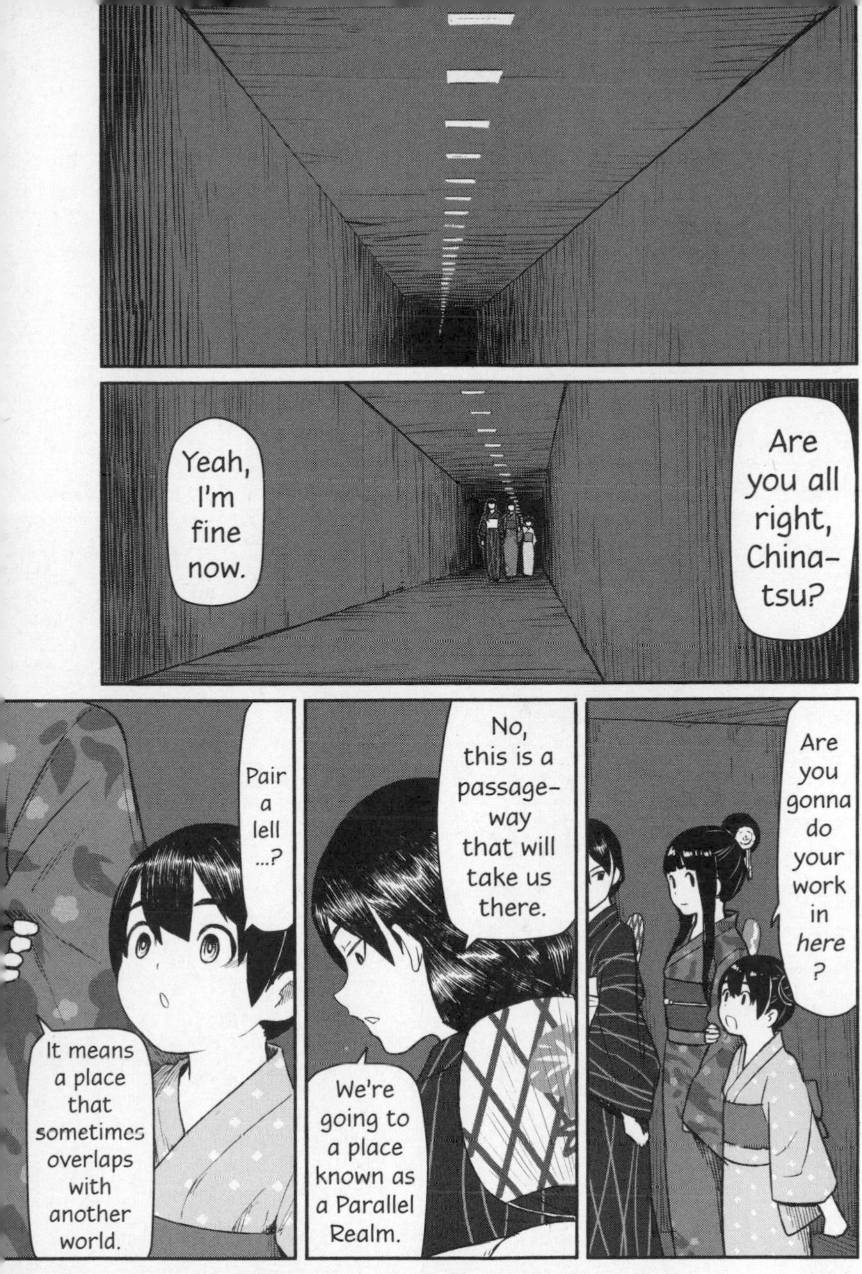
Are you all right, China-tsu?
Yeah, I'm fine now.
Are you gonna do your work in *here*?
No, this is a passage-way that will take us there.
We're going to a place known as a Parallel Realm.
Pair a lell ...?
It means a place that sometimes overlaps with another world.

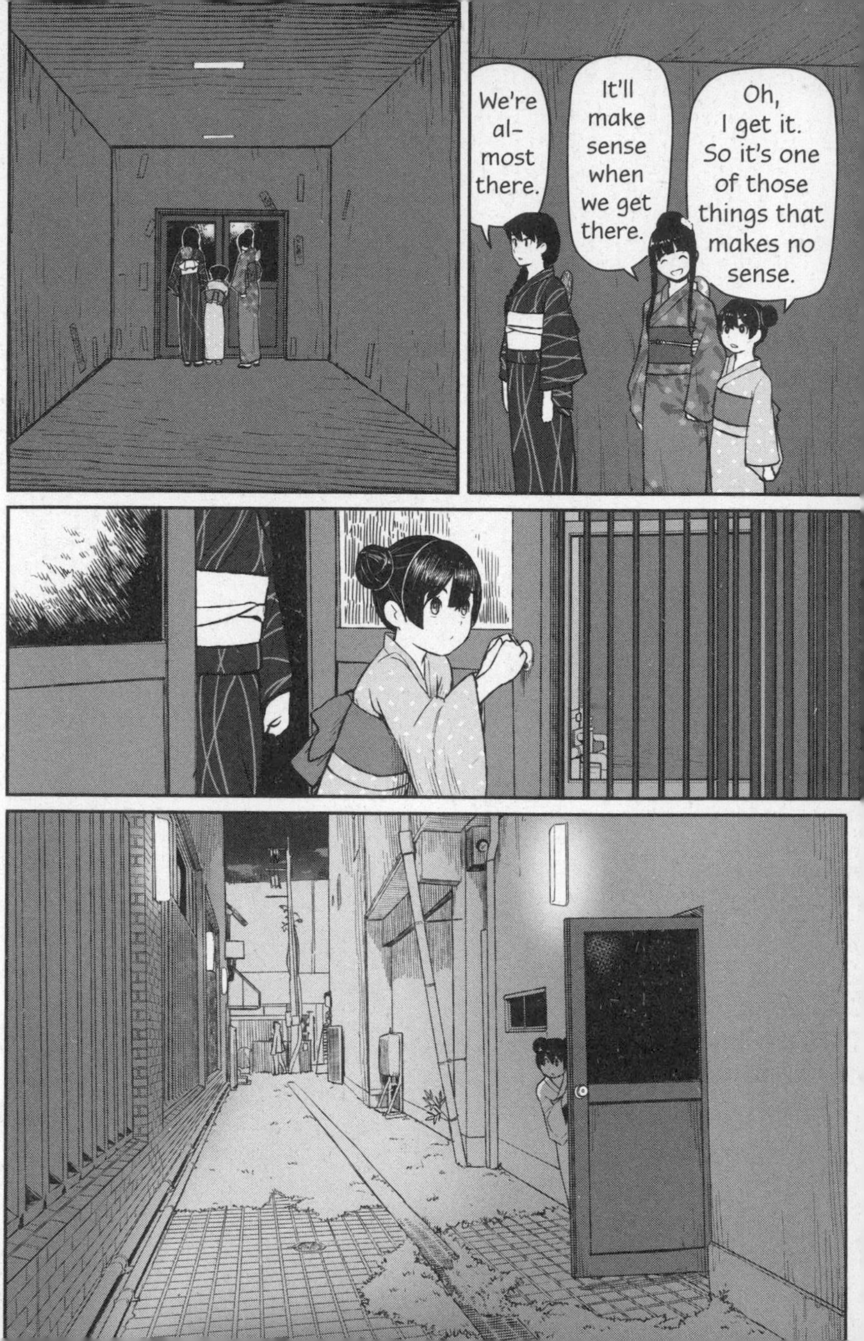
Oh, I get it. So it's one of those things that makes no sense.
It'll make sense when we get there.
We're al-most there.

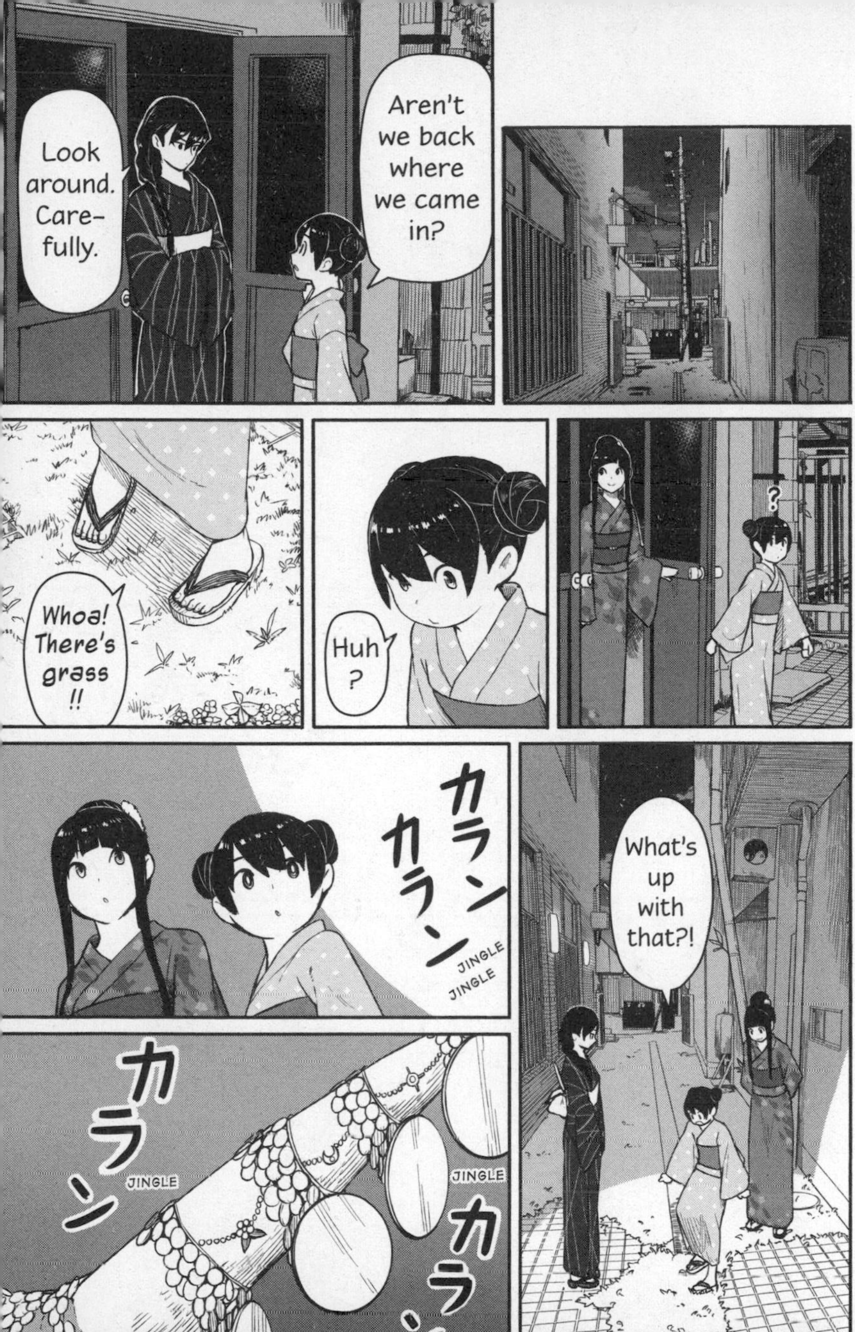
Aren't we back where we came in?
Look around. Care-fully.
?
Huh?
Whoa! There's grass!!
What's up with that?!
カランカラン
JINGLE JINGLE
JINGLE
カラン
JINGLE
カラン

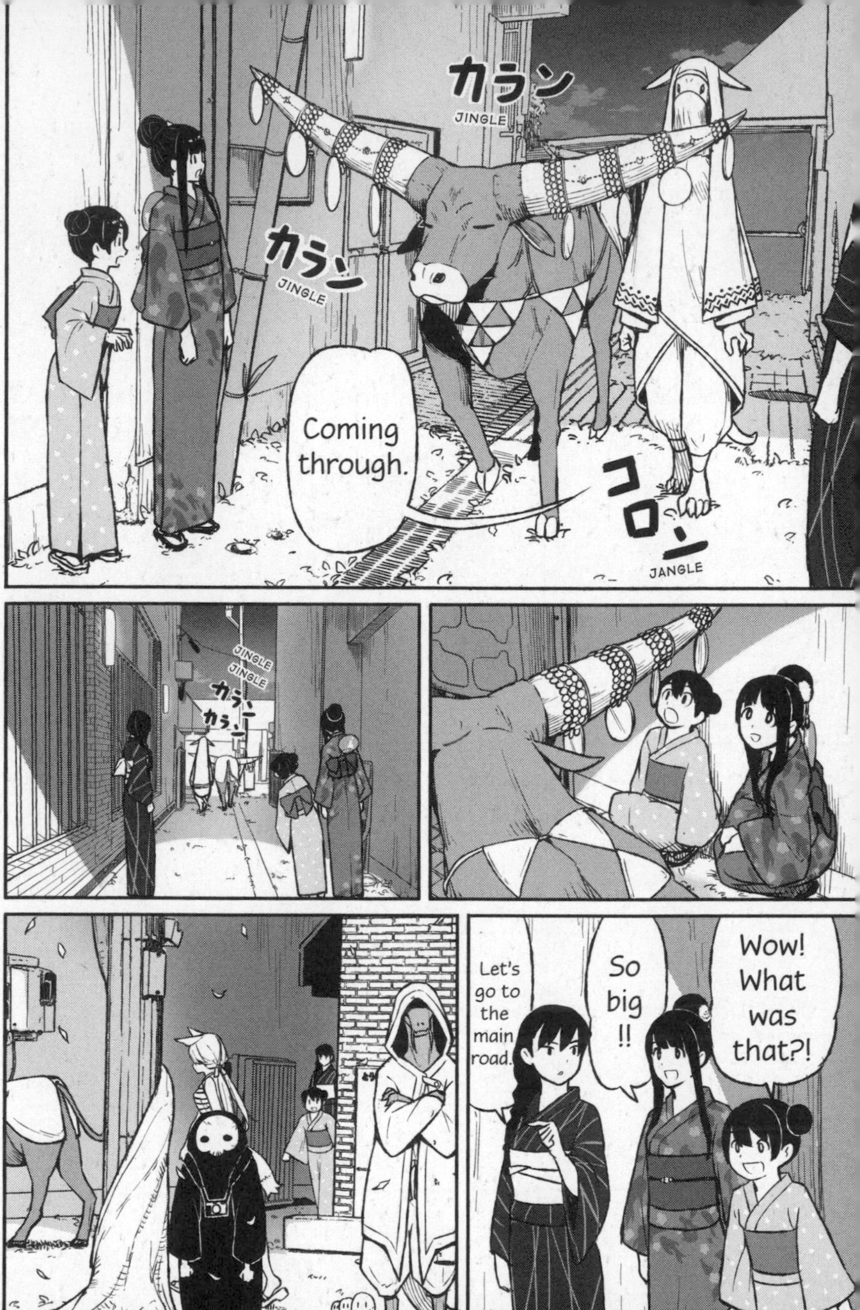

カラン
JINGLE
カラン
JINGLE
Coming through.
コロン
JANGLE
JINGLE
JINGLE
Wow! What was that?!
So big !!
Let's go to the main road.

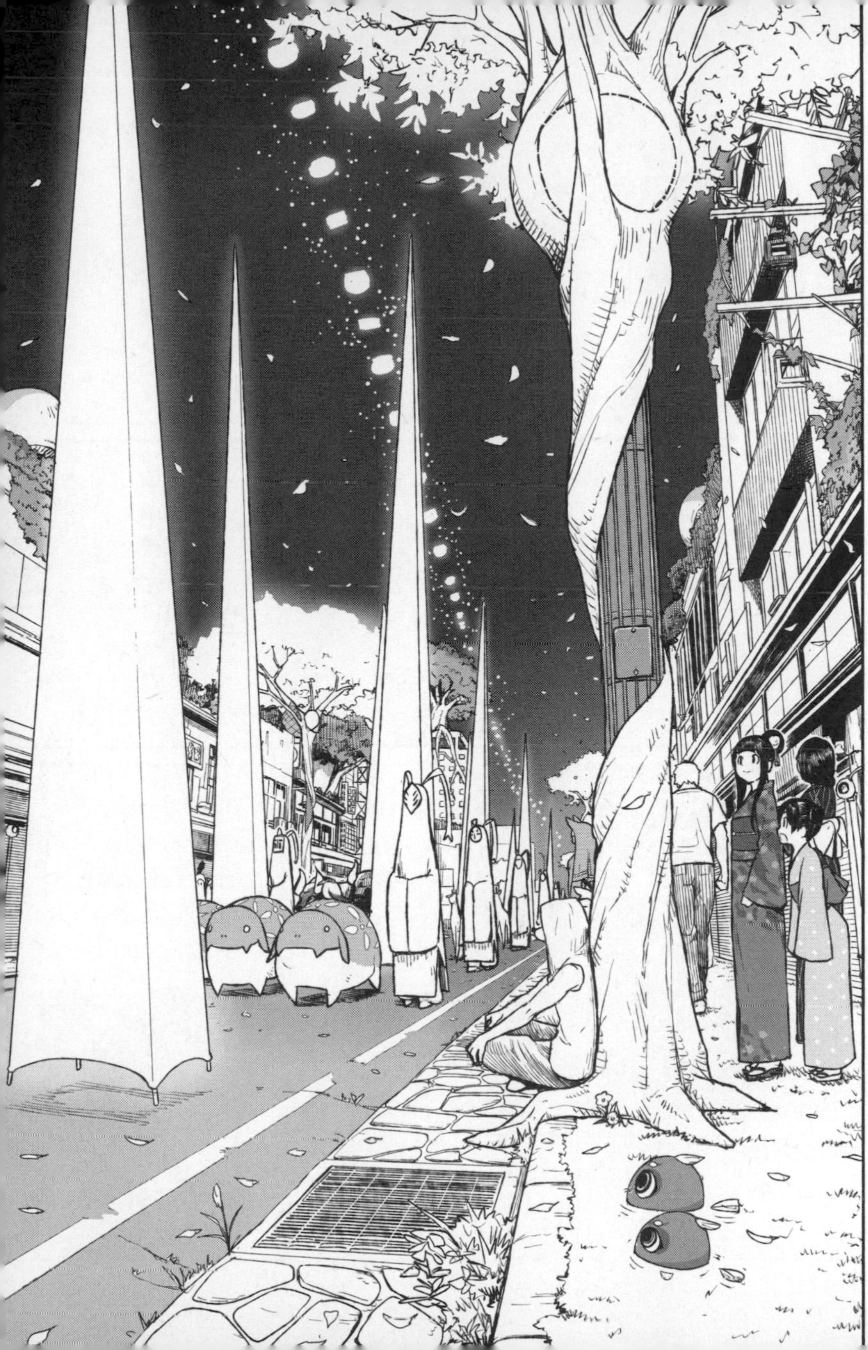

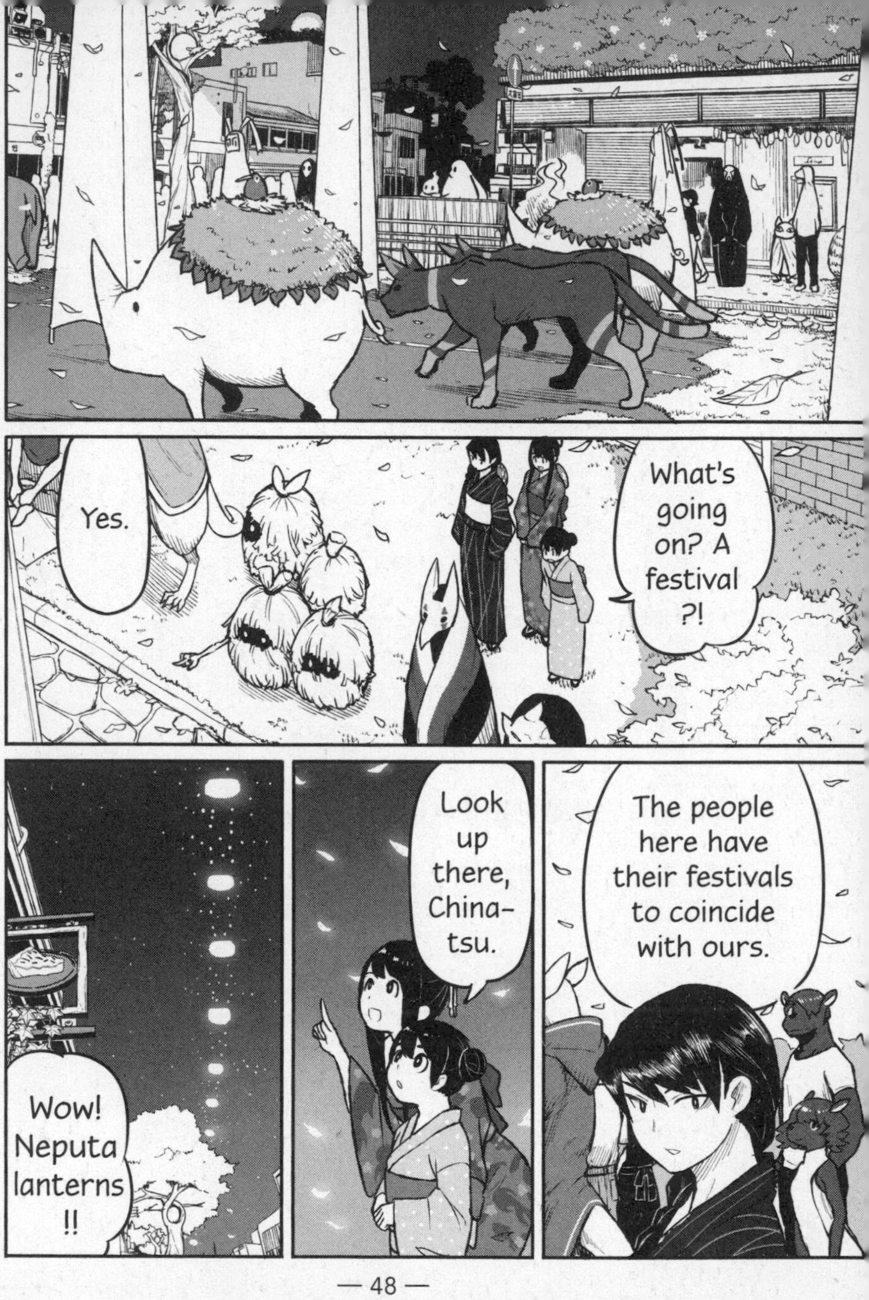
What's going on? A festival?!
Yes.
The people here have their festivals to coincide with ours.
Look up there, China-tsu.
Wow! Neputa lanterns!!

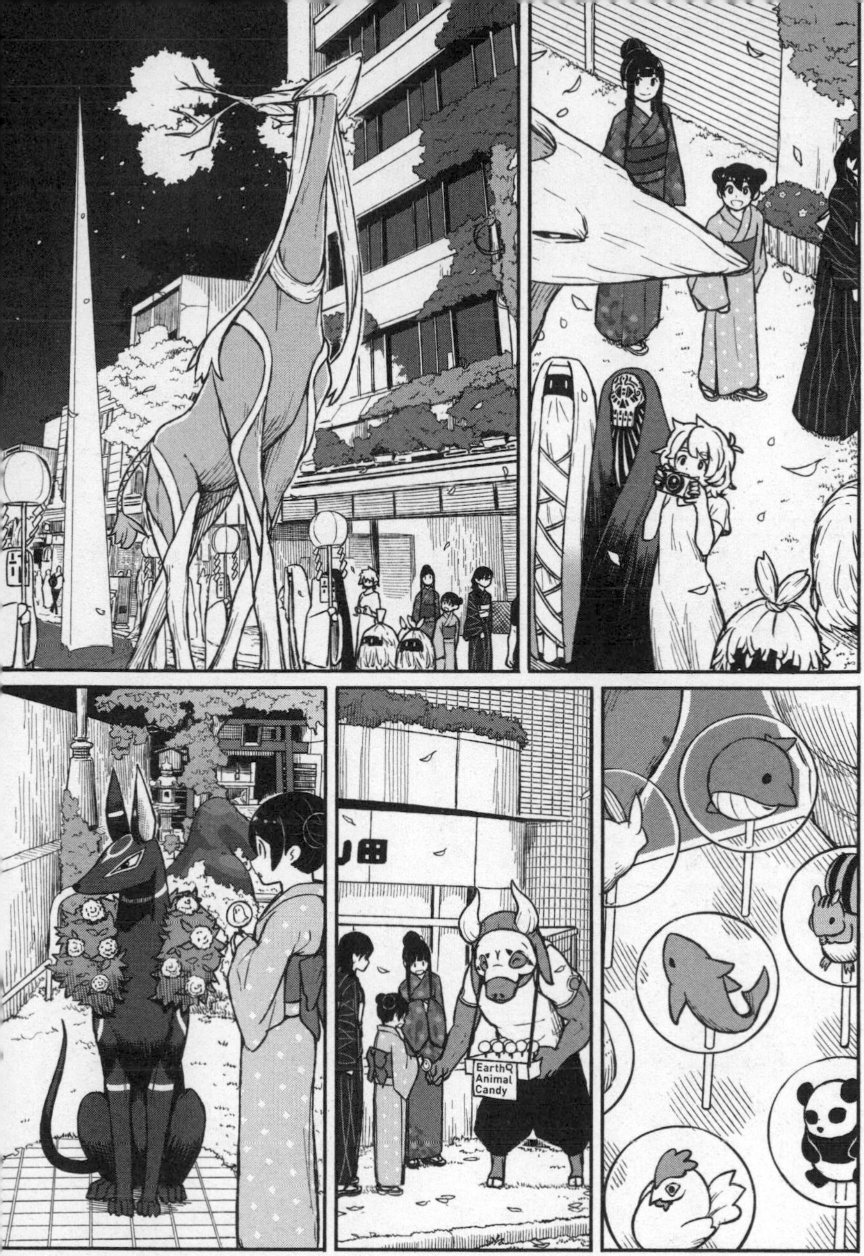
Earth Animal Candy

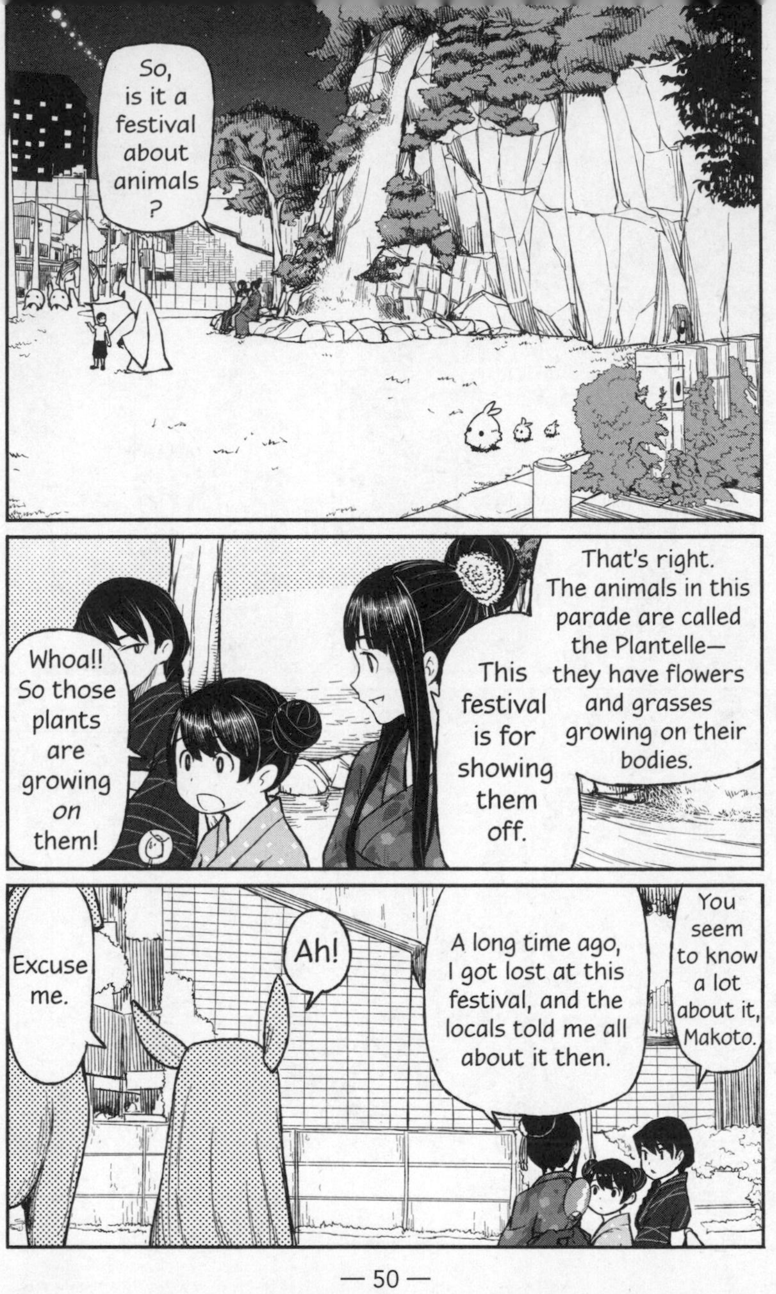
So, is it a festival about animals?
That's right. The animals in this parade are called the Plantelle—they have flowers and grasses growing on their bodies.
This festival is for showing them off.
Whoa!! So those plants are growing *on* them!
You seem to know a lot about it, Makoto.
A long time ago, I got lost at this festival, and the locals told me all about it then.
Ah!
Excuse me.

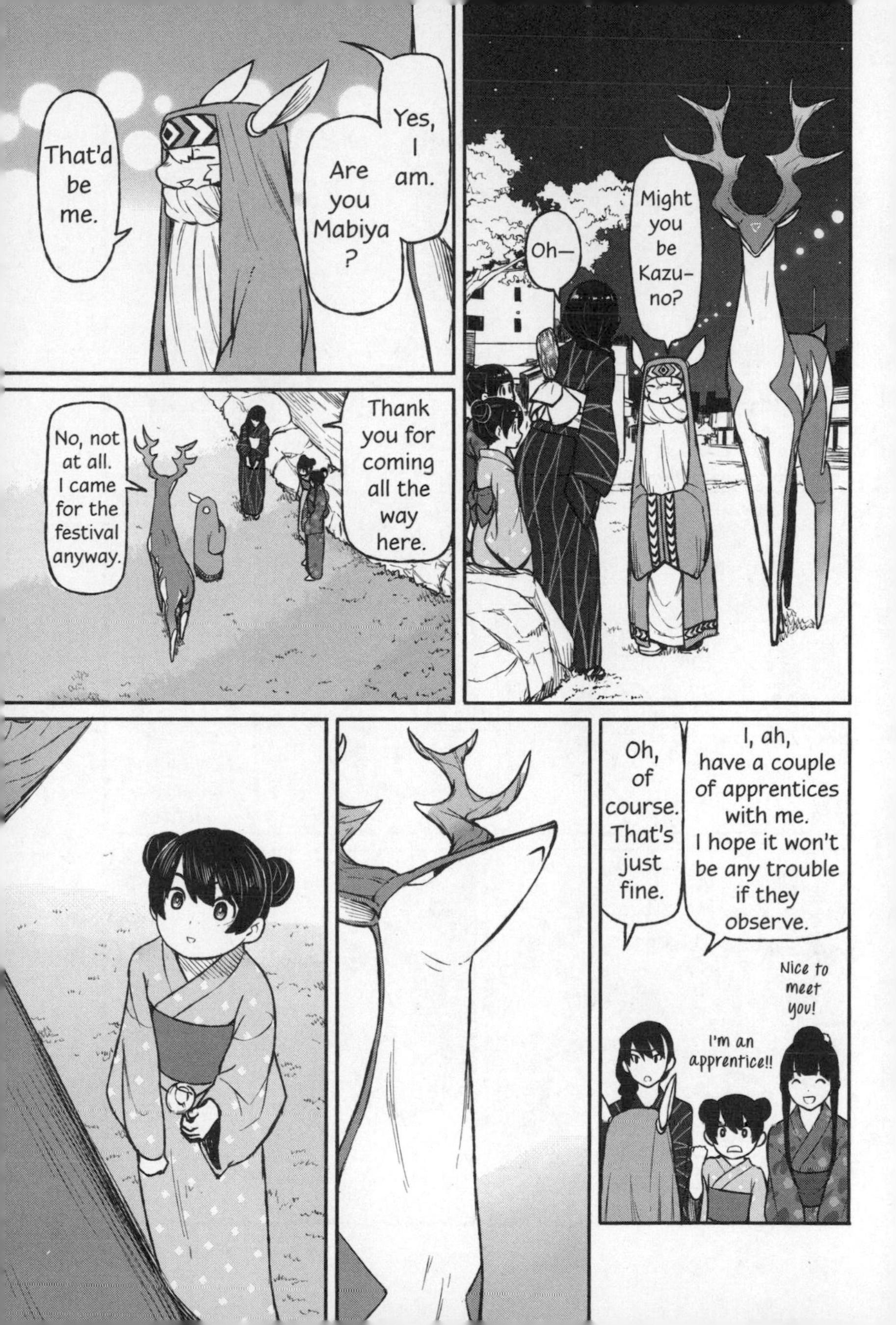
Might you be Kazuno?
Oh—
Yes, I am.
Are you Mabiya?
That'd be me.
Thank you for coming all the way here.
No, not at all. I came for the festival anyway.
I, ah, have a couple of apprentices with me. I hope it won't be any trouble if they observe.
Oh, of course. That's just fine.
Nice to meet you!
I'm an apprentice!!

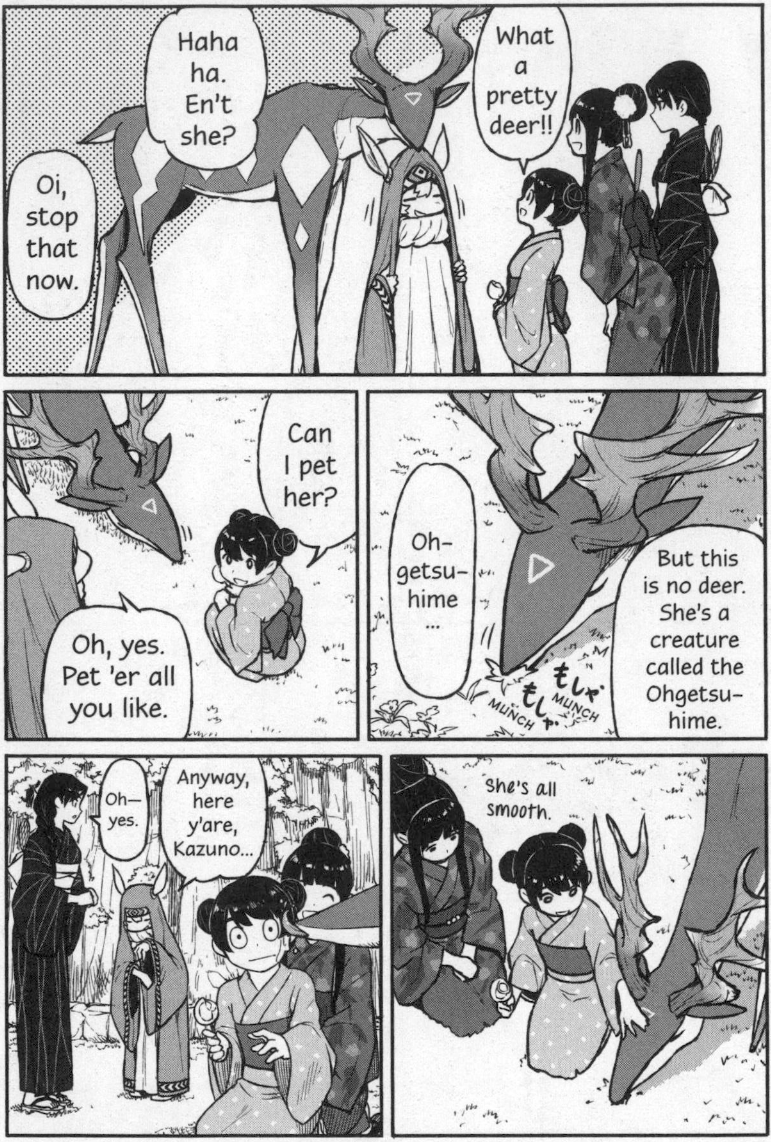
What a pretty deer!!
Haha ha. En't she?
Oi, stop that now.
But this is no deer. She's a creature called the Ohgetsu-hime.
Oh-getsu-hime...
もしゃ MUNCH
もしゃ MUNCH
Can I pet her?
Oh, yes. Pet 'er all you like.
She's all smooth.
Anyway, here y'are, Kazuno...
Oh— yes.

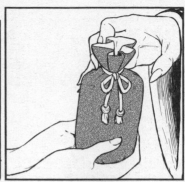

Just let me make sure. I hope you understand.

Of course.

What is it?

Sure.

Thank you so much.

Yes— This is it...!!

Yes. A highly prized variety— Ohgetsu-hime rice.

Getting this from Mabiya was my task today.

Oh, I see.

Rice?

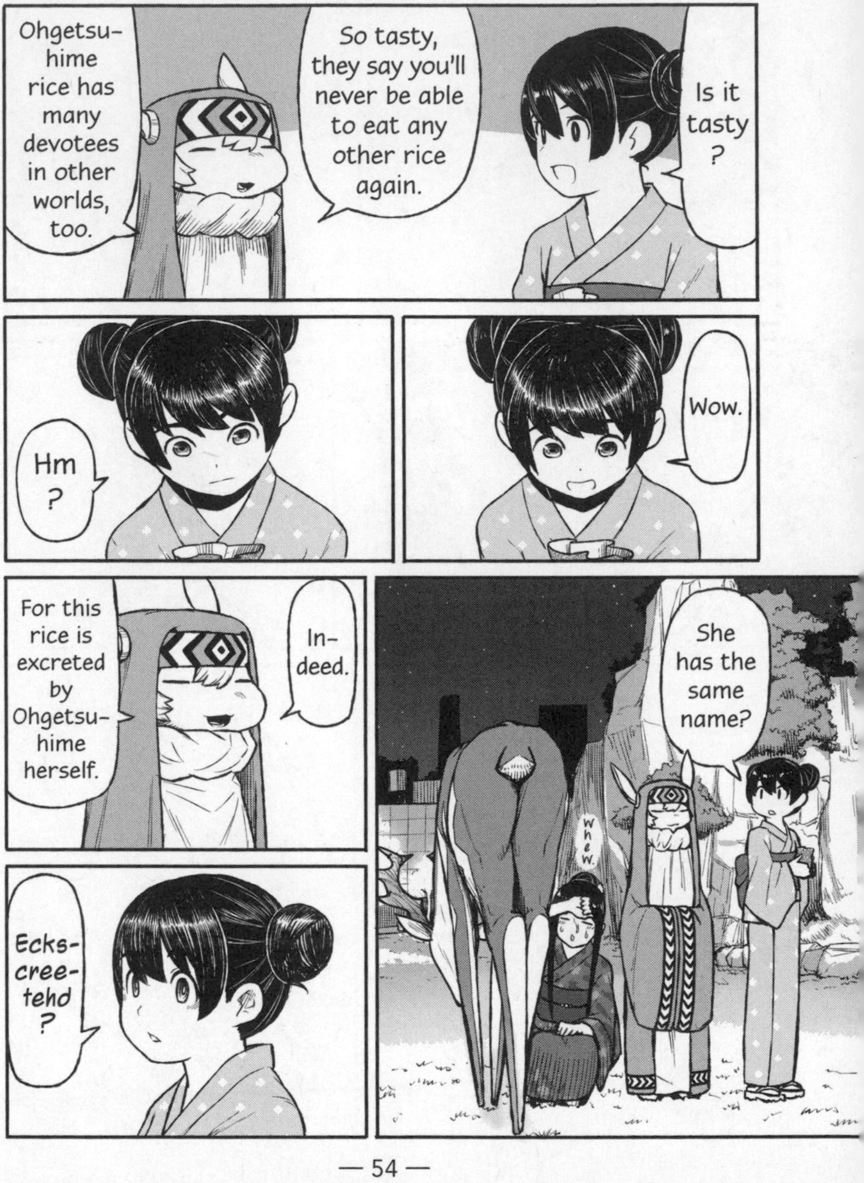
Is it tasty ?
So tasty, they say you'll never be able to eat any other rice again.
Ohgetsu-hime rice has many devotees in other worlds, too.
Wow.
Hm ?
She has the same name?
Whew.
In-deed.
For this rice is excreted by Ohgetsu-hime herself.
Ecks-cree-tehd ?

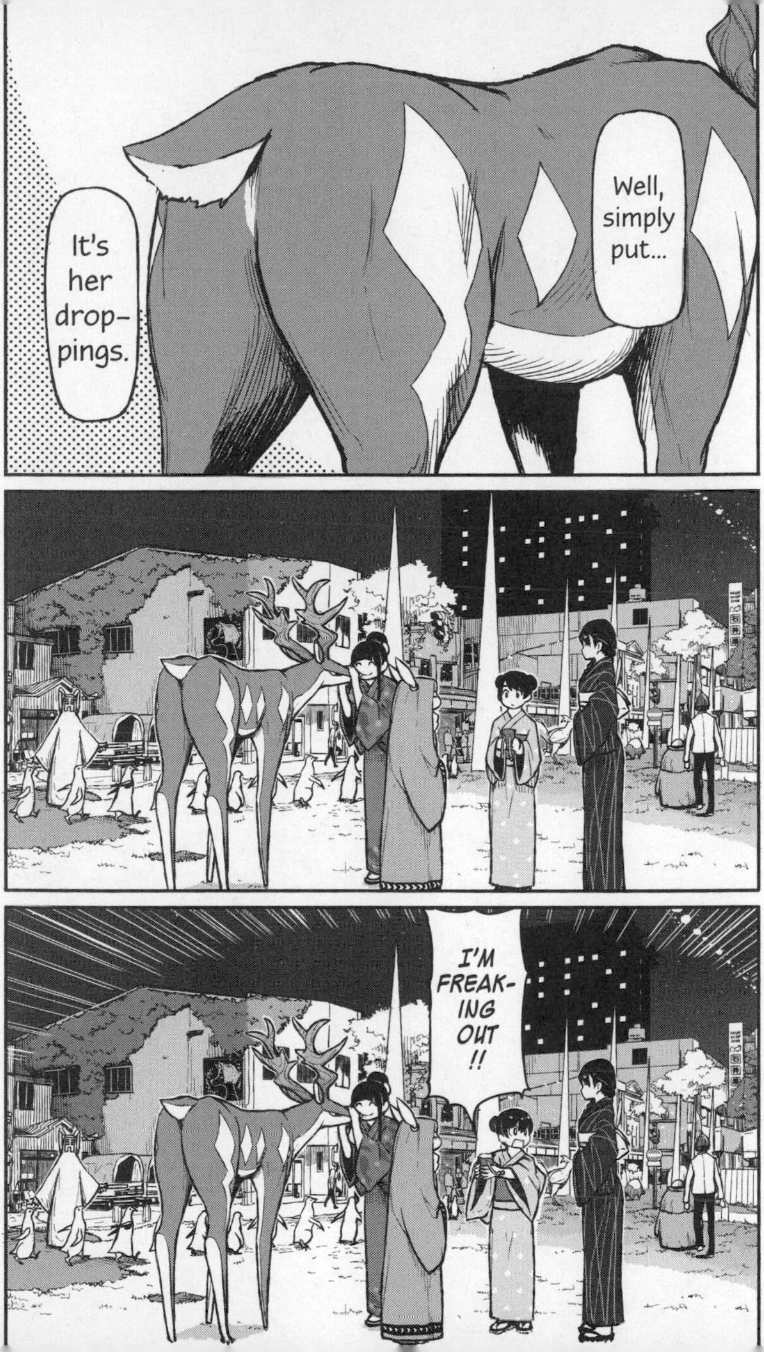
Well, simply put...
It's her drop-pings.
I'M FREAK-ING OUT !!

why, she's even in your old legends.

Chapter 51
Chomolungma Aspirations

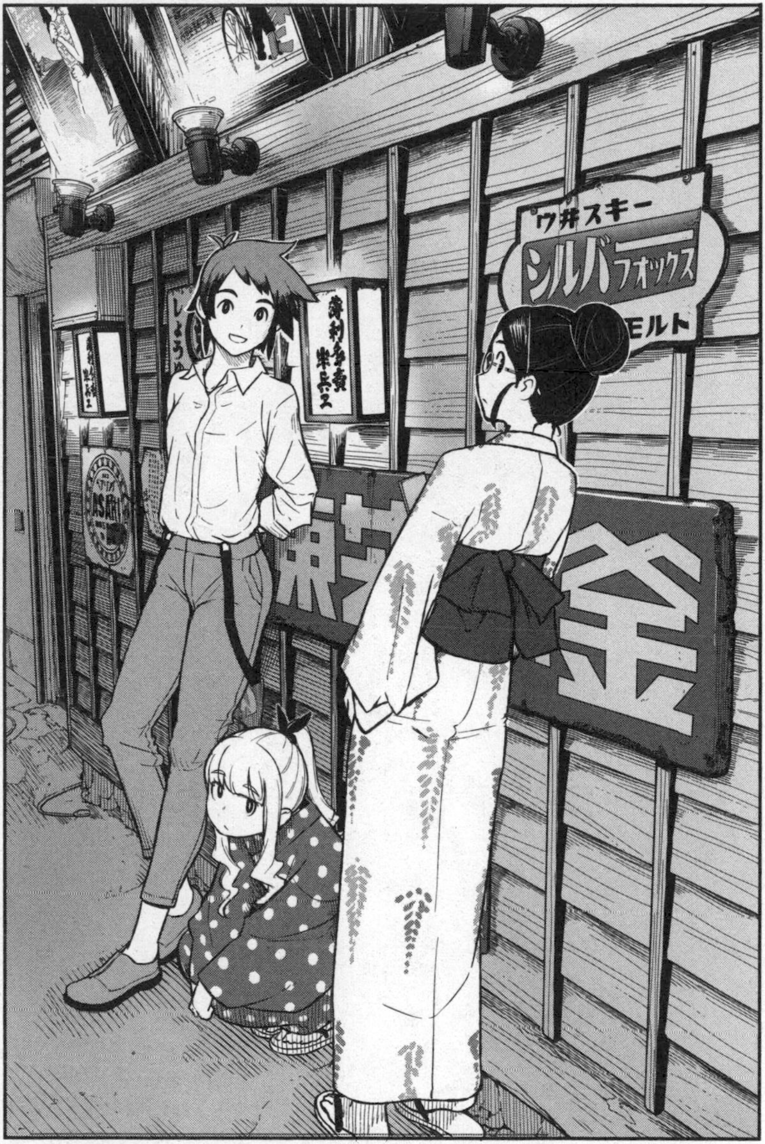

ウヰスキー
シルバフォックス
モルト

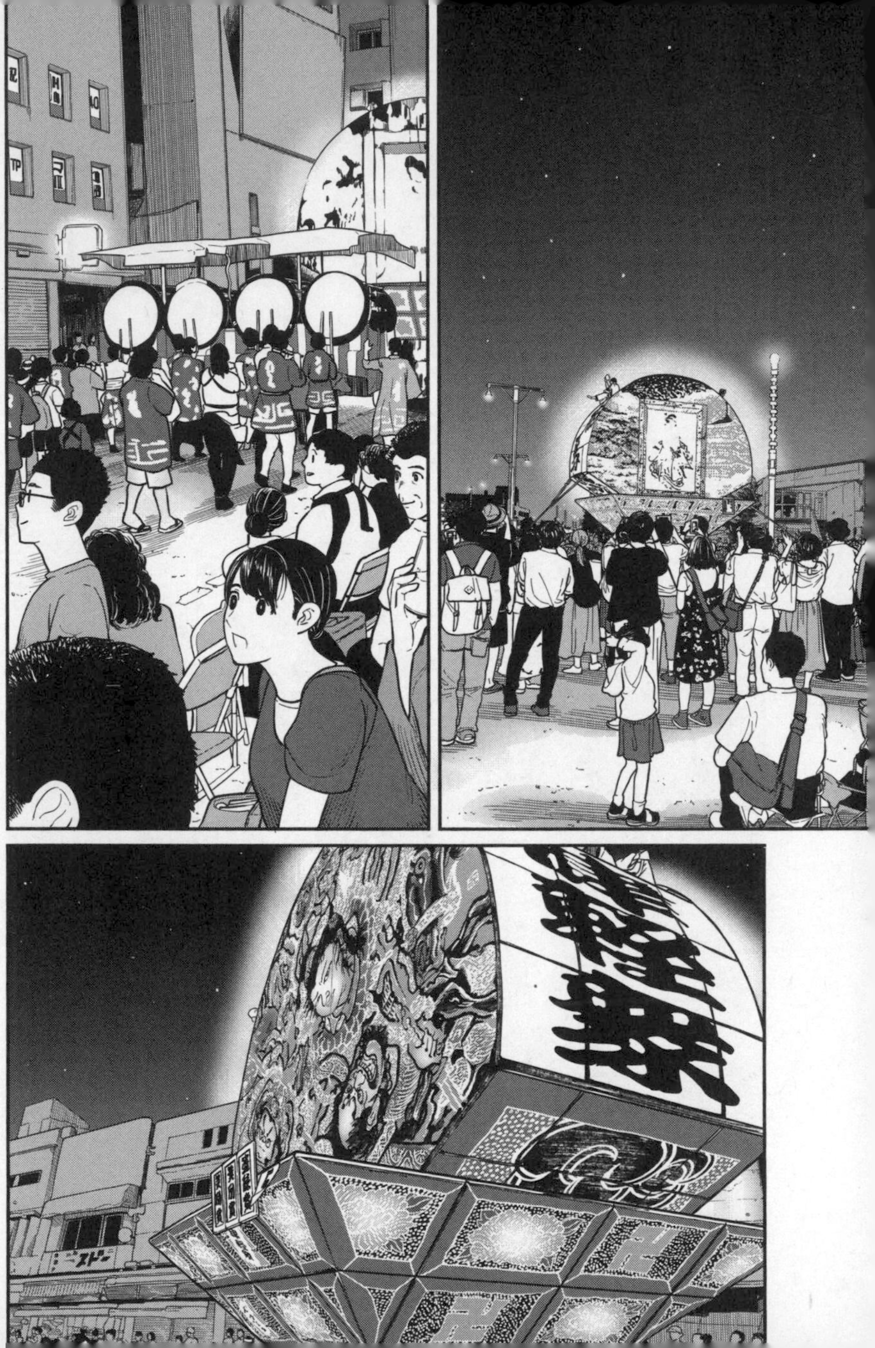

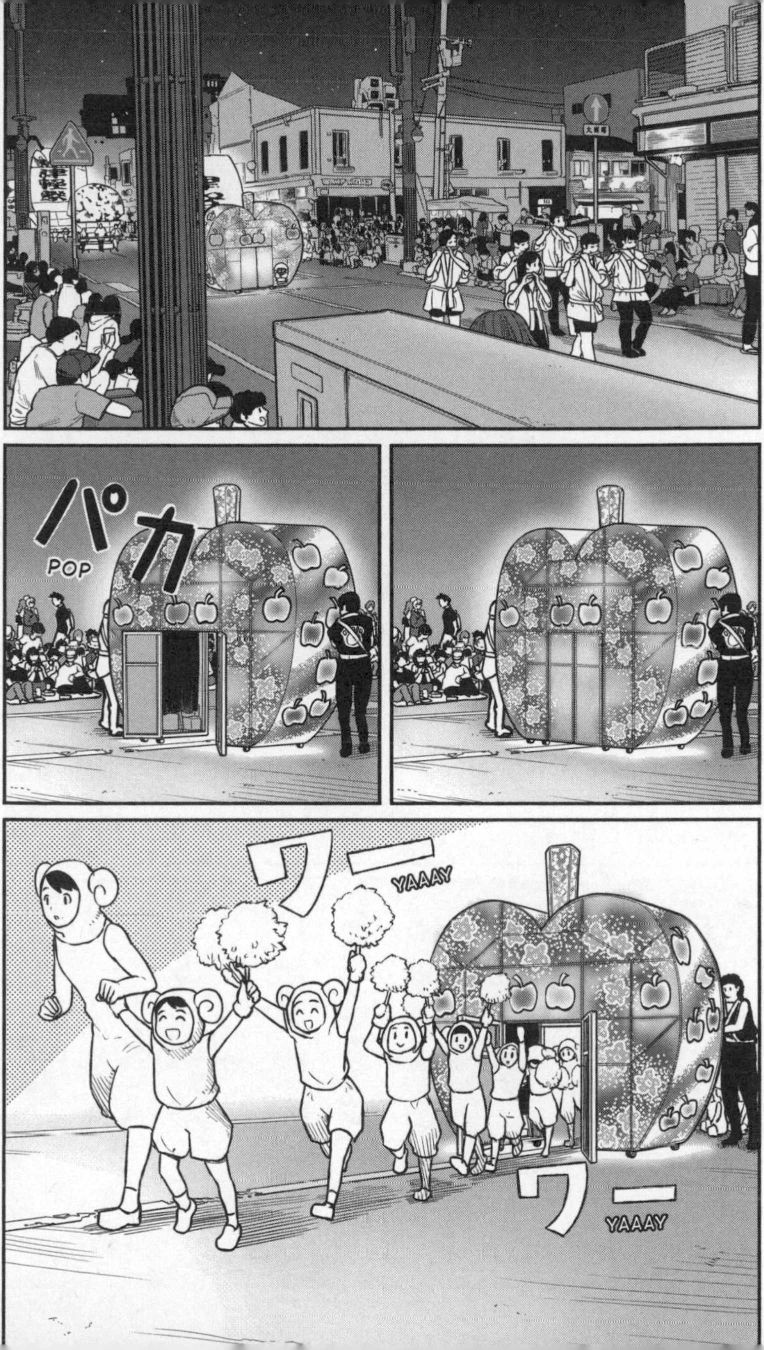
パカ
POP
ワー
YAAAY
ワー
YAAAY

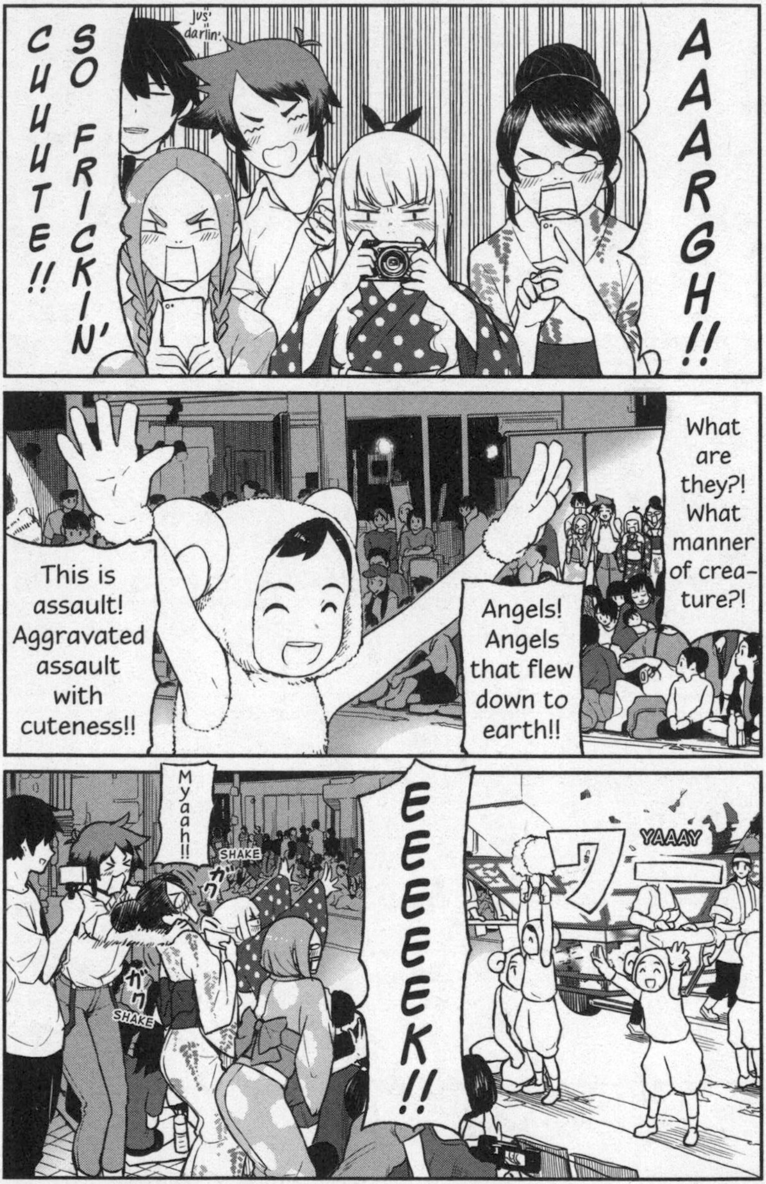
AAAARGH!!
jus' darlin'.
SO FRICKIN'
CUUUTE!!
What are they?! What manner of crea-ture?!
Angels! Angels that flew down to earth!!
This is assault! Aggravated assault with cuteness!!
YAAAY
ワー
EEEEEEK!!
Myaah!!
SHAKE
ガク
ガク
SHAKE

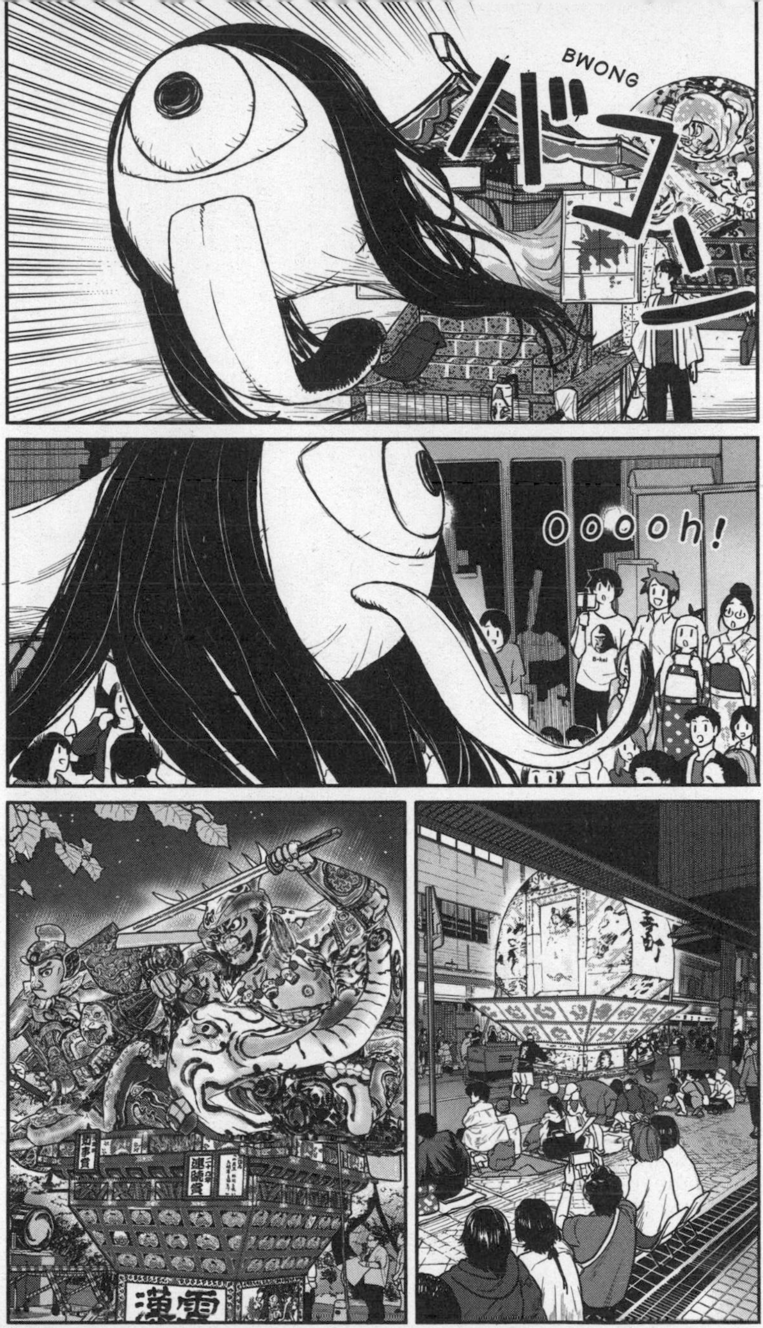
BWONG
Ooooh!

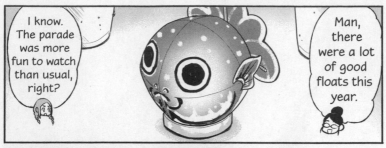

Man, there were a lot of good floats this year.
I know. The parade was more fun to watch than usual, right?
Hey, what's that, Tachibana? It looks tasty.
White sau-sage.
It's so good.
Ooh. I think I'll go grab one too.
They're selling them at the end of the street.
Oh, be careful, you guys.
We've still got the main event ahead of us...!!

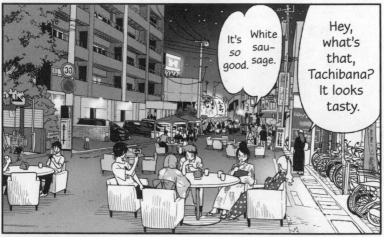

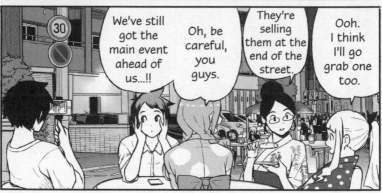

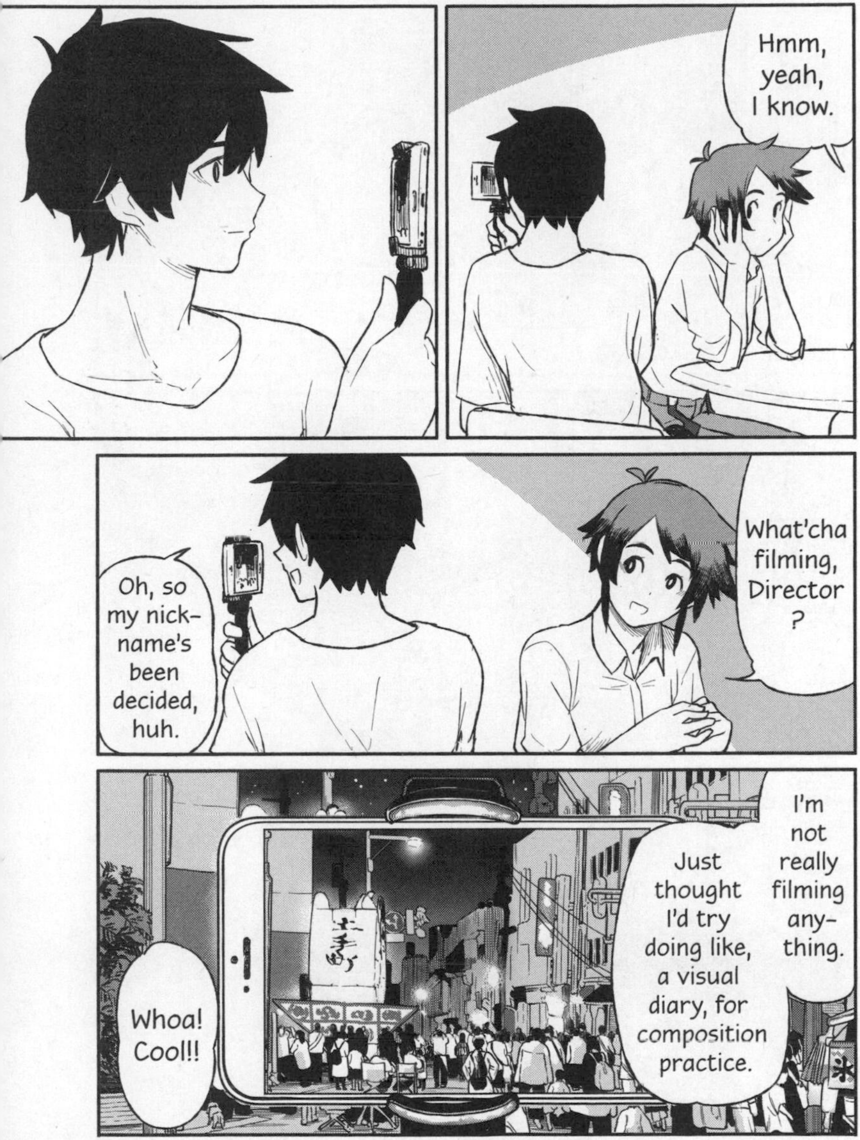
Hmm, yeah, I know.
What'cha filming, Director?
Oh, so my nick-name's been decided, huh.
I'm not really filming any-thing.
Just thought I'd try doing like, a visual diary, for composition practice.
Whoa! Cool!!

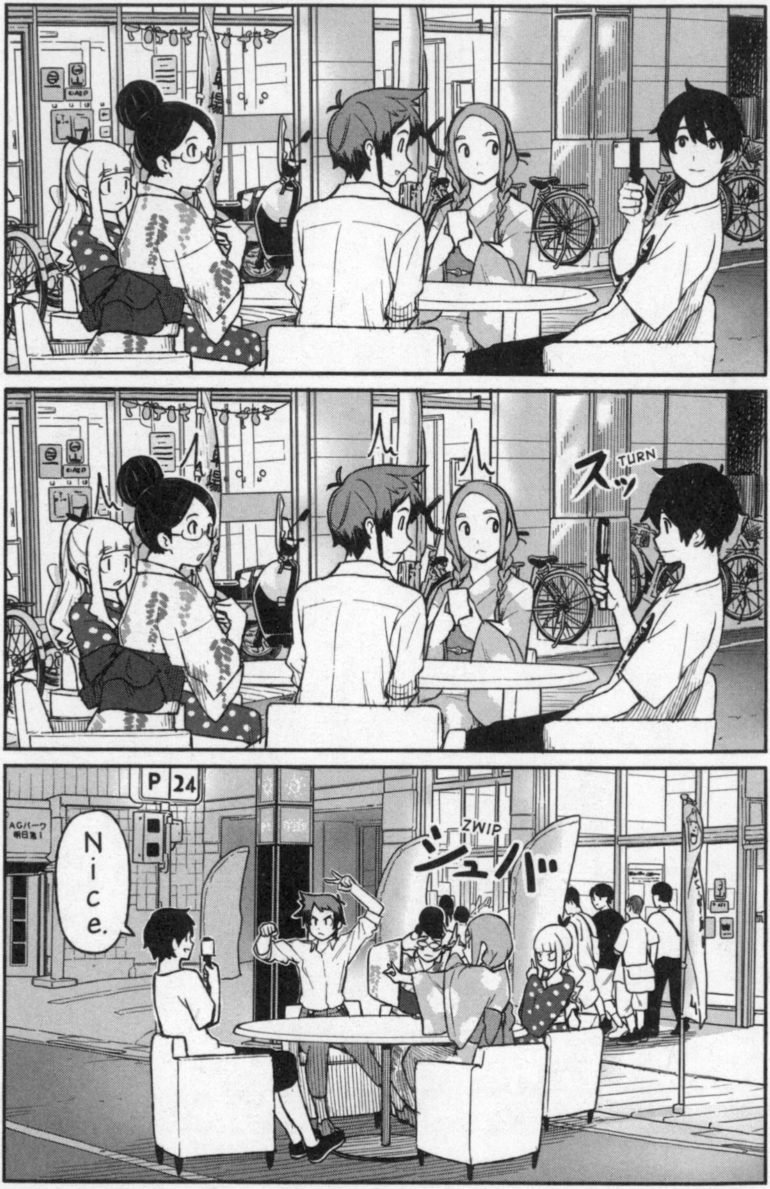
スッ
TURN
P 24
ジュバ
ZWIP
Nice.

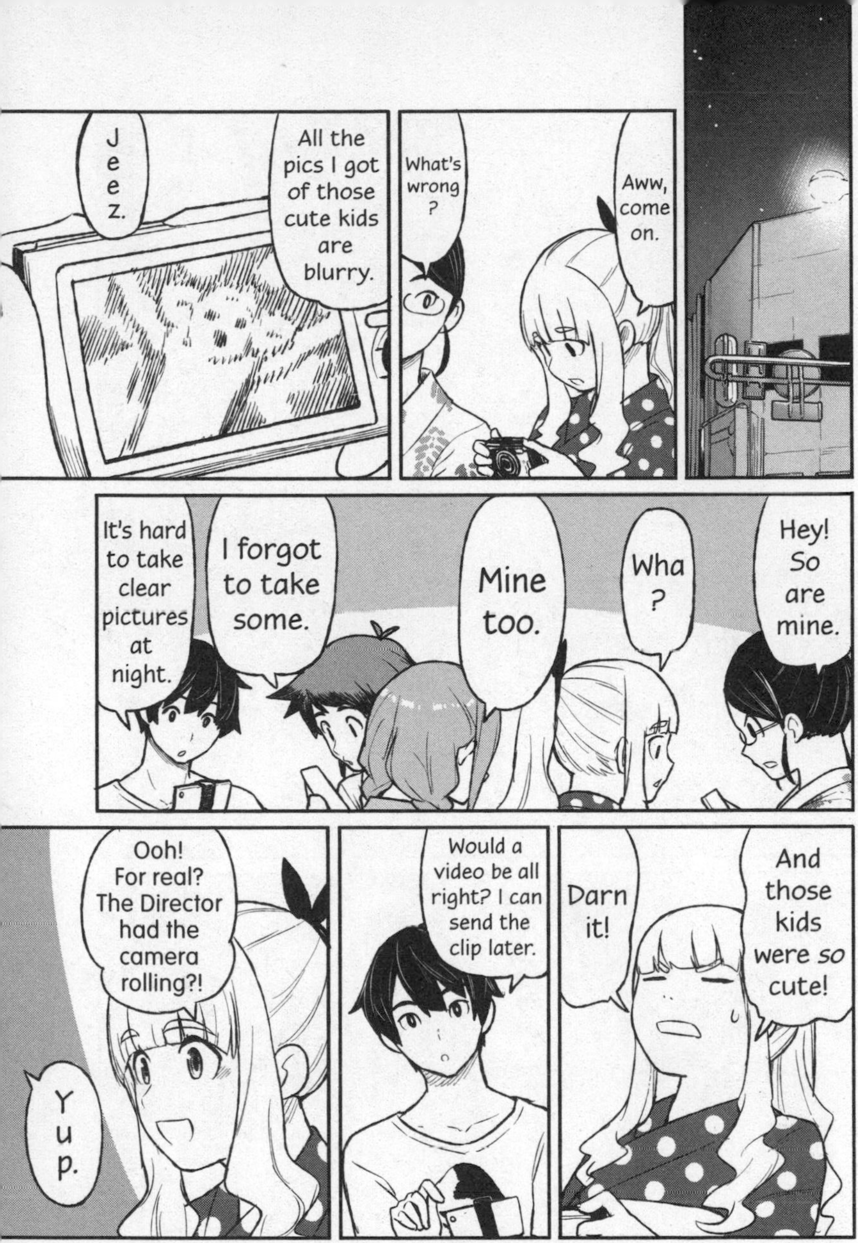
Aww, come on.
What's wrong?
All the pics I got of those cute kids are blurry.
Jeez.
Hey! So are mine.
Wha?
Mine too.
I forgot to take some.
It's hard to take clear pictures at night.
And those kids were *so* cute!
Darn it!
Would a video be all right? I can send the clip later.
Ooh! For real? The Director had the camera rolling?!
Yup.

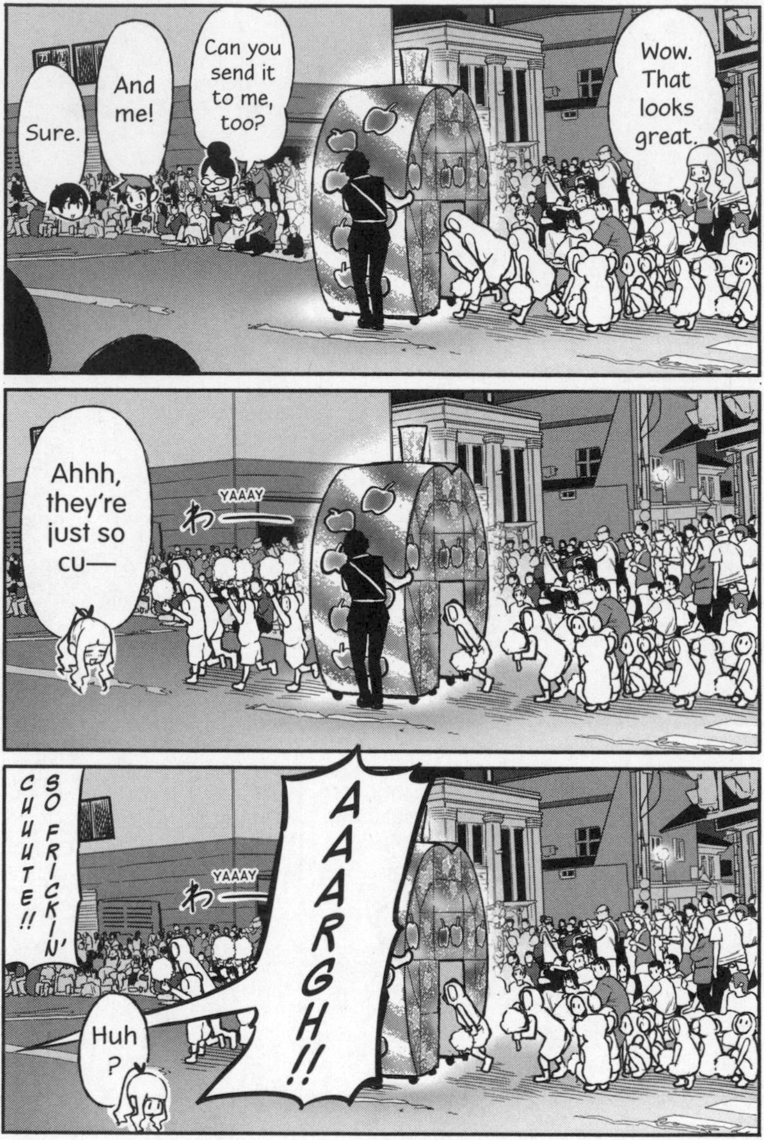
Wow. That looks great.
Can you send it to me, too?
And me!
Sure.
わー
YAAAY
Ahhh, they're just so cu—
AAARGH!!
SO FRICKIN' CUUUTE!!
わー
YAAAY
Huh?

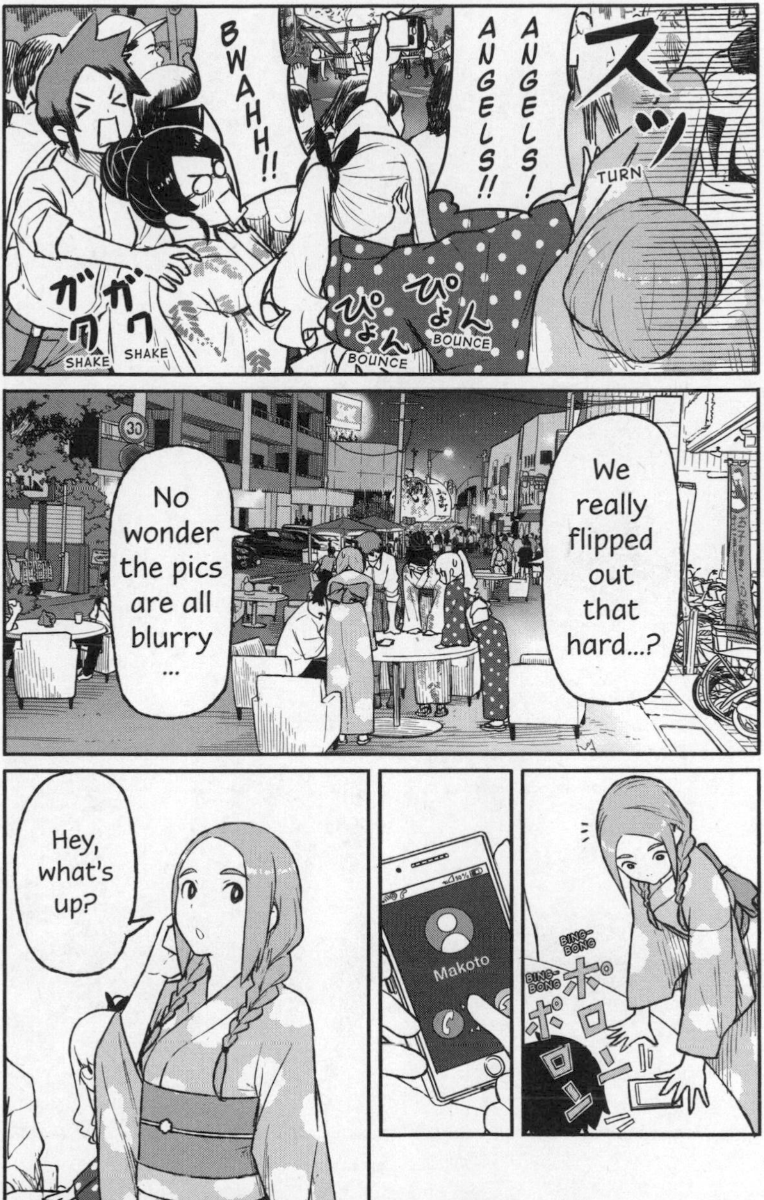
TURN
ANGELS! ANGELS!!
BWAHHH!!
ぴょん BOUNCE
ぴょん BOUNCE
ガク SHAKE
ガク SHAKE
We really flipped out that hard...?
No wonder the pics are all blurry ...
BING-BONG
BING-BONG
Makoto
Hey, what's up?

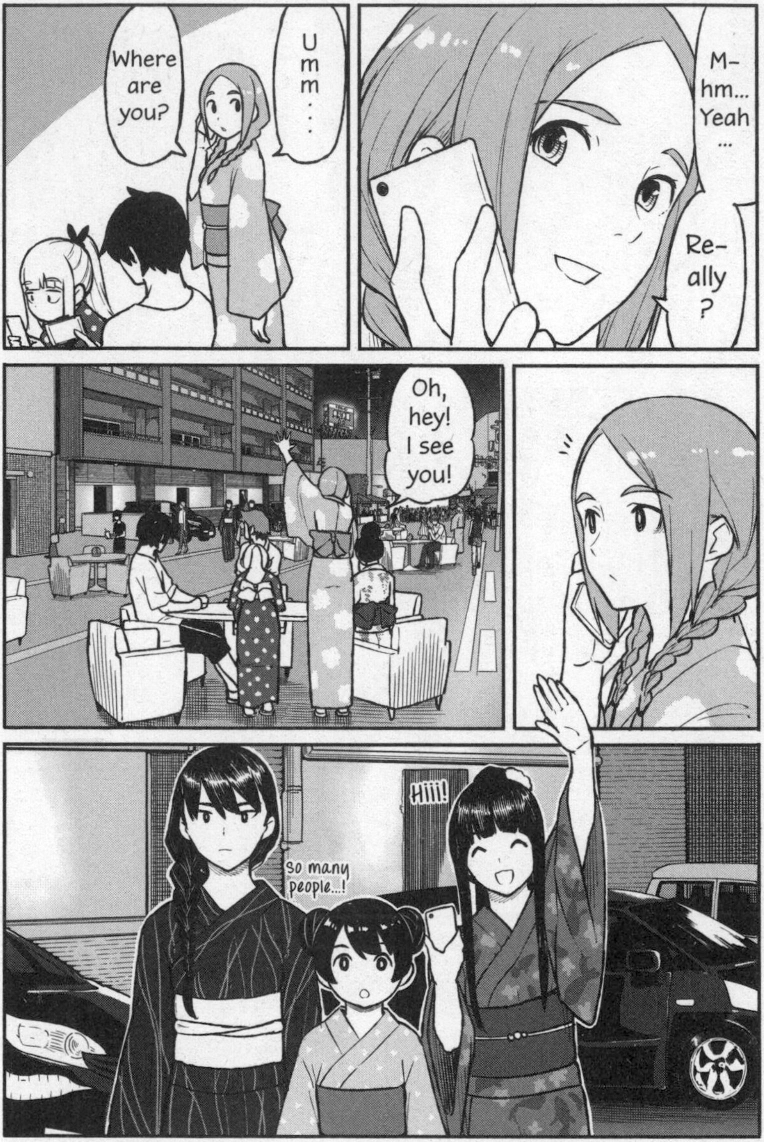
M-hm... Yeah ...
Re-ally?
Umm...
Where are you?
Oh, hey! I see you!
Hiii!
so many people...!

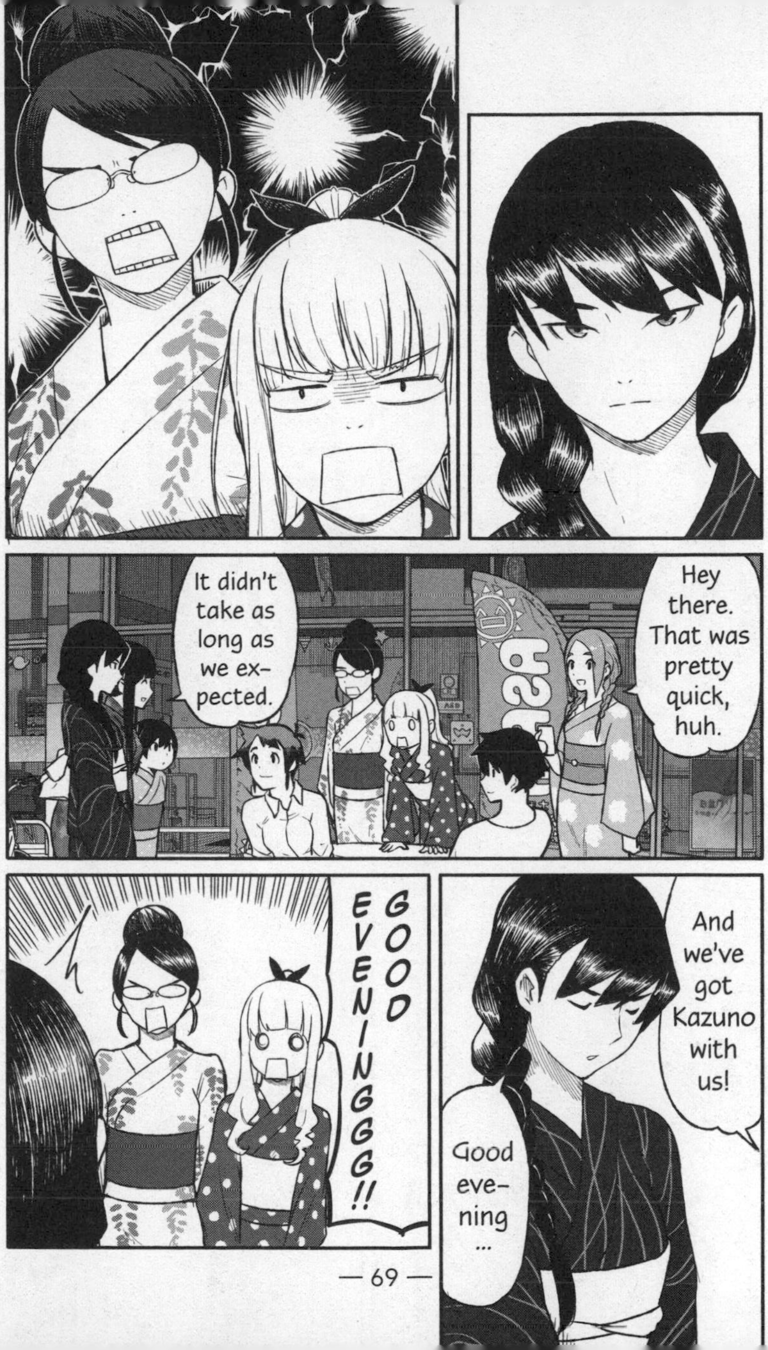
Hey there. That was pretty quick, huh.
It didn't take as long as we expected.
And we've got Kazuno with us!
Good evening...
GOOD EVENINGGGG!!

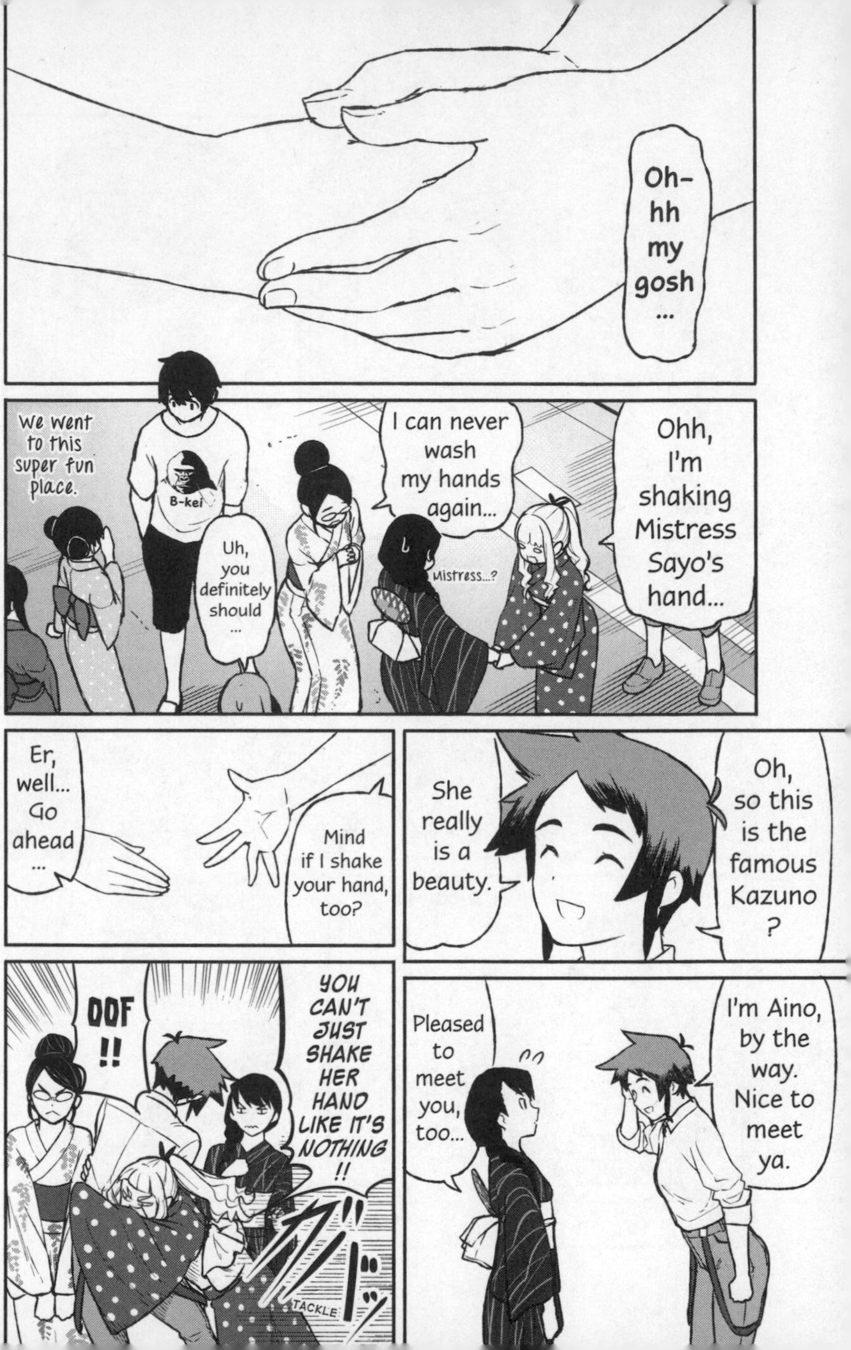
Oh-hh my gosh ...
Ohh, I'm shaking Mistress Sayo's hand...
Mistress...?
I can never wash my hands again...
B-kei
Uh, you definitely should ...
We went to this super fun place.
Oh, so this is the famous Kazuno ?
She really is a beauty.
Mind if I shake your hand, too?
Er, well... Go ahead ...
I'm Aino, by the way. Nice to meet ya.
Pleased to meet you, too...
YOU CAN'T JUST SHAKE HER HAND LIKE IT'S NOTHING !!
OOF !!
TACKLE

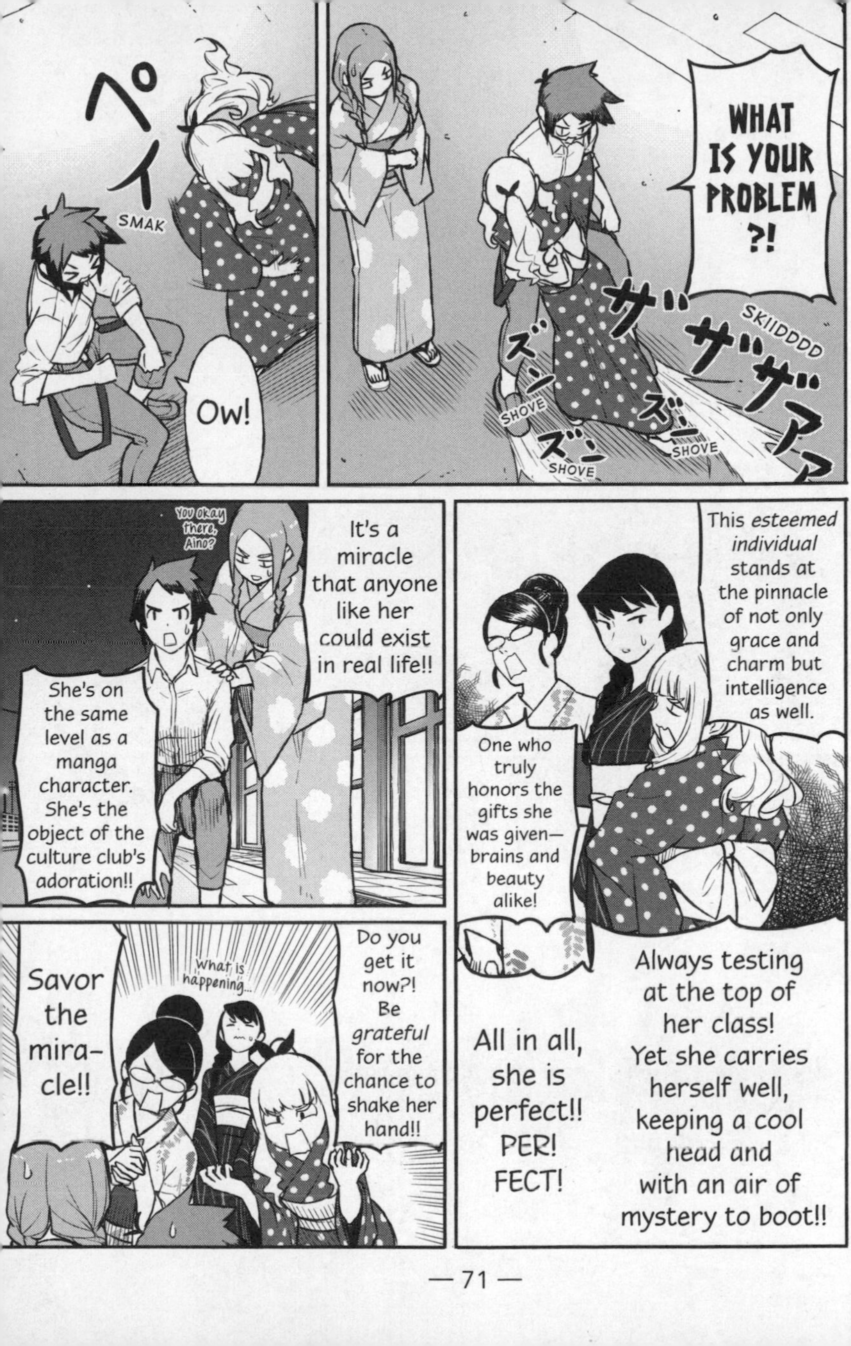
WHAT IS YOUR PROBLEM ?!
SKIIDDDD
SHOVE
SHOVE
SHOVE
ペイ
SMAK
Ow!
This esteemed individual stands at the pinnacle of not only grace and charm but intelligence as well.
One who truly honors the gifts she was given—brains and beauty alike!
Always testing at the top of her class! Yet she carries herself well, keeping a cool head and with an air of mystery to boot!!
All in all, she is perfect!! PER! FECT!
It's a miracle that anyone like her could exist in real life!!
You okay there, Aino?
She's on the same level as a manga character. She's the object of the culture club's adoration!!
Do you get it now?! Be grateful for the chance to shake her hand!!
What is happening...
Savor the mira-cle!!

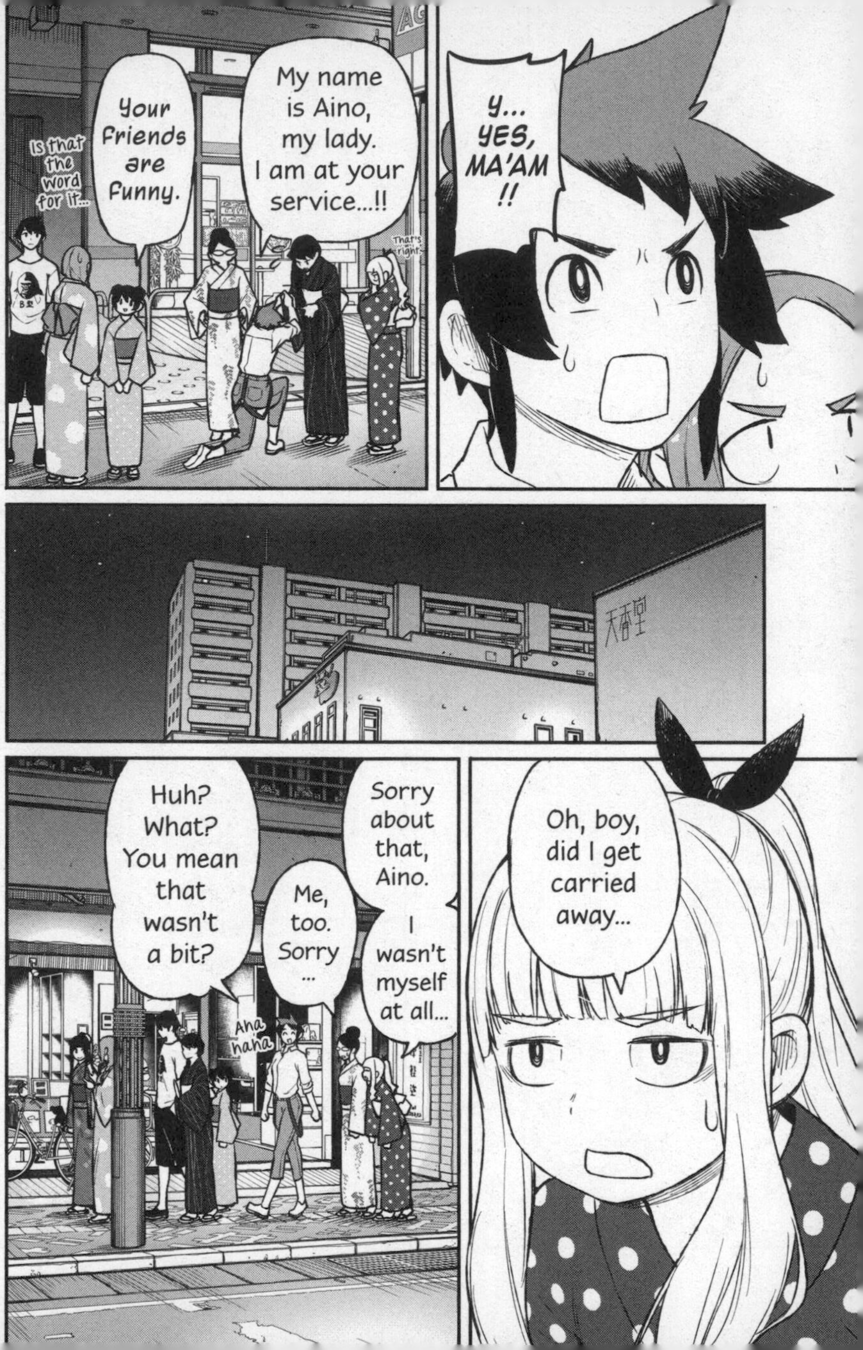
Y... YES, MA'AM !!
My name is Aino, my lady. I am at your service...!!
That's right.
Your friends are funny.
Is that the word for it...
天香堂
Oh, boy, did I get carried away...
Sorry about that, Aino.
I wasn't myself at all...
Me, too. Sorry ...
Huh? What? You mean that wasn't a bit?
Ahahaha

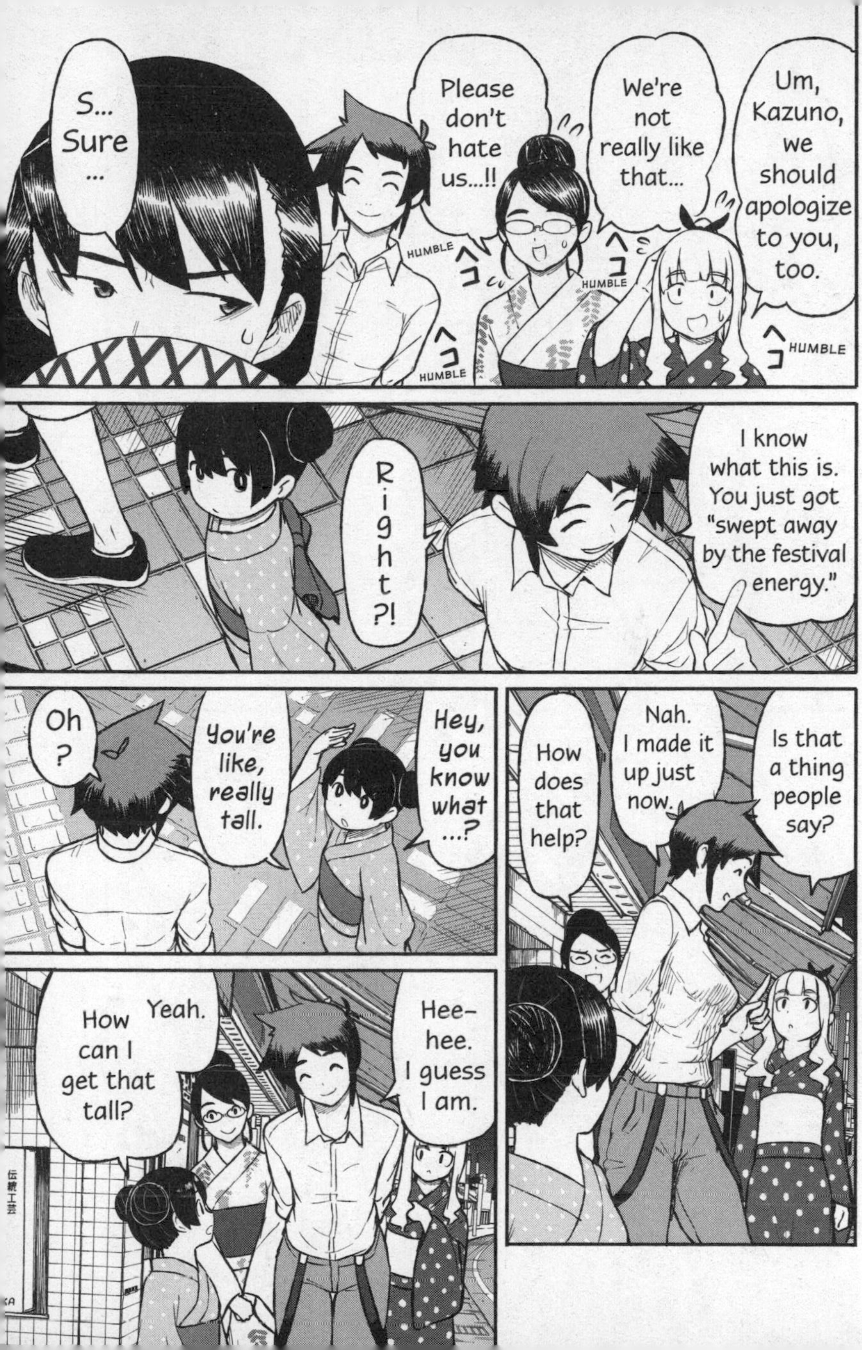
Um, Kazuno, we should apologize to you, too.
HUMBLE
We're not really like that...
HUMBLE
Please don't hate us...!!
HUMBLE
HUMBLE
S... Sure ...
I know what this is. You just got "swept away by the festival energy."
Right?!
Is that a thing people say?
Nah. I made it up just now.
How does that help?
Hey, you know what...?
You're like, really tall.
Oh?
Hee-hee. I guess I am.
Yeah. How can I get that tall?

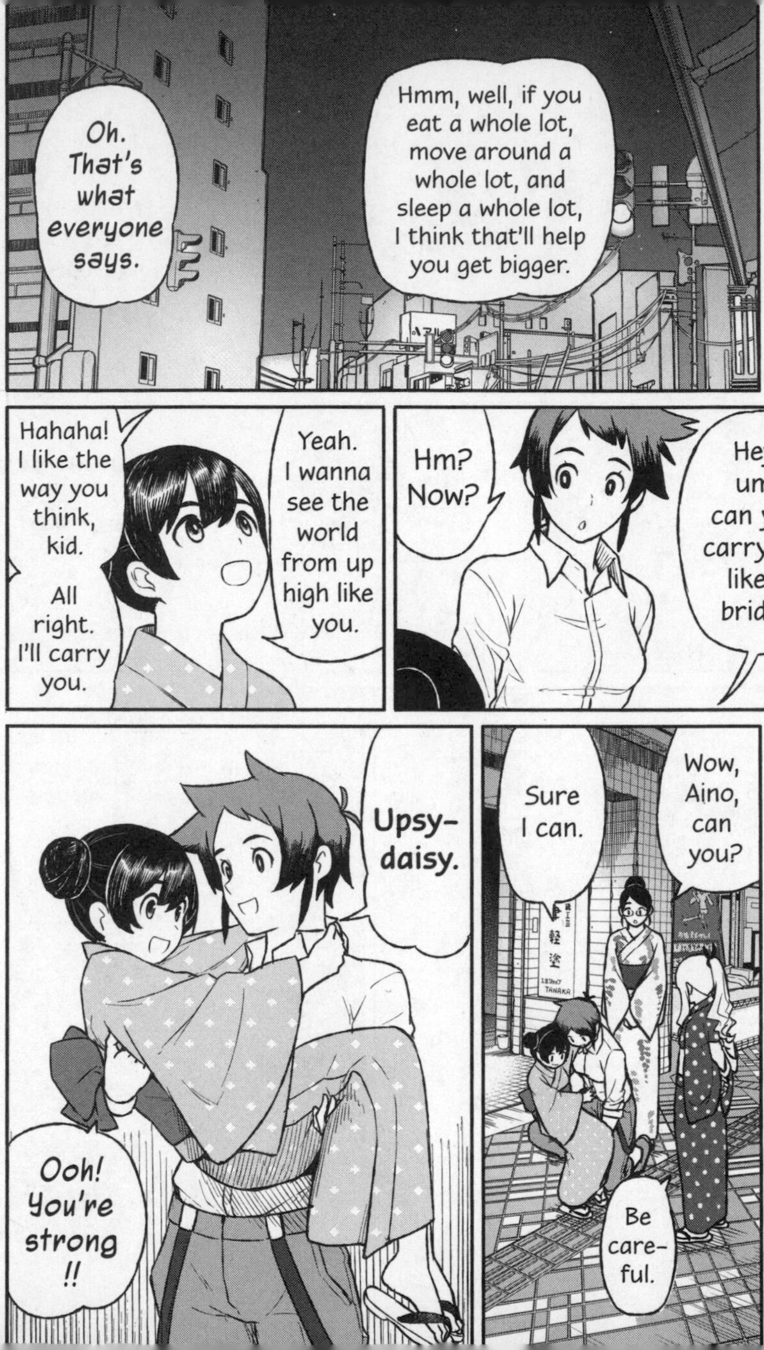
Hmm, well, if you eat a whole lot, move around a whole lot, and sleep a whole lot, I think that'll help you get bigger.
Oh. That's what everyone says.
Hey, um, can you carry me like a bride?
Hm? Now?
Yeah. I wanna see the world from up high like you.
Hahaha! I like the way you think, kid.
All right. I'll carry you.
Wow, Aino, can you?
Sure I can.
Be care-ful.
Upsy-daisy.
Ooh! You're strong!!

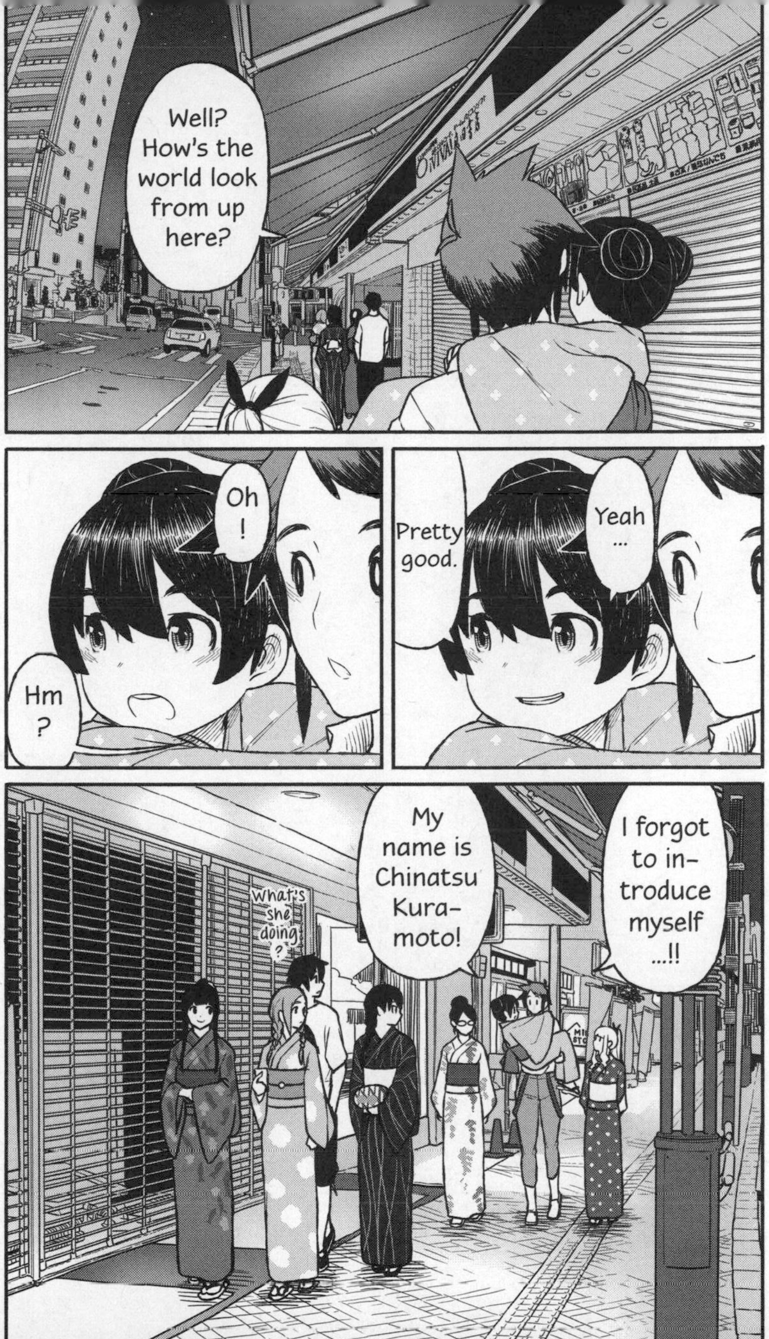
Well? How's the world look from up here?
Yeah ...
Pretty good.
Oh !
Hm ?
I forgot to in-troduce myself ...!!
My name is Chinatsu Kura-moto!
what's she doing ?

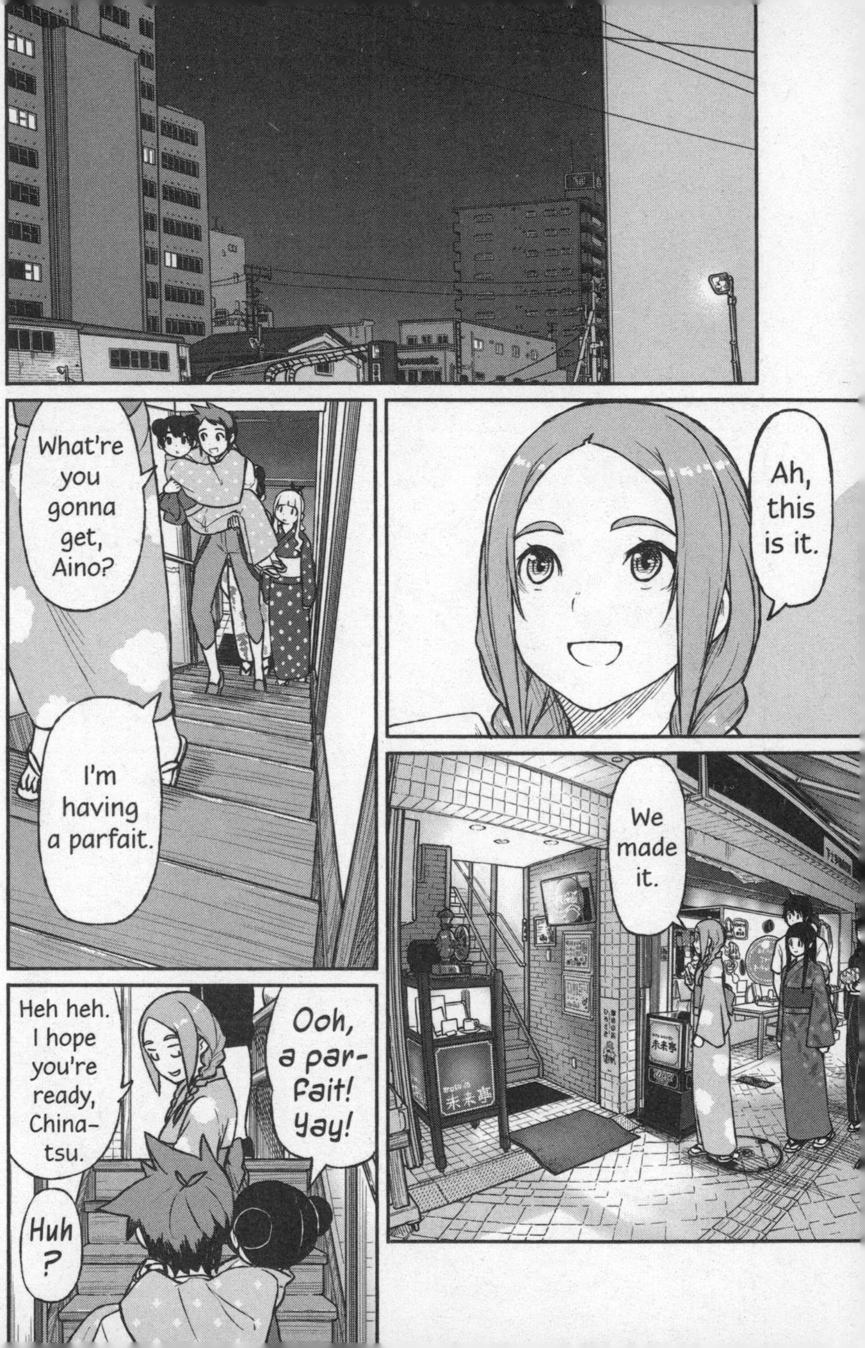
Ah, this is it.
We made it.
What're you gonna get, Aino?
I'm having a parfait.
Ooh, a par-fait! Yay!
Heh heh. I hope you're ready, China-tsu.
Huh?

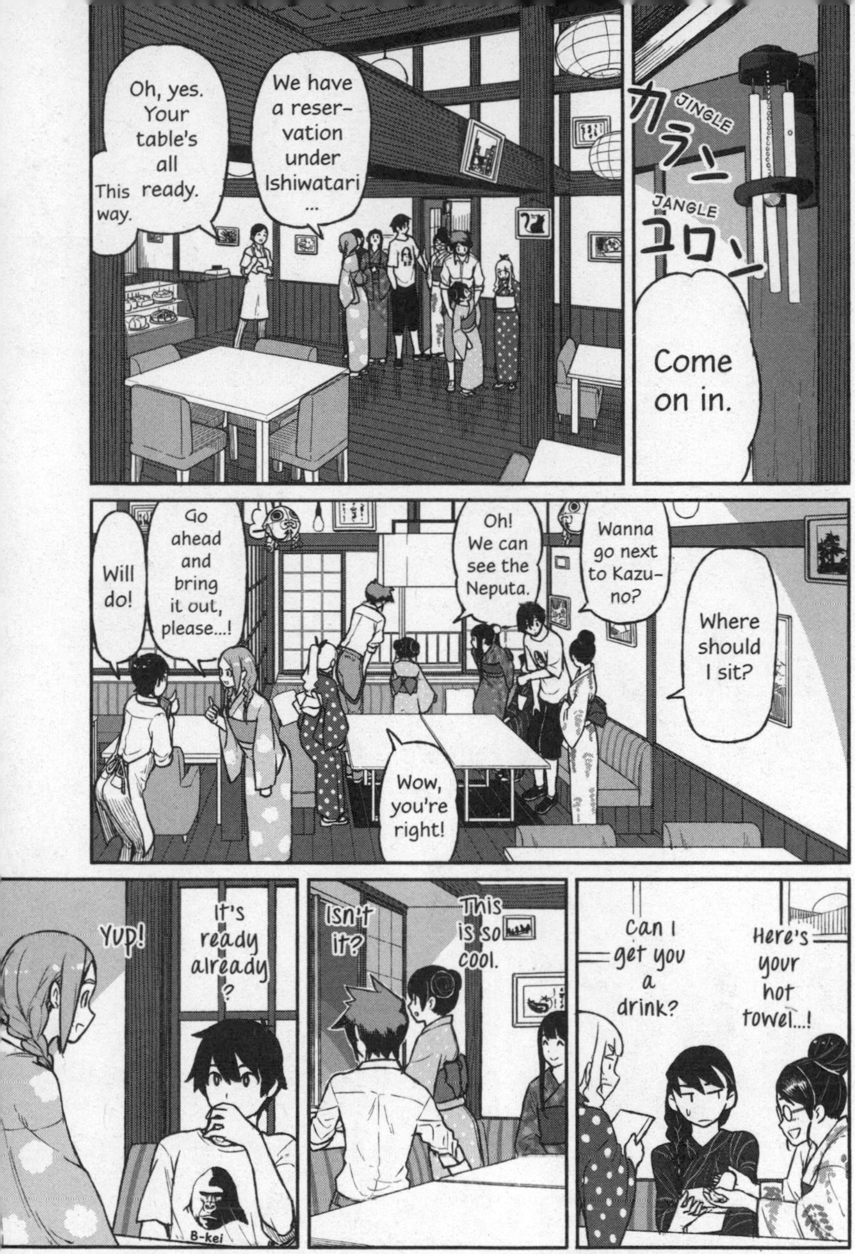
カラン JINGLE
コロン JANGLE
Come on in.
We have a reservation under Ishiwatari...
Oh, yes. Your table's all ready.
This way.
Where should I sit?
Wanna go next to Kazuno?
Oh! We can see the Neputa.
Wow, you're right!
Go ahead and bring it out, please...!
Will do!
Here's your hot towel...!
Can I get you a drink?
This is so cool.
Isn't it?
It's ready already?
Yup!
B-kei

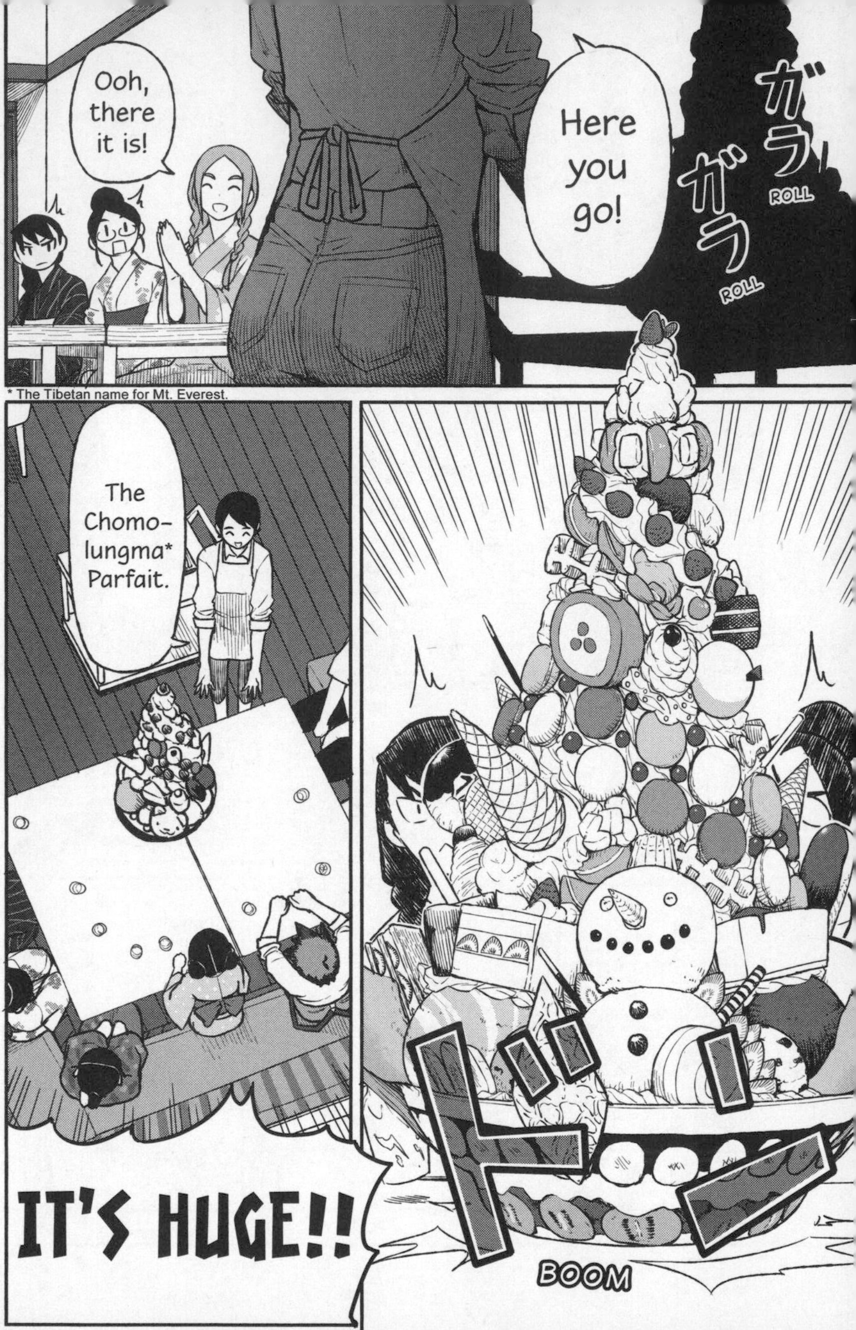
ガラ ガラ
ROLL ROLL
Here you go!
Ooh, there it is!
ドッ
BOOM
The Chomo-lungma* Parfait.
IT'S HUGE!!
* The Tibetan name for Mt. Everest.

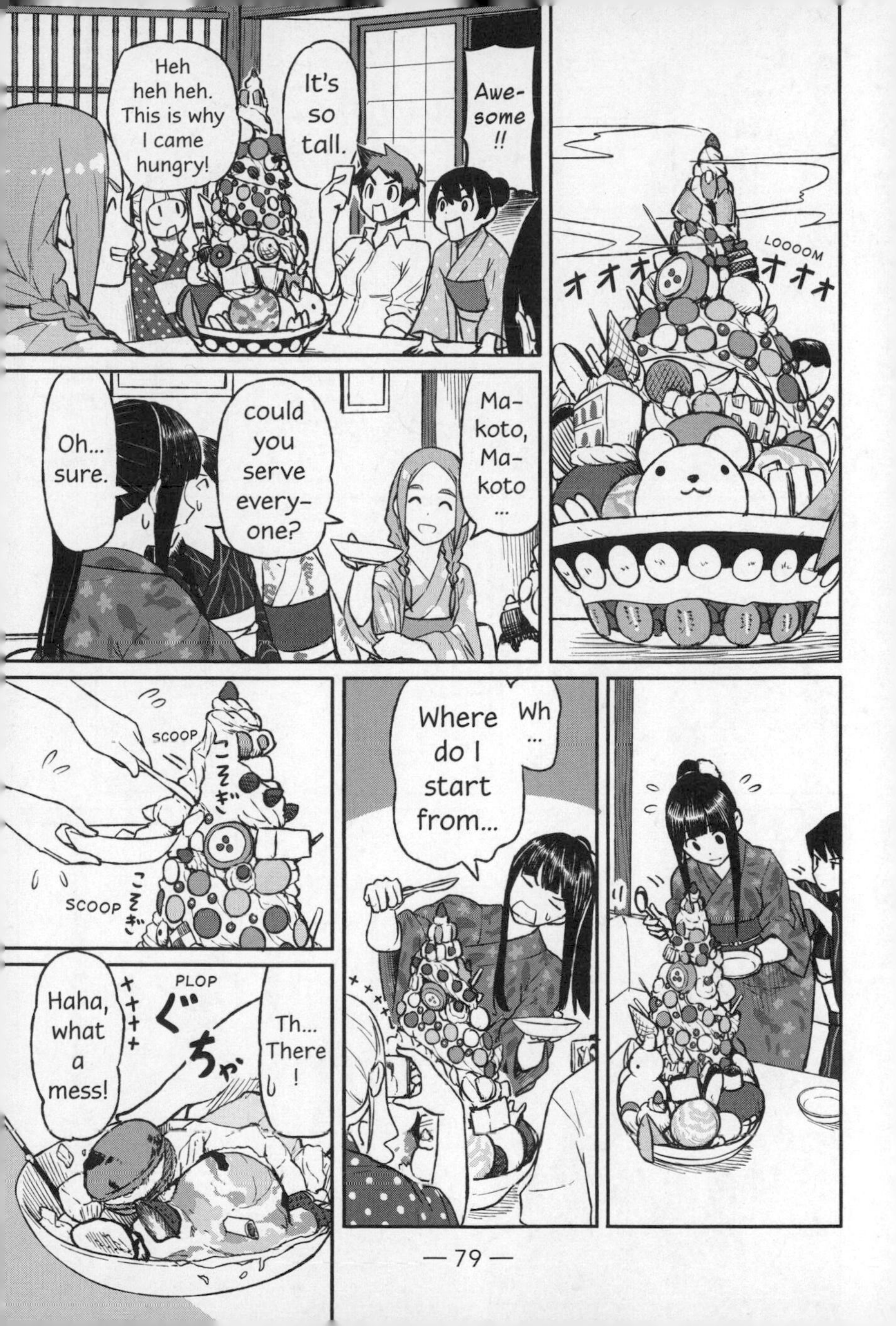
LOOOOM
オオオオオオ
Awe-some!!
It's so tall.
Heh heh heh. This is why I came hungry!
Ma-koto, Ma-koto...
could you serve every-one?
Oh... sure.
Wh...
Where do I start from...
SCOOP
こそぎ
SCOOP
こそぎ
Th... There!
PLOP
ぐちゃ
Haha, what a mess!

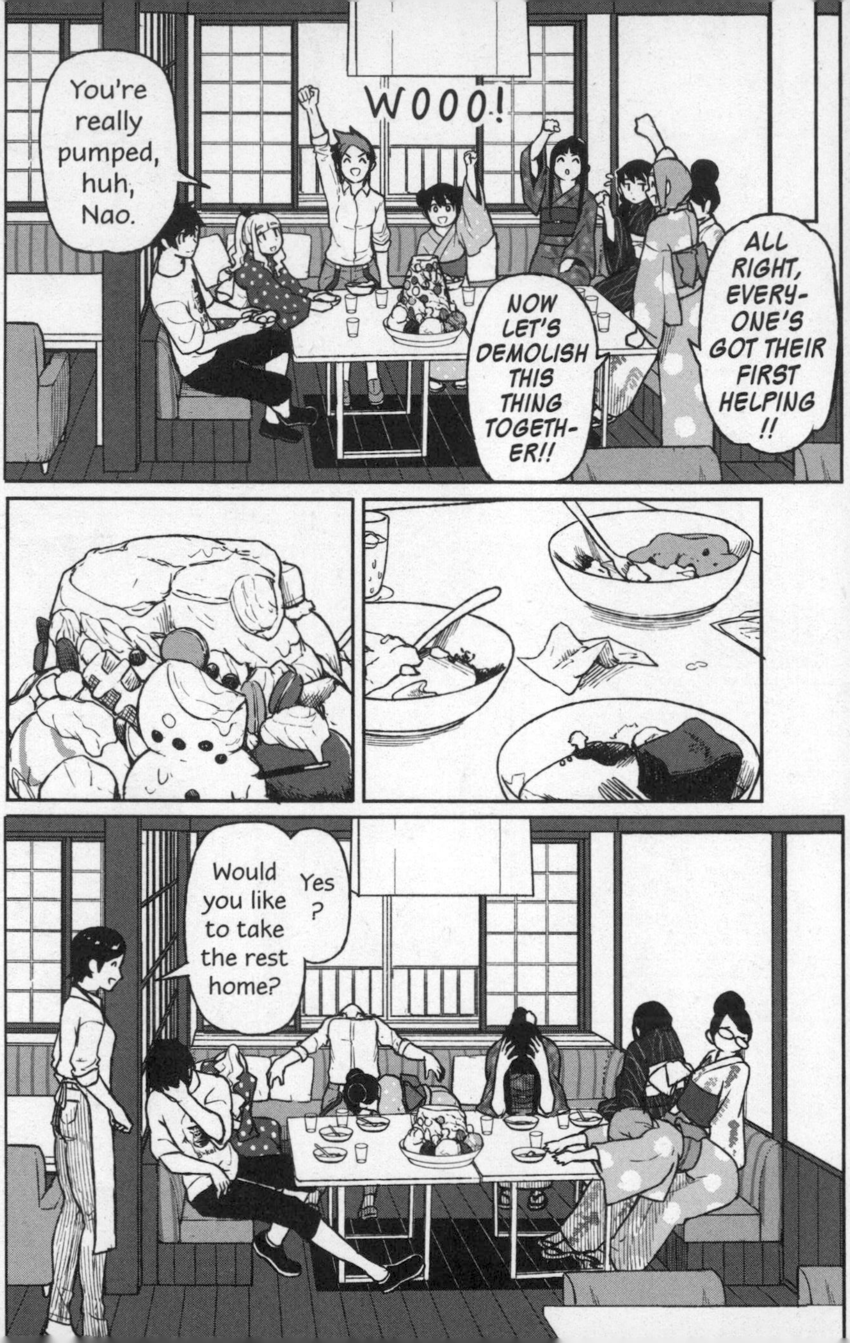
ALL RIGHT, EVERY-ONE'S GOT THEIR FIRST HELPING!!
NOW LET'S DEMOLISH THIS THING TOGETH-ER!!
WOOO!
You're really pumped, huh, Nao.
Yes?
Would you like to take the rest home?

Flying
Witch

urp

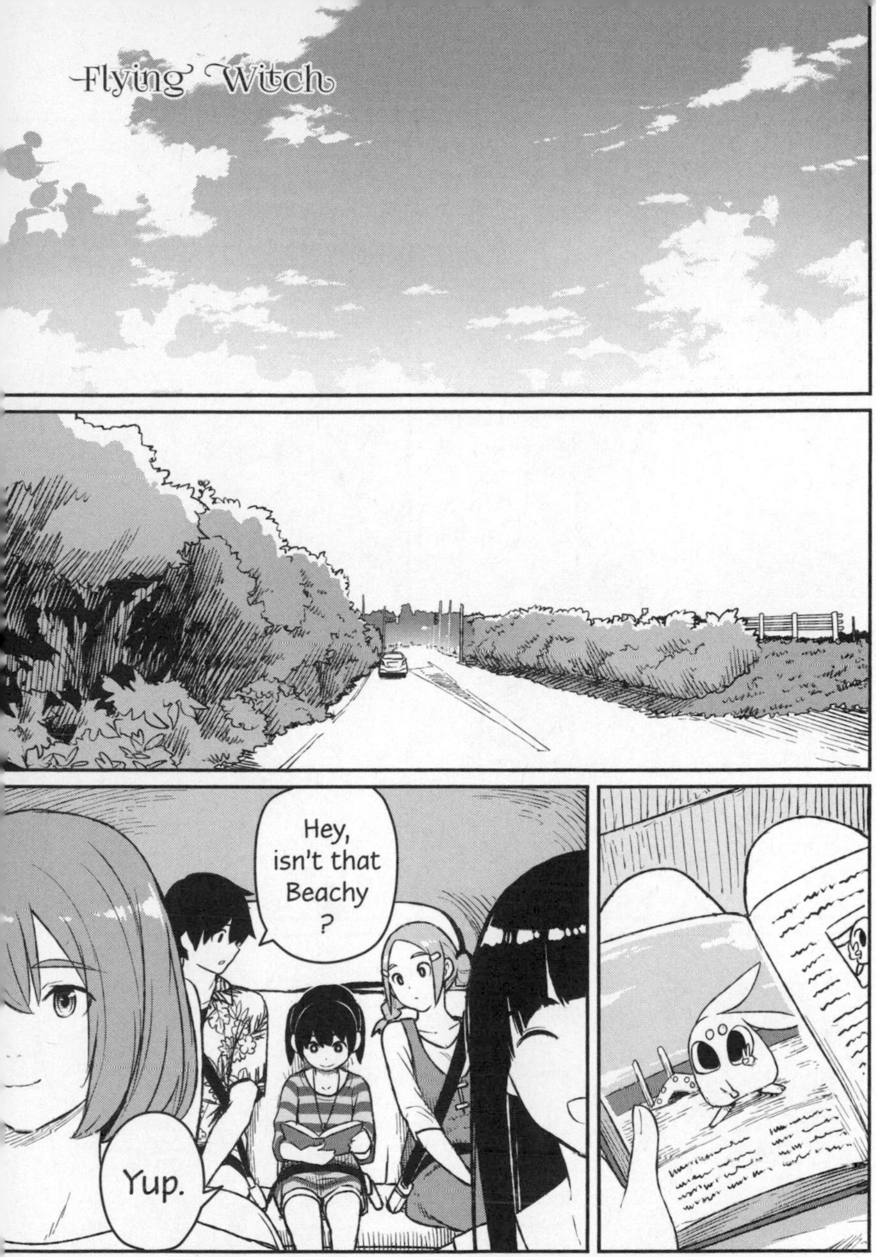
Flying Witch
Hey, isn't that Beachy?
Yup.

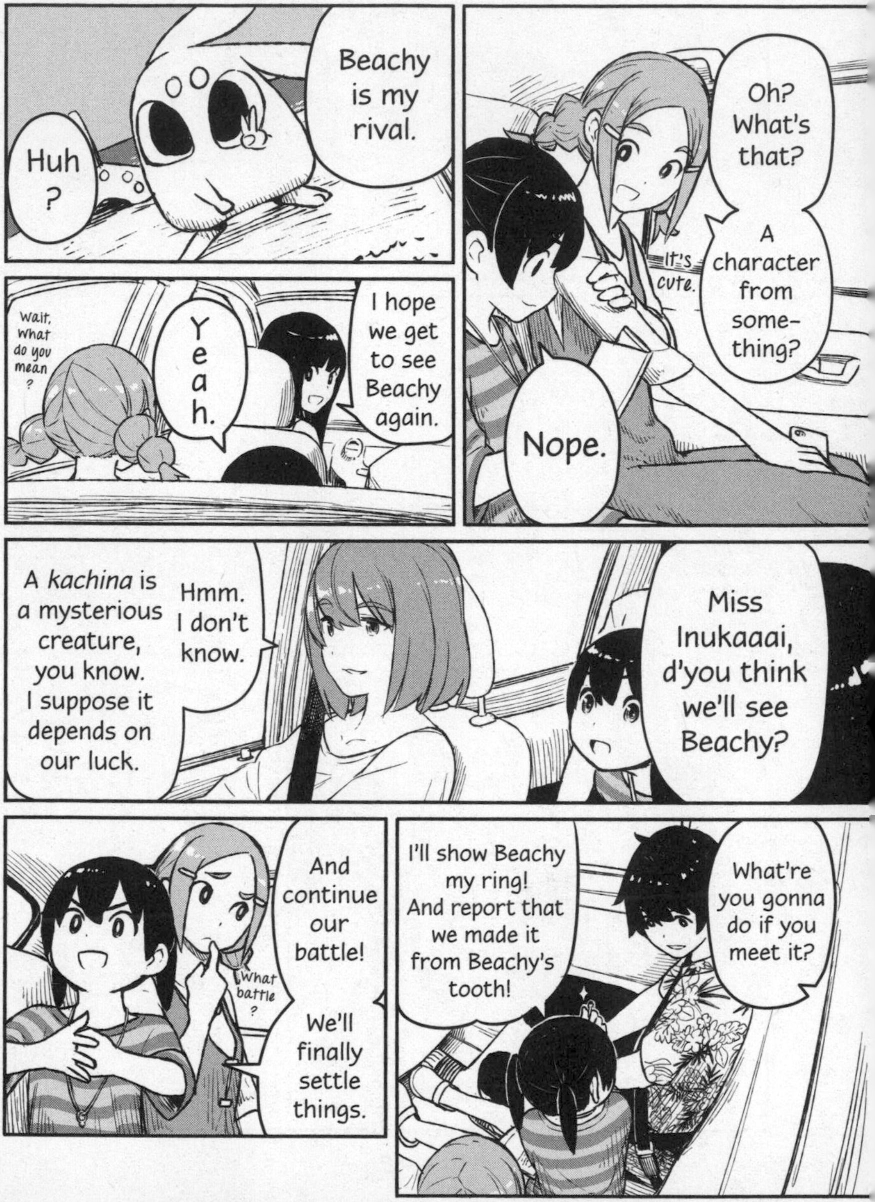
Oh? What's that?
A character from some-thing?
It's cute.
Nope.
Beachy is my rival.
Huh?
I hope we get to see Beachy again.
Yeah.
Wait, what do you mean?
Miss Inukaaai, d'you think we'll see Beachy?
Hmm. I don't know.
A *kachina* is a mysterious creature, you know. I suppose it depends on our luck.
What're you gonna do if you meet it?
I'll show Beachy my ring! And report that we made it from Beachy's tooth!
And continue our battle!
What battle?
We'll finally settle things.

Chapter 52
Our Friend, the Guardian Spirit of the Beach

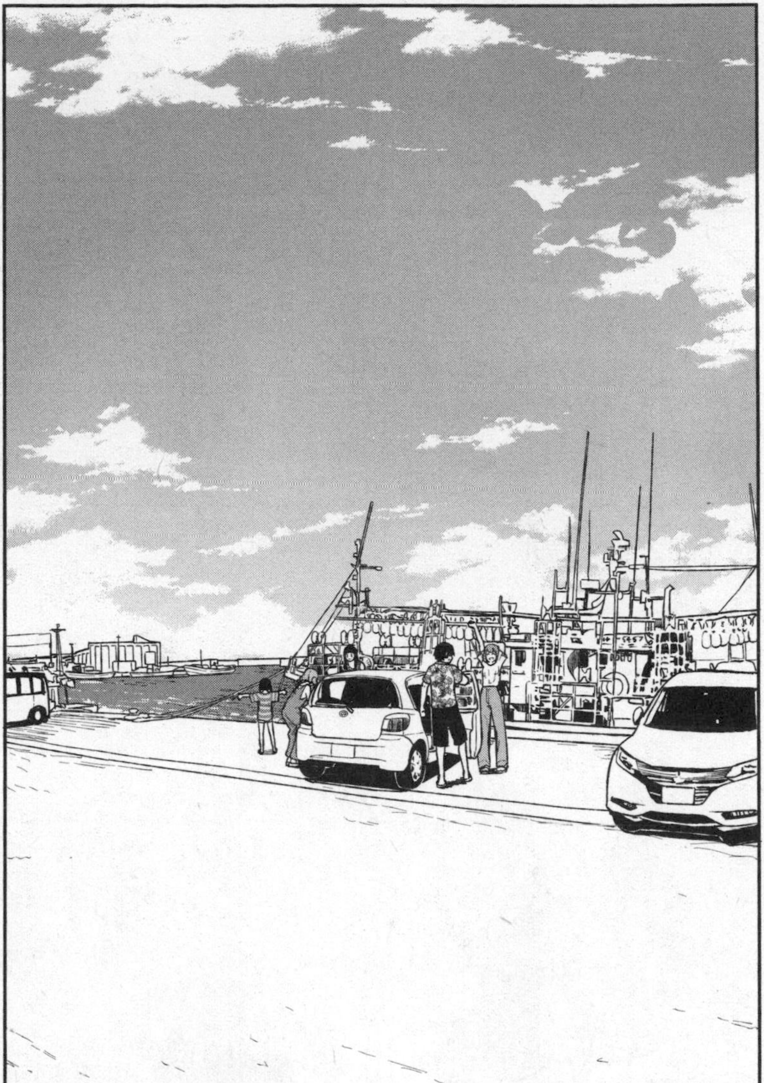

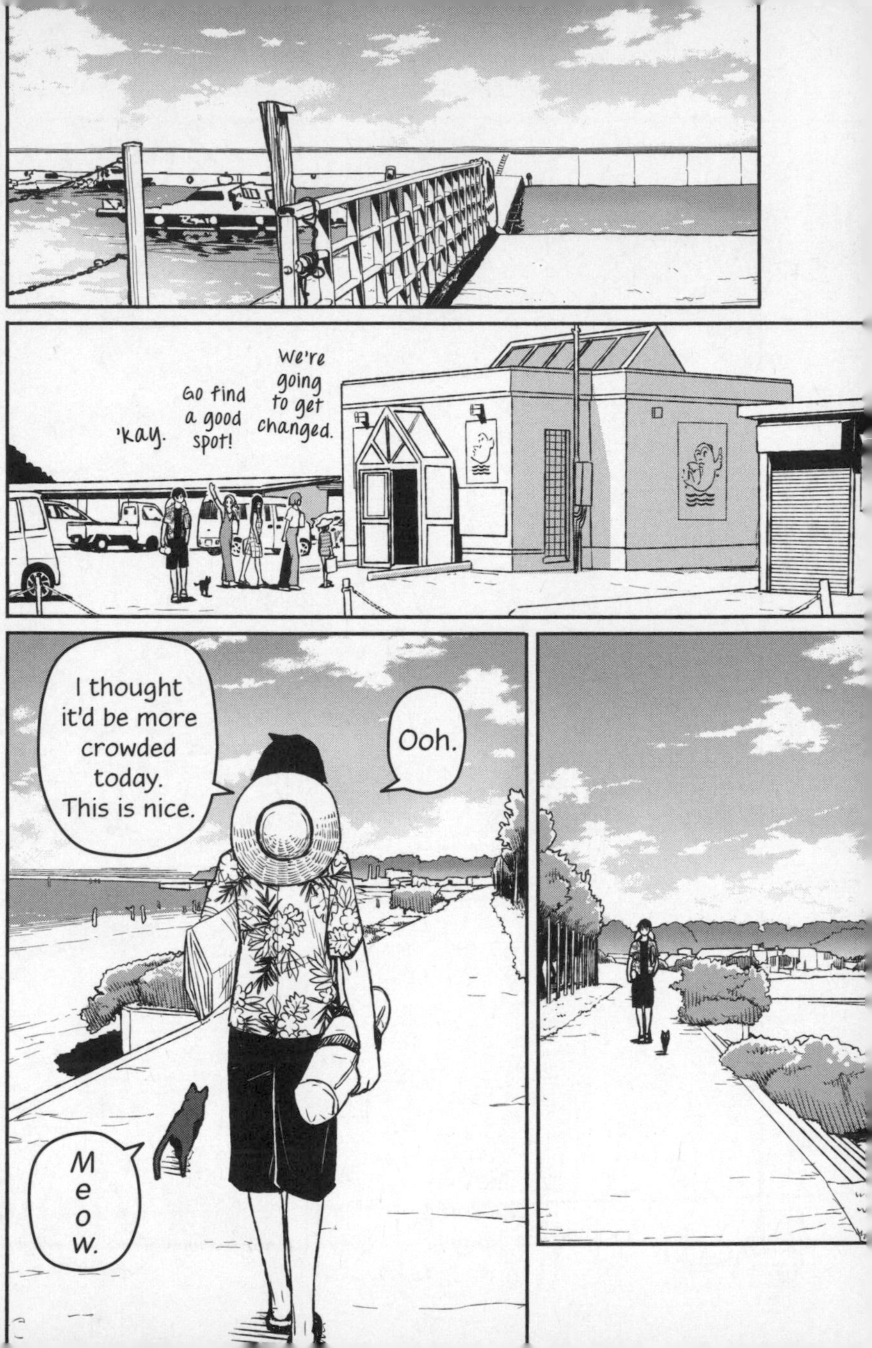
We're going to get changed.
Go find a good spot!
'kay.
Ooh.
I thought it'd be more crowded today. This is nice.
Meow.

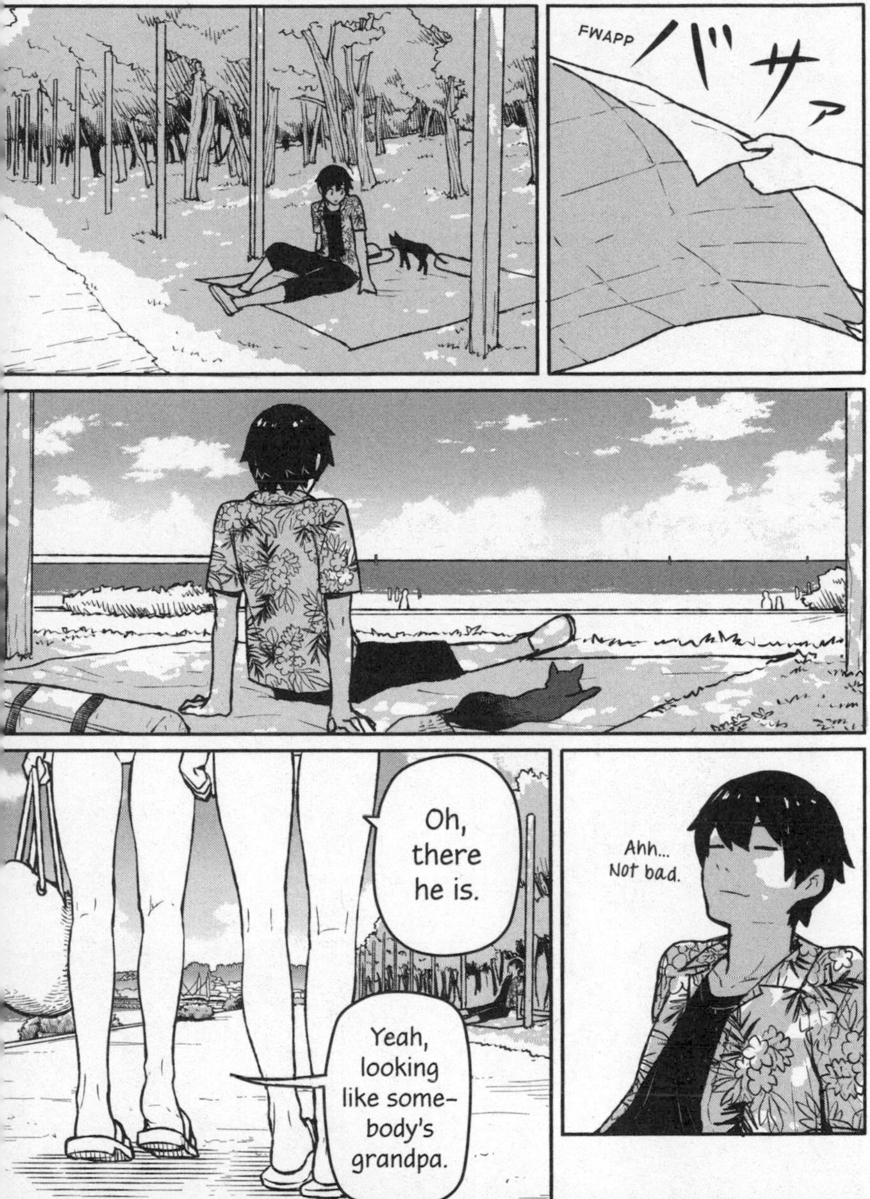
FWAPP
バサァ
Ahh... Not bad.
Oh, there he is.
Yeah, looking like some-body's grandpa.

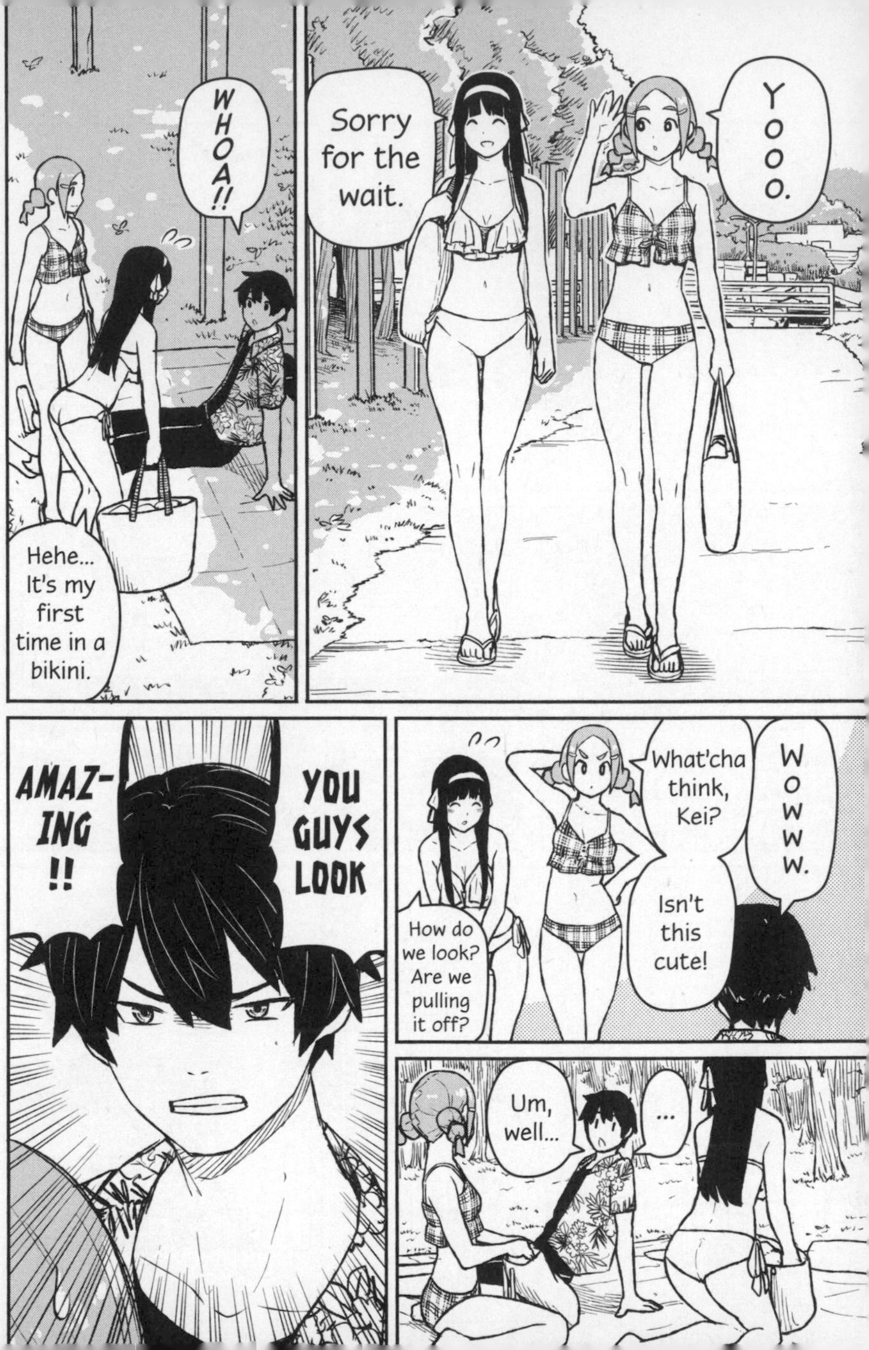
YOOO.
Sorry for the wait.
WHOA!!
Hehe... It's my first time in a bikini.
WOWWW.
What'cha think, Kei?
Isn't this cute!
How do we look? Are we pulling it off?
...
Um, well...
YOU GUYS LOOK
AMAZING!!

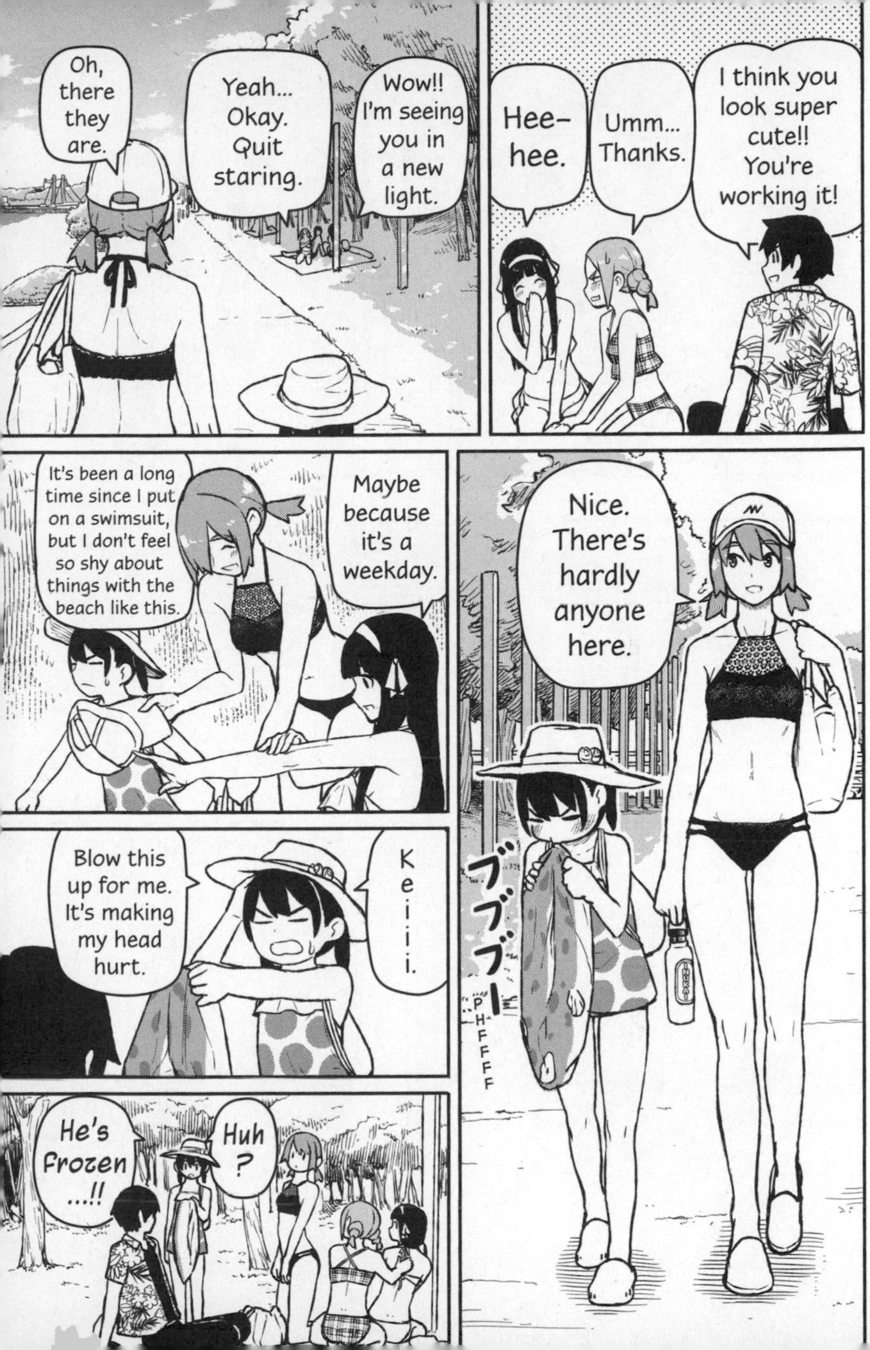
I think you look super cute!! You're working it!
Umm... Thanks.
Hee-hee.
Wow!! I'm seeing you in a new light.
Yeah... Okay. Quit staring.
Oh, there they are.
Nice. There's hardly anyone here.
ブブブー
PHFFFF
Maybe because it's a weekday.
It's been a long time since I put on a swimsuit, but I don't feel so shy about things with the beach like this.
Keiii.
Blow this up for me. It's making my head hurt.
Huh?
He's frozen...!!

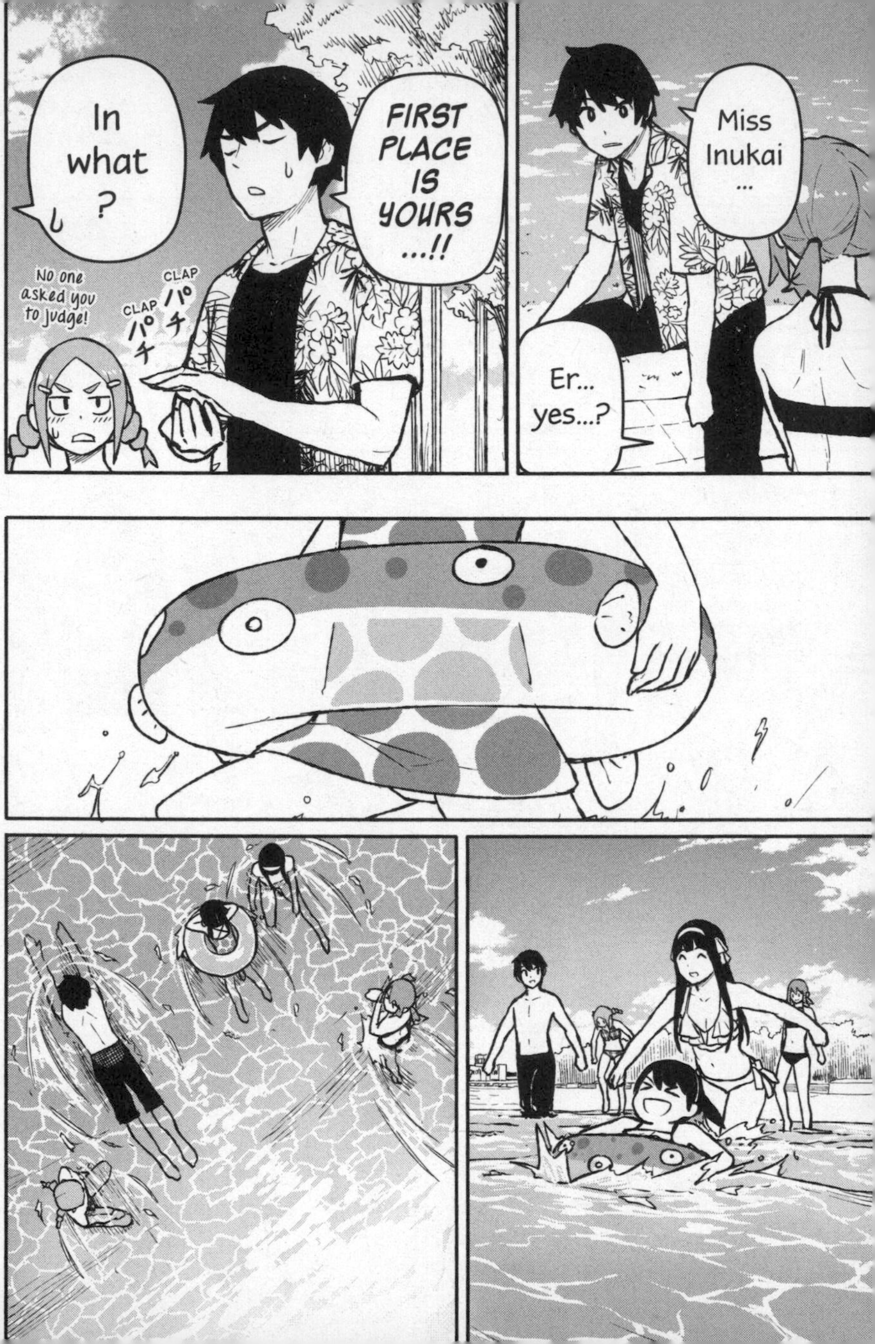

Miss Inukai ...
Er... yes...?
FIRST PLACE IS YOURS ...!!
In what?
CLAP パチ
CLAP パチ
No one asked you to judge!

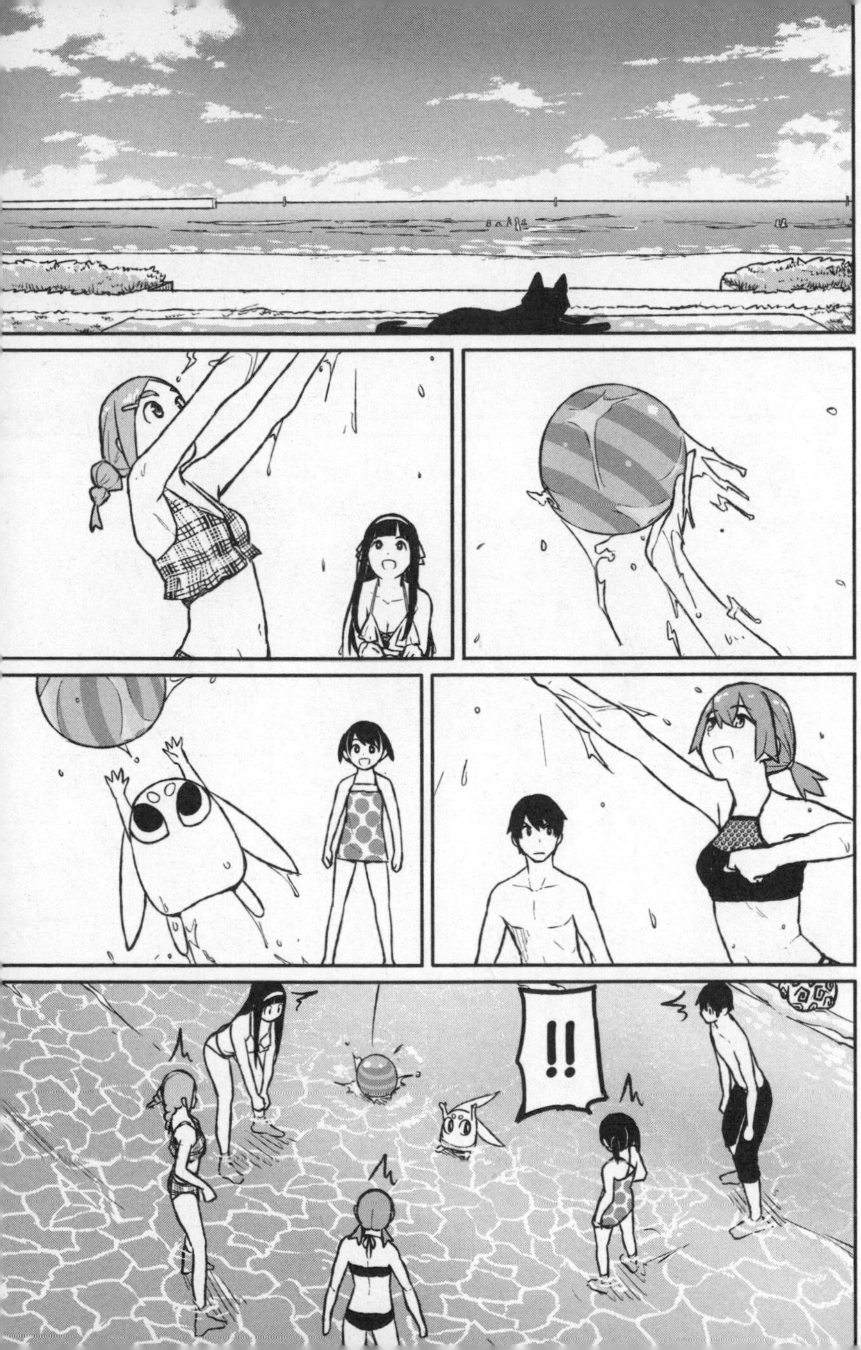
!!

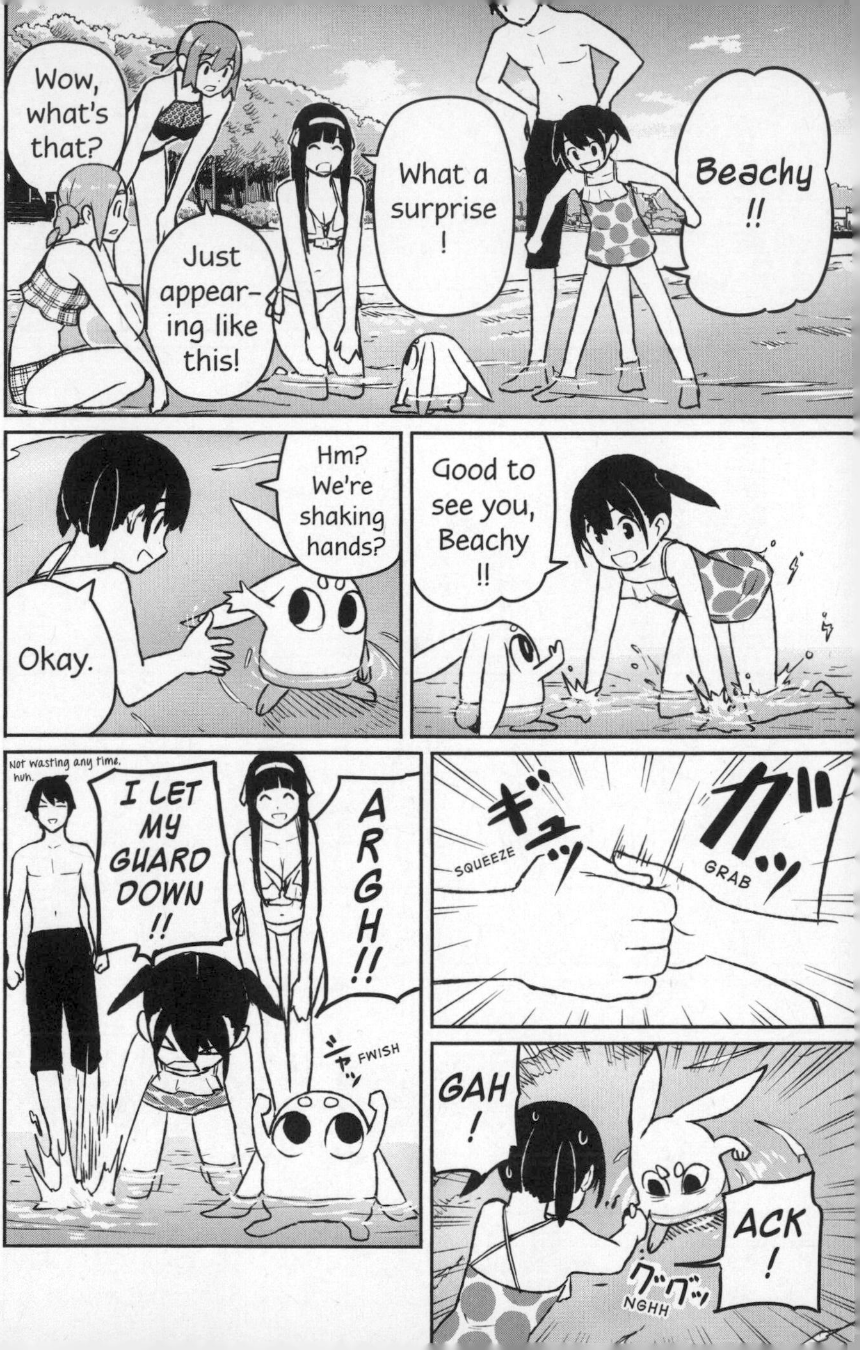
Beachy !!
What a surprise !
Just appear-ing like this!
Wow, what's that?
Good to see you, Beachy !!
Hm? We're shaking hands?
Okay.
ガッ
GRAB
ギュッ
SQUEEZE
ACK !
GAH !
グッグッ
NGHH
ARGH!!
I LET MY GUARD DOWN !!
シャッ
FWISH
Not wasting any time, huh.

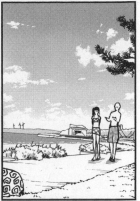

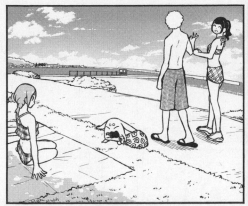

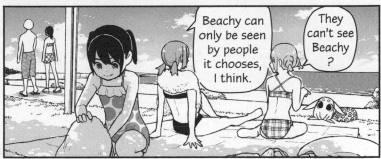

They can't see Beachy?
Beachy can only be seen by people it chooses, I think.
Look at this, Beachy!
This ring contains the *mana* from your tooth!
And I can make it shoot water. Is that cool or what!

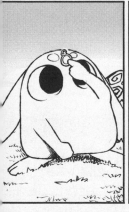

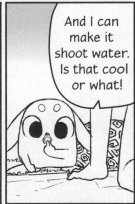

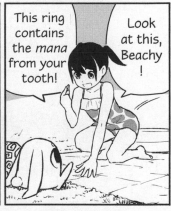

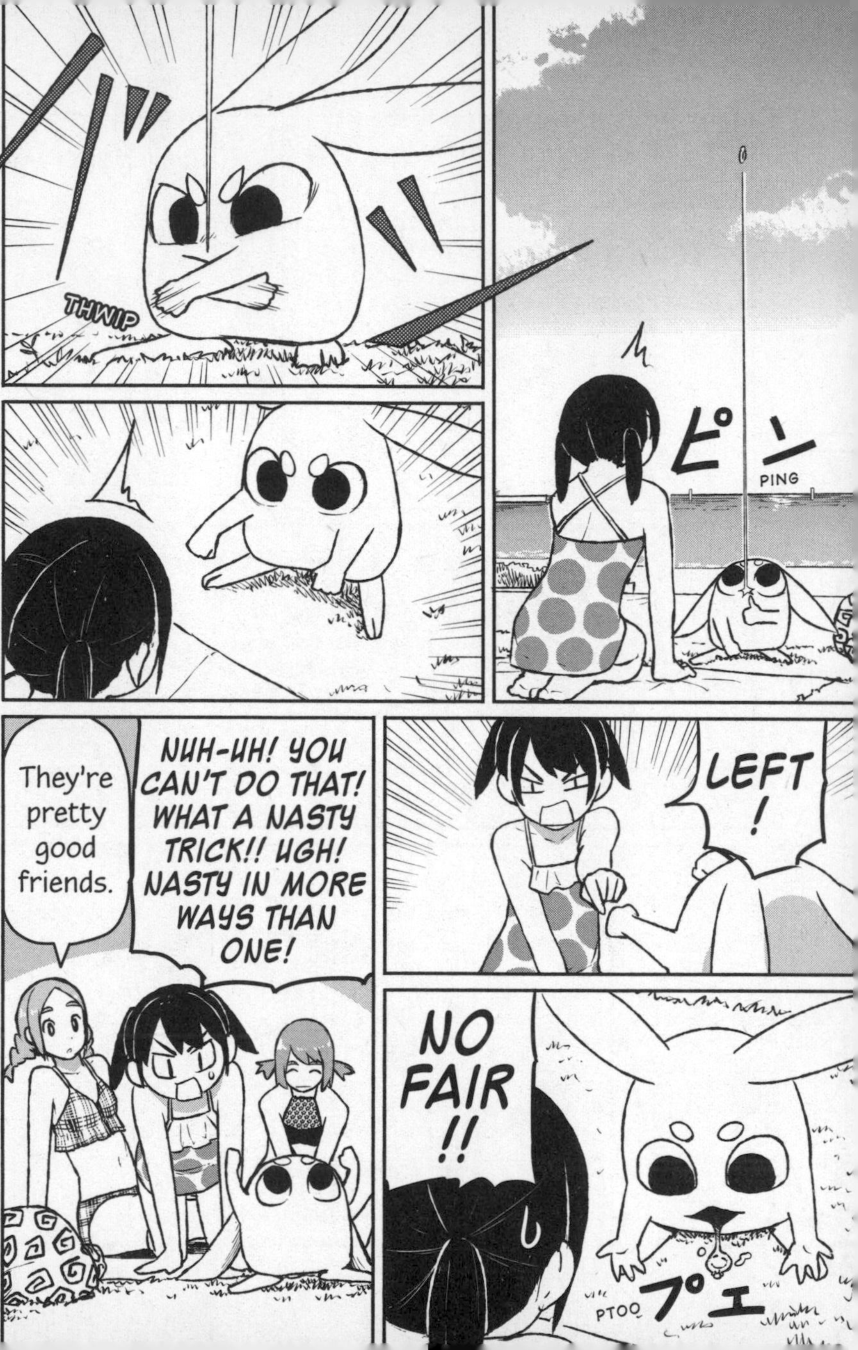
ピン
PING
THWIP
LEFT!
NO FAIR!!
プエ
PTOO
NUH-UH! YOU CAN'T DO THAT! WHAT A NASTY TRICK!! UGH! NASTY IN MORE WAYS THAN ONE!
They're pretty good friends.

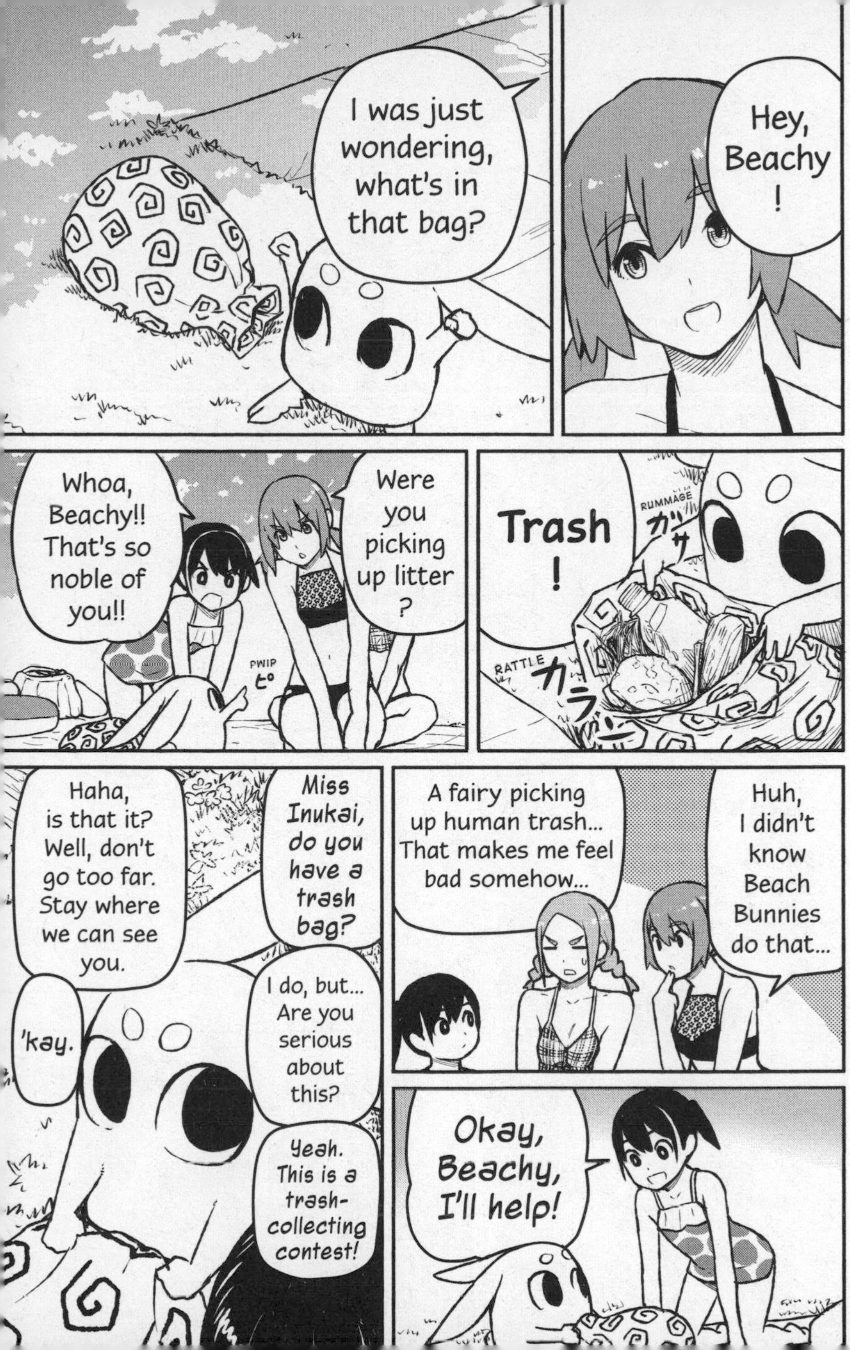
Hey, Beachy!
I was just wondering, what's in that bag?
RUMMAGE
ガサ
Trash!
RATTLE
カラ
Were you picking up litter?
Whoa, Beachy!! That's so noble of you!!
PWIP
ピ
Huh, I didn't know Beach Bunnies do that...
A fairy picking up human trash... That makes me feel bad somehow...
Okay, Beachy, I'll help!
Miss Inukai, do you have a trash bag?
Haha, is that it? Well, don't go too far. Stay where we can see you.
I do, but... Are you serious about this?
'kay.
Yeah. This is a trash-collecting contest!

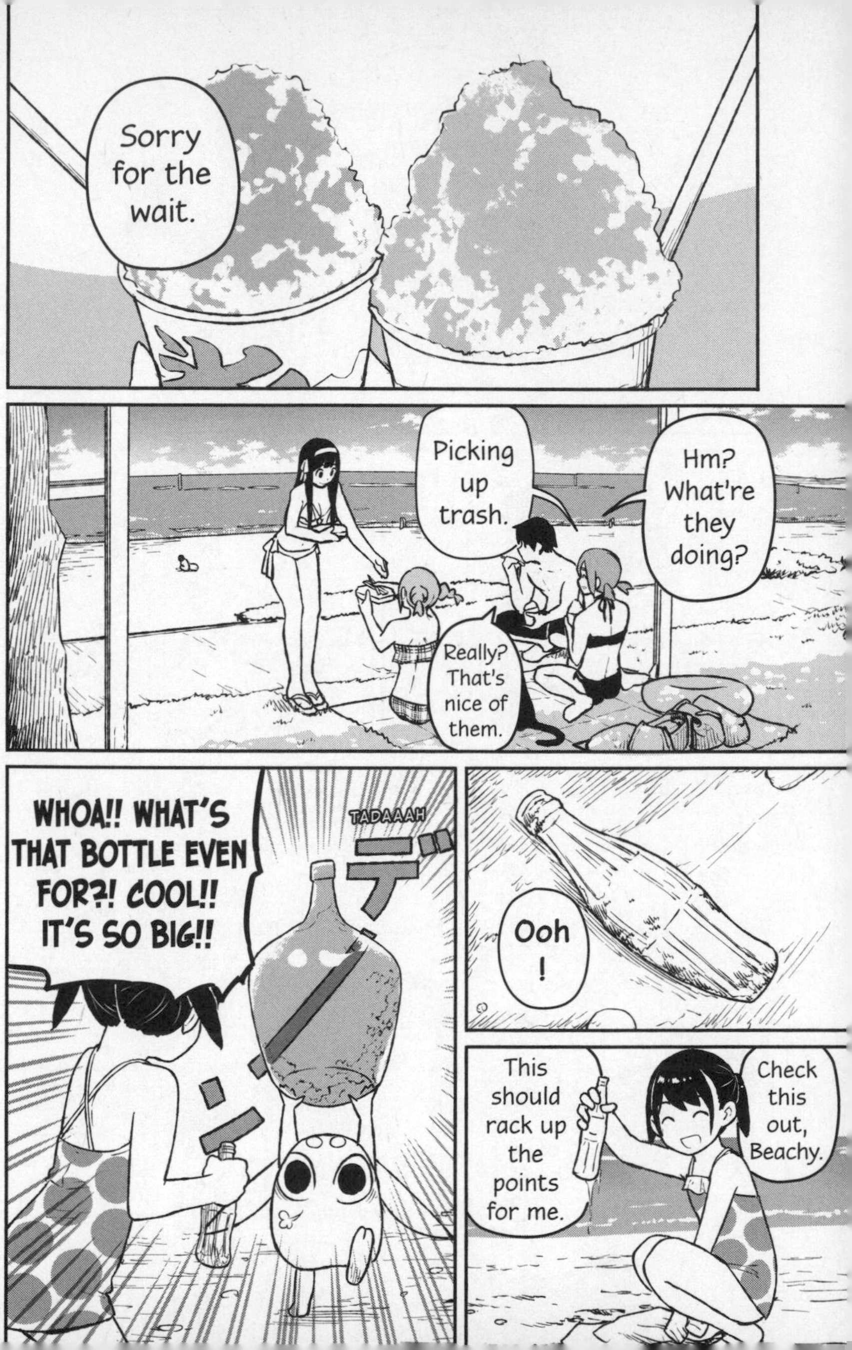
Sorry for the wait.
Hm? What're they doing?
Picking up trash.
Really? That's nice of them.
Ooh !
Check this out, Beachy.
This should rack up the points for me.
TADAAAH
WHOA!! WHAT'S THAT BOTTLE EVEN FOR?! COOL!! IT'S SO BIG!!

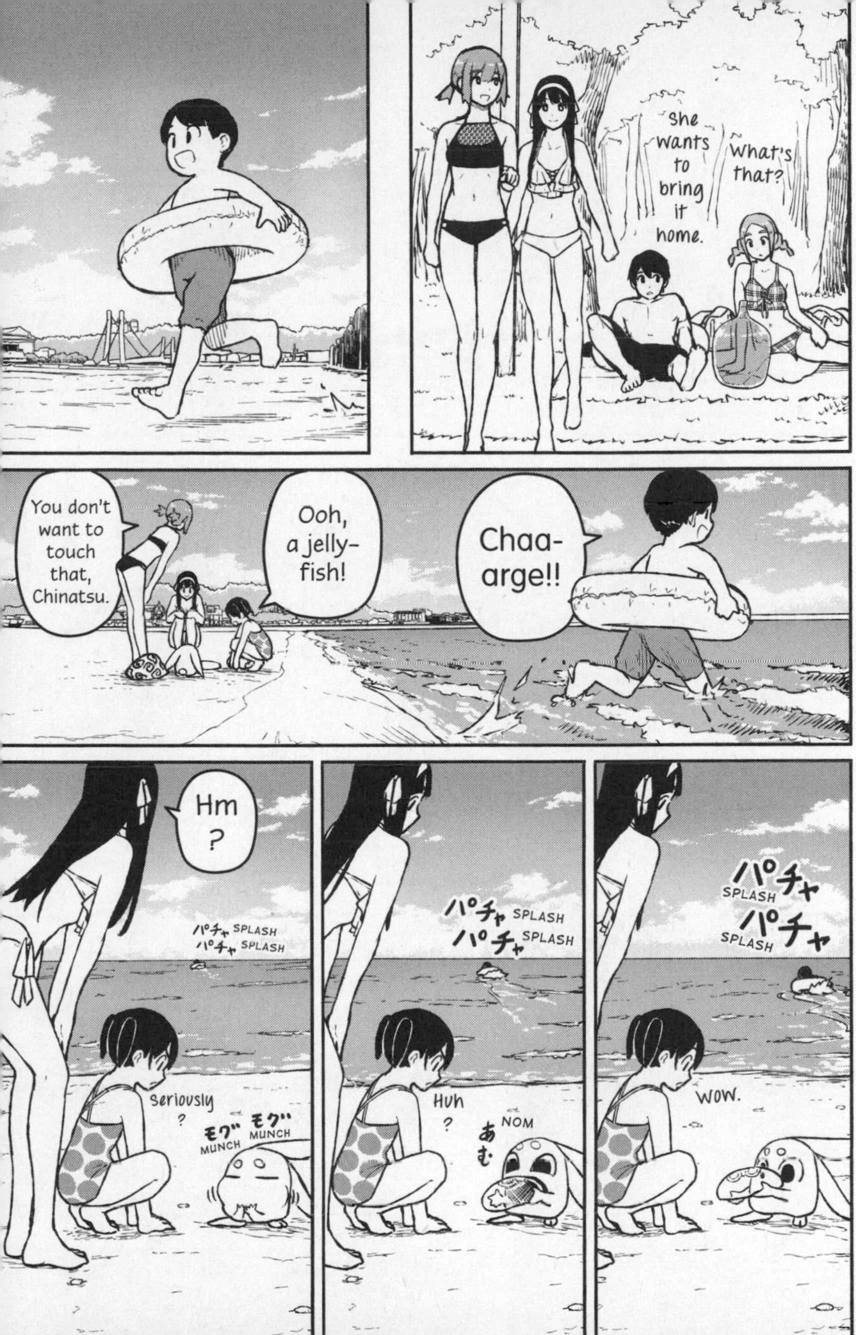
What's that?
She wants to bring it home.
Chaa-arge!!
Ooh, a jelly-fish!
You don't want to touch that, Chinatsu.
パチャ SPLASH
パチャ SPLASH
Wow.
パチャ SPLASH
パチャ SPLASH
Huh?
あむ NOM
Hm?
パチャ SPLASH
パチャ SPLASH
Seriously?
モグ MUNCH
モグ MUNCH

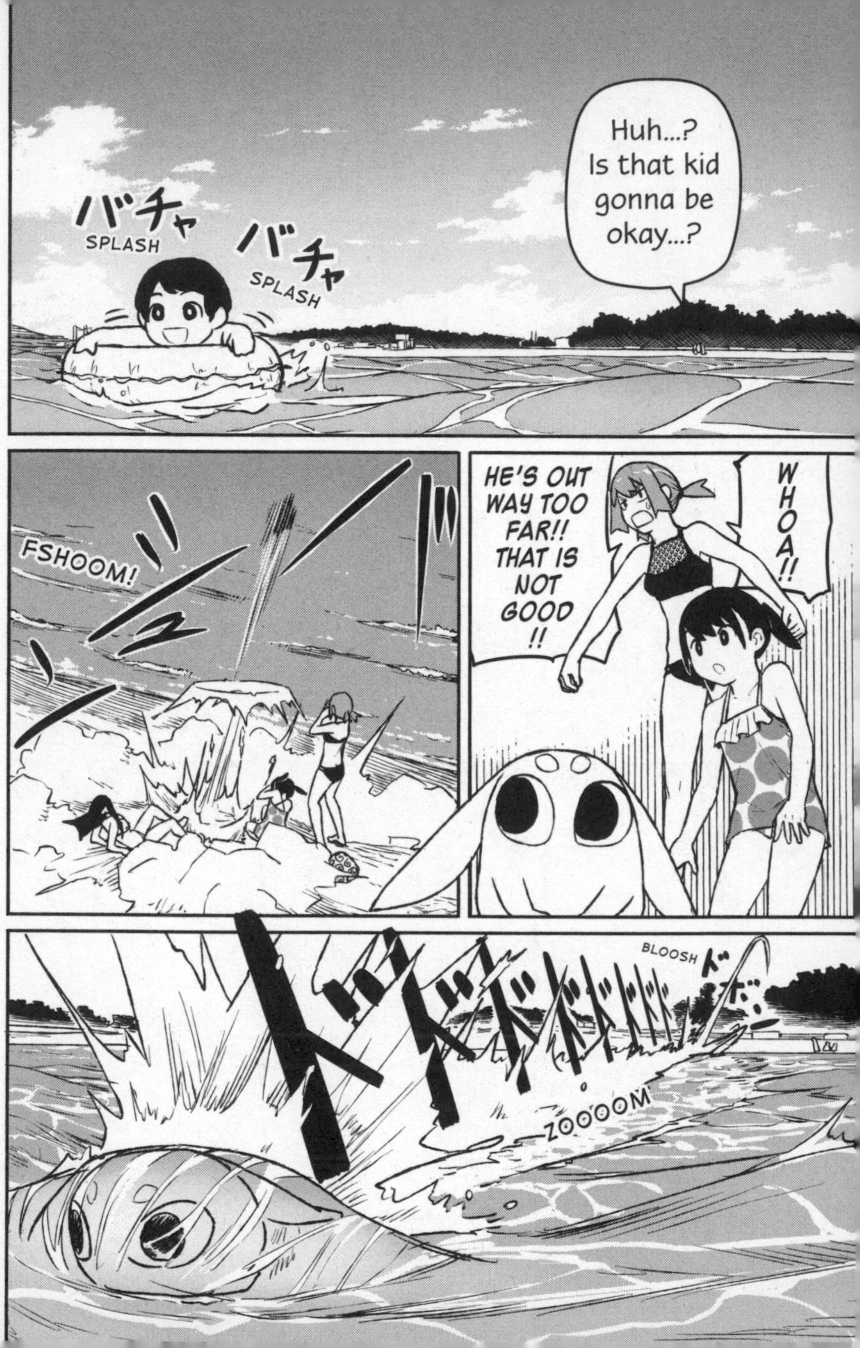
Huh...? Is that kid gonna be okay...?
バチャ
SPLASH
バチャ
SPLASH
WHOA!!
HE'S OUT WAY TOO FAR!! THAT IS NOT GOOD!!
FSHOOM!
BLOOSH
ZOOOOM

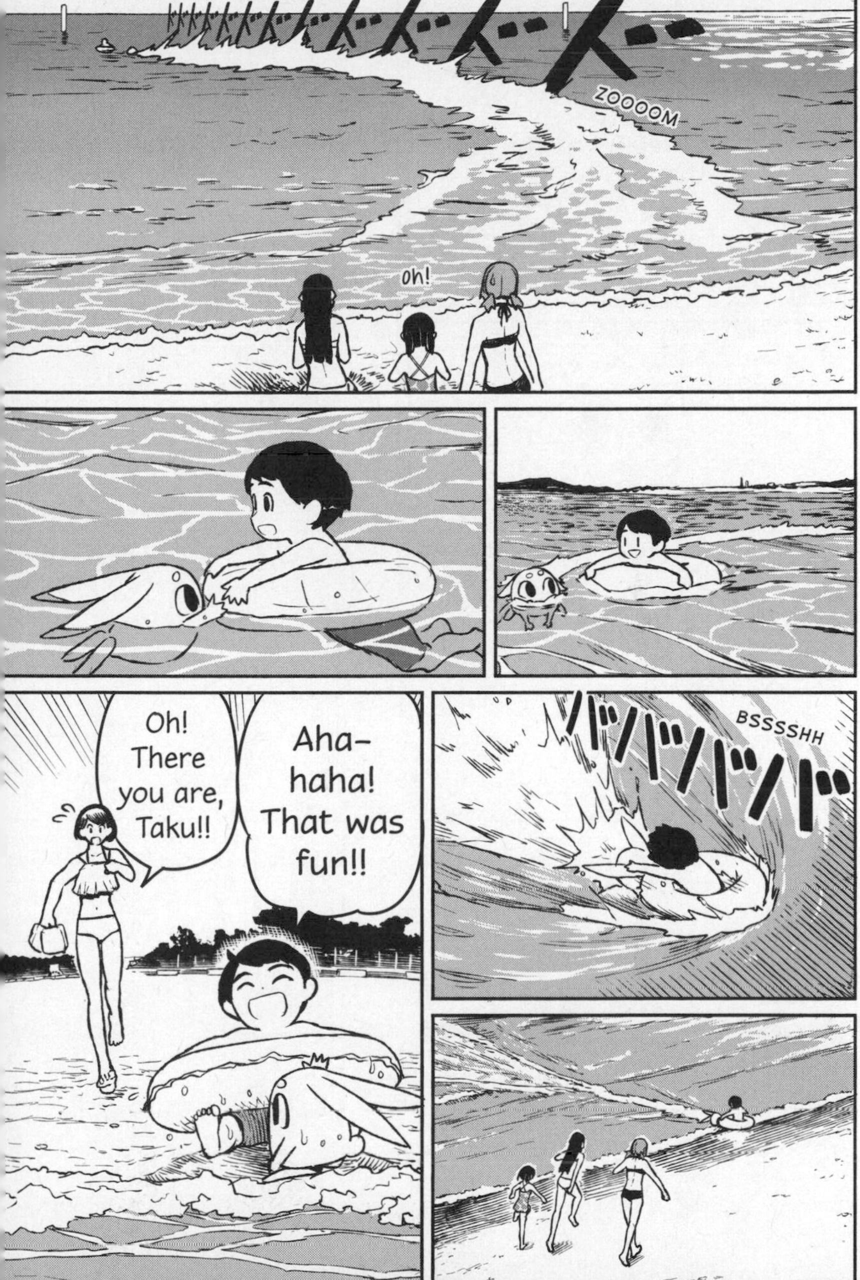
ZOOOOM
Oh!
BSSSSHH
Aha-haha! That was fun!!
Oh! There you are, Taku!!

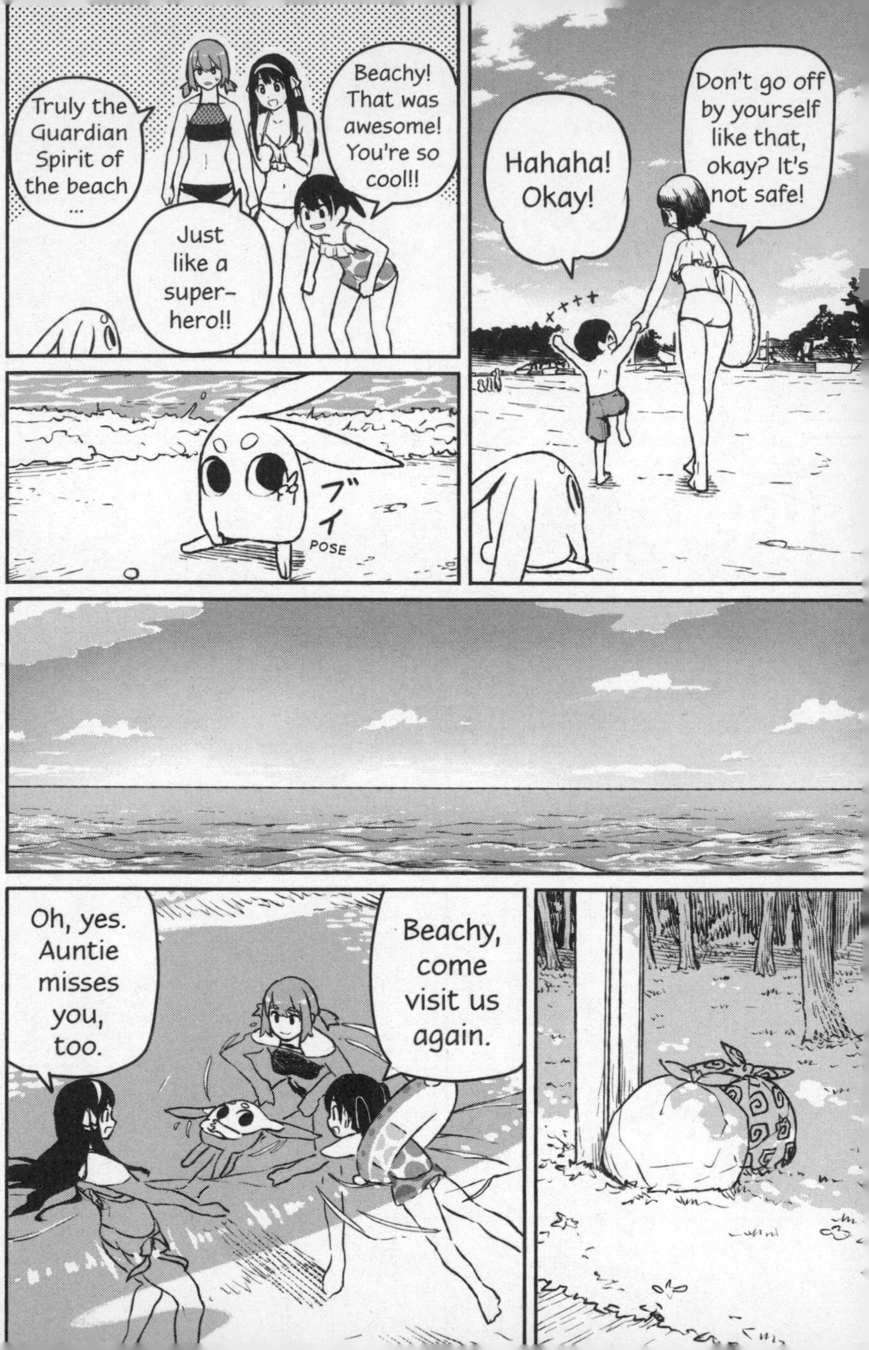
Don't go off by yourself like that, okay? It's not safe!
Hahaha! Okay!
Beachy! That was awesome! You're so cool!!
Truly the Guardian Spirit of the beach ...
Just like a superhero!!
ブイ
POSE
Beachy, come visit us again.
Oh, yes. Auntie misses you, too.

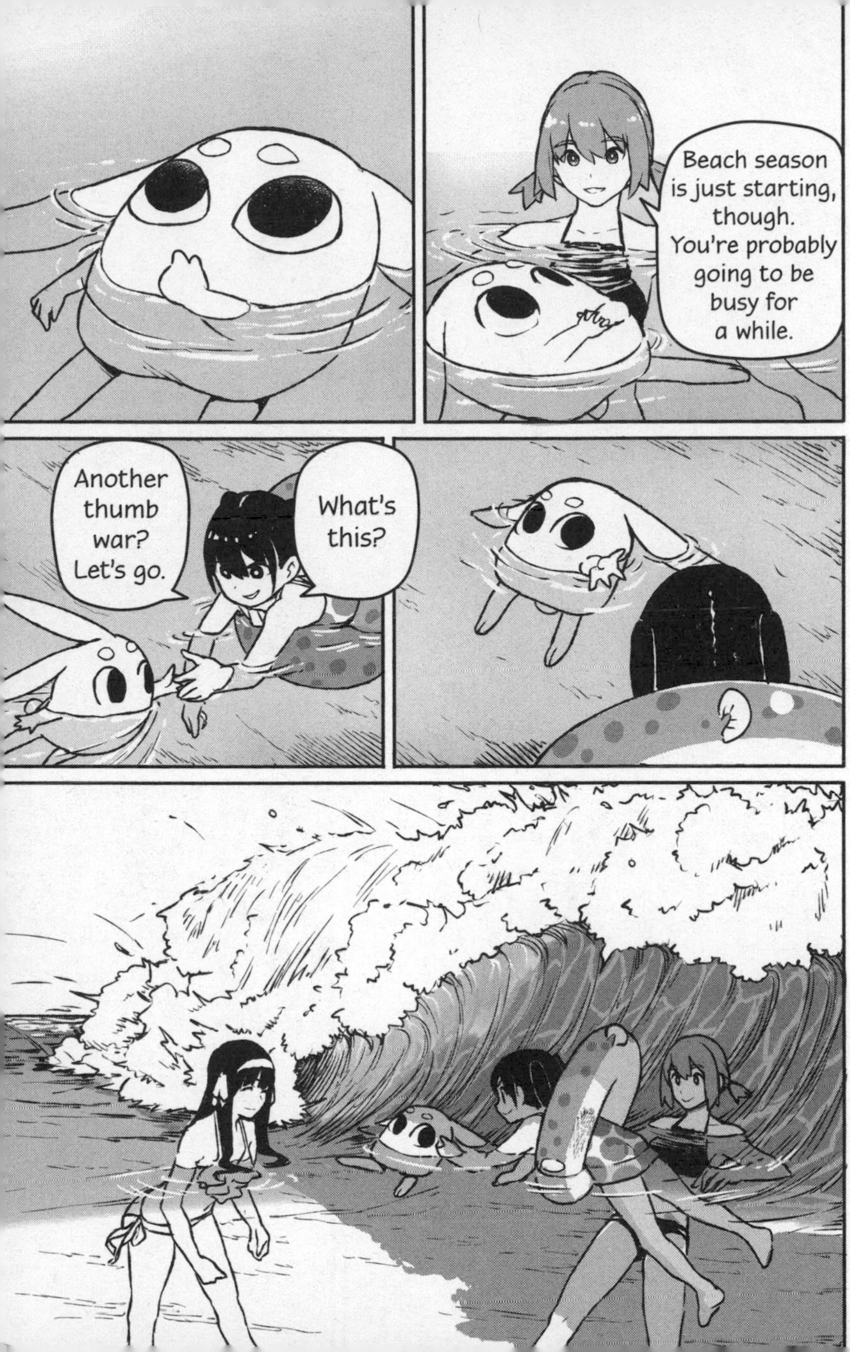
Beach season is just starting, though. You're probably going to be busy for a while.
What's this?
Another thumb war? Let's go.

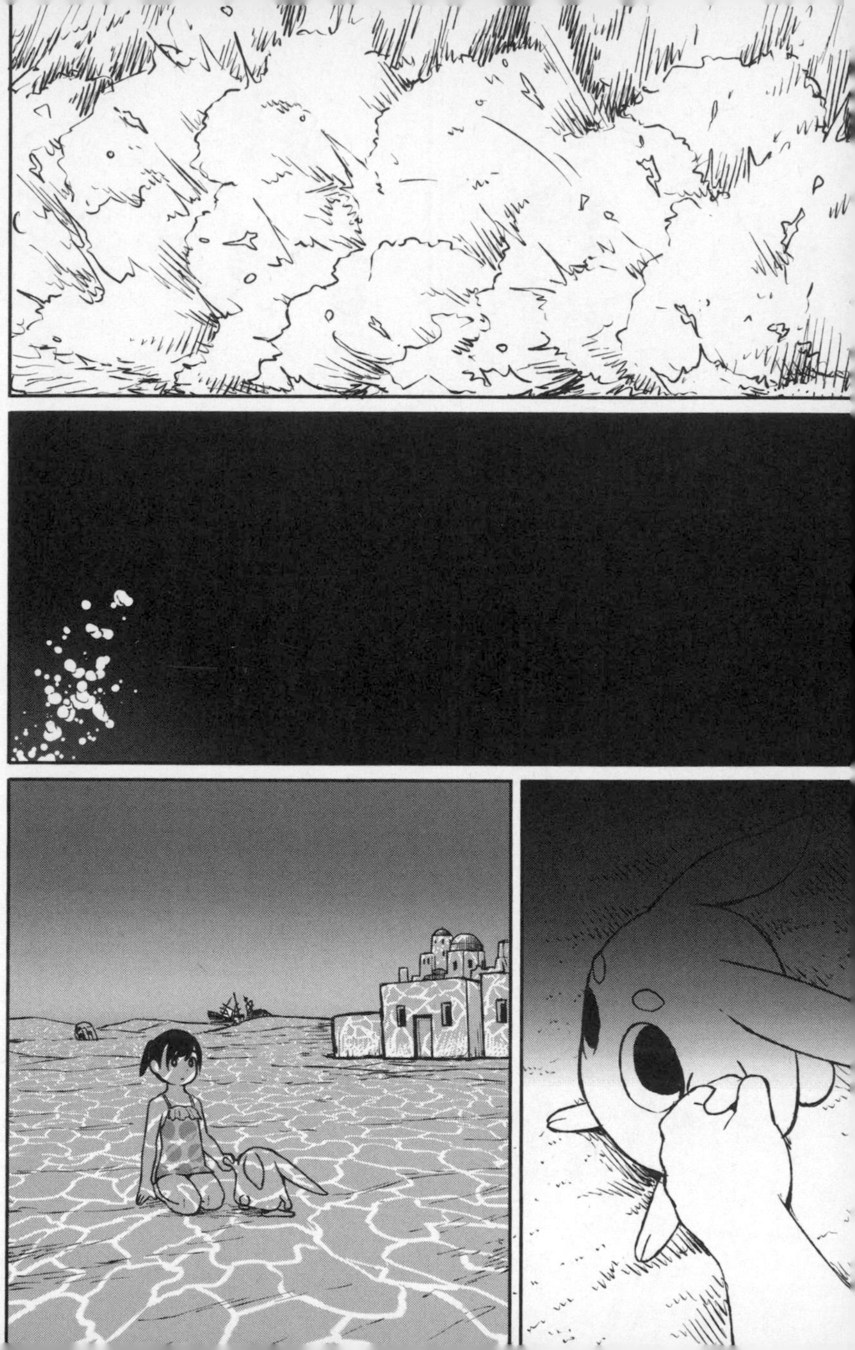

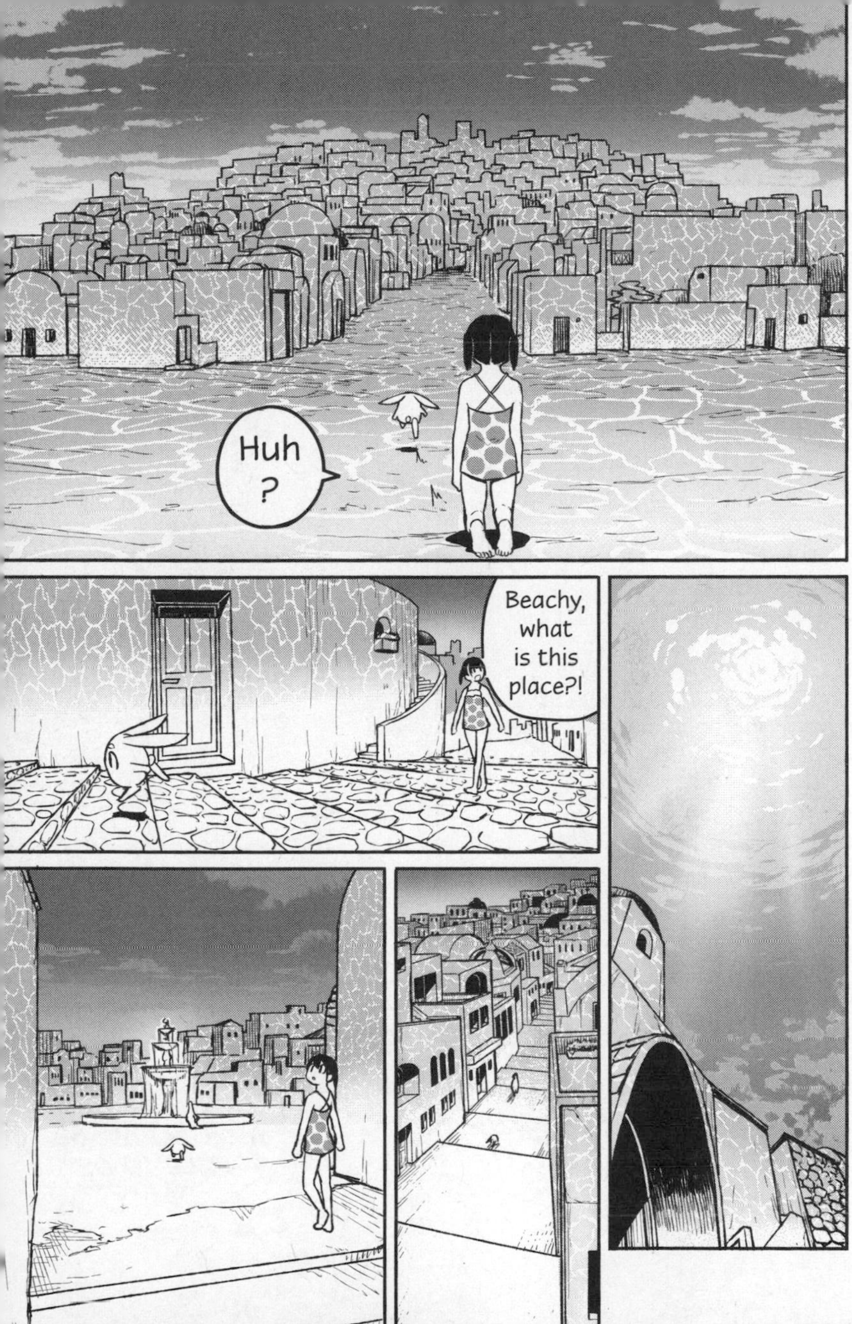
Huh
?
Beachy, what is this place?!

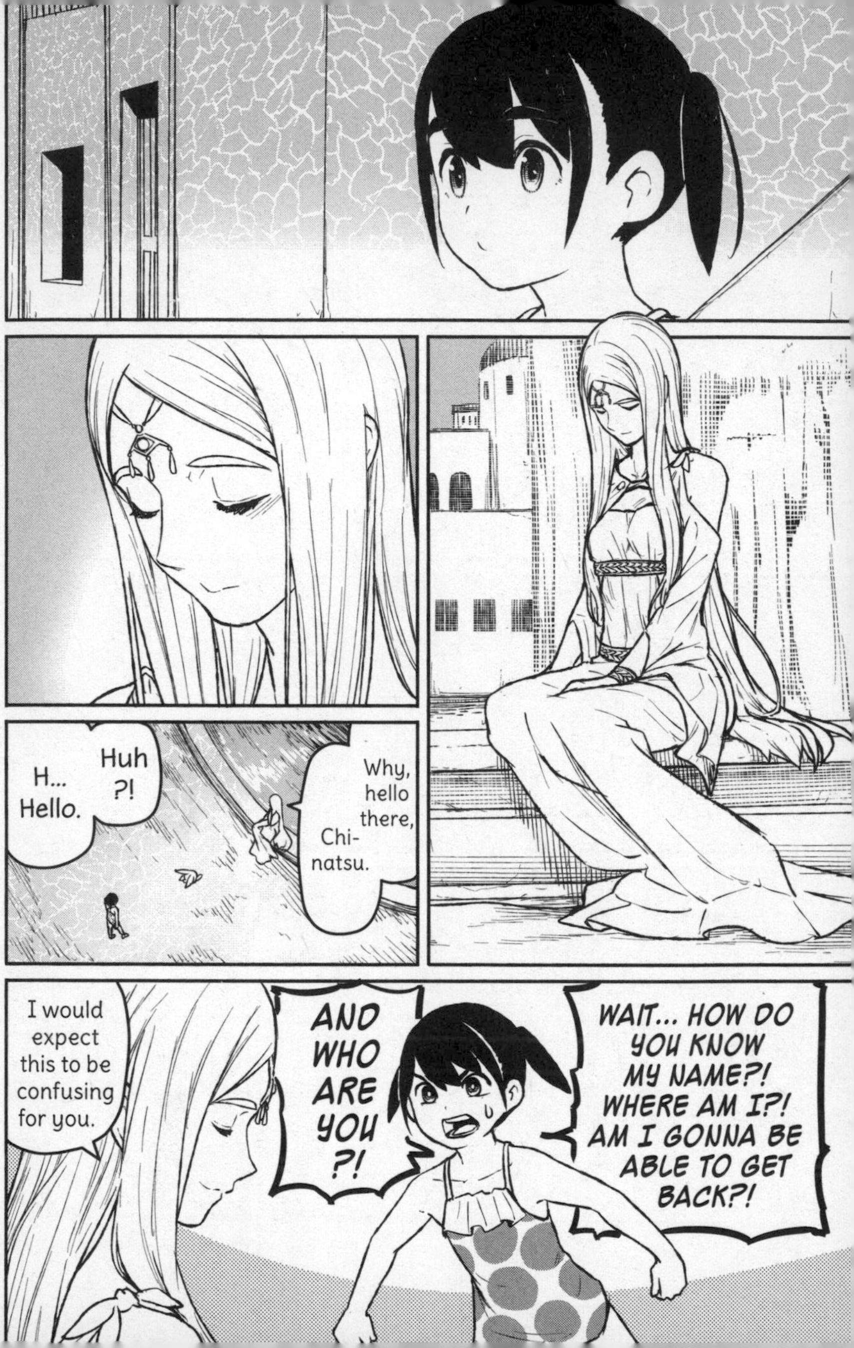
Why, hello there, Chinatsu.
Huh ?!
H... Hello.
WAIT... HOW DO YOU KNOW MY NAME?! WHERE AM I?! AM I GONNA BE ABLE TO GET BACK?!
AND WHO ARE YOU ?!
I would expect this to be confusing for you.

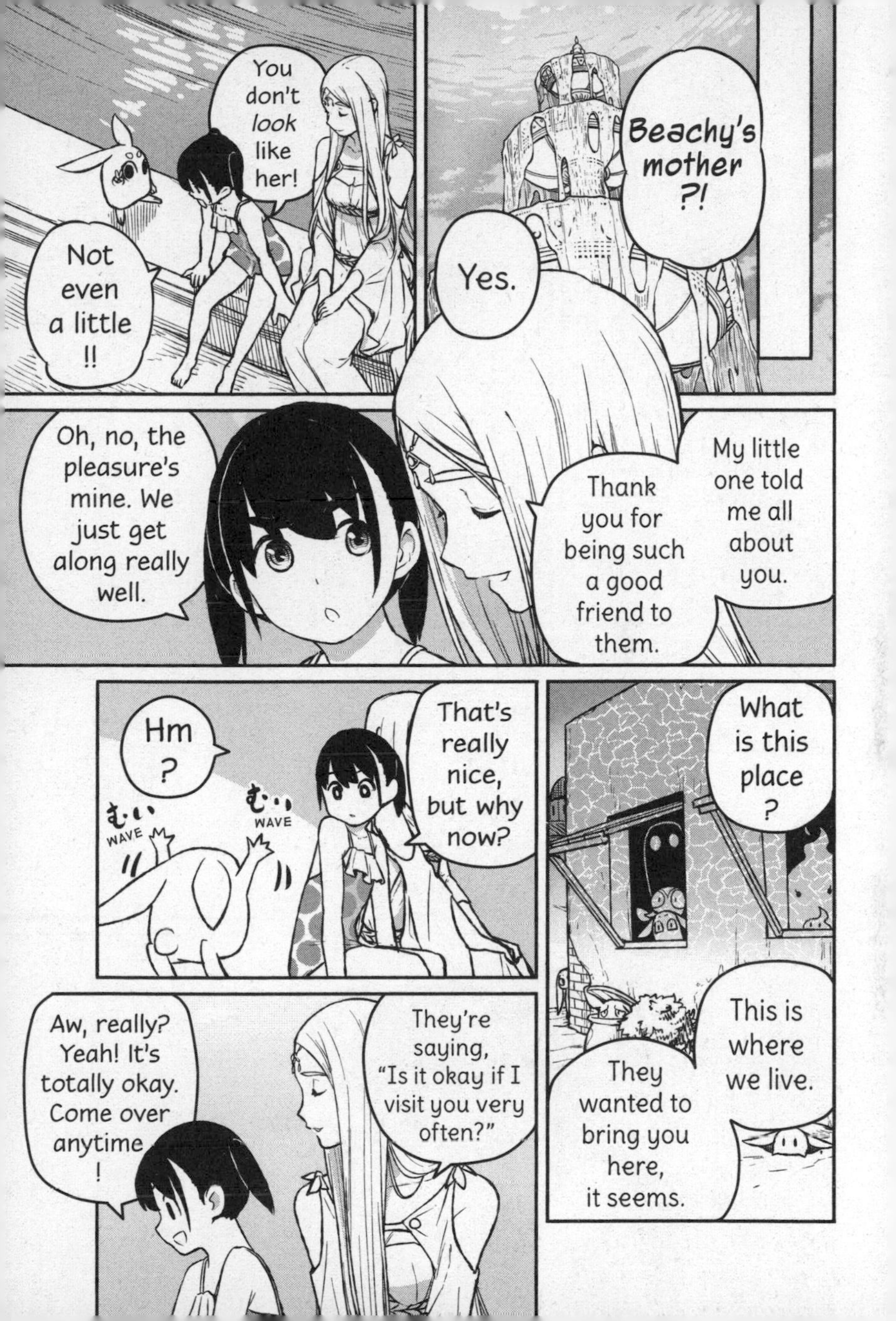
Beachy's mother ?!
Yes.
You don't *look* like her!
Not even a little !!
My little one told me all about you.
Thank you for being such a good friend to them.
Oh, no, the pleasure's mine. We just get along really well.
What is this place ?
This is where we live.
They wanted to bring you here, it seems.
That's really nice, but why now?
Hm ?
むい WAVE
むい WAVE
They're saying, "Is it okay if I visit you very often?"
Aw, really? Yeah! It's totally okay. Come over anytime !

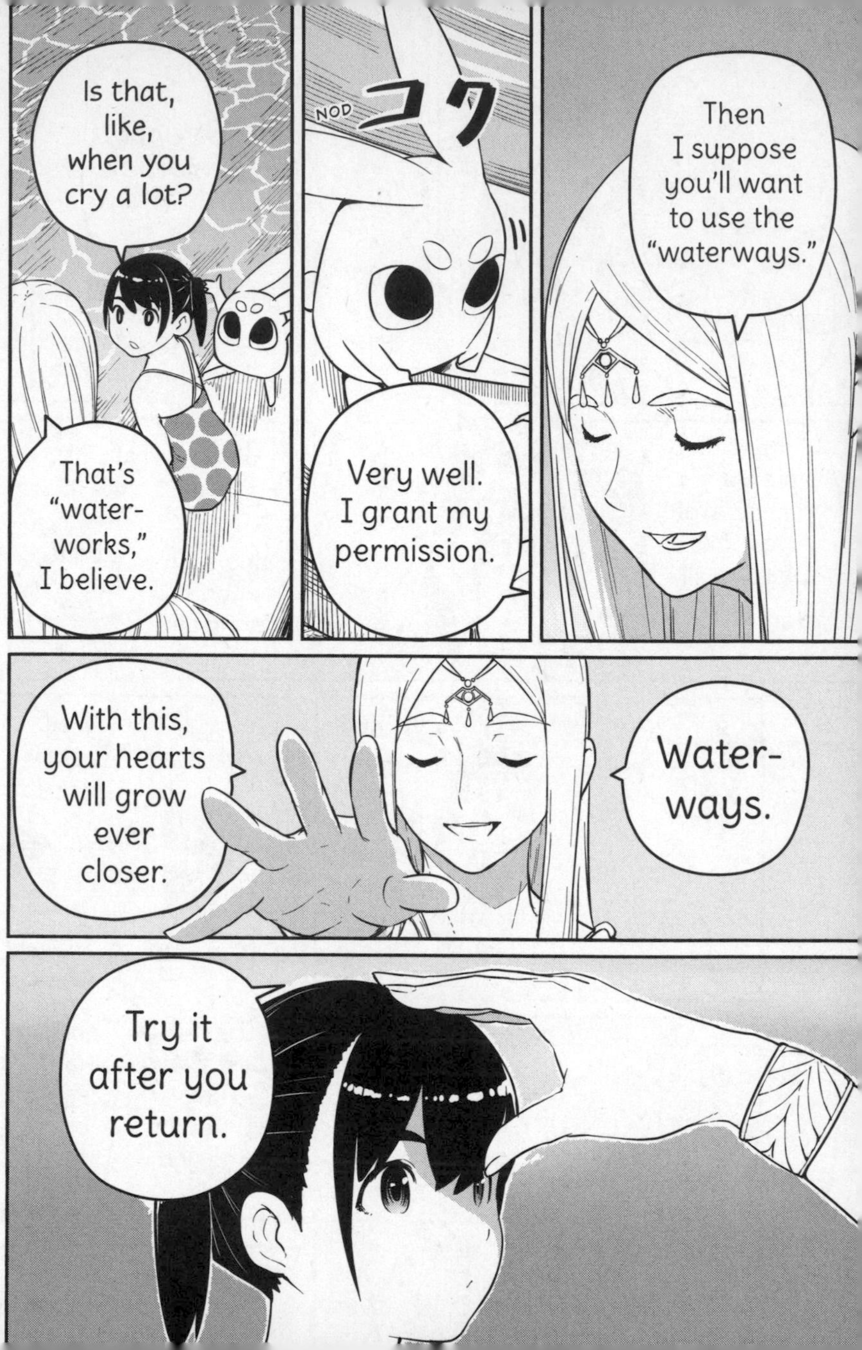
Then I suppose you'll want to use the "waterways."
NOD コク
Very well. I grant my permission.
Is that, like, when you cry a lot?
That's "water-works," I believe.
Water-ways.
With this, your hearts will grow ever closer.
Try it after you return.

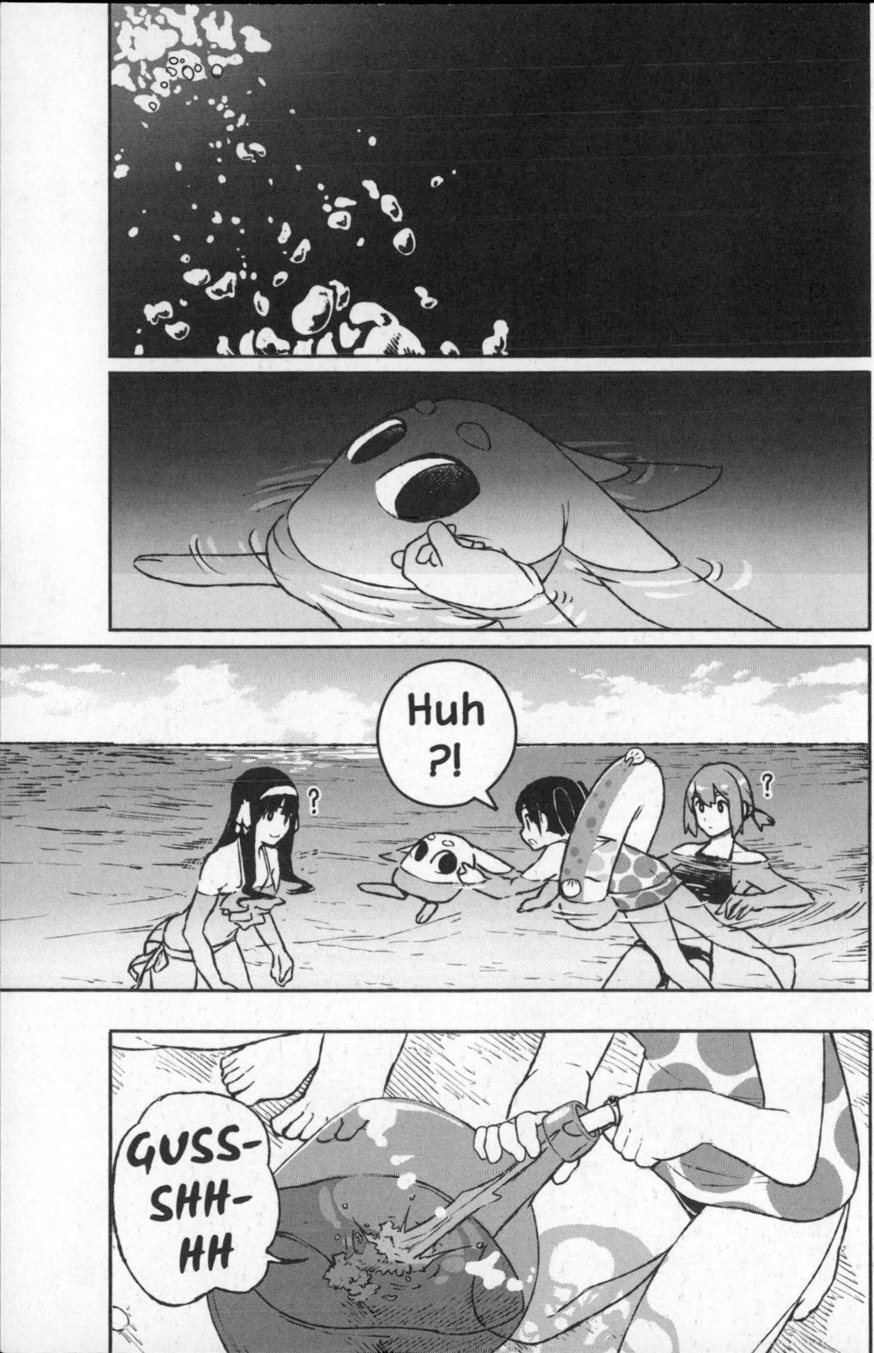
?
Huh ?!
?
GUSS-SHH-HH

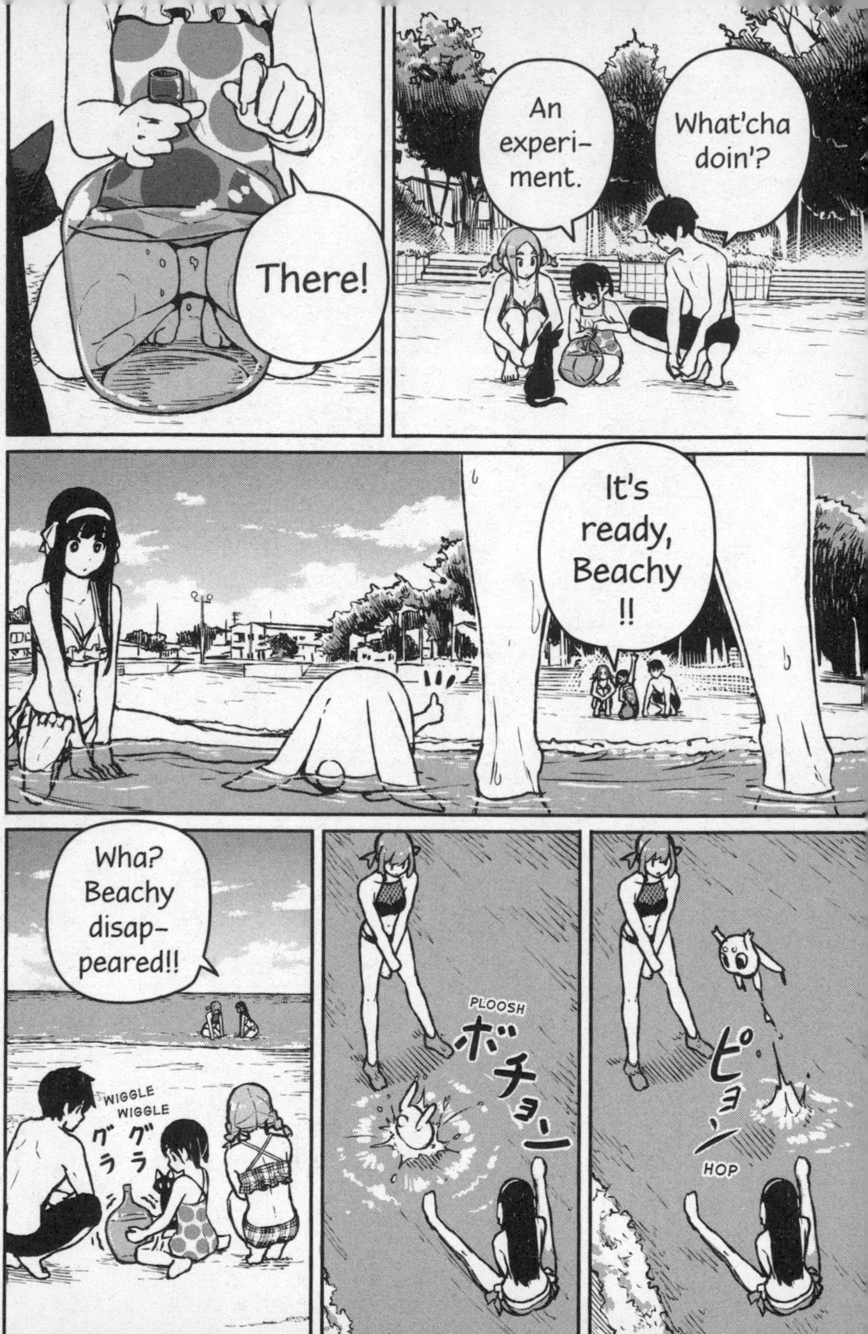
What'cha doin'?
An experi-ment.
There!
It's ready, Beachy !!
HOP
ピョン
PLOOSH
ボチョン
Wha? Beachy disap-peared!!
WIGGLE WIGGLE
グラグラ

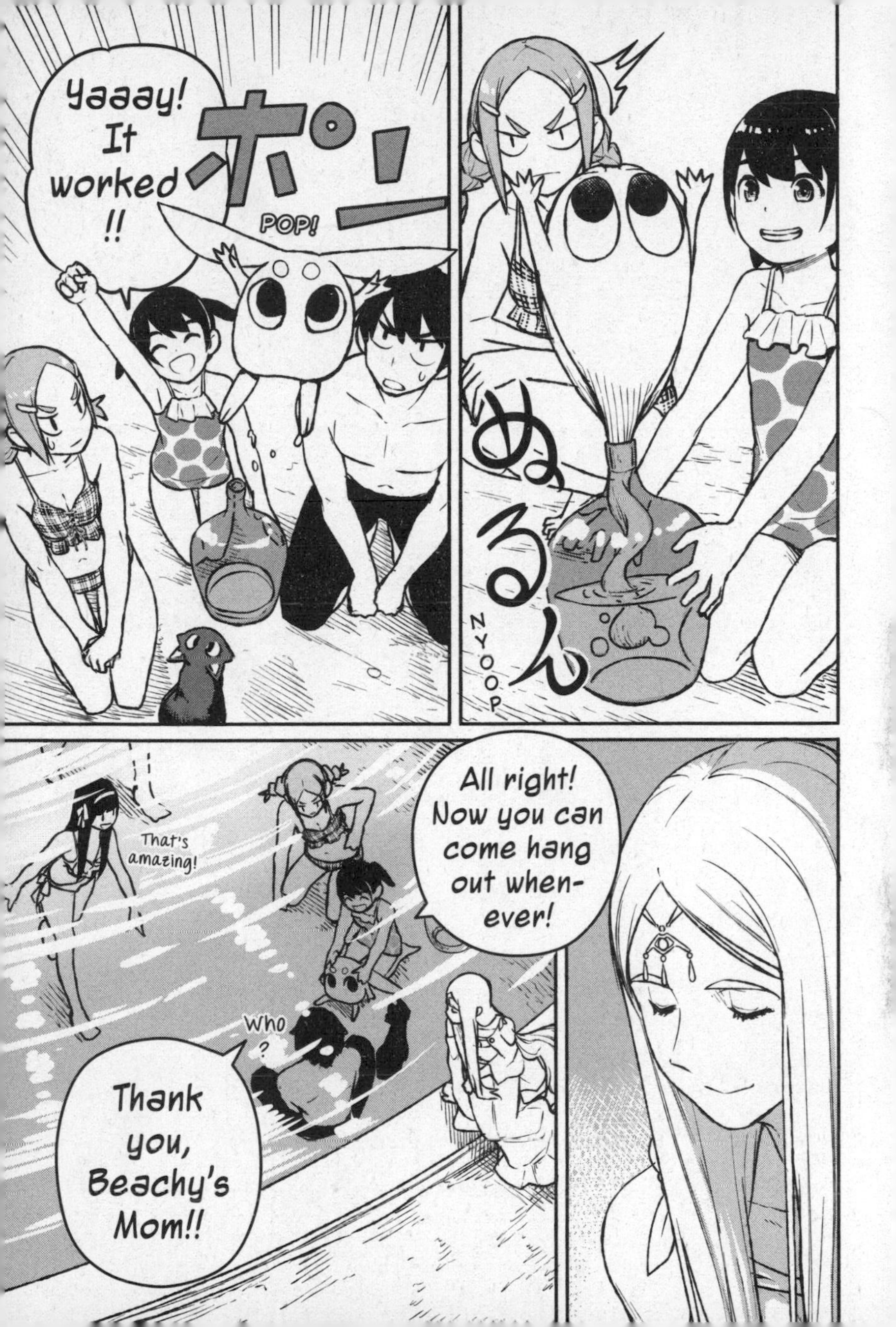
めるん
NYOOOP
Yaaay! It worked!!
ポー
POP!
All right! Now you can come hang out whenever!
That's amazing!
Who?
Thank you, Beachy's Mom!!

Chapter 53
Mandrake Evolution

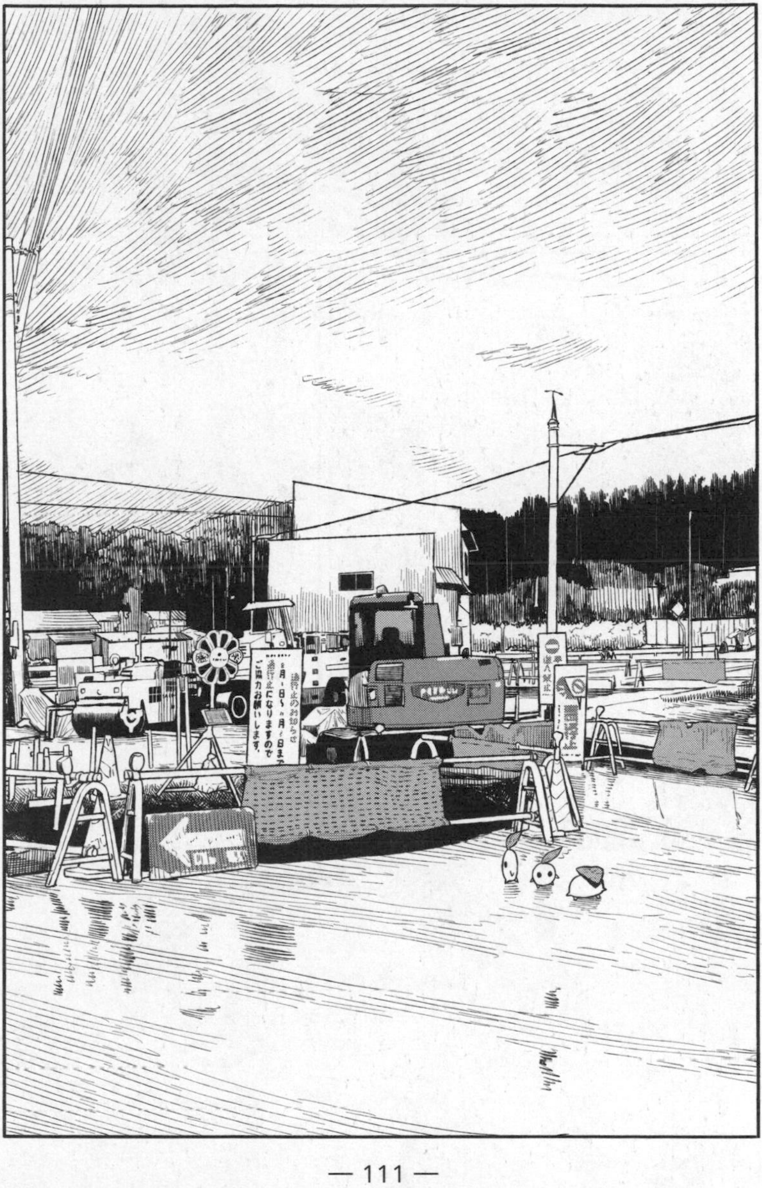
通行止のお知らせ
通行止になりますので
ご協力お願いします。

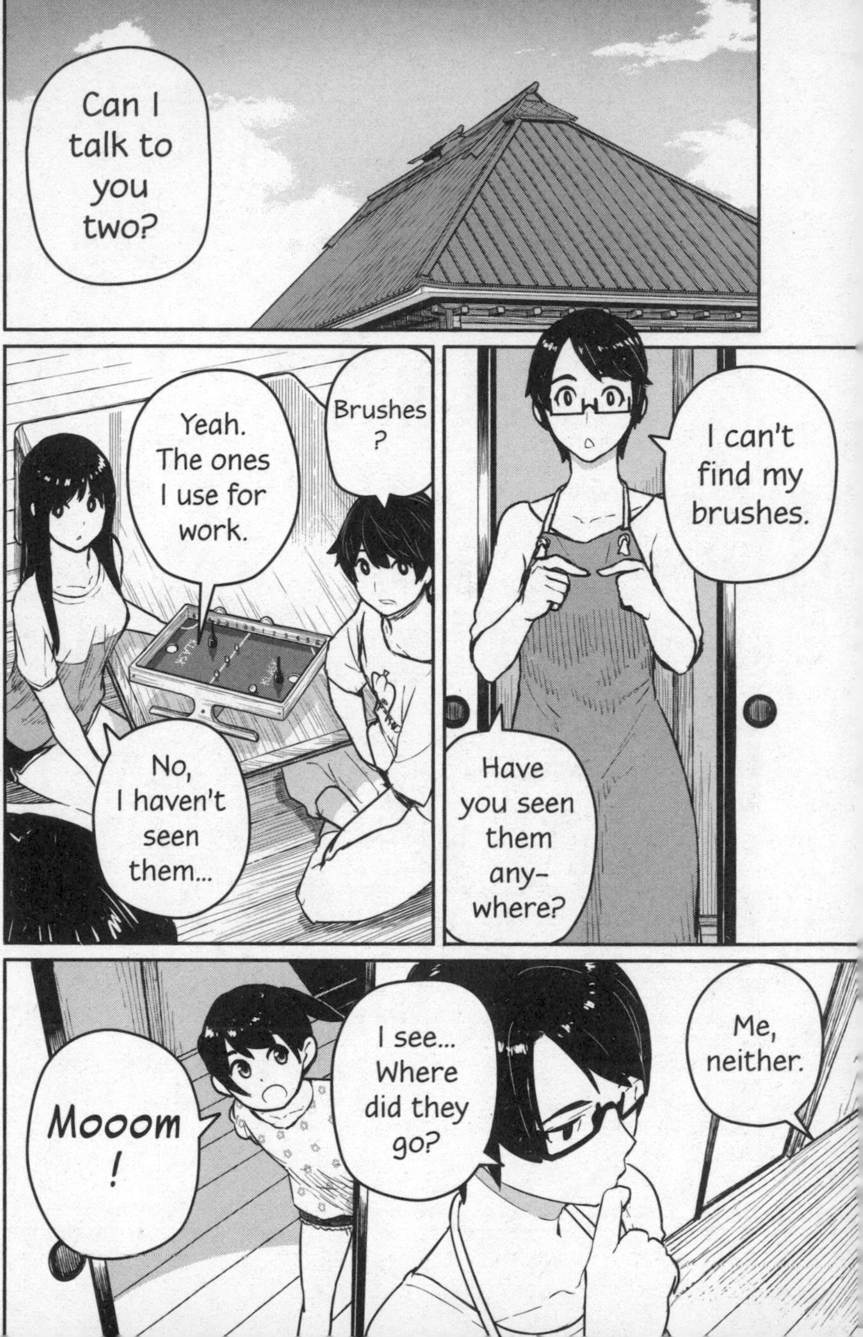
Can I talk to you two?
I can't find my brushes.
Have you seen them any-where?
Brushes?
Yeah. The ones I use for work.
No, I haven't seen them...
Me, neither.
I see... Where did they go?
Mooom!

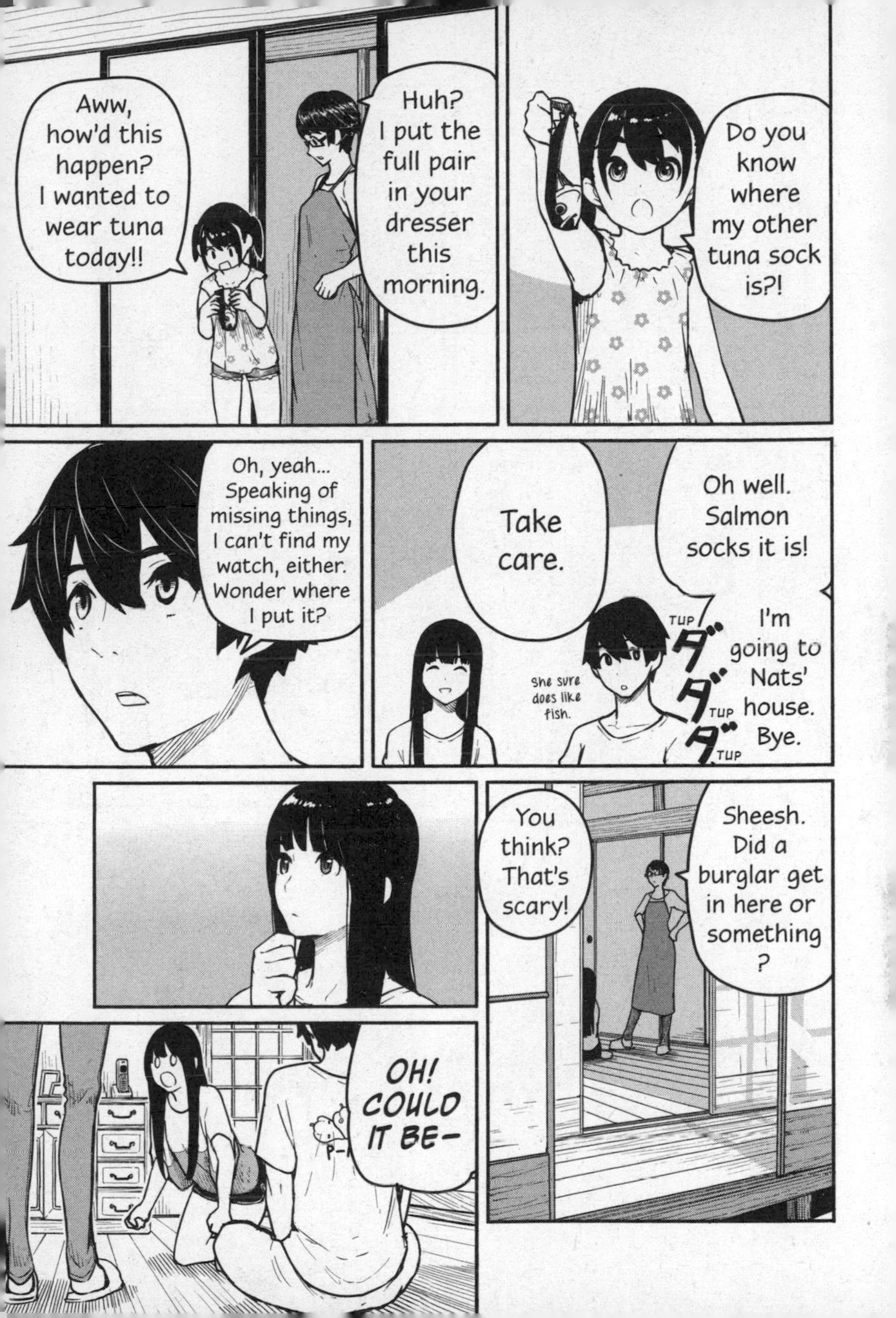
Do you know where my other tuna sock is?!
Huh? I put the full pair in your dresser this morning.
Aww, how'd this happen? I wanted to wear tuna today!!
Oh well. Salmon socks it is!
I'm going to Nats' house. Bye.
TUP ダ
TUP ダ
TUP ダ
Take care.
She sure does like fish.
Oh, yeah... Speaking of missing things, I can't find my watch, either. Wonder where I put it?
Sheesh. Did a burglar get in here or something?
You think? That's scary!
OH! COULD IT BE—

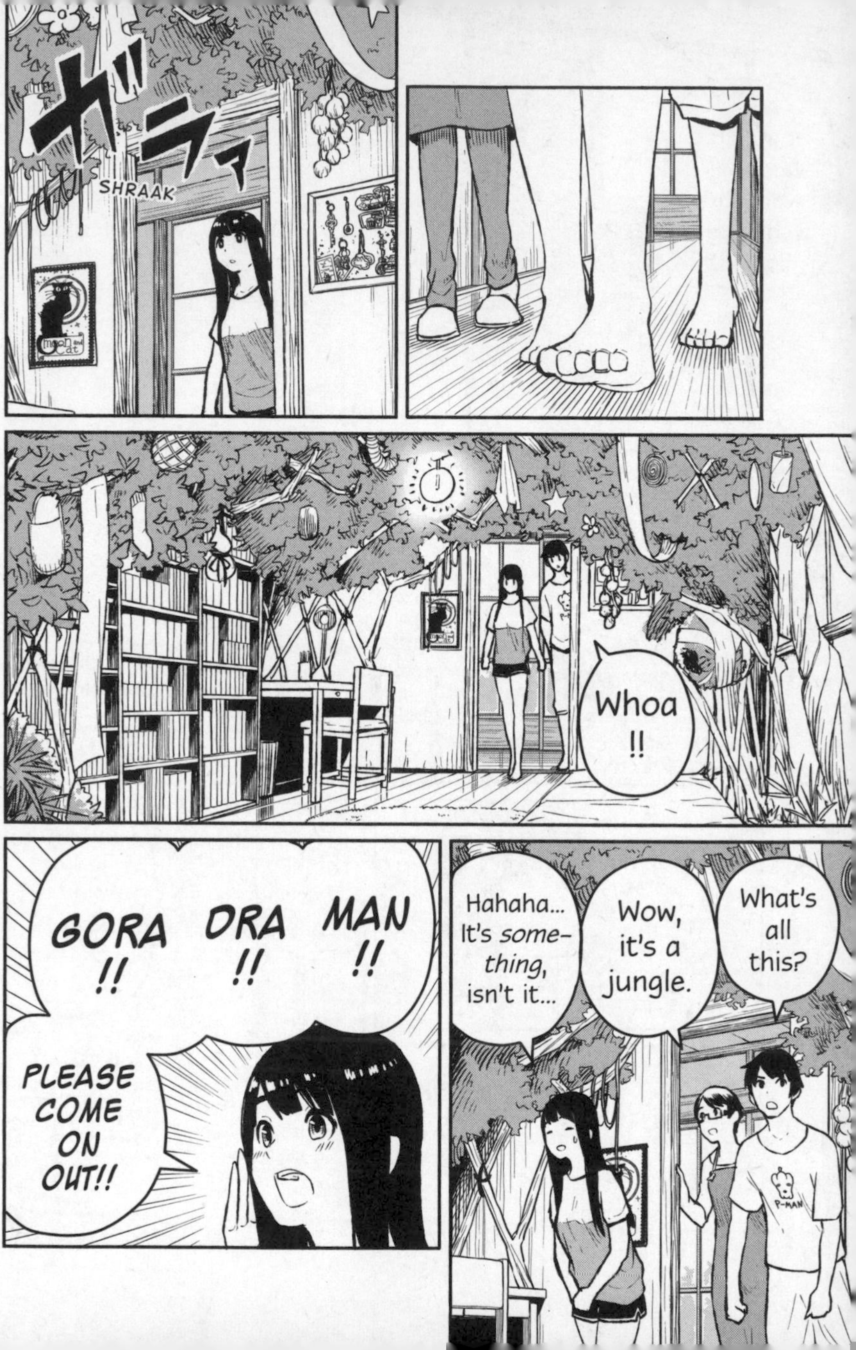
ガラァ
SHRAAK
Whoa!!
What's all this?
Wow, it's a jungle.
Hahaha... It's *something*, isn't it...
GORA!! DRA!! MAN!!
PLEASE COME ON OUT!!

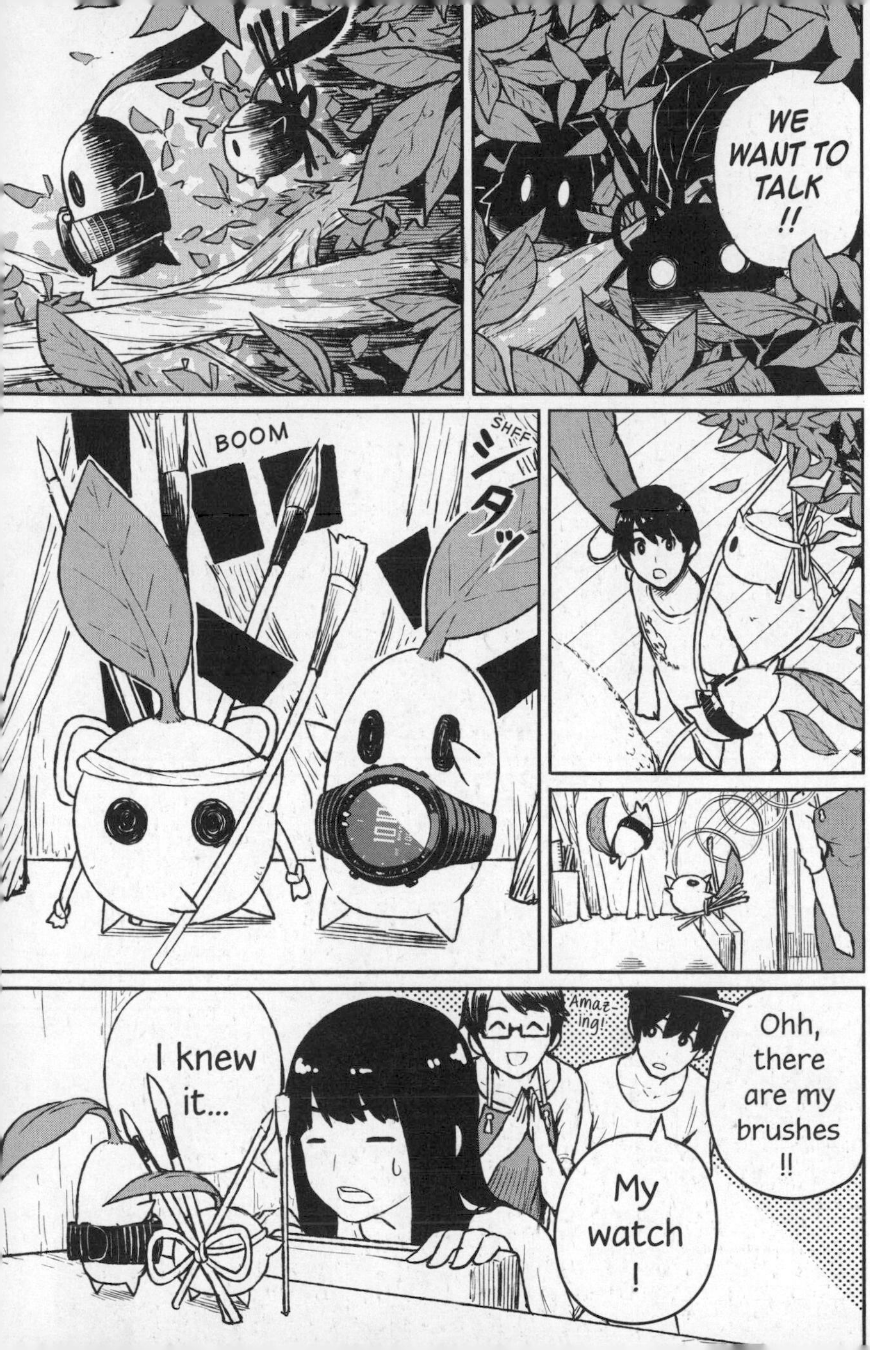
WE WANT TO TALK !!
SHFF
BOOM
Ohh, there are my brushes !!
Amaz-ing!
My watch !
I knew it...

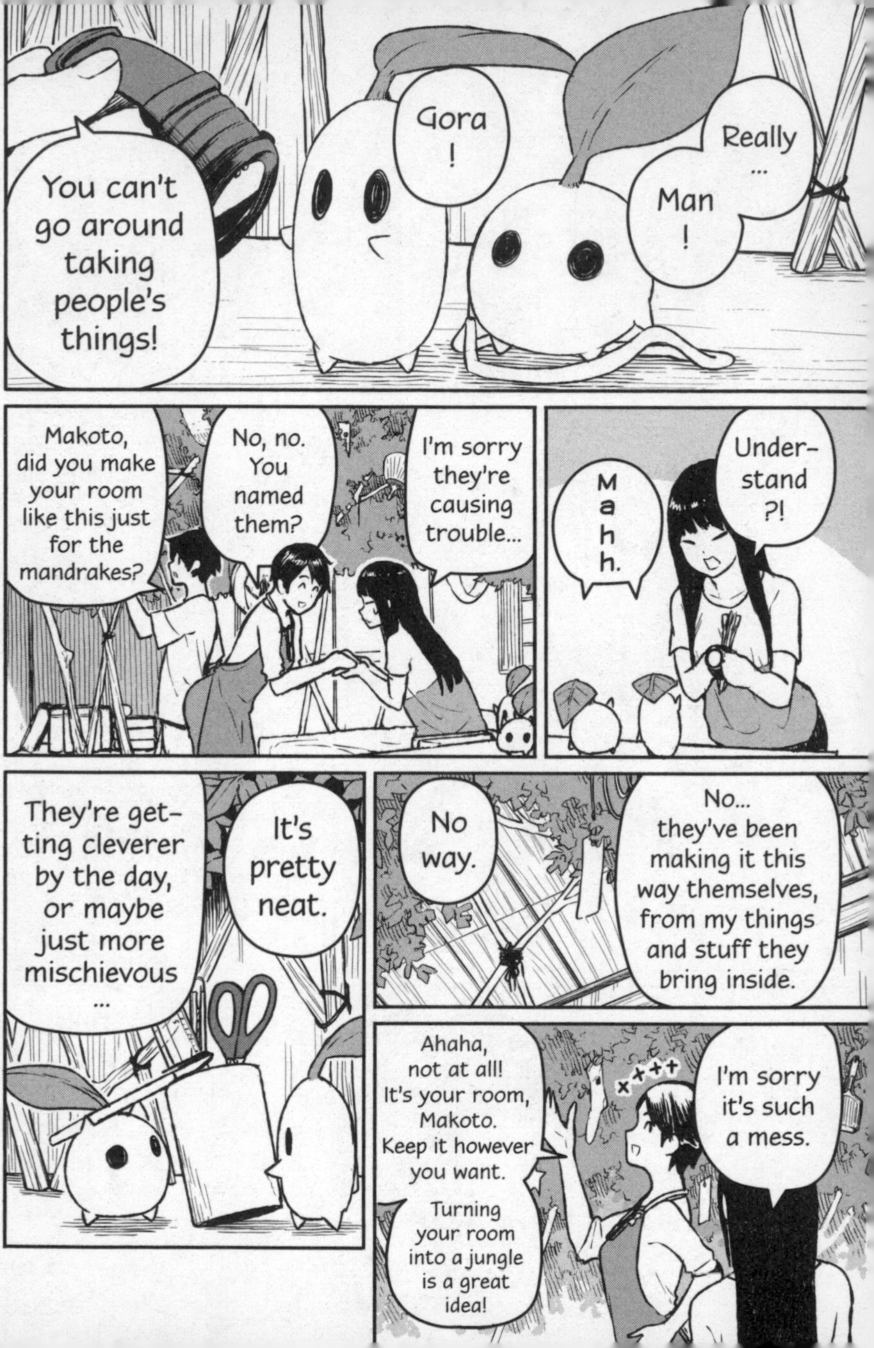
Really... Man!
Gora!
You can't go around taking people's things!
Under-stand?!
Mahh.
I'm sorry they're causing trouble...
No, no. You named them?
Makoto, did you make your room like this just for the mandrakes?
No... they've been making it this way themselves, from my things and stuff they bring inside.
No way.
I'm sorry it's such a mess.
Ahaha, not at all! It's your room, Makoto. Keep it however you want.
Turning your room into a jungle is a great idea!
It's pretty neat.
They're get-ting cleverer by the day, or maybe just more mischievous...

Mahh.

Wha? I don't see Dra...

?

クイ

TUG

Mahh.

I should pull on this?

Oh, there's the tuna sock.

FLUMP
パタ

スピ
BWEE

ゴワン
WOBBLE

ゴワン
WOBBLE

CLANG

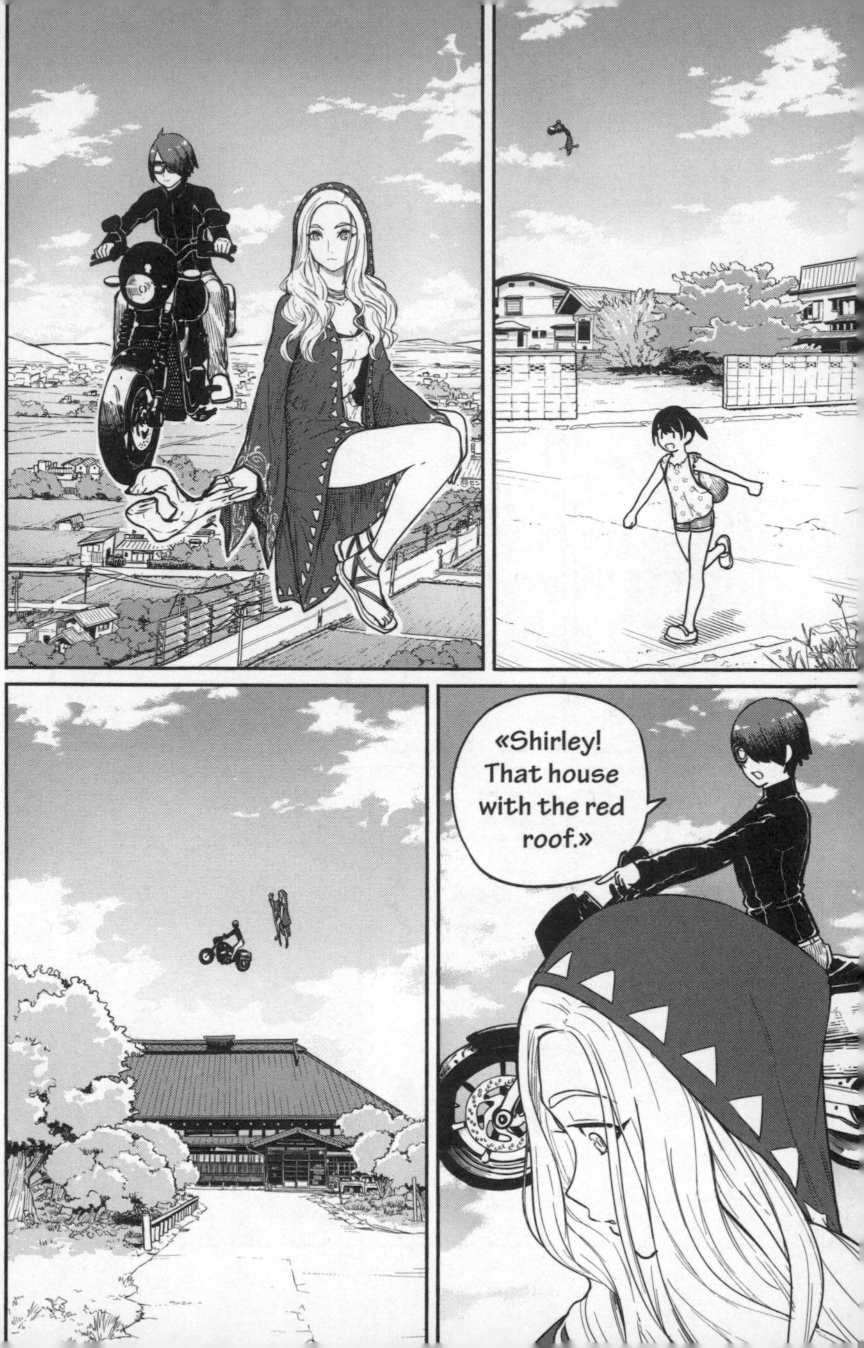
«Shirley! That house with the red roof.»

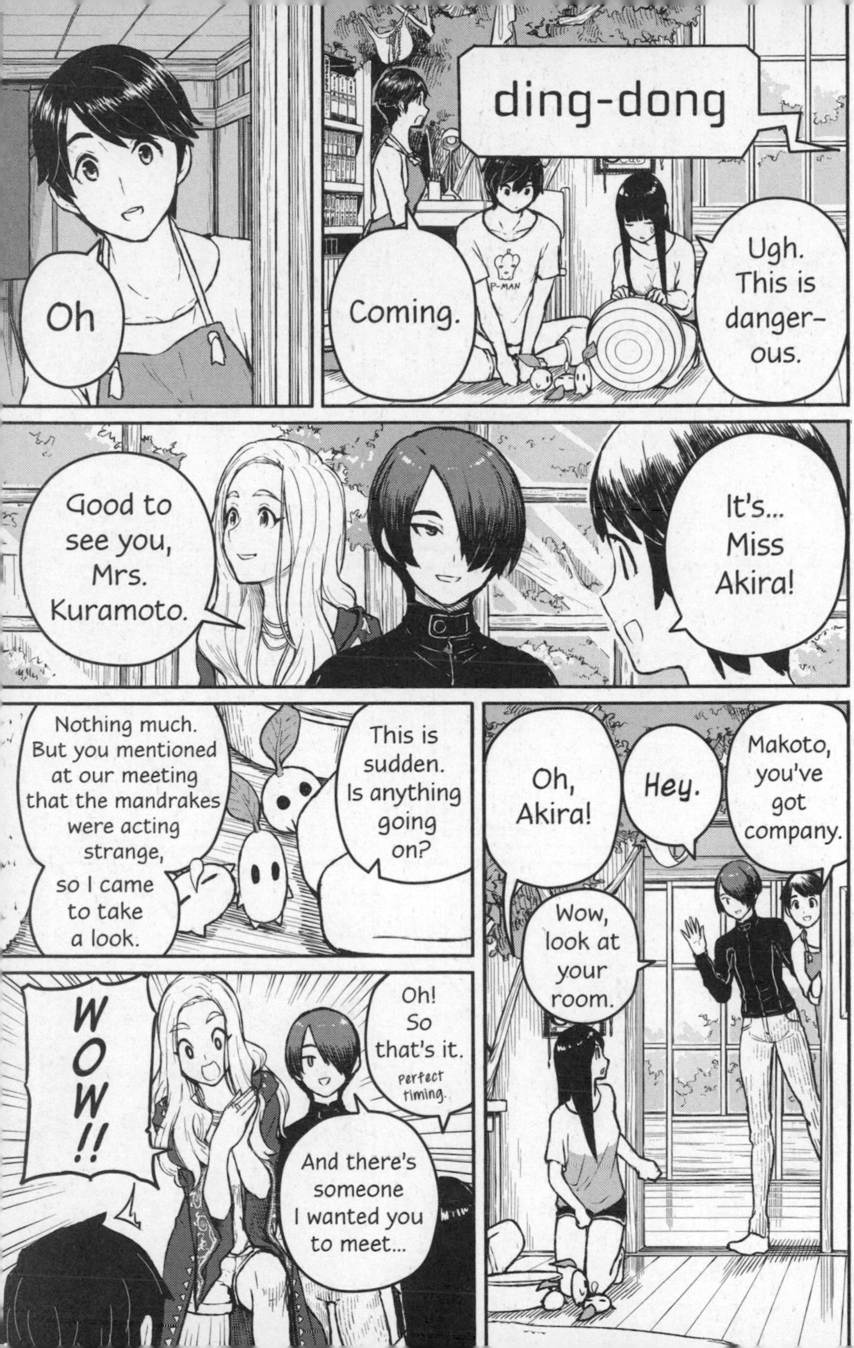
ding-dong
Ugh. This is danger-ous.
Coming.
Oh
It's... Miss Akira!
Good to see you, Mrs. Kuramoto.
Makoto, you've got company.
Hey.
Oh, Akira!
Wow, look at your room.
This is sudden. Is anything going on?
Nothing much. But you mentioned at our meeting that the mandrakes were acting strange,
so I came to take a look.
Oh! So that's it.
Perfect timing.
WOW!!
And there's someone I wanted you to meet...

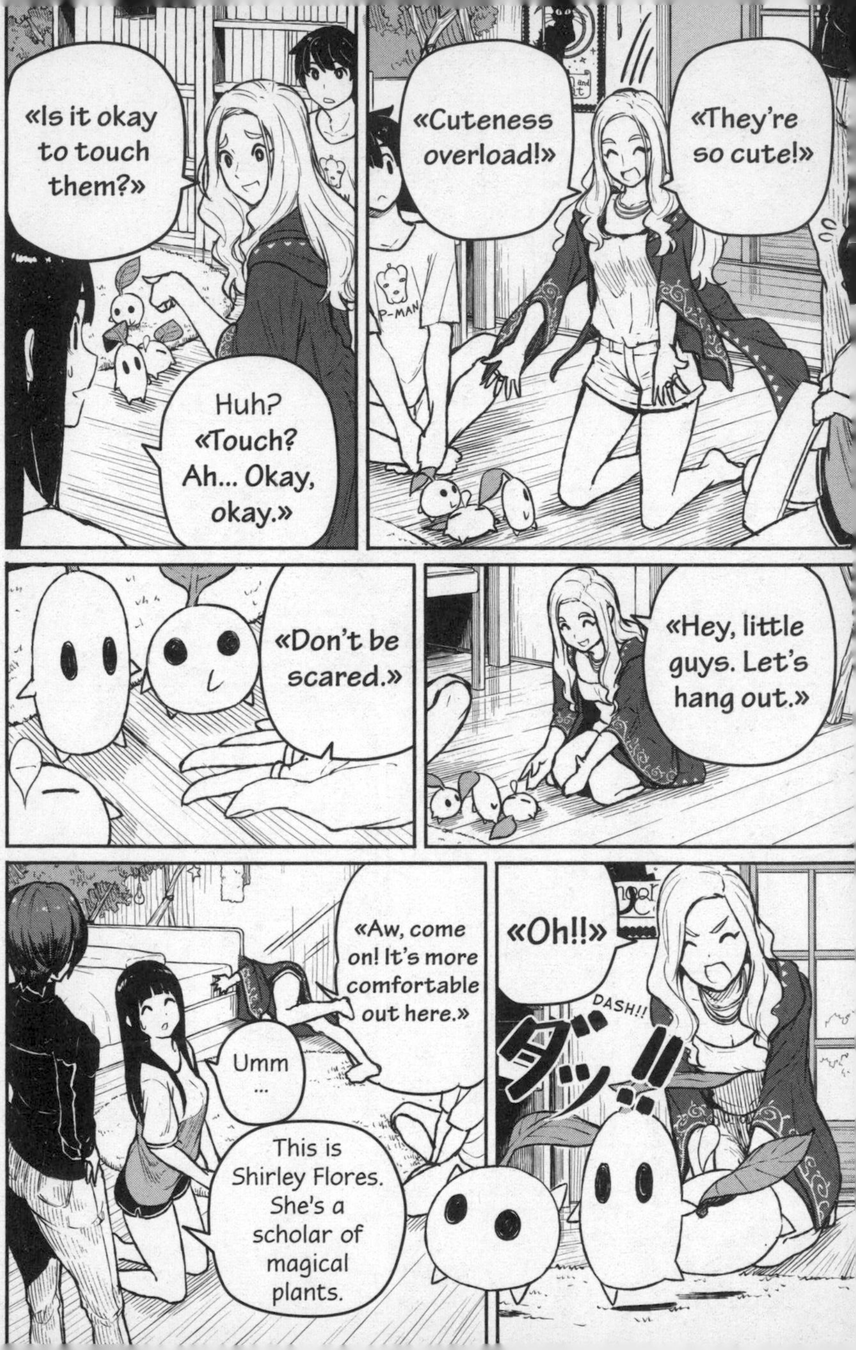
«They're so cute!»
«Cuteness overload!»
«Is it okay to touch them?»
Huh? «Touch? Ah... Okay, okay.»
«Hey, little guys. Let's hang out.»
«Don't be scared.»
«Oh!!»
DASH!!
ダッ!!
«Aw, come on! It's more comfortable out here.»
Umm ...
This is Shirley Flores. She's a scholar of magical plants.

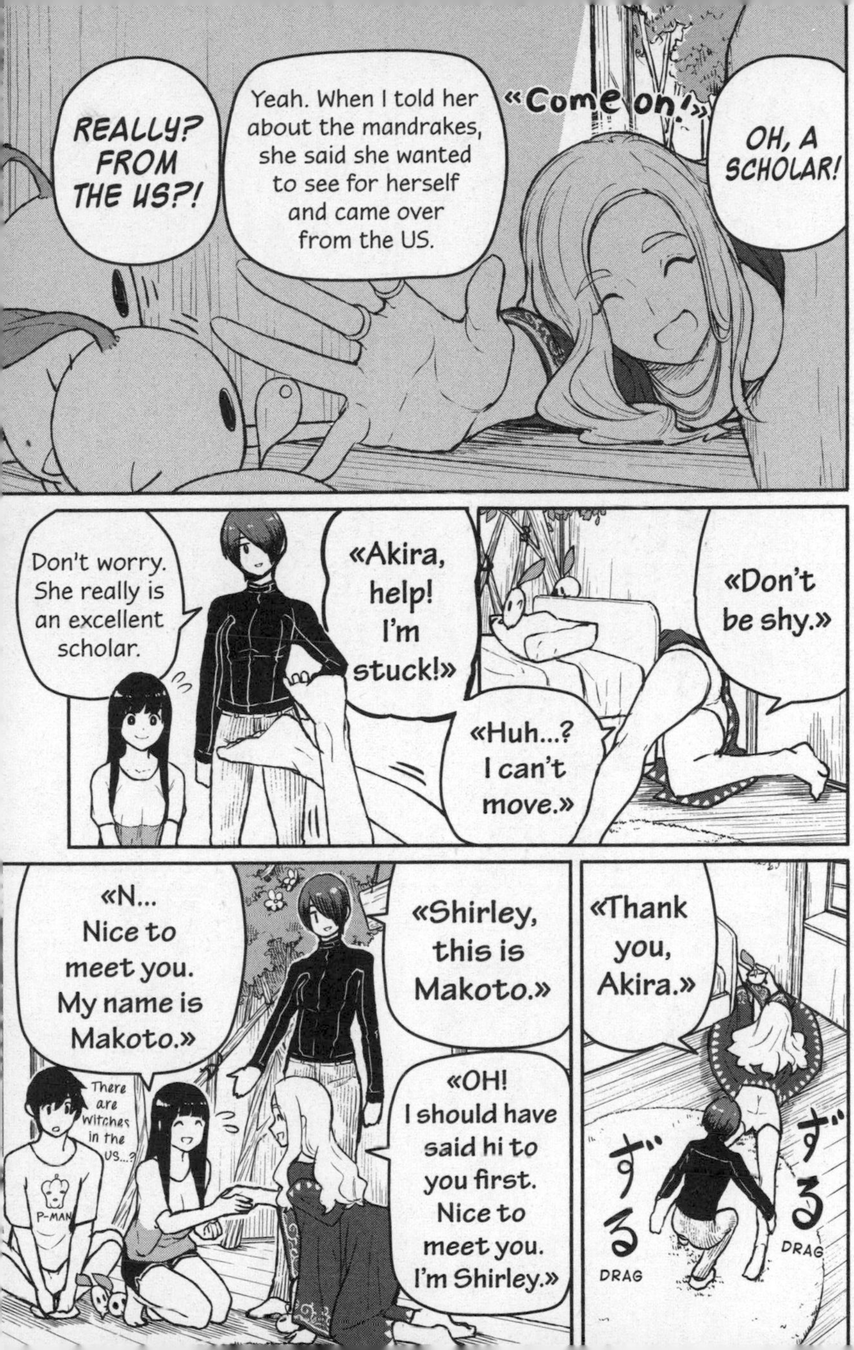
OH, A SCHOLAR!
«Come on!»
Yeah. When I told her about the mandrakes, she said she wanted to see for herself and came over from the US.
REALLY? FROM THE US?!
«Don't be shy.»
«Huh...? I can't move.»
«Akira, help! I'm stuck!»
Don't worry. She really is an excellent scholar.
«Thank you, Akira.»
ずる
DRAG
ずる
DRAG
«Shirley, this is Makoto.»
«N... Nice to meet you. My name is Makoto.»
«OH! I should have said hi to you first. Nice to meet you. I'm Shirley.»
There are witches in the US...?
P-MAN

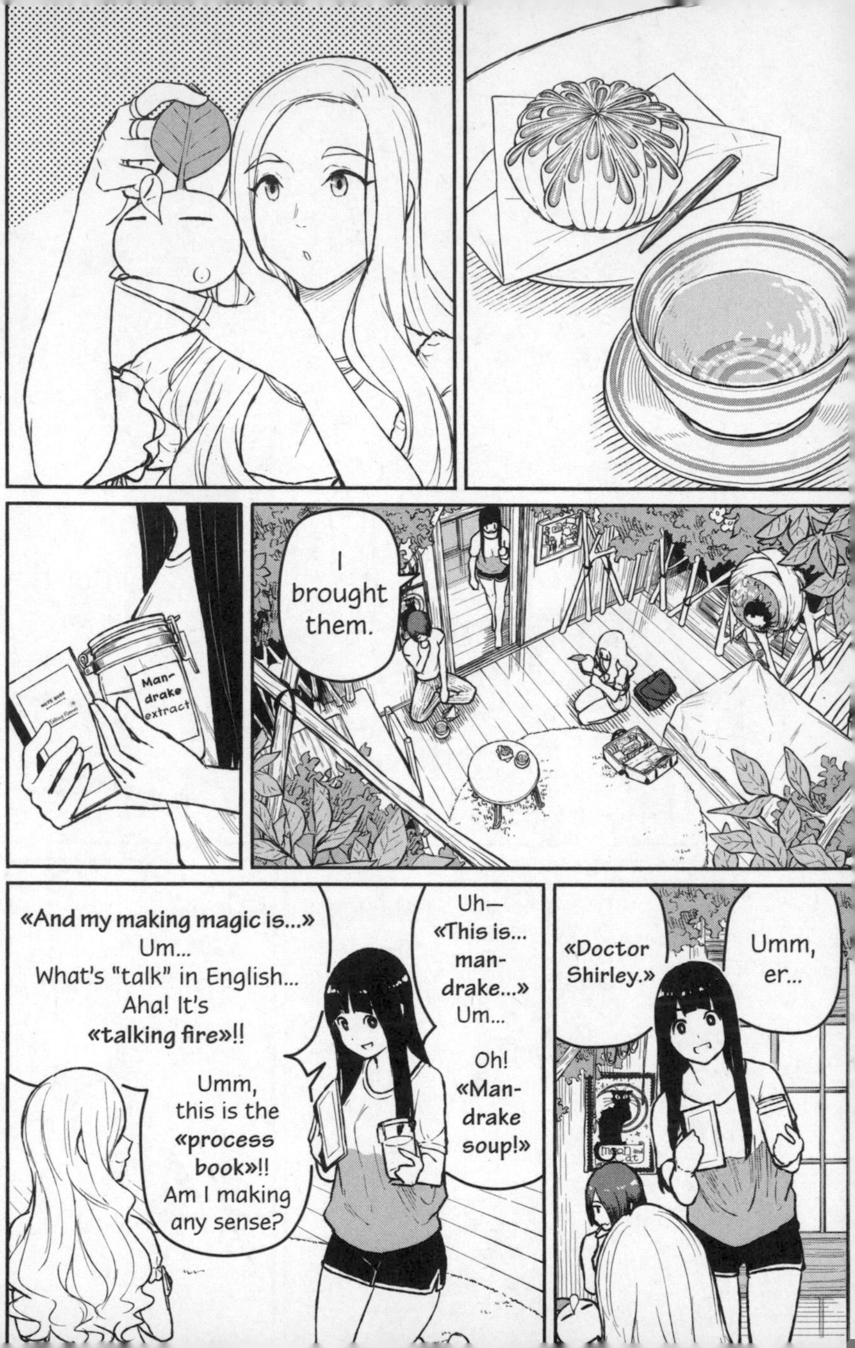

I brought them.
Man-drake extract
Umm, er...
«Doctor Shirley.»
Uh— «This is... man-drake...» Um...
Oh! «Man-drake soup!»
«And my making magic is...» Um... What's "talk" in English... Aha! It's «talking fire»!!
Umm, this is the «process book»!! Am I making any sense?

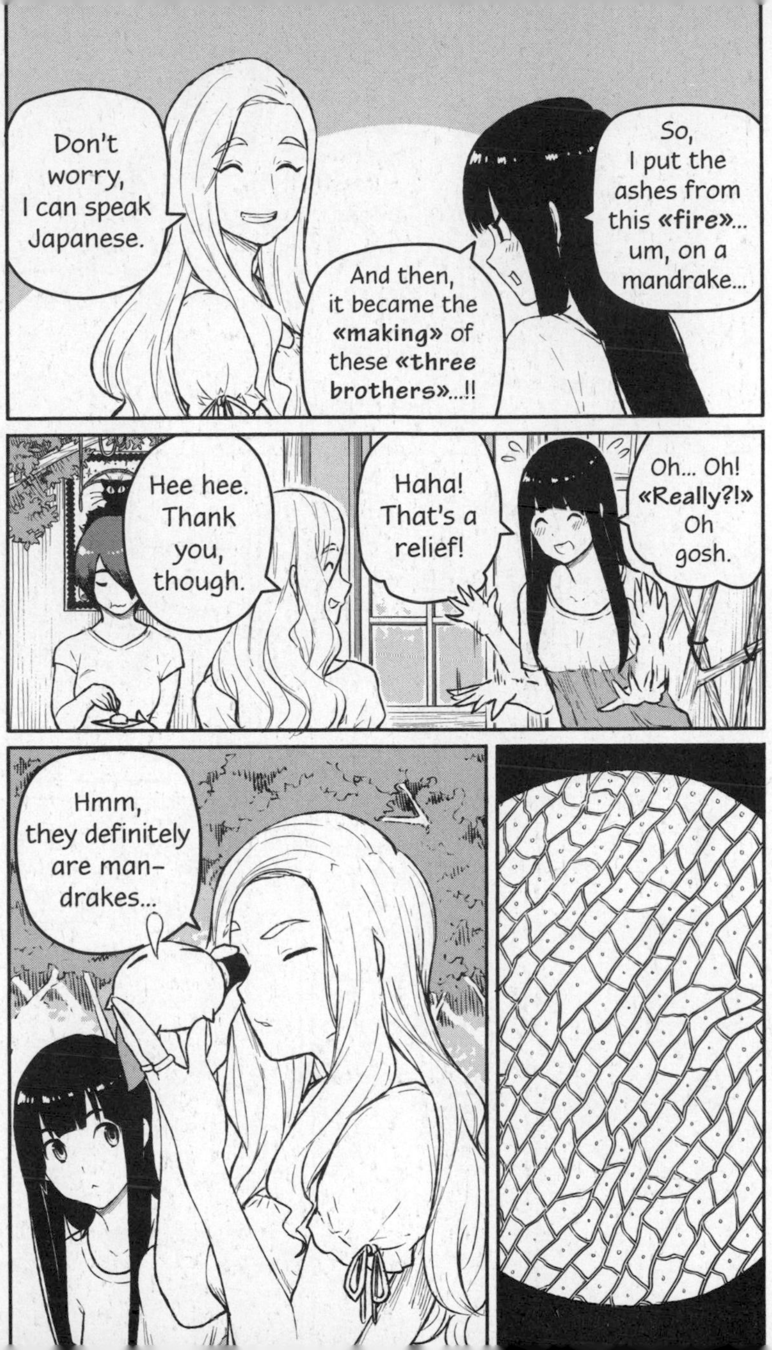
So, I put the ashes from this «fire»... um, on a mandrake...
And then, it became the «making» of these «three brothers»...!!
Don't worry, I can speak Japanese.
Oh... Oh! «Really?!» Oh gosh.
Haha! That's a relief!
Hee hee. Thank you, though.
Hmm, they definitely are man-drakes...

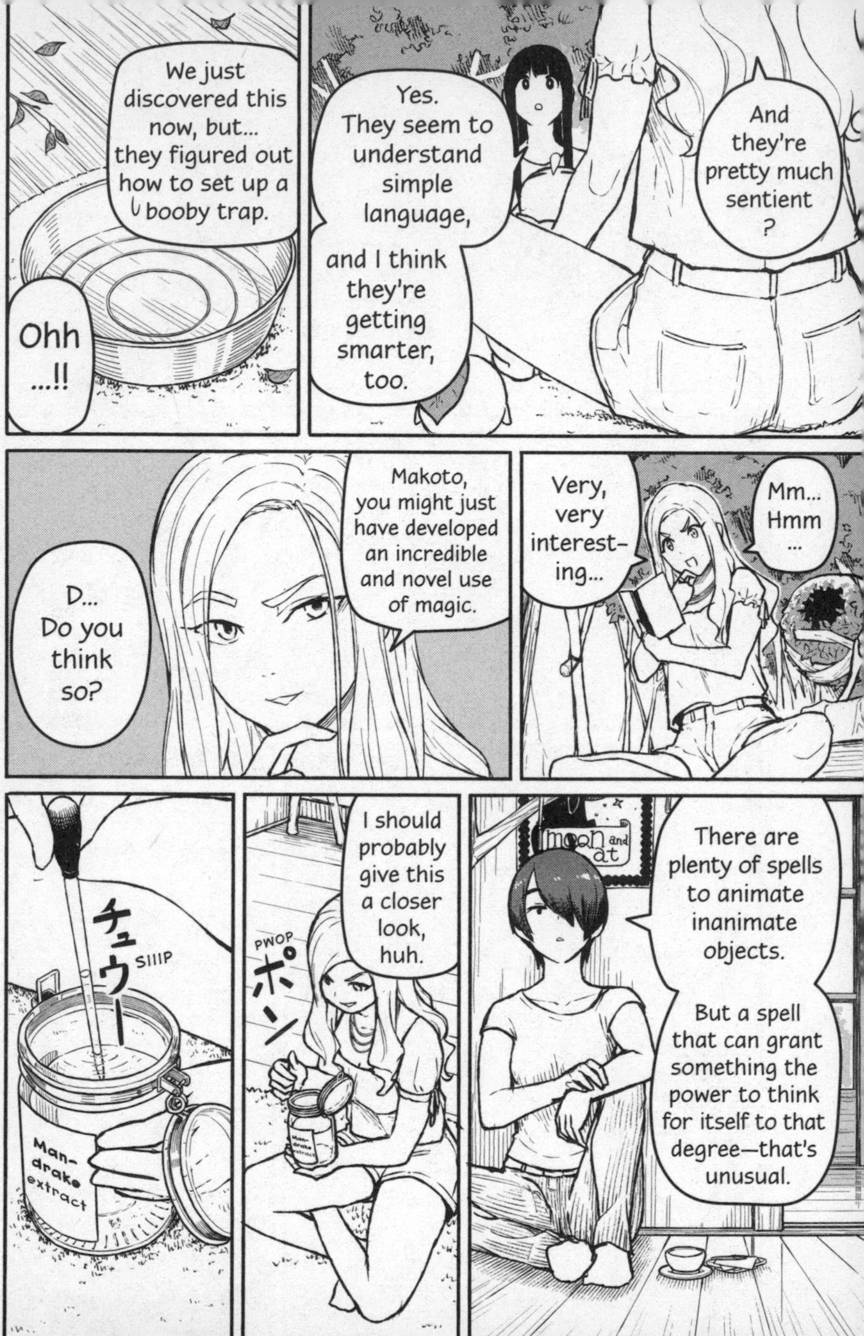
And they're pretty much sentient ?
Yes. They seem to understand simple language,
and I think they're getting smarter, too.
We just discovered this now, but... they figured out how to set up a booby trap.
Ohh ...!!
Mm... Hmm ...
Very, very interest-ing...
Makoto, you might just have developed an incredible and novel use of magic.
D... Do you think so?
There are plenty of spells to animate inanimate objects.
But a spell that can grant something the power to think for itself to that degree—that's unusual.
I should probably give this a closer look, huh.
ポン
PWOP
Man-drake extract
チュウー
SIIIP
Man-drake extract

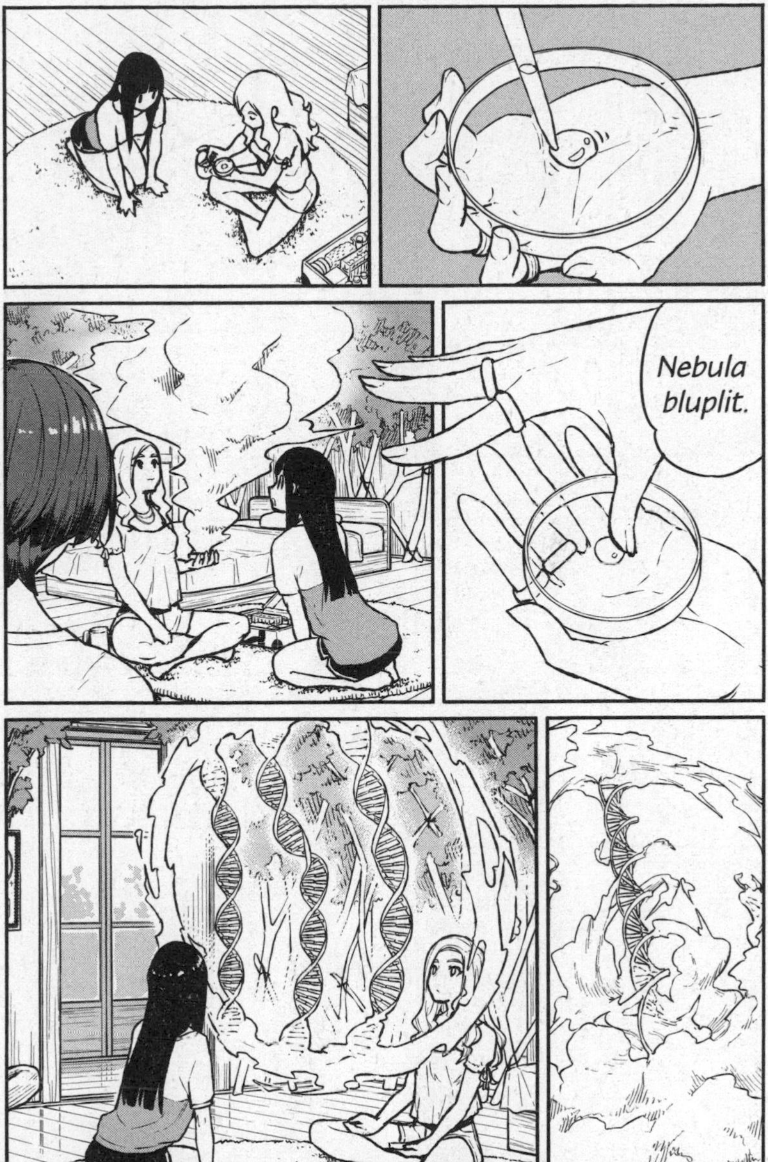
Nebula bluplit.

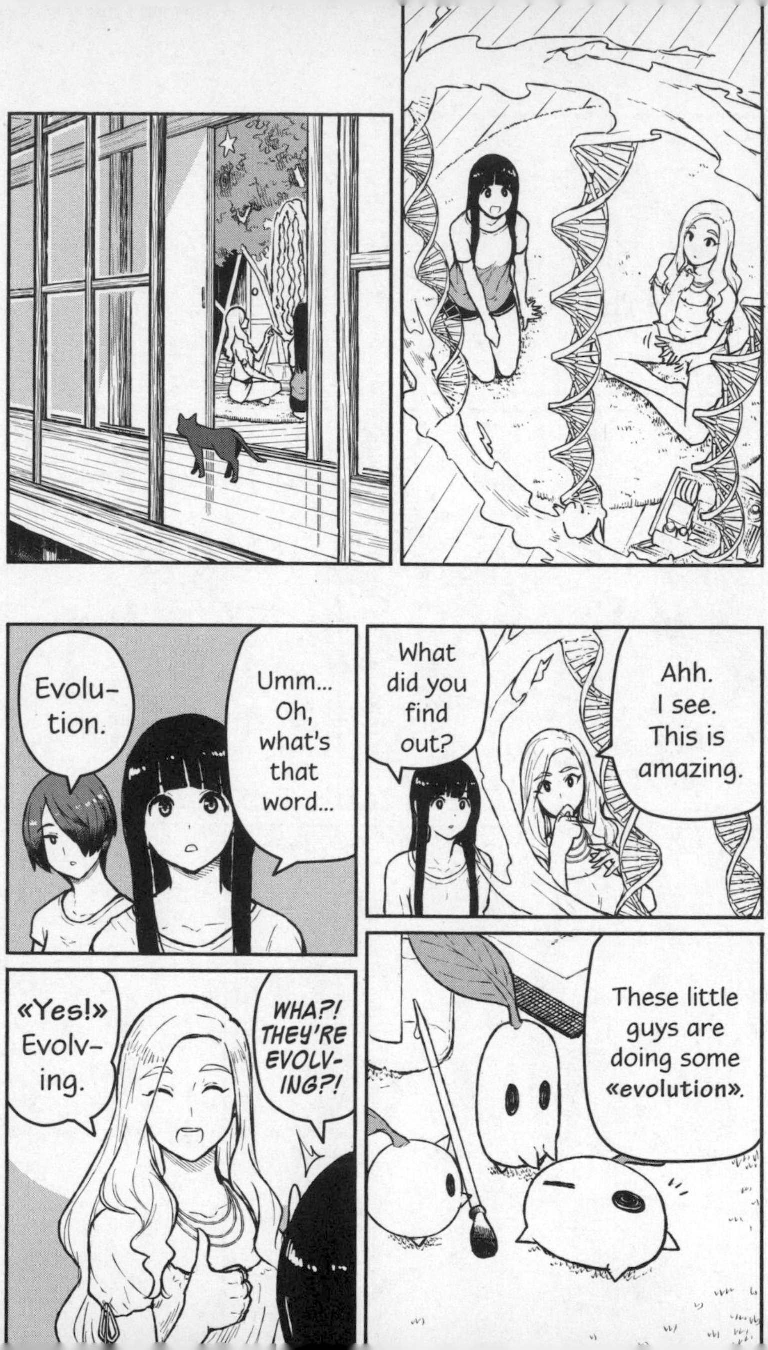
Ahh. I see. This is amazing.
What did you find out?
Umm... Oh, what's that word...
Evolu-tion.
These little guys are doing some «evolution».
WHA?! THEY'RE EVOLV-ING?!
«Yes!» Evolv-ing.

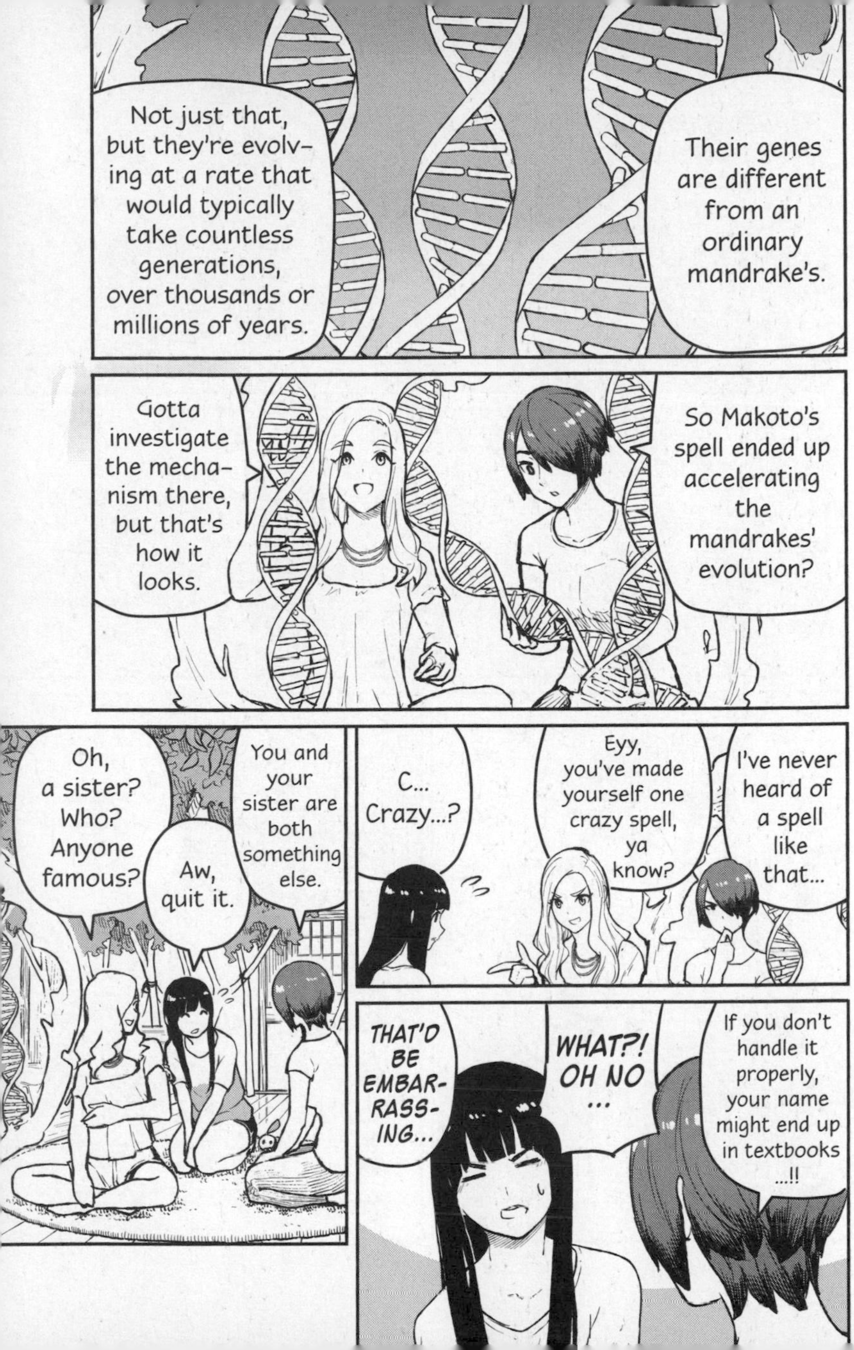
Their genes are different from an ordinary mandrake's.
Not just that, but they're evolving at a rate that would typically take countless generations, over thousands or millions of years.
So Makoto's spell ended up accelerating the mandrakes' evolution?
Gotta investigate the mechanism there, but that's how it looks.
I've never heard of a spell like that...
Eyy, you've made yourself one crazy spell, ya know?
C... Crazy...?
If you don't handle it properly, your name might end up in textbooks ...!!
WHAT?! OH NO ...
THAT'D BE EMBARRASSING...
You and your sister are both something else.
Aw, quit it.
Oh, a sister? Who? Anyone famous?

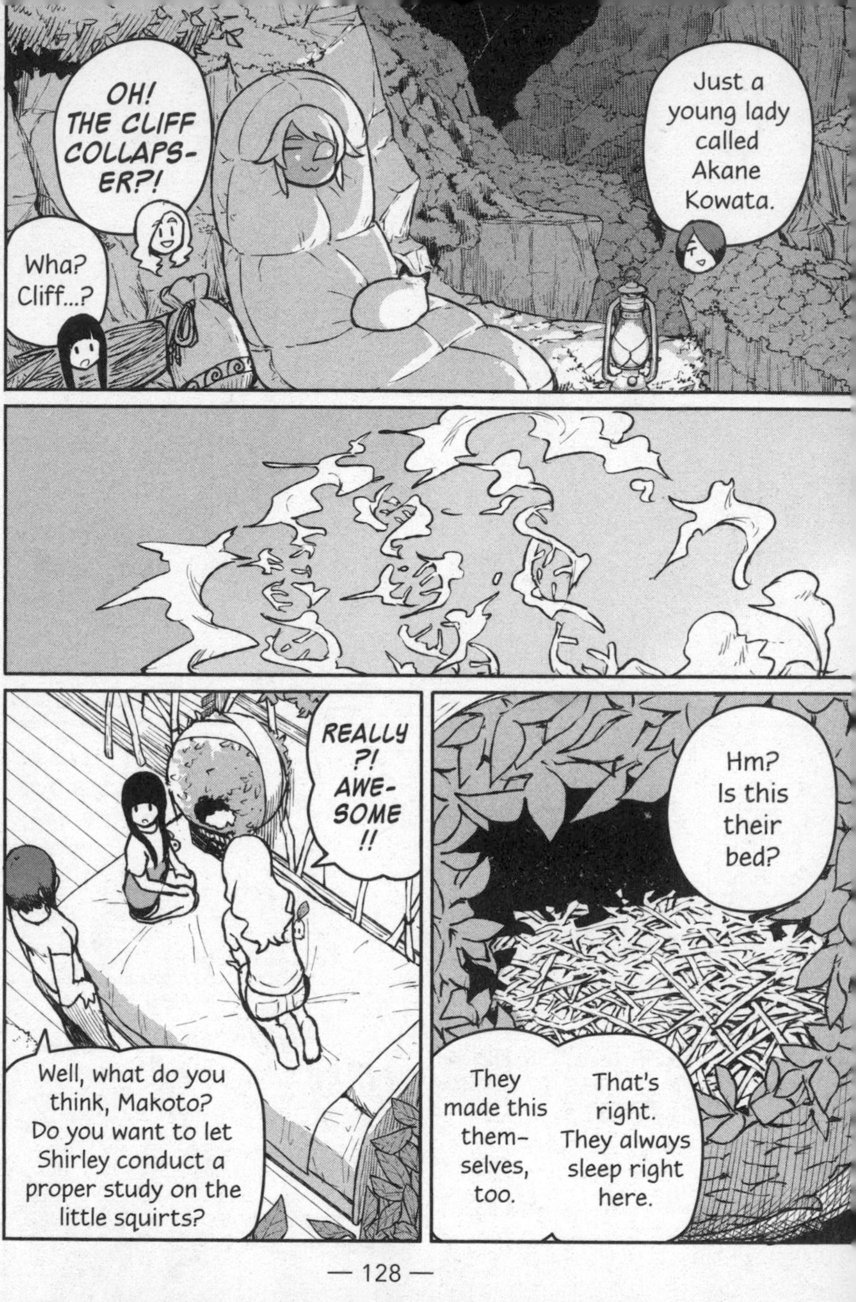
Just a young lady called Akane Kowata.
OH! THE CLIFF COLLAPSER?!
Wha? Cliff...?
Hm? Is this their bed?
That's right. They always sleep right here.
They made this themselves, too.
REALLY?! AWESOME!!
Well, what do you think, Makoto? Do you want to let Shirley conduct a proper study on the little squirts?

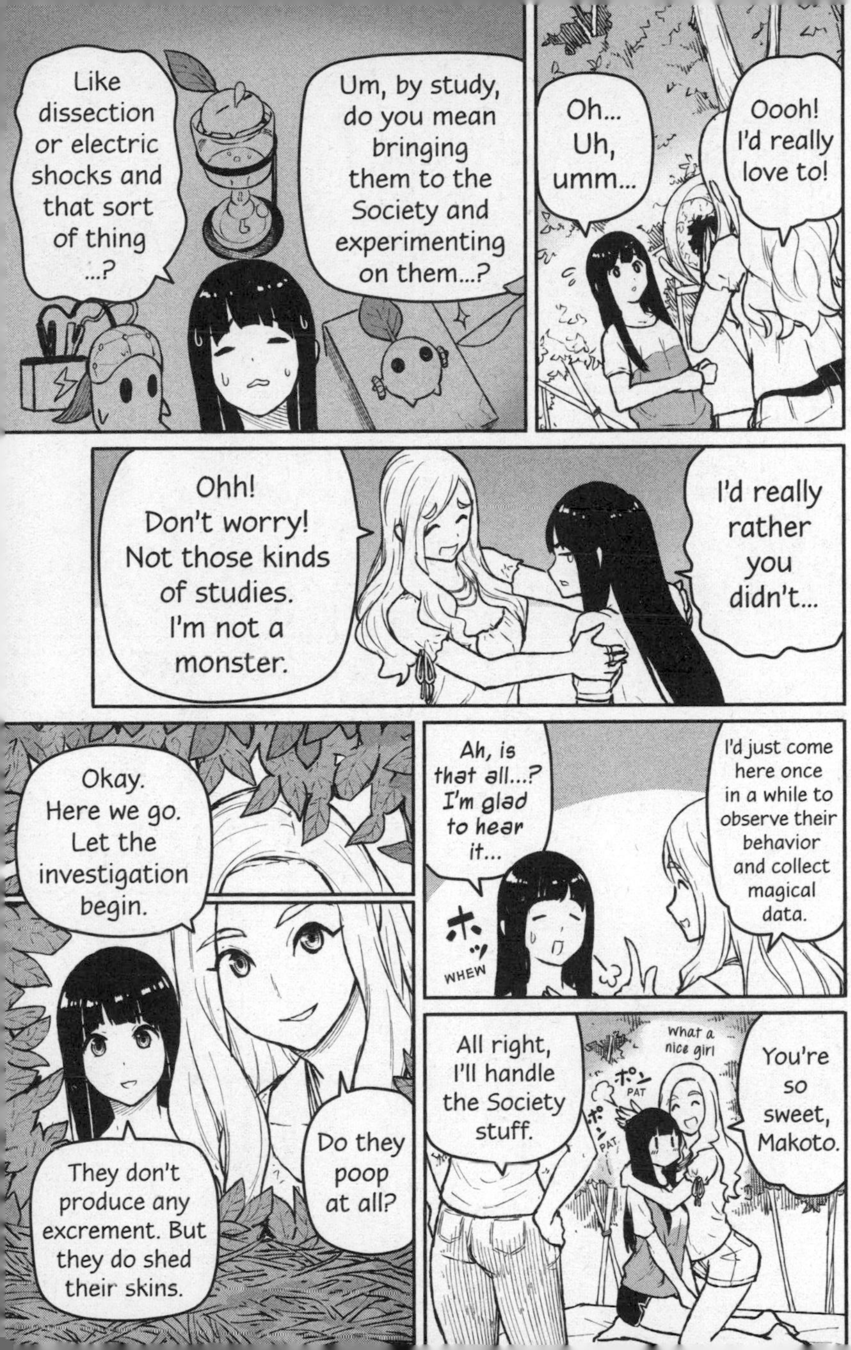

Oooh! I'd really love to!
Oh... Uh, umm...
Um, by study, do you mean bringing them to the Society and experimenting on them...?
Like dissection or electric shocks and that sort of thing ...?
I'd really rather you didn't...
Ohh! Don't worry! Not those kinds of studies. I'm not a monster.
I'd just come here once in a while to observe their behavior and collect magical data.
Ah, is that all...? I'm glad to hear it...
ホッ
WHEW
You're so sweet, Makoto.
What a nice girl
ポン
PAT
ポン
PAT
All right, I'll handle the Society stuff.
Okay. Here we go. Let the investigation begin.
Do they poop at all?
They don't produce any excrement. But they do shed their skins.

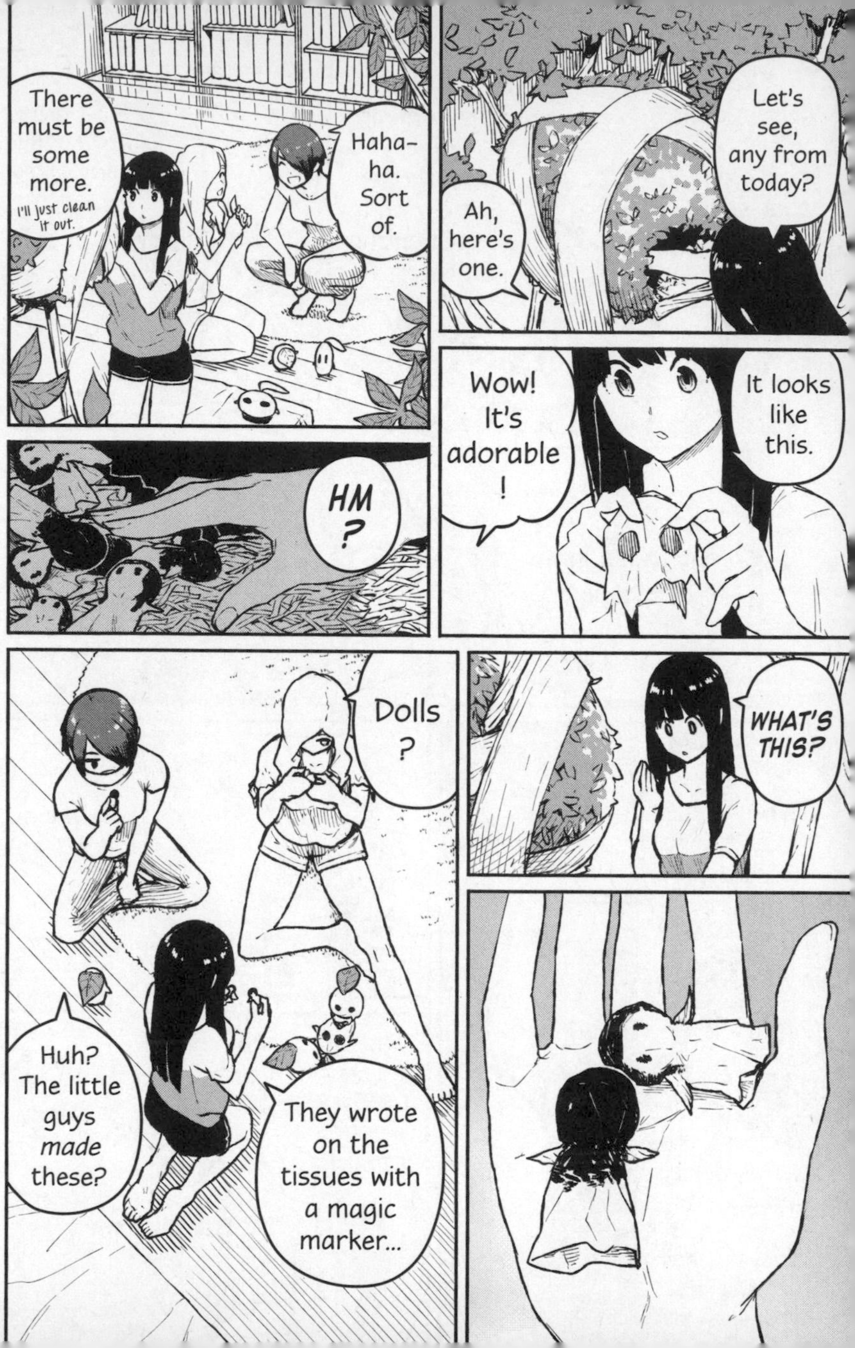
Let's see, any from today?
Ah, here's one.
Haha-ha. Sort of.
There must be some more.
I'll just clean it out.
It looks like this.
Wow! It's adorable!
HM?
WHAT'S THIS?
Dolls?
Huh? The little guys *made* these?
They wrote on the tissues with a magic marker...

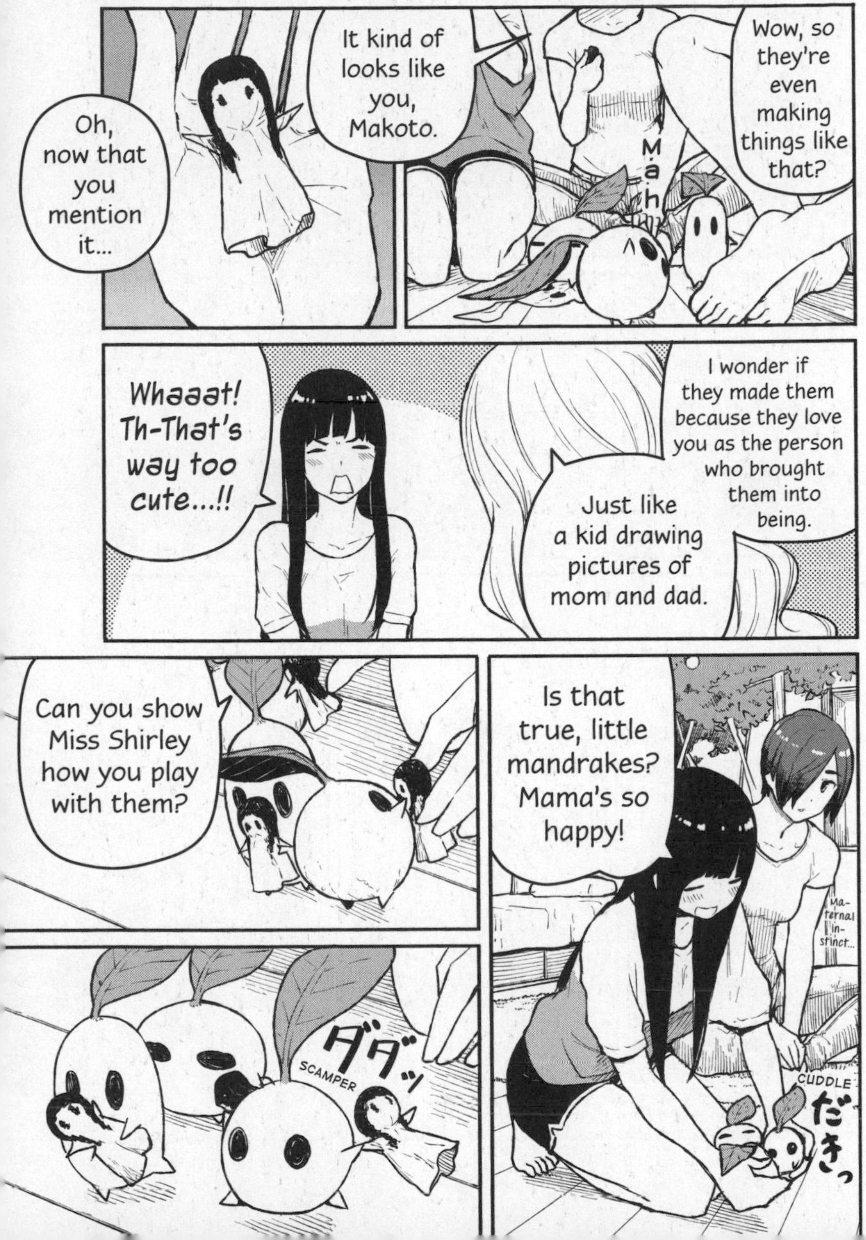

Wow, so they're even making things like that?
Mah
It kind of looks like you, Makoto.
Oh, now that you mention it...
I wonder if they made them because they love you as the person who brought them into being.
Just like a kid drawing pictures of mom and dad.
Whaaat! Th-That's way too cute...!!
Is that true, little mandrakes? Mama's so happy!
Maternal instinct...
CUDDLE
だきっ
Can you show Miss Shirley how you play with them?
ダダッ
SCAMPER

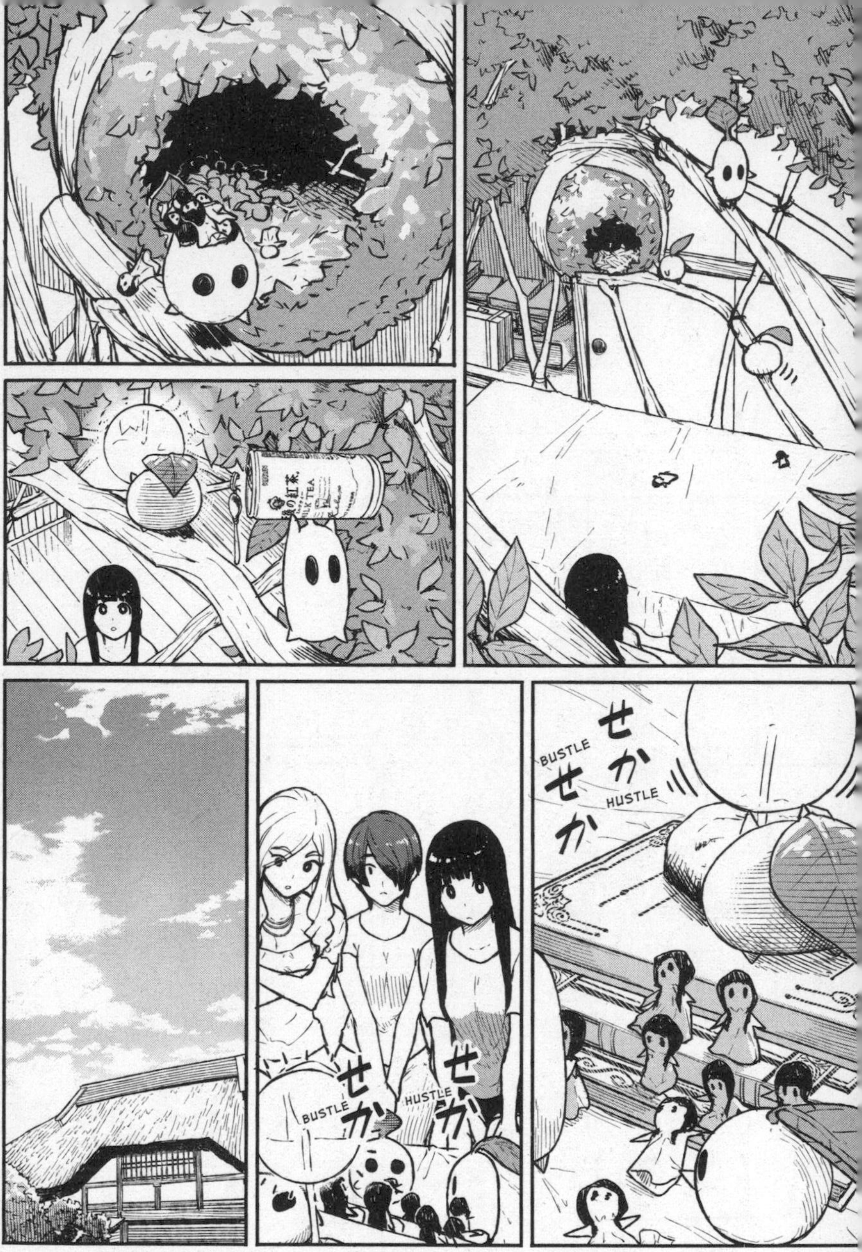
せか
せか
BUSTLE
HUSTLE
せか
HUSTLE
せか
BUSTLE

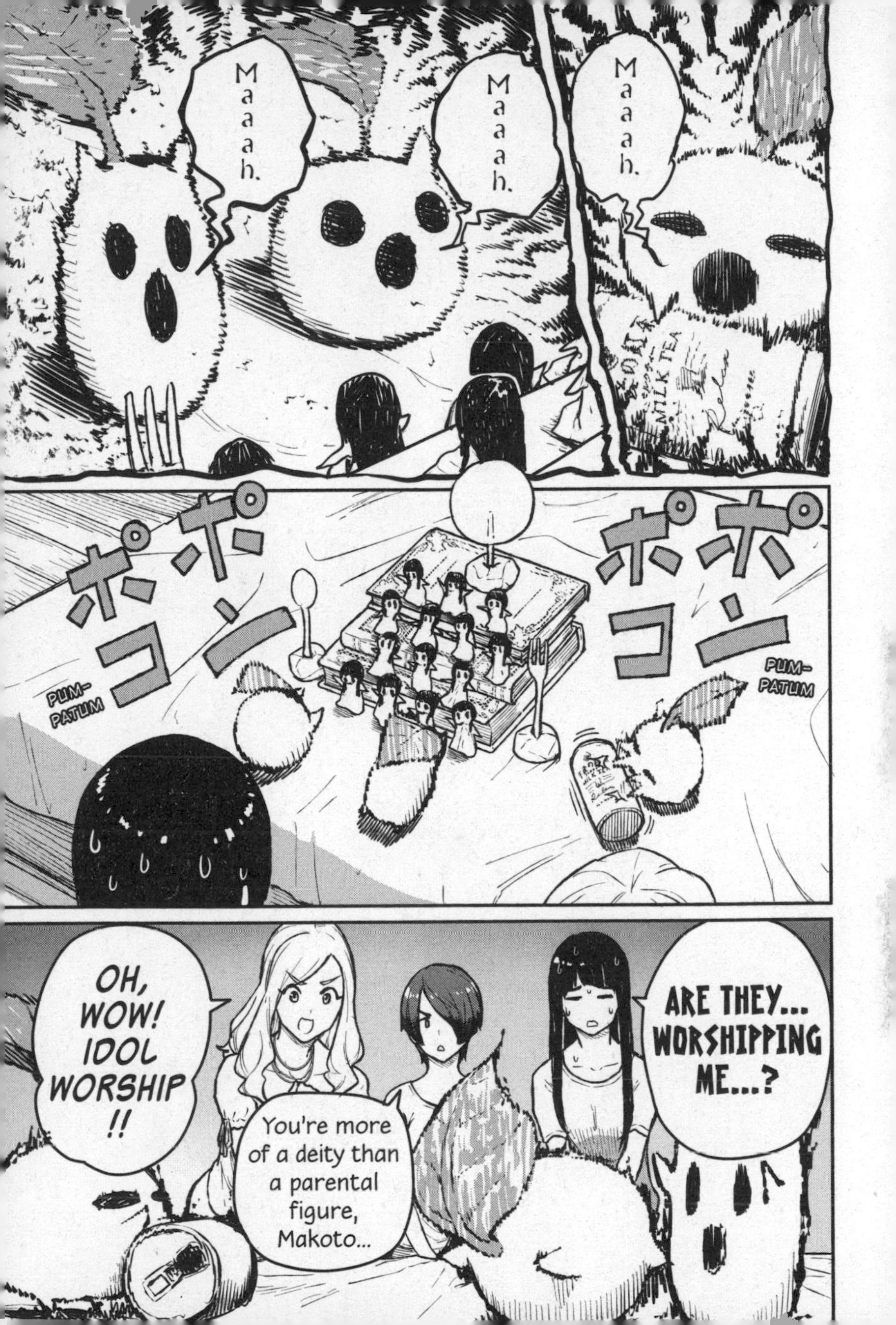
Maaaah.
Maaaah.
Maaah.
MILK TEA
ポコポン
PUM-PATUM
ポコポン
PUM-PATUM
ARE THEY... WORSHIPPING ME...?
OH, WOW! IDOL WORSHIP!!
You're more of a deity than a parental figure, Makoto...

Chapter 54
The Deva Kings are Foodies

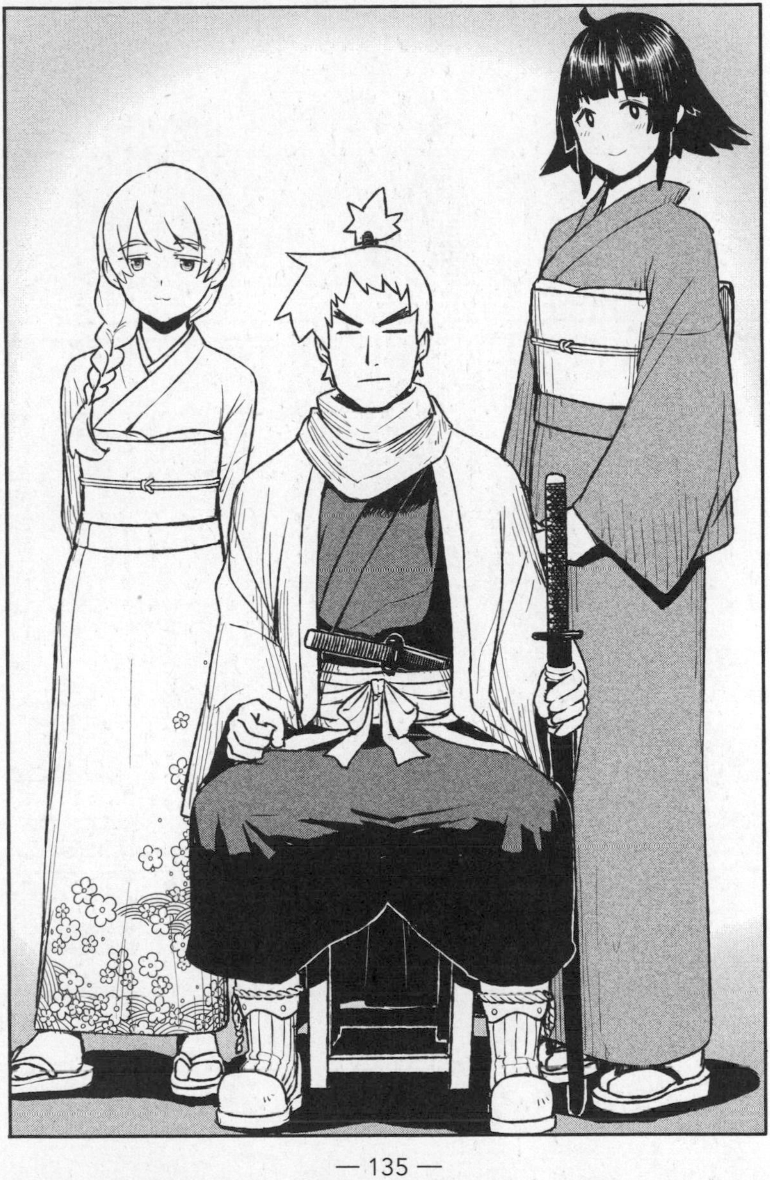

A game of shogi.

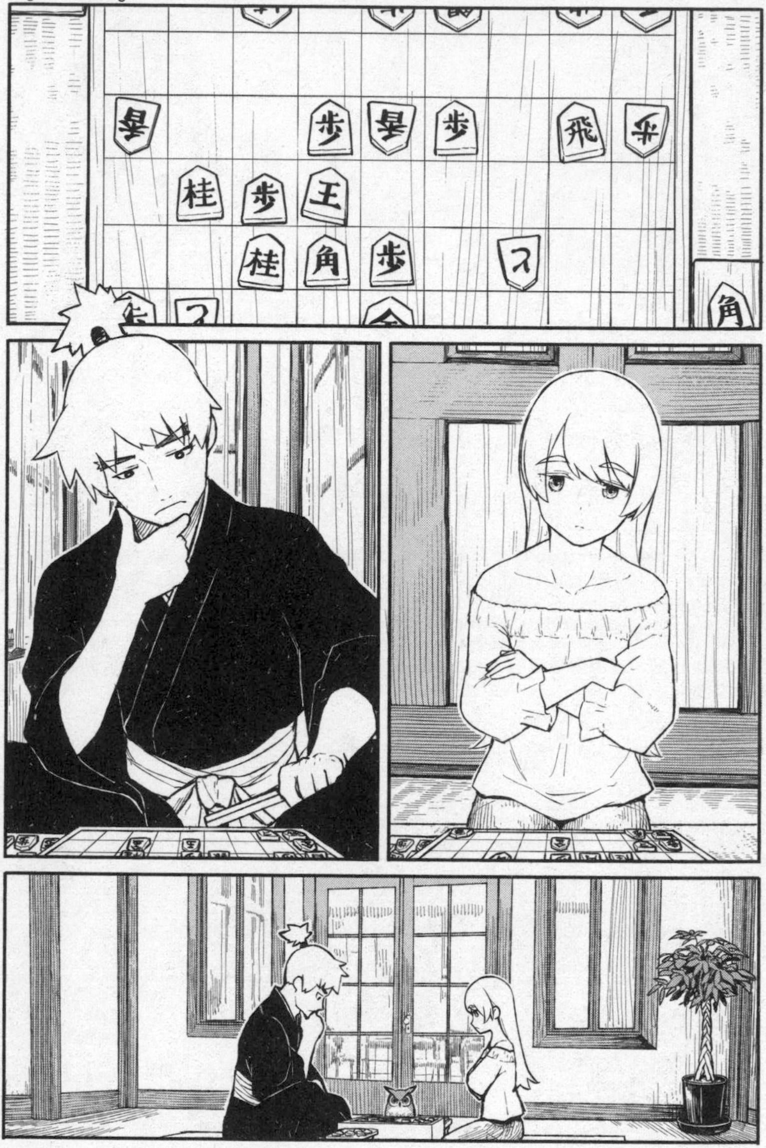

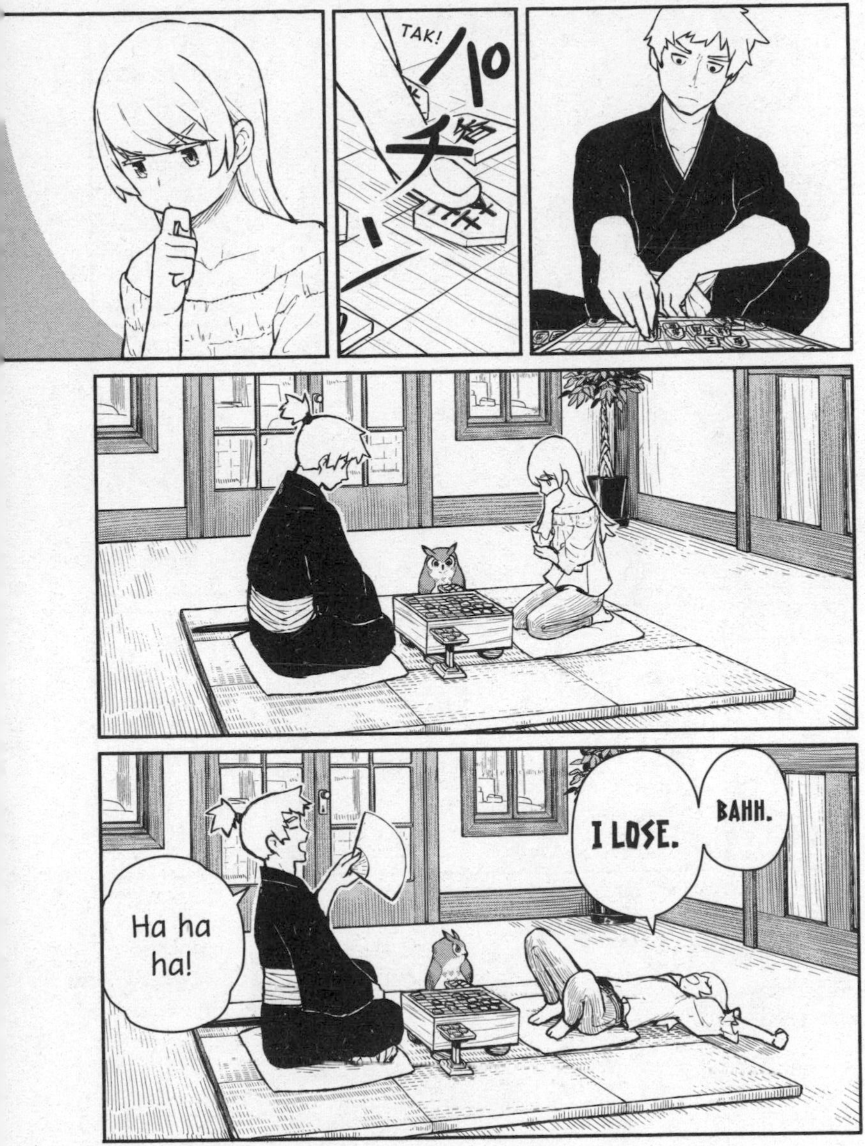
TAK!
パチ
BAHH.
I LOSE.
Ha ha ha!

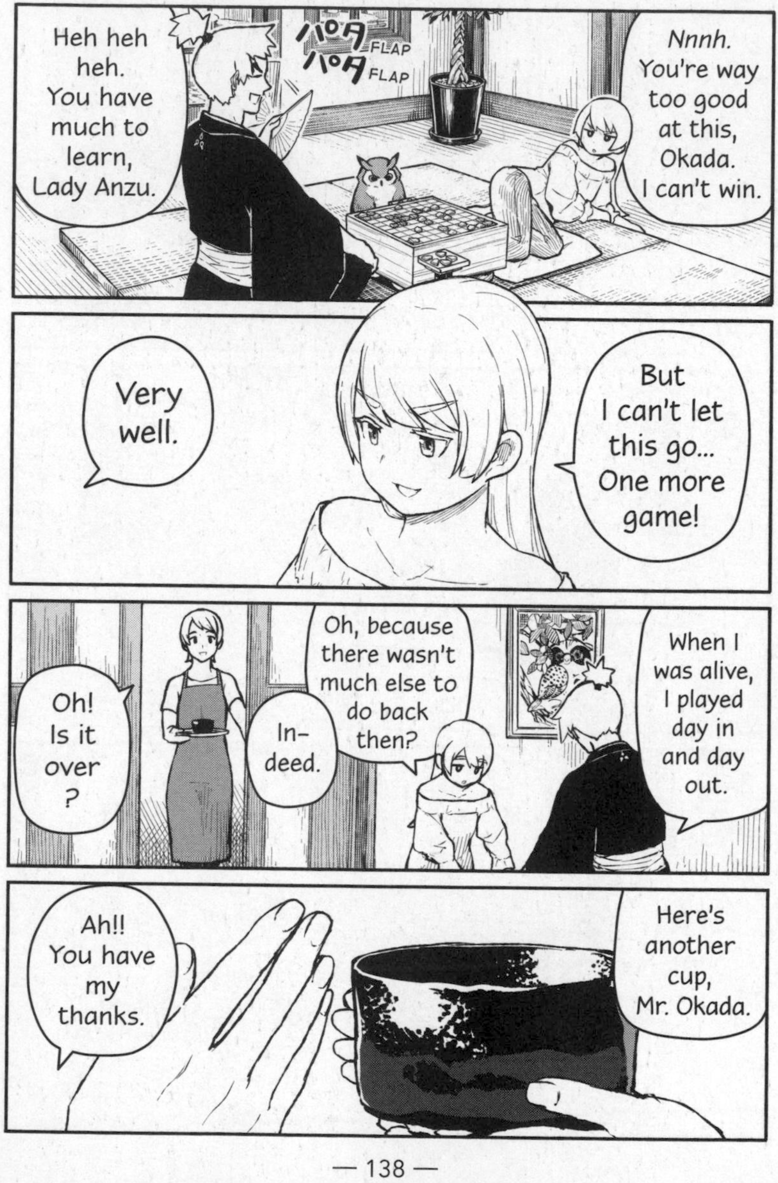

Nnnh. You're way too good at this, Okada. I can't win.
パタ FLAP
パタ FLAP
Heh heh heh. You have much to learn, Lady Anzu.
But I can't let this go... One more game!
Very well.
When I was alive, I played day in and day out.
Oh, because there wasn't much else to do back then?
In-deed.
Oh! Is it over?
Here's another cup, Mr. Okada.
Ah!! You have my thanks.

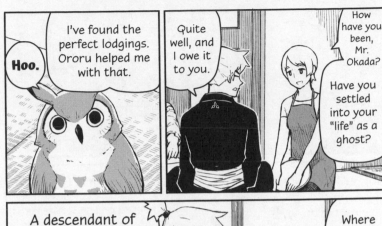

How have you been, Mr. Okada?
Have you settled into your "life" as a ghost?
Quite well, and I owe it to you.
I've found the perfect lodgings. Ororu helped me with that.
Hoo.
Where are you staying now?
A descendant of the Okada clan is living nearby, so I've taken up residence in a vase there.
Ah, so your home is an object.
It must feel nice to have one with a family connection.
Indeed. I never thought I'd find a dwelling so comfortable.
Oh, yes— I did have one request, Mistress.
Yes?

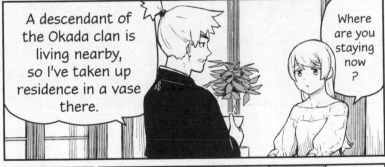

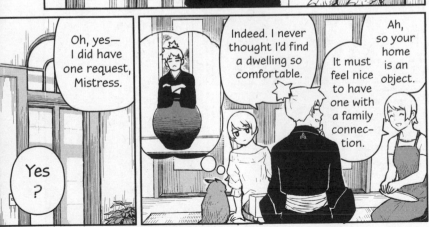

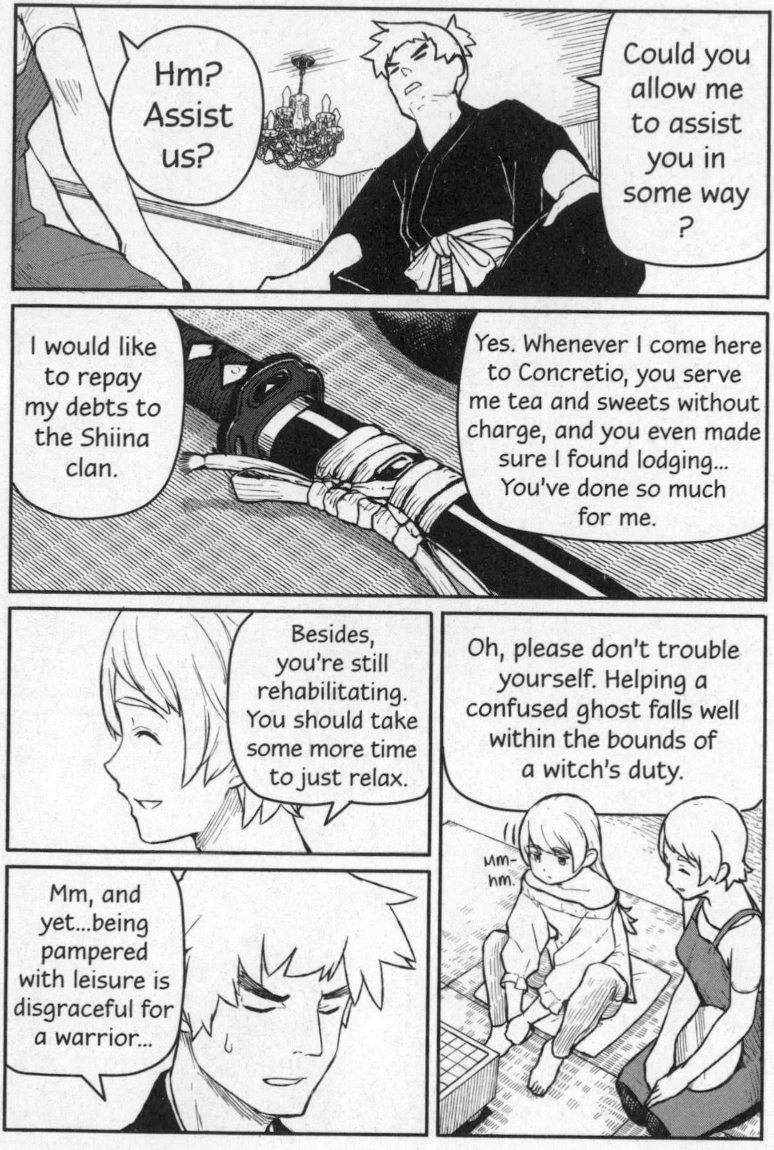
Could you allow me to assist you in some way?
Hm? Assist us?
Yes. Whenever I come here to Concretio, you serve me tea and sweets without charge, and you even made sure I found lodging... You've done so much for me.
I would like to repay my debts to the Shiina clan.
Oh, please don't trouble yourself. Helping a confused ghost falls well within the bounds of a witch's duty.
Mm-hm.
Besides, you're still rehabilitating. You should take some more time to just relax.
Mm, and yet...being pampered with leisure is disgraceful for a warrior...

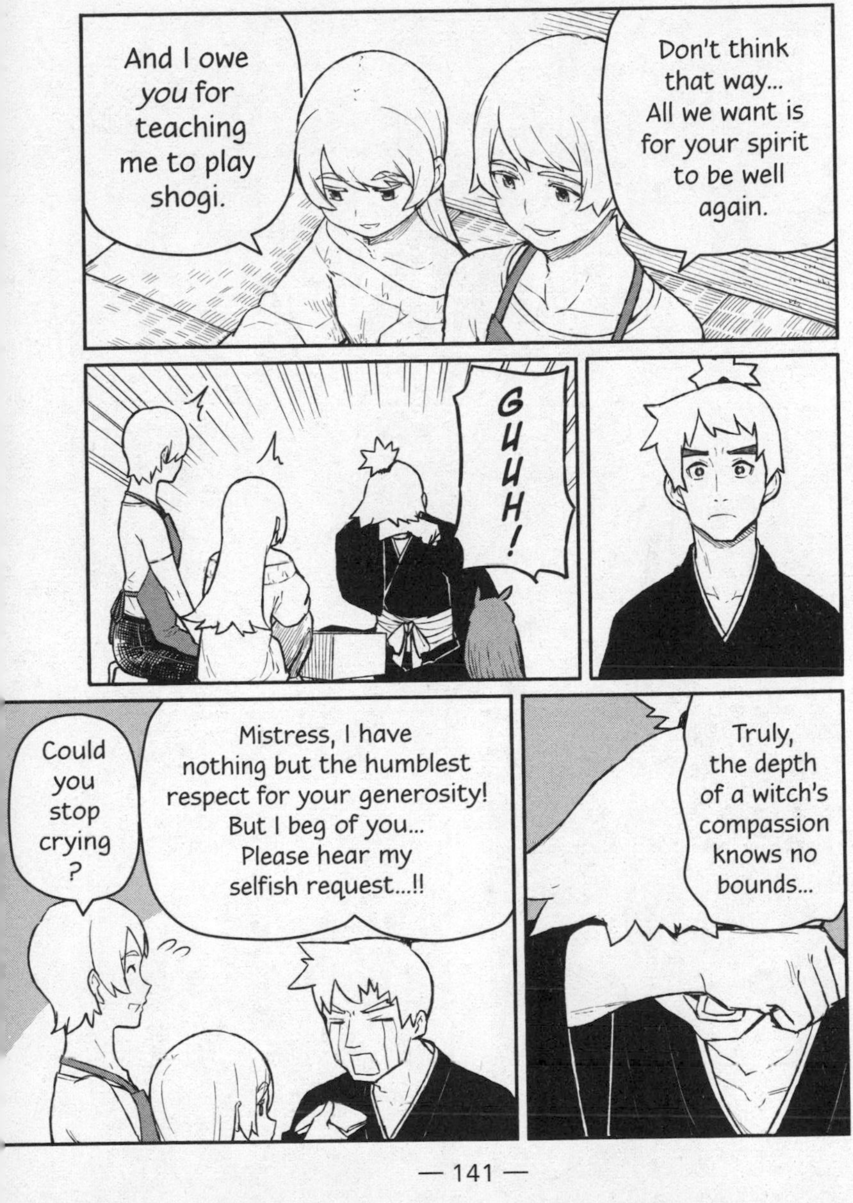
Don't think that way... All we want is for your spirit to be well again.
And I owe *you* for teaching me to play shogi.
GUUH!
Truly, the depth of a witch's compassion knows no bounds...
Mistress, I have nothing but the humblest respect for your generosity! But I beg of you... Please hear my selfish request...!!
Could you stop crying ?

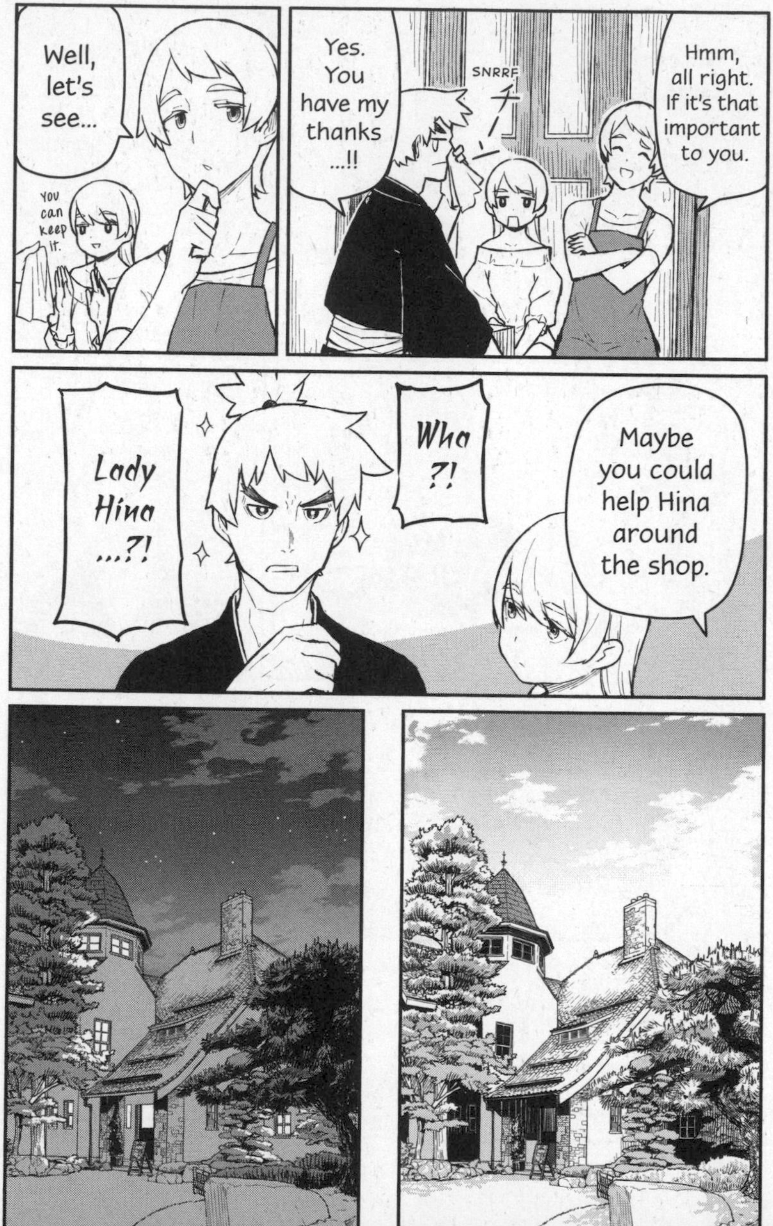
Hmm, all right. If it's that important to you.
SNRRF
Yes. You have my thanks ...!!
Well, let's see...
You can keep it.
Maybe you could help Hina around the shop.
Wha ?!
Lady Hina ...?!

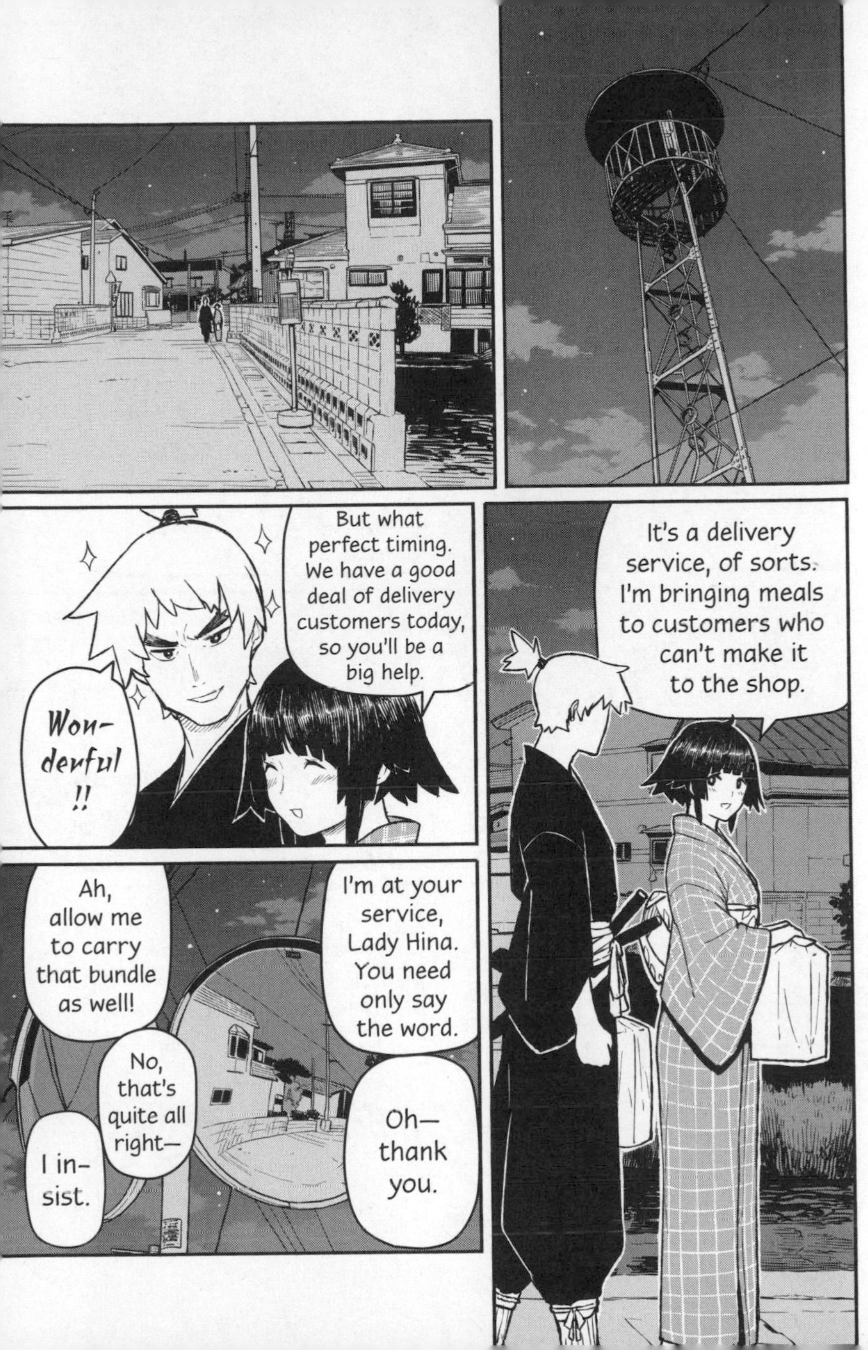
It's a delivery service, of sorts. I'm bringing meals to customers who can't make it to the shop.
But what perfect timing. We have a good deal of delivery customers today, so you'll be a big help.
Won-derful !!
I'm at your service, Lady Hina. You need only say the word.
Ah, allow me to carry that bundle as well!
Oh— thank you.
No, that's quite all right—
I in-sist.

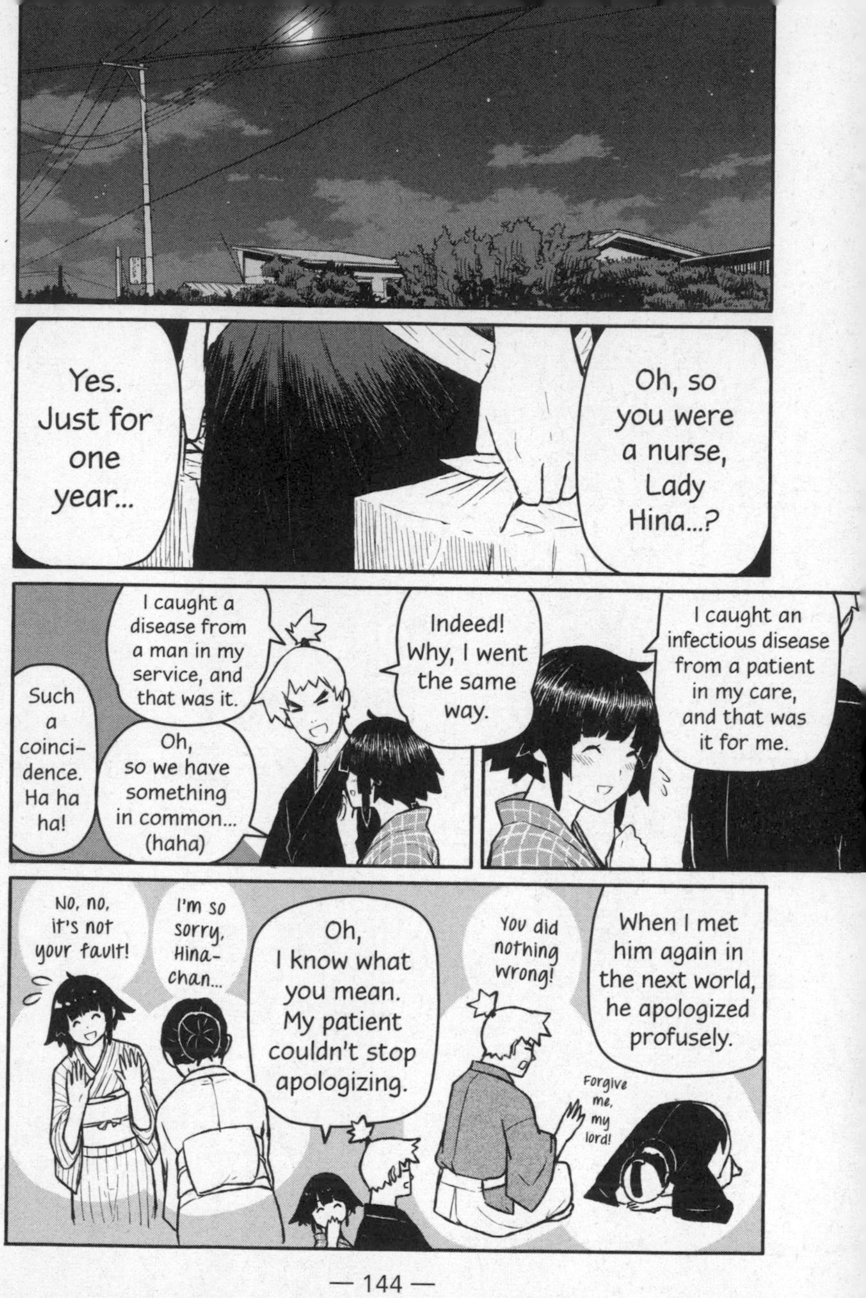

Oh, so you were a nurse, Lady Hina...?
Yes. Just for one year...
I caught an infectious disease from a patient in my care, and that was it for me.
Indeed! Why, I went the same way.
I caught a disease from a man in my service, and that was it.
Oh, so we have something in common... (haha)
Such a coincidence. Ha ha ha!
When I met him again in the next world, he apologized profusely.
You did nothing wrong!
Forgive me, my lord!
Oh, I know what you mean. My patient couldn't stop apologizing.
I'm so sorry, Hina-chan...
No, no, it's not your fault!

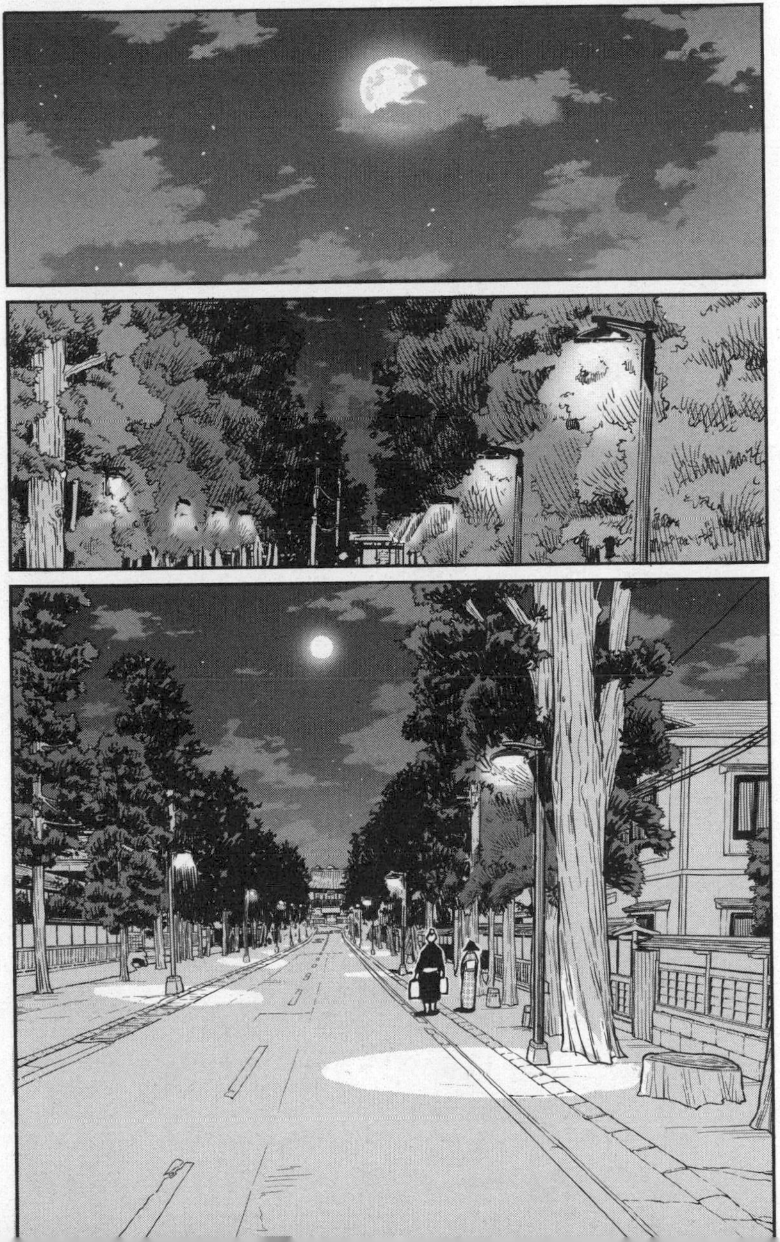

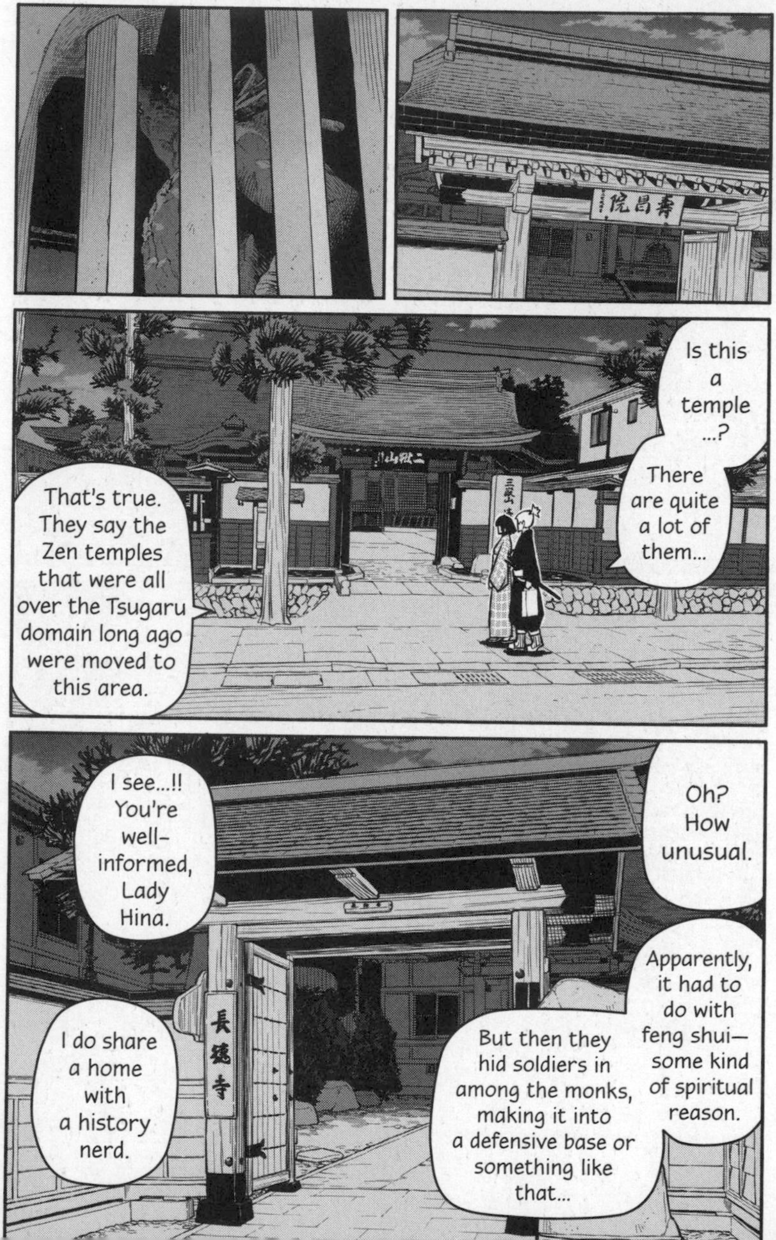
寿昌院
Is this a temple ...?
There are quite a lot of them...
That's true. They say the Zen temples that were all over the Tsugaru domain long ago were moved to this area.
Oh? How unusual.
Apparently, it had to do with feng shui— some kind of spiritual reason.
But then they hid soldiers in among the monks, making it into a defensive base or something like that...
I see...!! You're well-informed, Lady Hina.
I do share a home with a history nerd.

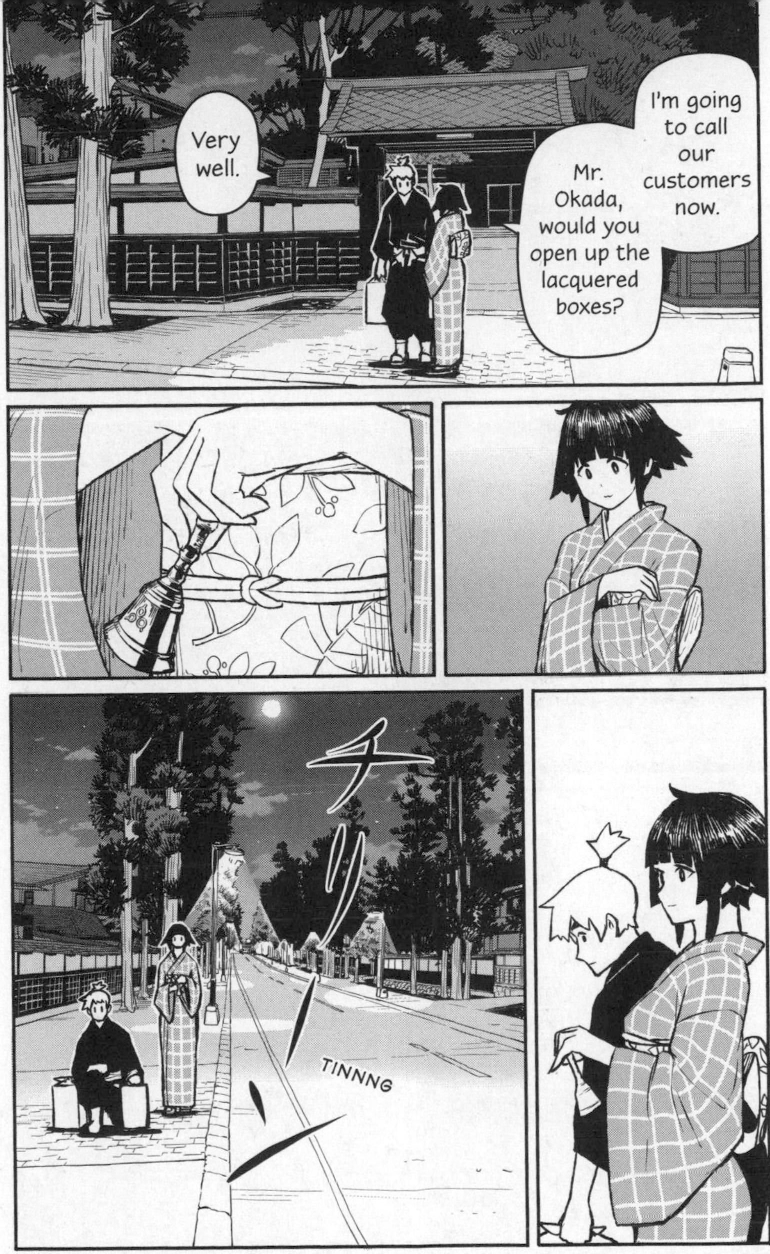
I'm going to call our customers now.
Mr. Okada, would you open up the lacquered boxes?
Very well.
TINNNG

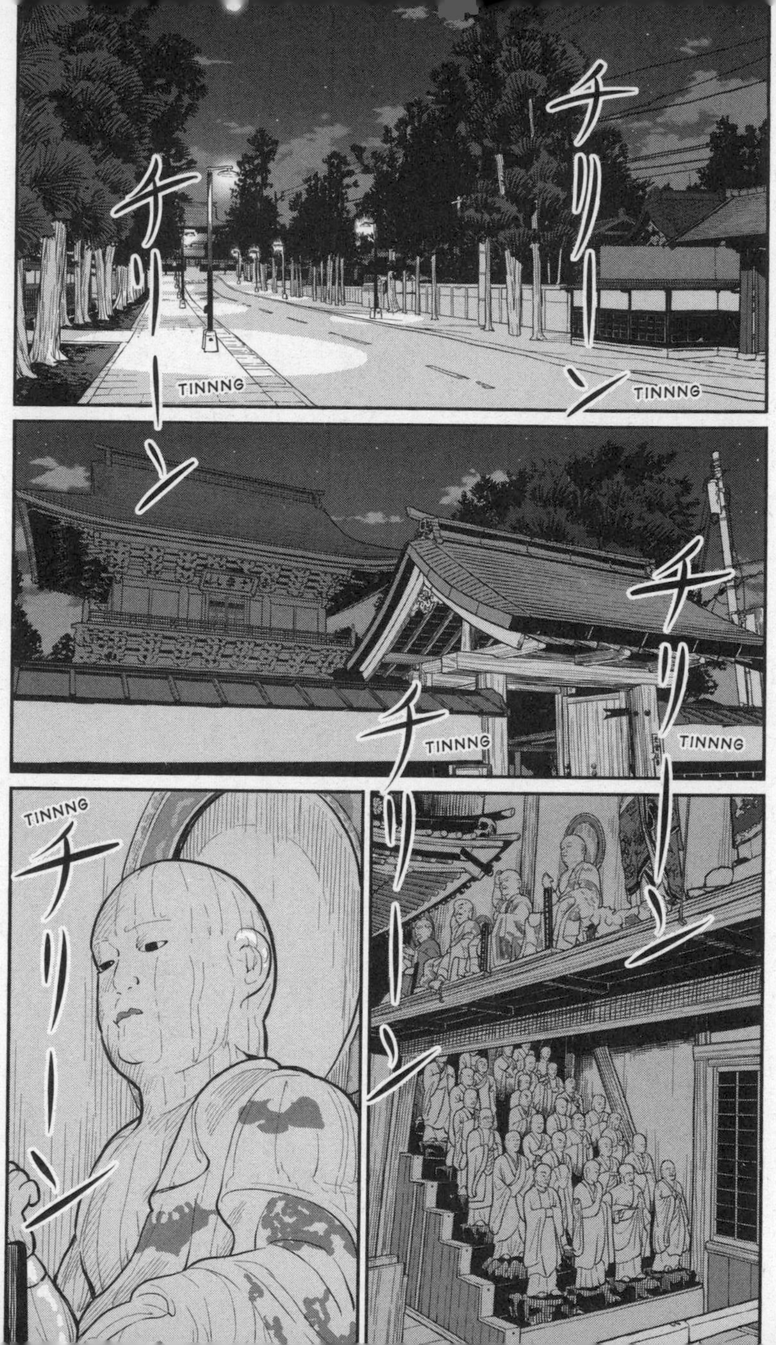
チリーン
TINNNG
チリーン
TINNNG
チリーン
TINNNG
チリーン
TINNNG
チリーン
TINNNG

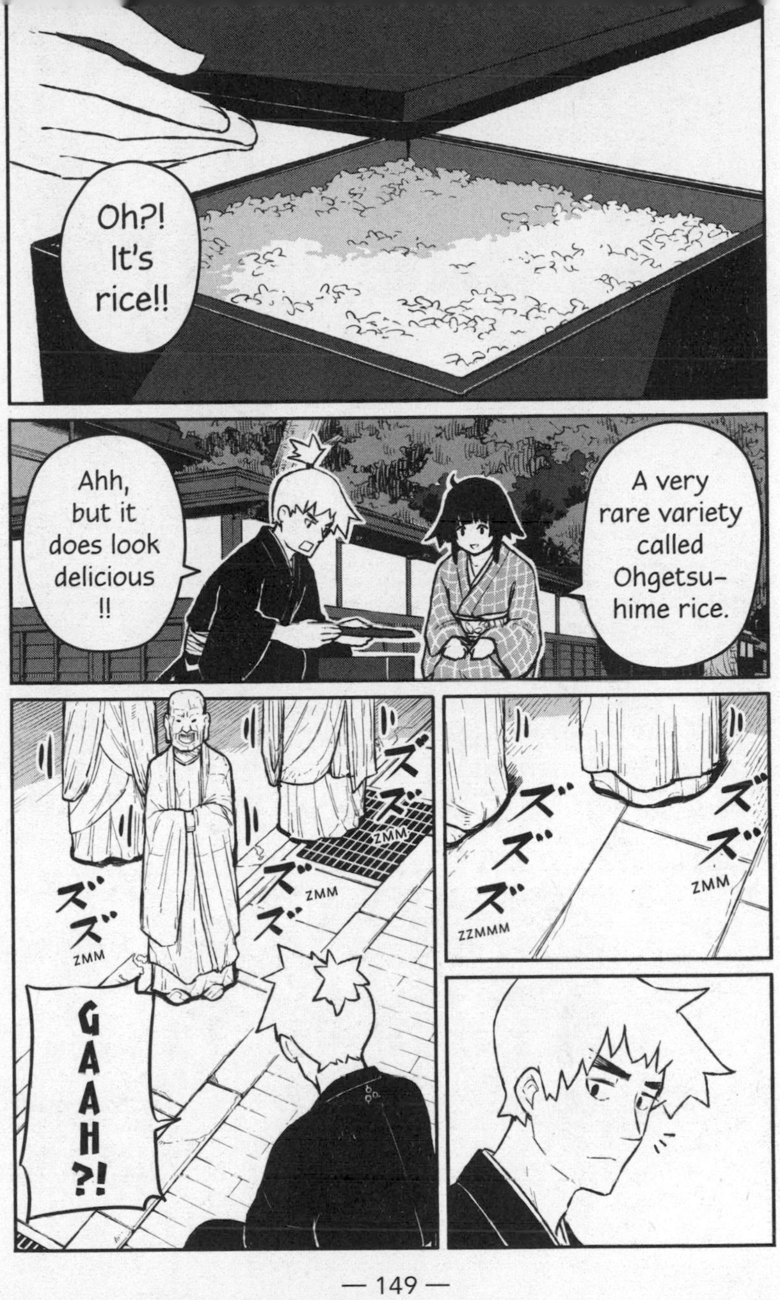
Oh?! It's rice!!
A very rare variety called Ohgetsu-hime rice.
Ahh, but it does look delicious !!
ズズ
ZMM
ズズズ
ZZMMM
ズズ
ZMM
ズズ
ZMM
ズズ
ZMM
GAAH?!

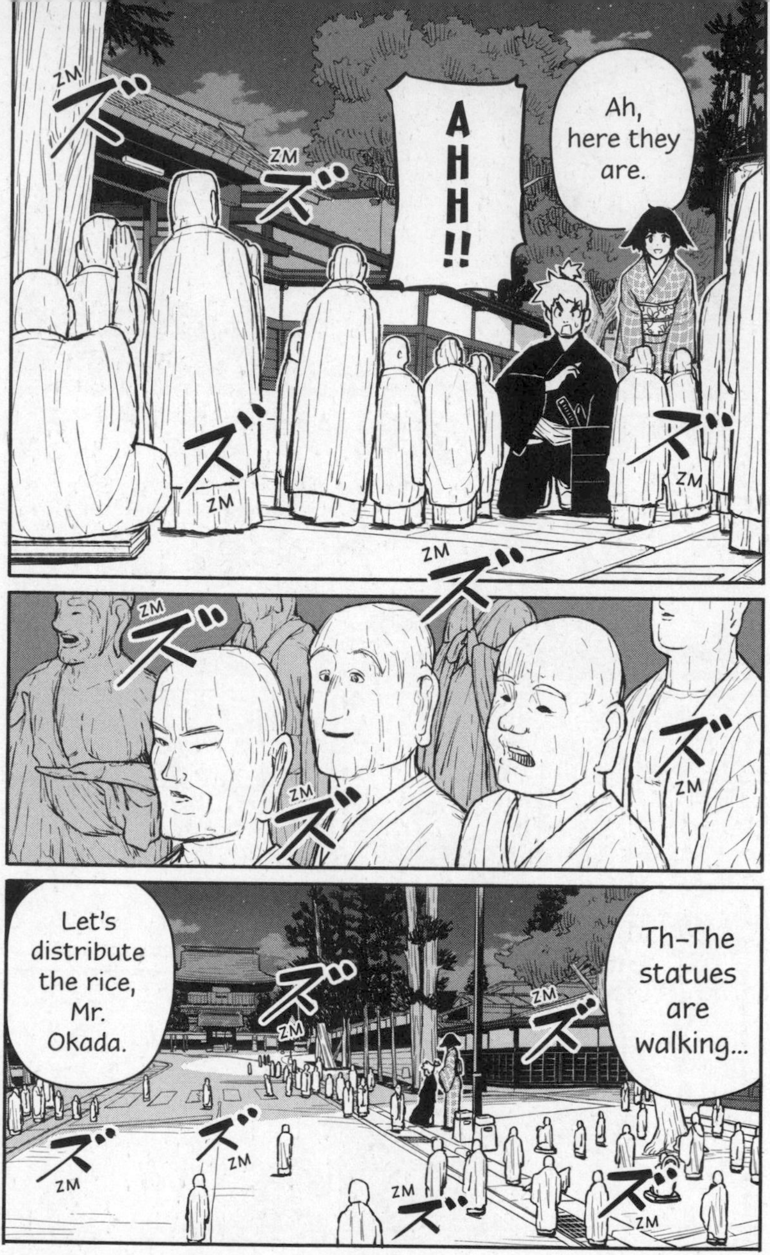
Ah, here they are.
AHH!!
ズ ZM
ズ ZM
ズ ZM
ズ ZM
ズ ZM
ズ ZM
ズ ZM
ズ ZM
Th–The statues are walking...
Let's distribute the rice, Mr. Okada.
ズ ZM
ズ ZM
ズ ZM
ズ ZM
ズ ZM
ズ ZM

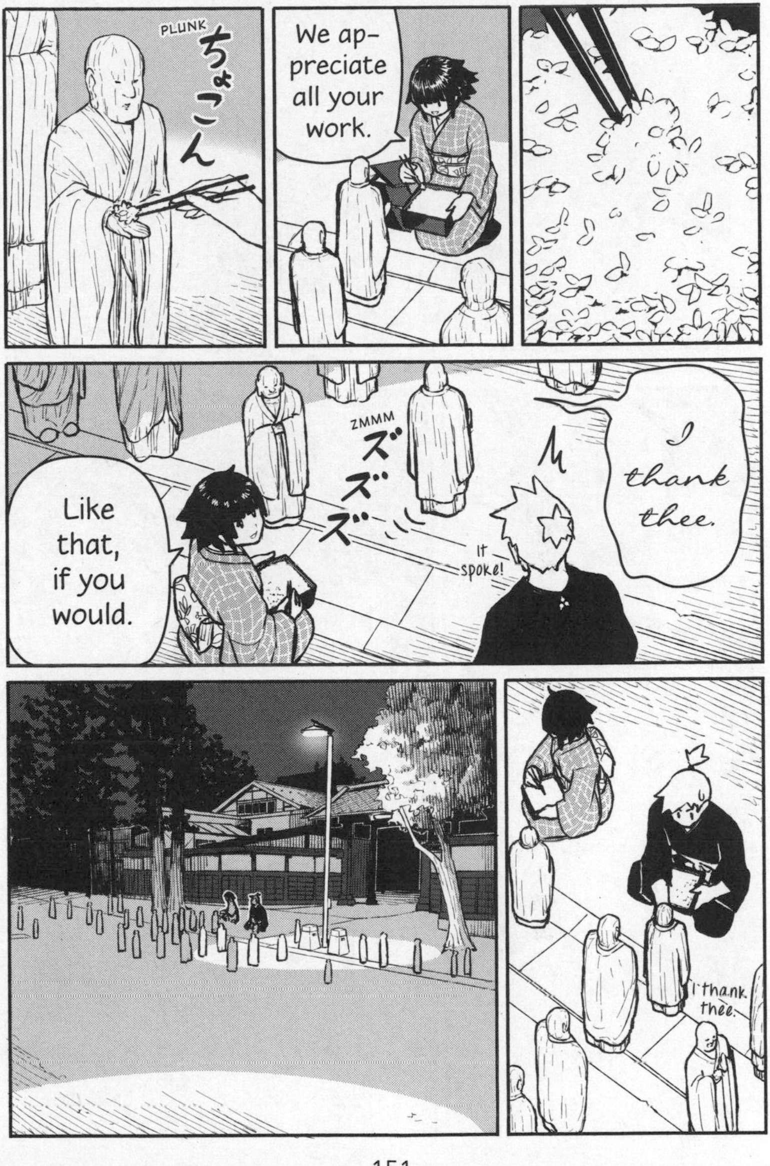
We appreciate all your work.
PLUNK
ちょこん
I thank thee.
ɯ
It spoke!
ZMMM
ズズズ
Like that, if you would.
I thank thee.

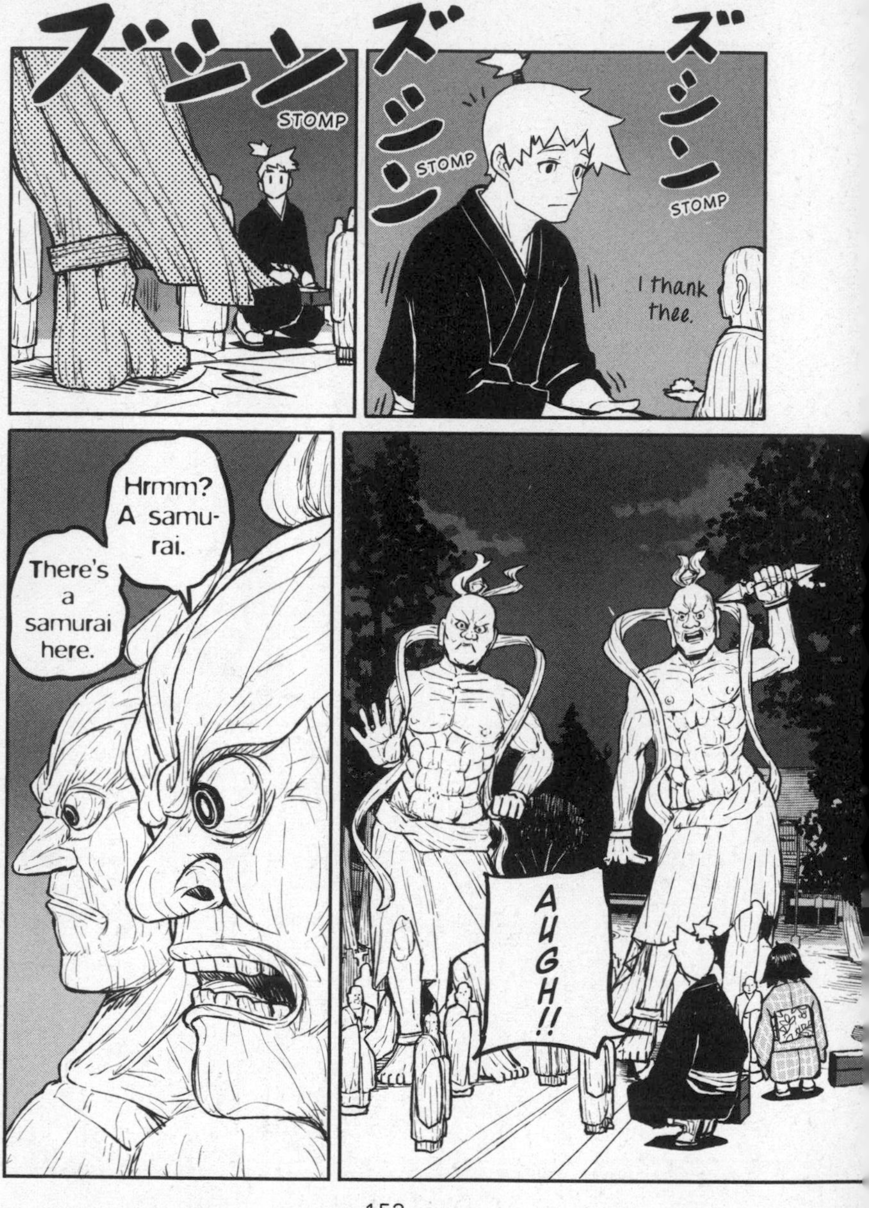
ズシン
STOMP
ズシン
STOMP
I thank thee.
ズシン
STOMP
AUGH!!
Hrmm? A samurai.
There's a samurai here.

No. Just a bandit.
Are you blind? That's a samurai.
You dullard. It's a bandit.
Are you a samurai ?
Are you a bandit ?
I... I am a samurai ...
Aha! You see? Who's the dullard now?
...
You'd better have your eyes restored! Hah!
KLONK

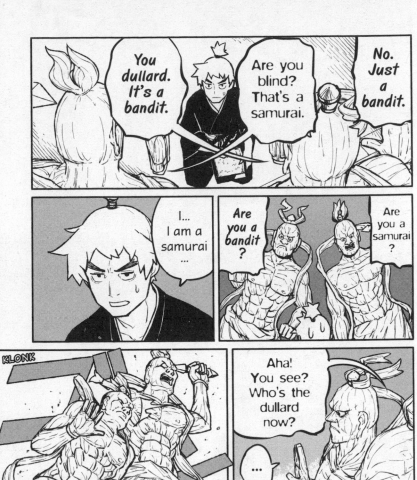

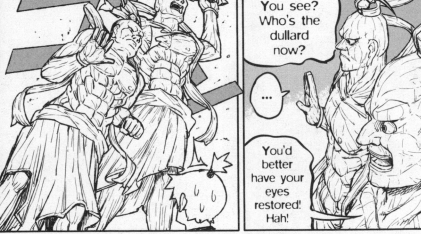

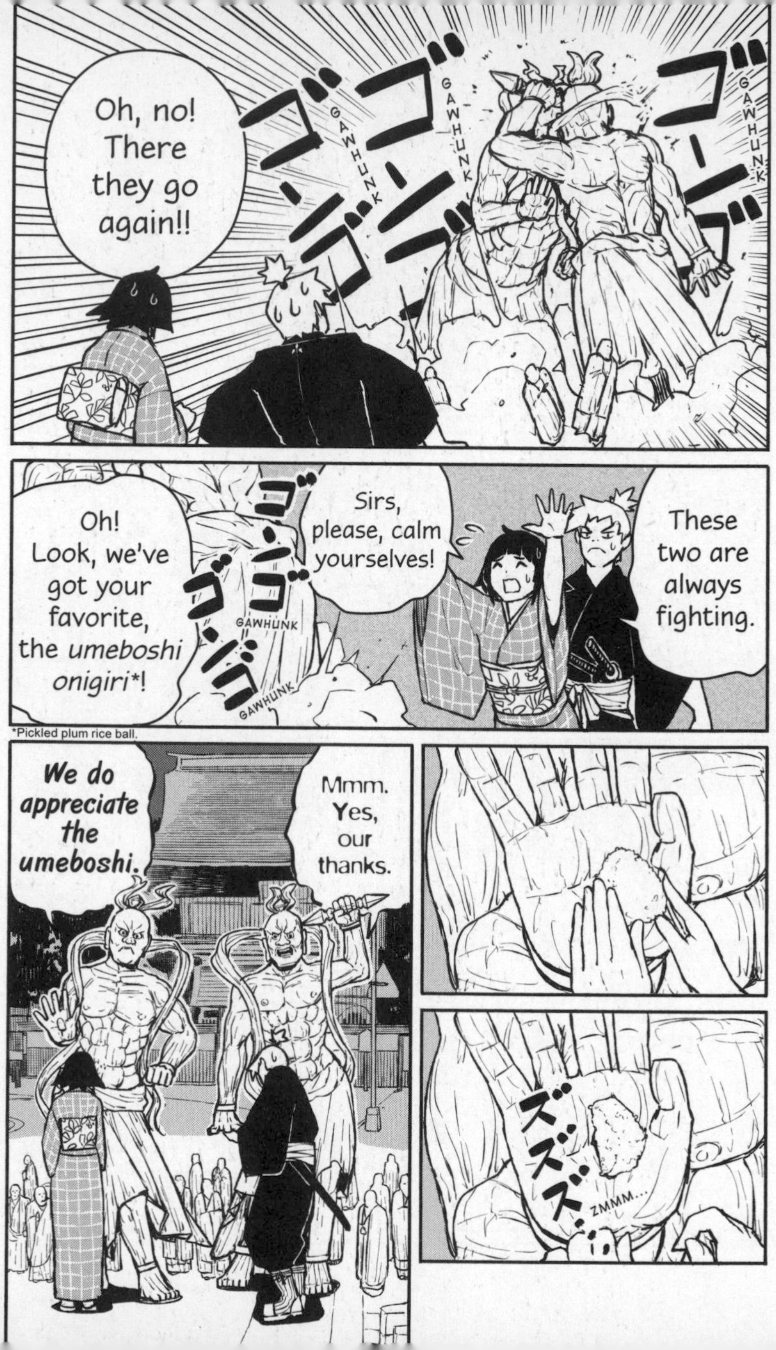
GAWHUNK
GAWHUNK
GAWHUNK
Oh, no! There they go again!!
These two are always fighting.
Sirs, please, calm yourselves!
GAWHUNK
GAWHUNK
Oh! Look, we've got your favorite, the *umeboshi onigiri**!
ZMMM...
Mmm. Yes, our thanks.
We do appreciate the umeboshi.

*Pickled plum rice ball.

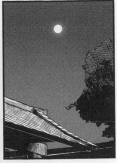

Ah, I never imagined that temple statues eat...
Are they actually Buddhas ...?
ズズ…
ZMM...
Our shopkeeper said they were more along the lines of *tsukumo-gami**.
They heal the flow of energy through the land and bring peace.
Ah, so they're quite important.
Oh— thank you for helping today, Mr. Okada. It went so quickly, thanks to you.
Not at all.

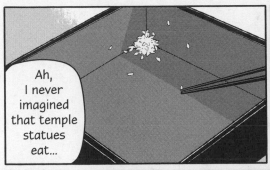

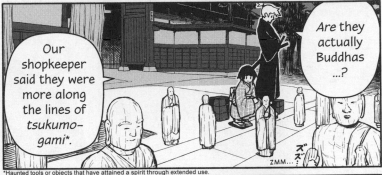

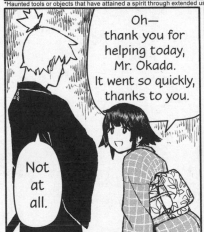

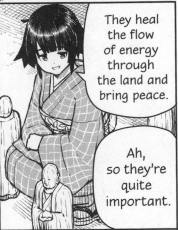

*Haunted tools or objects that have attained a spirit through extended use.

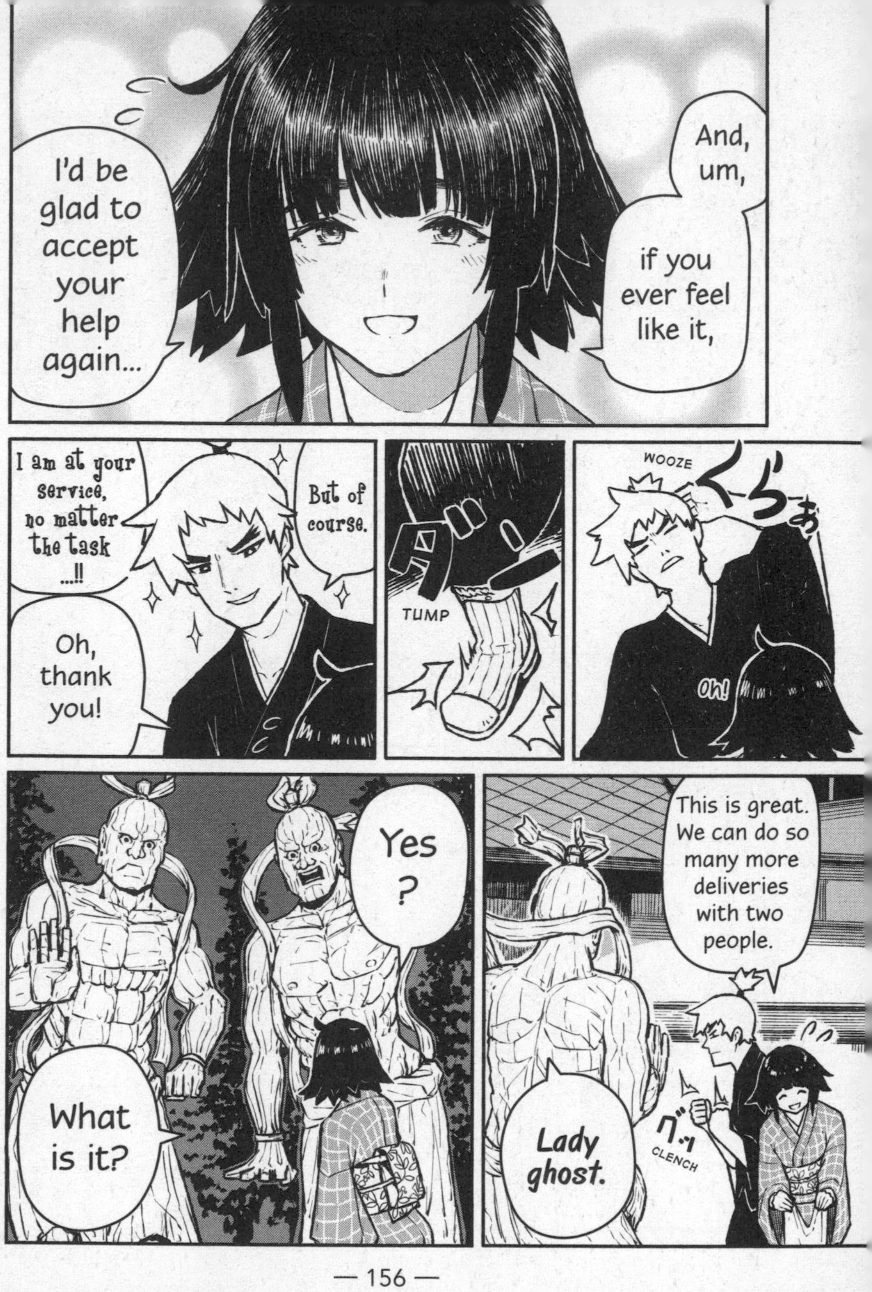
And, um,
if you ever feel like it,
I'd be glad to accept your help again...
WOOZE
くらぁ
Oh!
TUMP
But of course.
I am at your service, no matter the task ...!!
Oh, thank you!
This is great. We can do so many more deliveries with two people.
Lady ghost.
グッ
CLENCH
Yes?
What is it?

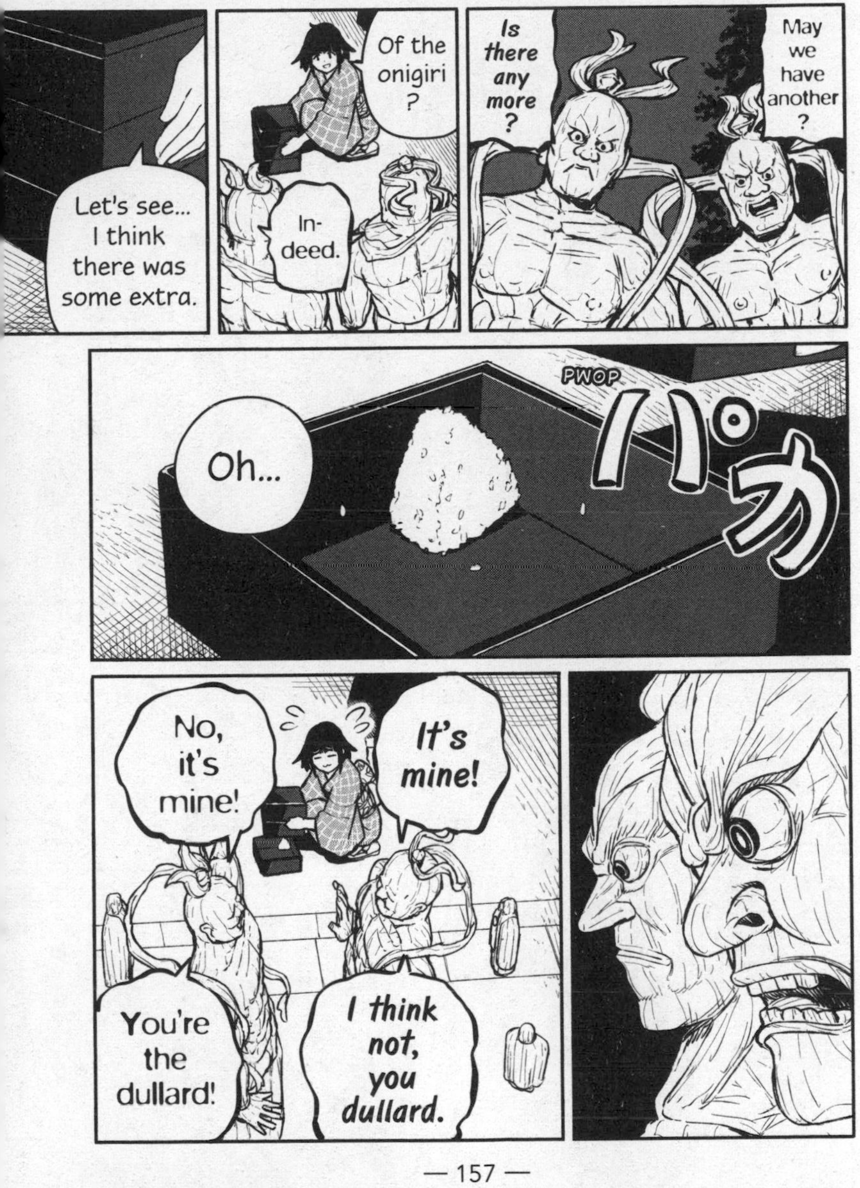
May we have another?
Is there any more?
Of the onigiri?
In-deed.
Let's see... I think there was some extra.
PWOP
パカ
Oh...
It's mine!
No, it's mine!
I think not, you dullard.
You're the dullard!

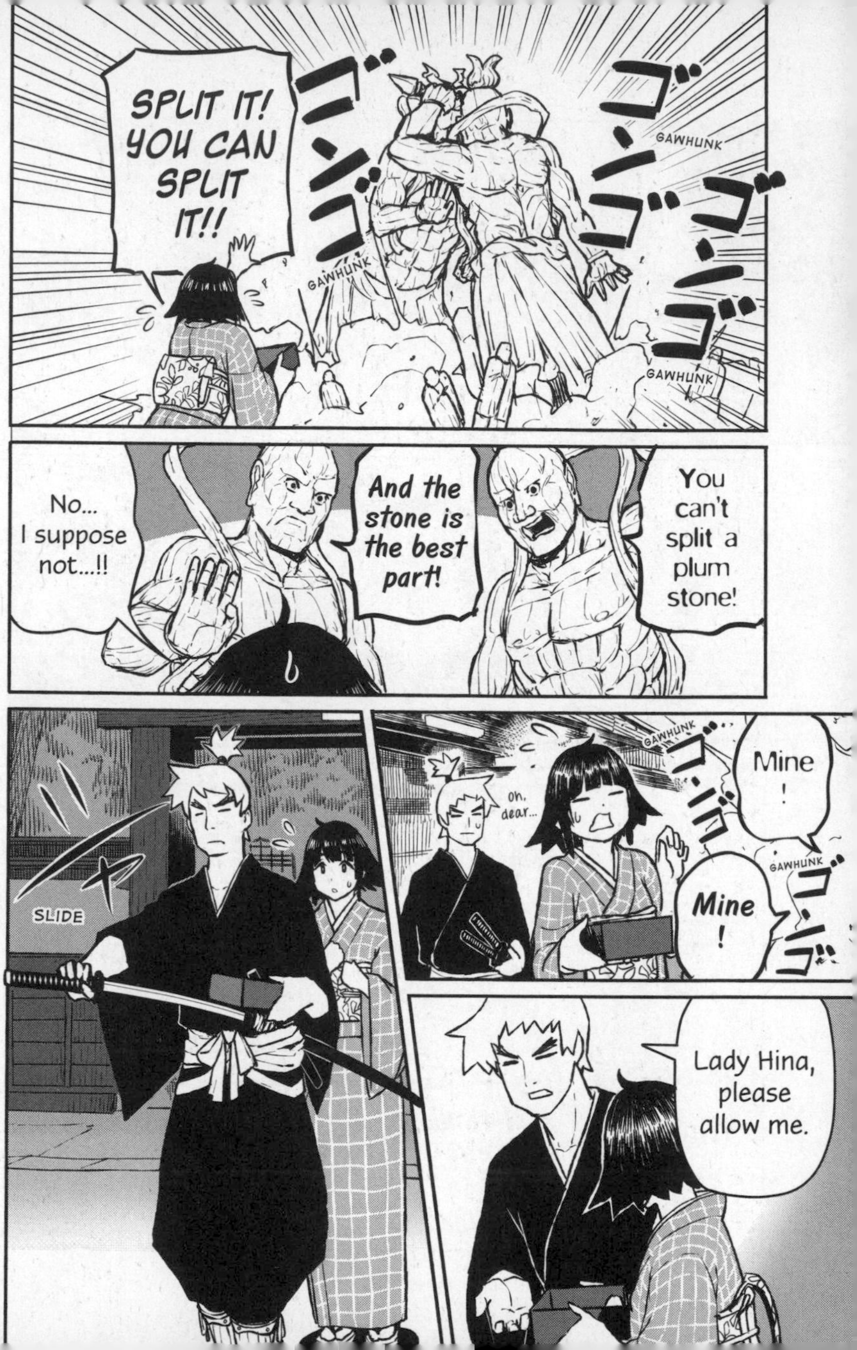

GAWHUNK
GAWHUNK
GAWHUNK
SPLIT IT! YOU CAN SPLIT IT!!
You can't split a plum stone!
And the stone is the best part!
No... I suppose not...!!
GAWHUNK
Mine!
Mine!
GAWHUNK
oh, dear...
Lady Hina, please allow me.
SLIDE

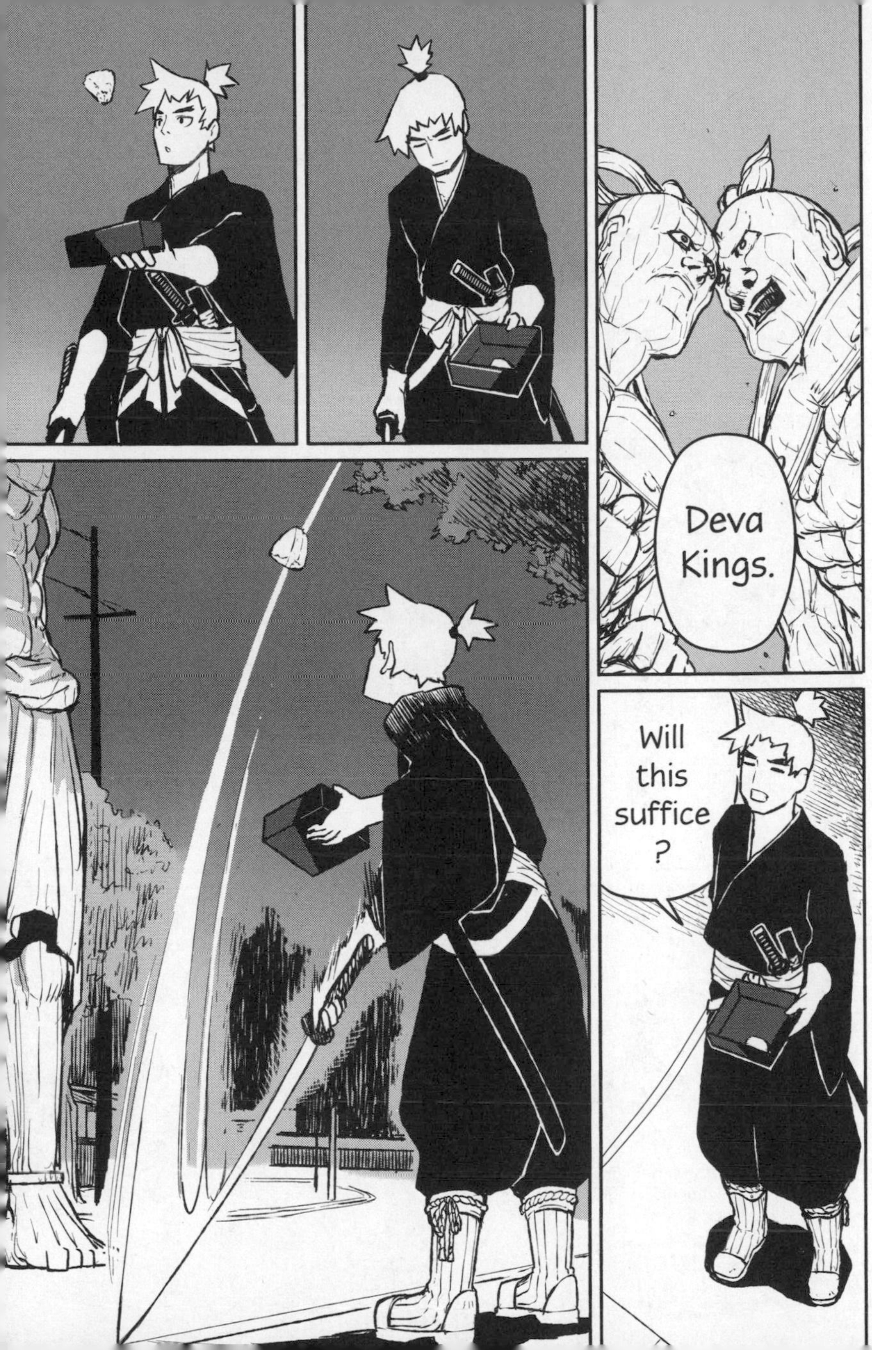
Deva Kings.
Will this suffice?

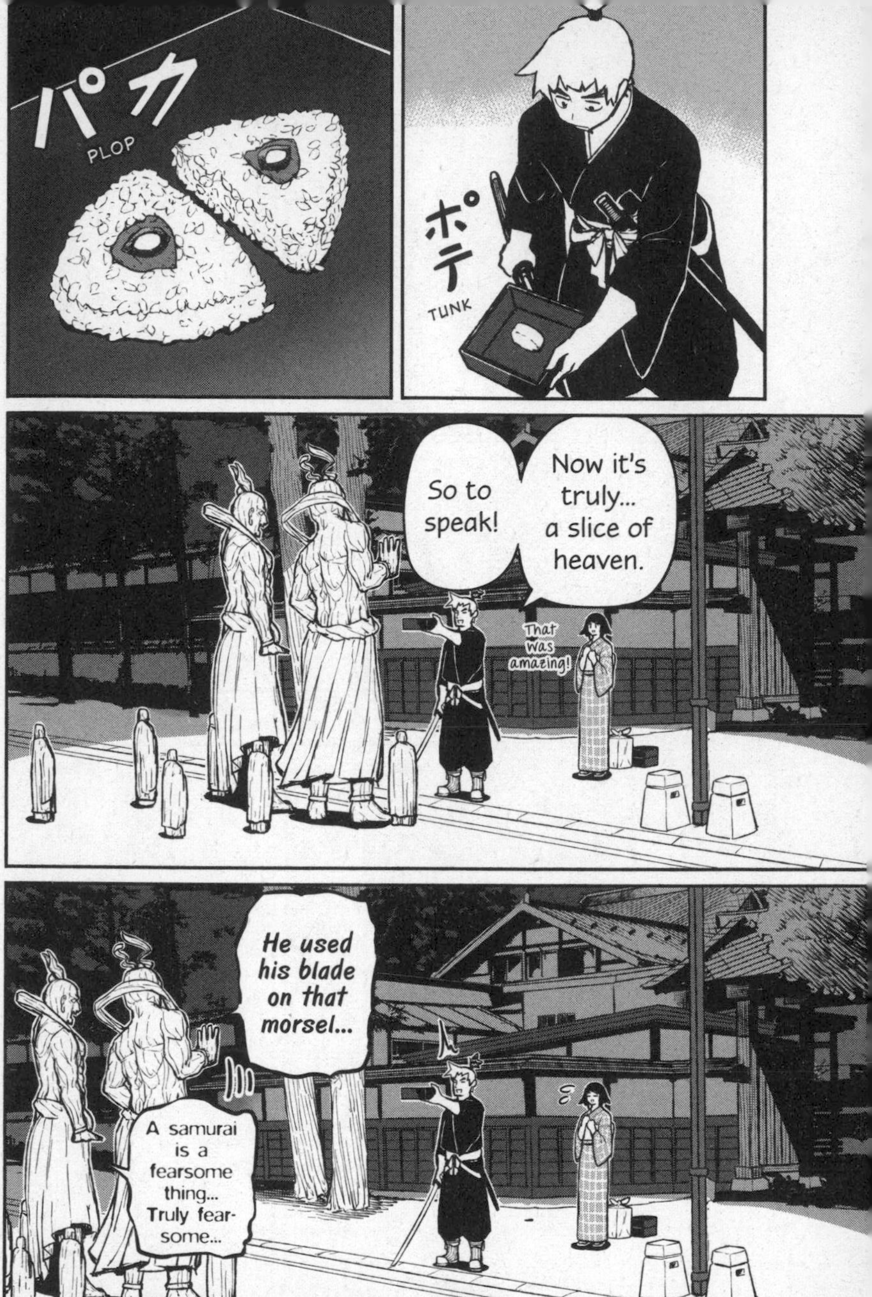
ポテ
TUNK
パカ
PLOP
Now it's truly... a slice of heaven.
So to speak!
That was amazing!
He used his blade on that morsel...
A samurai is a fearsome thing... Truly fear-some...

Fly again in Volume 10

Flying
Witch

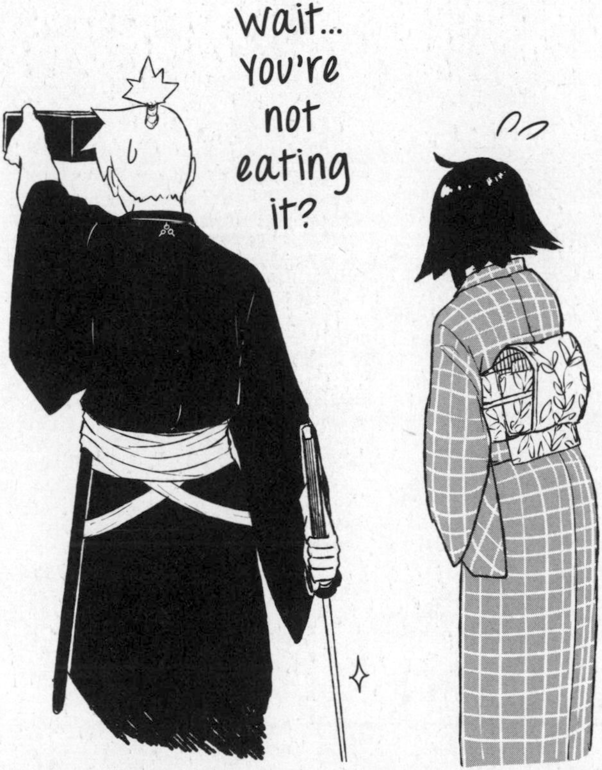
Wait... You're not eating it?

flying witch ✳ kcm flying witch preview for next volume ✳

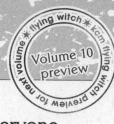

Volume 10 preview

Hello everyone.
The time has come at last!

The field where Kei, Uncle, and so many others helped out is about to yield its crop. It's the moment I've been waiting for—the harvest. Fresh-picked summer vegetables are so delicious.

I'll be sharing it all with the friends and neighbors who have taken such good care of me, too. Happiness only grows when it's shared!

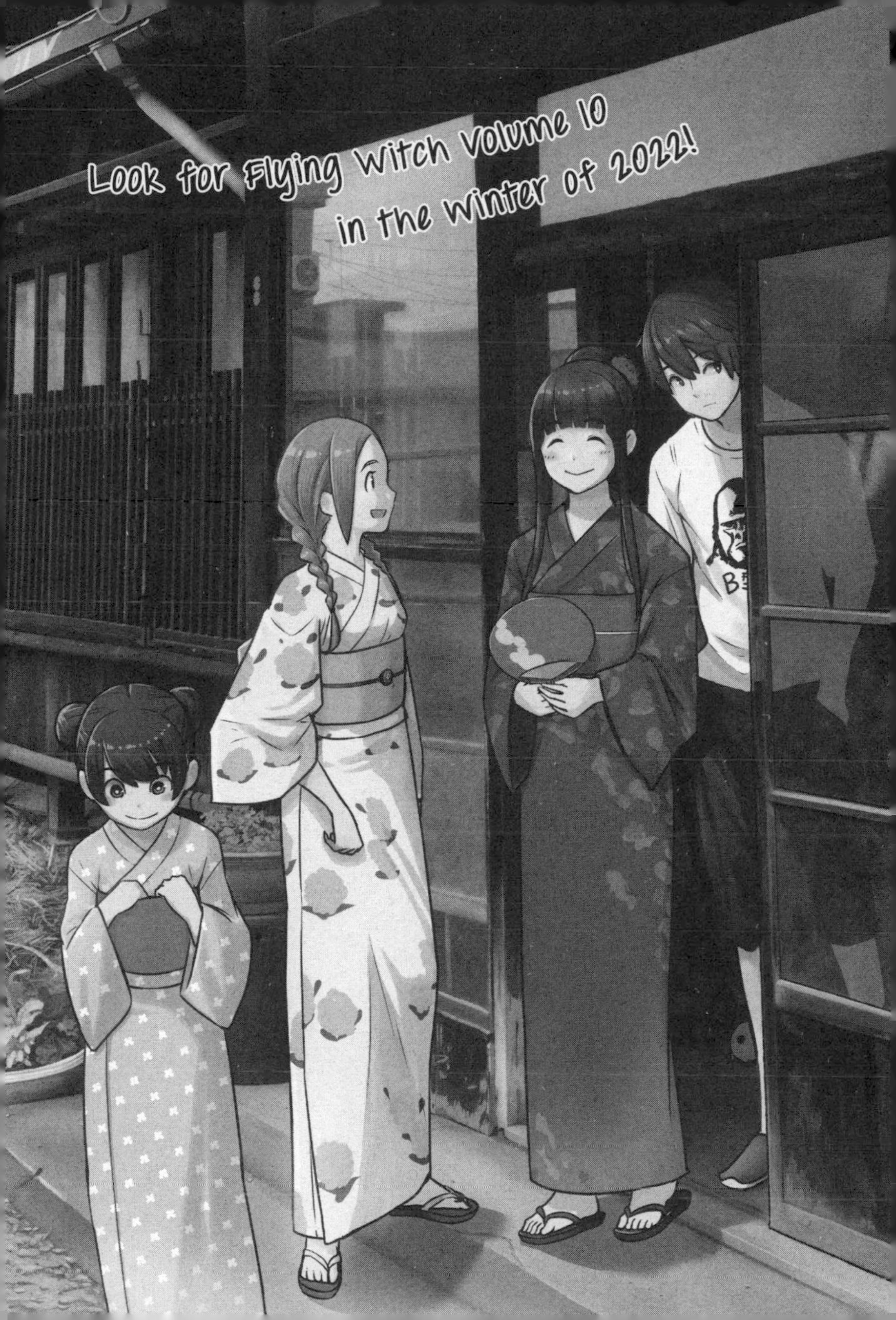
Look for Flying Witch Volume 10
in the winter of 2022!

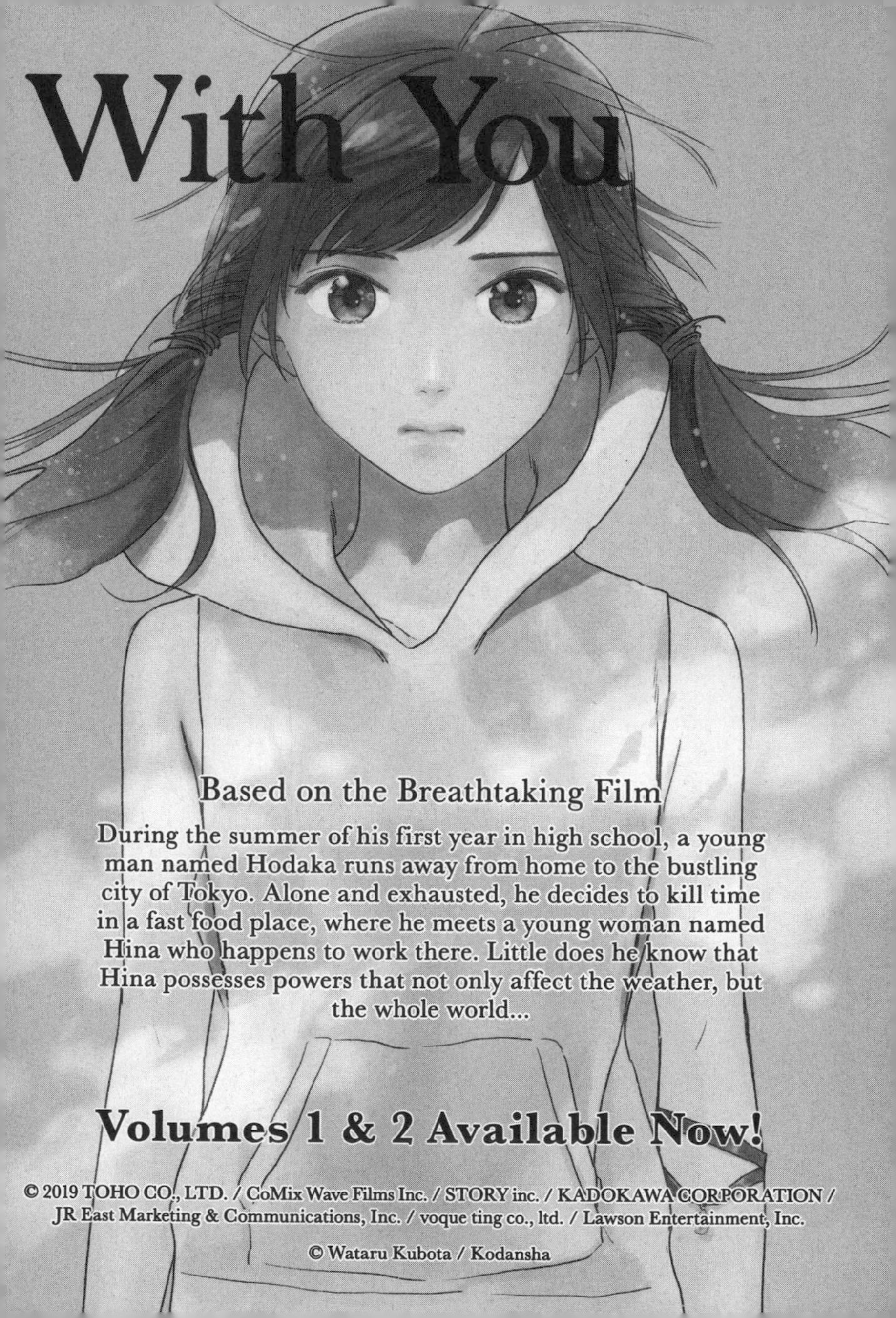
With You
Based on the Breathtaking Film
During the summer of his first year in high school, a young man named Hodaka runs away from home to the bustling city of Tokyo. Alone and exhausted, he decides to kill time in a fast food place, where he meets a young woman named Hina who happens to work there. Little does he know that Hina possesses powers that not only affect the weather, but the whole world...
Volumes 1 & 2 Available Now!
© 2019 TOHO CO., LTD. / CoMix Wave Films Inc. / STORY inc. / KADOKAWA CORPORATION / JR East Marketing & Communications, Inc. / voque ting co., ltd. / Lawson Entertainment, Inc.
© Wataru Kubota / Kodansha

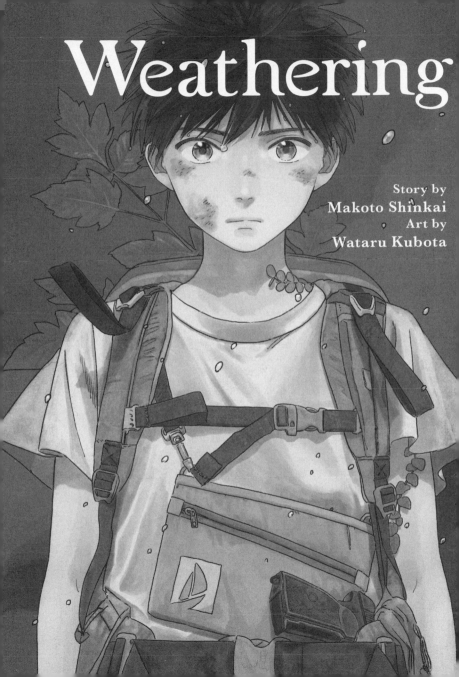

Weathering

Story by
Makoto Shinkai
Art by
Wataru Kubota

Flying Witch 9

Editor - Ajani Oloye
Translation - Melissa Tanaka
Production - Grace Lu
Tomoe Tsutsumi

First published in Japan in 2020 by Kodansha, Ltd., Tokyo
Publication for this English edition arranged through Kodansha, Ltd., Tokyo
English language version produced by Vertical Comics,
an imprint of Kodansha USA Publishing, LLC

Translation provided by Vertical Comics, 2021
Published by Kodansha USA Publishing, LLC, New York

Originally published in Japanese as *Flying Witch 9* by Kodansha, Ltd., 2020
Flying Witch first serialized in *Bessatsu Shonen Magazine*, Kodansha, Ltd., 2013-

ISBN: 978-1-949980-97-4

Manufactured in the United States of America

First Edition

Kodansha USA Publishing, LLC
451 Park Avenue South, 7th Floor
New York, NY 10016
www.readvertical.com

Vertical books are distributed through Penguin-Random House Publisher Services.